In 1857, Ross Nickerson, a young man with—as the deans of Harvard College describe it—"an undue bent toward mischief," leaves school and his wealthy New England inheritance in search of broader fields for his adventurous nature.

Drinking, gambling, dueling, killing and breathless adventure are what he finds in the mountains of Montana. Miners, mountain men, thieves, Indians, saloon girls, gamblers, quack doctors and stern vigilantes are the people he encounters. And one young, beautiful, untamed daughter of the West.

The ingredients that made THE TRAVELS OF JAIMIE McPHEETERS a worldwide success—sheer entertainment carved out of authentic history, with a rollicking humor reminiscent of Mark Twain and Bret Harte—make A ROARING IN THE WIND a rich and racy tale for all who love an exciting story, nostalgia and rip-roaring drama.

A ROARING IN THE WIND

by
Robert Lewis Taylor

(Being a History of Alder Gulch, Montana,
in its great and shameful days.)

ace books
A Division of Charter Communications Inc.
A GROSSET & DUNLAP COMPANY
360 Park Avenue South
New York, New York 10010

A ROARING IN THE WIND

An ACE Book

First ACE Printing: February, 1979

Printed Simultaneously in Canada

Printed in U.S.A.

CHAPTER I

MY INTRODUCTION TO the Duncan Brothers, Grantly and James, bordered on the comic, if the trials of a dying man may be dismissed thus lightly. The year is 1857, the setting California, my name—Ross Nickerson, of a hopeful Bostonian family.

Harvard College had "reluctantly" concluded that I "needed a broader field for operations." The phrases "undue bent toward mischief" and "a disruptive inability to conform to the spirit of a great institution" came into play during my valedictory chat with the president. So— shrinking from the thunders to come, I decided to seek without too much delay the broader fields mentioned. California, of course, was the place. Nearly everybody, it seemed, was going to California, and the editor Horace Greeley had only recently boomed out the now historic charge: "Go West, young man! Go West!" It was generally overlooked that Greely meant Pennsylvania, but it was one of those catch cries to be borne down the generations as the very kernels of wisdom.

Quickly, then, I borrowed $200 from a deaf aunt (who confused the loan with some charitable venture), resettled some bric-a-brac, and picked up traveling clothes at a point when my family were absent in the Berkshires. I left a note that struck me, in modesty, as exceptional in harmless mendacity.

After a ride by rail to St. Louis and a convalescence from straw seats (which had induced a hemorrhoidal threat), I took a paddle-wheeler up the ugly Missouri to St. Joseph; thence north to strike the wagon-trail road along the Carson River. It might be said that, in St. Joe, I was misinformed two or three dozen times, by both wags and touts, so that I probably chose the worst possible route to Sacramento, a decade after the rush to Sutter's Mill.

Finally (omitting the details) I arrived in American Valley, near the still-frenzied digs— and quickly learned that I had about as much chance of enrichment by gold as I had of selling snow by the pound.

In brief, I rushed (with others) from one El Dorado to another—Bidwell's Bar, White Rock Camp, Little Butte Creek, Tom Neal's Dry Diggins—and worse—but was slowed by my clothes falling to shreds, my funds spent on two-dollar meals (when available), and general ignorance of how to proceed amongst the placers, gulches, and quartz-blossoms. Add to this that I never owned more than a pan and a spade, or a spoon for crevicing, and you have a student in search of a campus, any campus.

Meanwhile I lost weight, felt always exhausted, slept shallowly, and, at last, fell to that curse of all local miners—the ague. Through many nights I shook with cold then burned with fever, drenching sweat, until I was unable to rise, even to eat.

No finer group ever existed than the California

miners, and those, later, in Montana. They took turnabout caring for me, with solicitude, often ignoring their own interests. But they were a restless population, and I saw them come and go, leaving me always in responsible hands. This despite the fact that life had small value in such a setting. Often, dimly, I heard strange tongues; I was nursed by Chileans, Frenchmen, Germans, Chinese (serfs sent by overlords in China), and, at last, by Indians.

In a valley where hope for wealth and good health trickled pretty thin, an entirely nude, comely, and intelligent tribe—akin but superior to Diggers—took on the chore of saving my life. They'd been told (by a miner), "He'll likely turn in his water-pail inside three or four days." Despite his advice, the Indians worked hard, but their nostrums, mixed from bark, roots and unmentionable parts of small animals, brought no rally. Nor could I eat their nutritious food, which took the form of acorns pestled to a paste, enriched by angleworms, and cooked as flat cakes over stones. All tribes—not only red but white—have their gourmet side, and my benefactors also kept busy chasing grasshoppers. These they roasted then shook in baskets so that the legs and wings blew off—leaving what they saw as a great delicacy, or, for all I know, dessert.

When a shapely nude girl bent over with food and a melting look and failed to rouse an appetite—or anything else—I concluded it was time to start digging a grave. However, nothing availing, my friends—for they *were* friends—insisted I be moved, by travois, to the next ravine but one. There dwelt two white brothers building a permanent (more or less) log home. From a distance of years, I see this decision as among the happiest of my life.

A travois, or *Teet-sock* in the Snake, or Shoshone, dialect (the Indian *lingua franca* of the country toward Montana) is a hide, generally elk, stretched across two poles. The front ends are carried, or attached to a horse, and the aft ends trail the ground. It will support heavy loads, and it had no trouble with me. Since the tribe neither had nor desired horses, two nude males lifted and two more trotted at the rear (to ease bumps).

In this manner we crossed a pleasant little valley and, breasting a rocky rise, descended into another even more handsome. It was wooded with sugar pines 300 feet high, smaller yellow pines, firs, black oaks, laurels, manzanita, and dogwood dazzling white with blossoms as large as silver dollars. Along a winding stream were flowering shrubs, and in the parklike stretches wildflowers dotted the grass everywhere you looked—the whole set to birdsong, over which, I fear, the rat-a-tat-tat of woodpeckers prevailed.

These natural delights I enjoyed later. At the moment, I was vaguely aware of a listing, lop-grained log dwelling and of two men, one tall and spare, the other of medium height though broad and strong-looking, who seemed bent on setting it right. Even in my low state I could see that they had inferior tools for the job. The brother last-mentioned was on the roof, wielding a homemade saw whose teeth might have roused interest from a quack dentist. He was

unsuccessfully trying to haggle free a loose end
of ridge-board. The other, carrying a
sledgehammer, was driving wooden pegs into,
or at, holes for which they were imperfectly fitted.

Both, however, dusted themselves off (the
shorter clambering down with great agility) and
came forward with concerned looks. They exchanged rapid Indianese with my porters, after
the standard "How, Cola!" greeting; then one
said, "In the house, on the double!"

"The Gold Room?" inquired the saw-wielder,
but the peg-driver replied, holding his chin,
"Providentially, the bunks are completed, at
least one is. As of this moment the other has a
tilt—by my reckoning without a level—of approximately eight degrees at the head." As an
afterthought he said, "Give two degrees either
way."

He had what struck me as a professorial manner, copied after some schoolmaster or cleric
he'd known in his youth. His statements were
delivered as judgments, with a considered air of
finality.

I was installed on a buffalo robe, with a second
robe on top, and, despite my feeble protests (for a
fit of shakes was on me), my Indian friends flatly
refused to accept payment. After patting my
head, they disappeared toward their acorn-
and-grasshopper heaven.

The shorter brother, James—he was the older,
but I thought of him as younger for some reason,
and Montana historians have made the same
mistake—the shorter, I say, now came to the bed
and drew up a wobbly three-legged stool, upon
which he sat, studying me gravely.

"You'll take the case, I assume?" inquired his brother, standing behind him. "Or is he too far descended into 'that bourne from which no traveler returneth'?"

"Ague, and a bad ague at that."

"I can hope that your remark is not in the nature of a pun; if so, a most untimely one. Then you recommend—"

"The Presnitz Water Cure System—last chance, German, wonderful results there. Fetch the blankets, Grantly." As sick as I was, I gathered that brother James disliked to talk more than needed, a quirk offset by brother Grantly's semi-learned garrulity. I thought, too, that the latter, at least, aspired to become a scholar and to achieve both riches and fame. With all the adversity that dogged him, he nearly succeeded in all lines.

But with great bustle they fetched four or five blankets and commenced the Presnitz Water Cure System, which I figured would finish me off without much trouble, and they could get back to work on the house. Soaking one blanket with water, they rolled me up then piled on others, cheerfully tucking them in, and spooned scalding hot tea into me at intervals. I recall that I hoped some day to catch up with Mr. Presnitz, in an isolated place, Mr. Presnitz unarmed and myself equipped with a variety of club, or mace.

Apparently the indefatigable brothers took turns, re-wetting the one blanket, drying the others, continuing the stream of tea for twenty-four hours without let-up. They forgot all else including the fact, I noticed once, that the cabin as yet had no door. Then I was put to bed for a night, and the process resumed early the next morning. This continued for four days when suddenly, at about dawn, I felt a bounding of spirit, refreshed, cool, relaxed, and altogether hopeful of brighter times to come.

"Fever's gone; we can start to feed him; load him up," said James with a kind of professional satisfaction, and brother Grantly closed a book he'd been studying, his lips moving in concert with the text. Later I found it to be a Bible and the text under scrutiny a litany for burial—in case Presnitz fell down on the job.

CHAPTER II

DURING THE NEXT two weeks I was given the livers and steaks of antelope, elk, and deer, and on one occasion—courtesy of James—a haunch of grizzly bear, which was stringy and tough and had a strong flavor of salmon. But more especially my diet consisted of fat gray squirrels, used here for more than a single purpose, as I would find.

On these premises they had a dog rather curiously named Watch, an amiable creature of blurred antecedents. Its sole, happy motive was to scent squirrels to the tall sugar pines, then sit, resting, while awaiting the shot that followed. These brothers could be taken as miners, or frontiersmen, only by a person critically nearsighted. They belonged to that handicapped class known as gentry, though both had become expert marksmen. One could ascribe to this, and to little else, the fact that they were still alive—after three years spent wandering about California. Their milieu was the diggings, and they remained ever hopeful, durably optimistic, never panning more than a few dollars a day (if that), often resorting to smaller devices for survival. They had two muzzle-loading rifles and two hand-sized revolvers of .25 calibre. These last used black powder and round balls—Maynard's Patent, they were called, lately invented and soon supplanted by the Colt.

Currently the pair were making "gold bags," with shoulder straps, out of gray squirrel skins. These had a brisk sale with more dedicated miners; and the squirrel meat, cooked in bacon fat, was the staple of our diet. I thought it ironic that, while solvent miners eagerly bought the bags, my hosts saw their time better spent in sewing. As California prospectors, they never rose above my bungling efforts of the pre-ague era.

"Assemble our panning gear, without delay," said Grantly, returning to the valley on a morning spent collecting potential squirrel bags, five sources dangling from his belt. "A bonanza has emerged at a hidden retreat four miles distant, bearing the place-name of Hogan's Gulch—"

"New to me," said James drily, "and I thought I knew the area."

"Yes, called after a Captain Hogan (late of the U.S. Army) who against advices ventured out after dark and fell eighty feet into the gulch, coming to rest on a rock. He was buried," said Mr. Duncan, musing, ever alert for unusual facts, "with full military honors."

"Military honors?"

"Two miners—former deserters, I'm informed—fired three shots into the air, one rifle misfiring on the first and second rounds but snapping to salute, as it were, on the third."

Infinite detail would doubtless have followed, for his curiosity was limitless, but James interrupted with a sigh, collecting our pans and spades, and three spoons, and would have dragged along a homemade cradle but the bottom fell out.

"Frankly, I think there's a million in it, possibly two, for when I arrived only three men were washing. Good fellows! They cried 'Come one, come all; there's enough to go thrice around the mulberry bush!' I wonder what they meant. Could they have been drunk? To the best of my knowl—"

"Let's go," said James briefly.

We made an odd sight tramping along, for no one's costume was ordinary. Mr. Grantly Duncan, somewhere on the San Francisco trail, had collected a tall hat, and this—with a shrunken Army jacket, frayed jeans with leggings, and boots from which toes leaked at the right foot—formed his mining ensemble. James, better equipped, wore a suit of buskskins he'd made himself. At no particular point did it fit; around his flat belly and burly arms it stretched tight, while the seat hung down like an elephant's folds. As to myself, two woolen shirts and a faded Harvard blazer remained. For the rest, Indian friends had covered me here and there, and a drunken trapper in Dog Town had presented me, after several drinks (and a freshet of tears), his coonskin cap, which felt uncomfortably warm, now in summer.

"Whoop-de-doodle-frisky-warts!" cried a grizzled old ruin standing ankle deep in the stream when we half-skidded down the gulch. "I've panned everything from carpet tacks to dandruff, and I aim to buy a knee-high squaw and ride first-class around the world, plying

spurs all the way. Eee-yow!" He was obviously
drunk, though the hour was short of noon. Two
companions lay asleep, or comatose, in the
shade of a cottonwood.

"Hogan's Gulch?" inquired James.

"Throughout my years in California," replied
his brother, in his half-pedantic tone, "I've never
laid eyes on a prospect this fine. Yes, I see it
clearly at last—we have the world prostrate at
our feet."

But it was shortly evident that neither would
enrich himself that day. Grantly had a careless
habit, while twirling the pan, of wandering
ashore to inspect some oddity of growth or insect
life. James, on the other hand, was explicit about
the frigid condition of his feet, which were bare
in loose moccasins. There was no question that
Hogan's Gulch (marked by a rude cross, with
rawhide thongs) contained gold, but not in
abundance.

After noon the three miners sobered up and
fell to with vigor, and complaints about the quality of the liquor they'd drunk. They formulated
three or four blood-curdling plans for the man
who sold it to them, next time they saw him. But
they "found the color," which they sifted out
and placed—ironically—in squirrel bags made
by my friends. I thought it odd that the Duncans
lacked confidence enough to bring bags of their
own.

At one point, James had a promising pan-full,
rich glints showing at the bottom, but wading
out he slipped on a moss-covered stone and lost
the lot, including the pan. Grantly, meanwhile,
came within a wisp of distinguishing himself

and making news in the towns.* He lifted one
end of a slab, over which the shallow water
purled, then dropped it as being bothersome. A
miner of eighty or eighty-five, behind him,
turned it over later, after some effort, and picked
up a nugget weighing twelve ounces. With gold
at $16 an ounce, this came, of course, to $192—a
good day's haul in that year. (The nugget, with
an addition of dust, would be stamped into oc-
tagonal $50 coins at the San Francisco mint.)

Homeward bound, we'd amassed perhaps
$1.20 worth of dust, as well as a badly-skinned
knee, stone-bruises (James'), a painful case of
sunburn (mine), and two dents in Grantly's hat;
as the sun sank the miners returned to the bottle,
whatever its quality, and began shying rocks. If
one reckons our time was worth, say, fifty cents
each per hour, we'd gone into the hole $14.80

But Grantly Duncan viewed our outing as hopeful in the extreme. "Frankly [this was a favorite
word] I see destiny to lie in that general area.
True, we had mishaps, but I might remark, helping the Bard, that 'now, praise God, we join the
very lists of woe'; we've learned a number of
things not to do—"

"Such as go back to Hogan's Gulch," his
brother suggested, unheard.

"My hat seemed to attract them; I wonder
why?" He took it off and dusted it, trying without success to remove the dents. "It was made,"
he said, consulting the inside band, "by Genin of
New York, whose establishment, I believe, fur-

* At that time in the West, unlike New England, there were
no such things as villages; a collection of a dozen shanties
was a "town," and nothing else. Dogtown, for example, had
ten huts and sixteen dogs, hence the name.

nished head-gear for Phineas T. Barnum. It is, of
course, possible that they'd never seen a tile of
this sheen. The advantages are not," he emphasized, "equally distributed at birth. That was
a popular remark of our father, who had, if memory serves, no advantages whatever except an
itch to remove from Point A to Point B and a stout
pair of legs to get him there. Those and an eccentric taste for reading. I recall—" but James abruptly made off in one direction and I, to my
shame, sheered away in another. My forehead
was blistered and I was scratchy with fatigue.

James, while broody, going virtually silent for
days, wandered often on his own. Nevertheless
he was, as an historian would write, "a very
prince of good fellows." At a time when his
looks seemed blackest, and I thought I'd displeased him, he'd break into the sunniest of
smiles, clap me on the back, and say something
like, "Good chap; have fun while you're young."
On one occasion, at least, this appeared strange,
for I was caught midway in Grantly's clapboard
period. The Duncans sometimes enjoyed credit
in Dogtown, and Grantly had wangled a two-
handled saw, an axe, a wedge, and other tools,
and had actually completed a dozen clapboards
from the pines. With these, he meant to make a
door and patch our roof. His elation was such
that he promptly embarked on a program to provide clapboards for all the towns around. And
they were badly needed here.

"I dislike, on ethical grounds, to establish a
monopoly, but this district is starving for clapboards. Frankly, I regard roof leakage as the basis
of most mountain ague, and Brother James,
versed in medical lore, has supported that view.

[James, by the way, had done no such thing.] In the pecuniary sense, there are several ways to skin a cat, not to mention two roads to Scotland. Clapboards can be made to serve in lieu of shingles. An example comes to—"

But James had bawled a deafening "Gee haw!" at a span of rented oxen, and another batch of clapboards began their drag toward town. In the end this work proved so backbreaking and comparatively profitless—for the miners turned out not to give a tinker's curse whether their roofs leaked or not—that Grantly switched to "provisioning"—with the Indians' help. To his credit, he—and we—briefly made a good thing out of this. It was enough, in fact, for our grubstake to Montana. The Indians were usually anxious to work, meaning to hunt. Forbidden firearms, they could kill little more than pigeons with their awkward bows and arrows. But they contributed their share toward our cache and, I thought, perhaps a trifle more.

For one thing, they always spotted game first; their eye-sight was uncanny. Like bird-dogs, they would freeze, then point at an apparent empty clump of alders. Then a deer, an antelope, even an elk might spring out, and the bombardment commenced. Using one of our knives, an Indian could butcher a deer within three or four minutes. Routinely he cleaned the paunch first and filled it with blood—this was part of his pay. Converted to blood pudding, it proved a wholesome addition to the acorns and grasshoppers. So they told me; I became nimble at refusing the mess without hurting their feelings.

The Indians took each animal we shot, tied its feet together, and lugged it to our camp. For this,

their regional pay was the head, neck, and hide.
But it was typical of the Duncans that, ignoring
the local scale, they added a quarter of meat. I
never asked what was done with the head, especially not wishing to know. For fetching
supplies from town, six miles each way, the fee
was a swappable hickory shirt worth seventy-
five cents. These trips often involved one man's
carry of fifty pounds in flour, bacon, beans, and
other edibles, the whole loaded onto his back.
I might note that most members became terribly
stooped in old age, not from their work for us but
from a lifetime of bending over searching for
grasshoppers.

All were strickly honest, unlike the Modocs
and Rogues, who had caused such havoc in these
valleys before the miners, with the military,
combined to drive them out.

Since the organized hunts produced far more
than our needs and those of our helpers, our
trade prospered in the towns. For three-quarters
of a deer we received an average of twenty-five
dollars, and our "pile" began to grow. The
brothers took the line, of course, that I was a full
partner, though I was then much the inferior
shot.

Now the miners could easily have supplied
themselves, but in the mountain-man phrase,
that "ain't the way our stick floats." The truth is
that their gold-seeking was a mixture of sport,
lust, and addiction. And when absent from digs,
they stuck close to the gambling saloons. There
they drank "Valley Tan," a semi-poisonous brew
wrought with some malice by the Mormons, or
"Tanglefoot," origin unknown, or other potables
that bore equally descriptive names. Let a sour-

dough with a sackful of dust "unstick his waggle-board" at the bar and he promptly made for the tables, where he usually lost his "poke" in less than an hour. Daunted? Not even slightly; he'd had a wonderful time and was ready to dig the next morning (still moderately drunk, as a rule). The life suited those men to perfection.

CHAPTER III

[1]

SHORTLY PAST MID-SUMMER, our water ran thin, and a group of men came by en route to Montana. Flour in their region had been exhausted for months, they said, the lack offset by imports from Chile, at robbery prices. The flour in our area, too, would be Chilean during the coming severe winter. The men, our visitors, were exploding with rumors of gold in Montana, or that land east of Idaho known as Montana.

Some time previously a man called Benetsee had discovered "float gold" in a stream of the Deer Lodge area, not far from where Butte would spring up. His name is remembered by Montana, but at no time did I hear that odd, reclusive fellow referred to as anything but "Benetsee the half-breed," as if he were somehow crippled, or that half of him might be missing. Usually he was mentioned acrimoniously, and I soon learned why. Benetsee, or François Finlay, was a half-breed in that his mother had been French and his father Scottish—hold-overs from a period when the Hudson's Bay Company controlled the region. The son made matters worse, I expect, by choosing to live with the Flathead

Indians, of whose blood he also had a share, he liked to hint.

Altogether, the fact of Benetsee's division and the cranial nature of his hosts might suggest a barrelful of anatomic curiosities. But since he was perfectly sound, and the heads of his associates normally formed, racial feeling could hardly cause his unpopularity.*

The truth is that Benetsee (his Indian name) hated prospecting, and even gold itself, and he stoutly refused to point ravening arrivals on the right path. Indeed, he frequently directed them a hundred or so miles north or east, with some hope that they might fall into a ravine. It is not divinely decreed that people must lust after gold; indeed, scriptural advice to the contrary exists, as Grantly said. Benetsee enjoyed trapping for furs, and his desires were ungluttonous. For the rest of his life he regretted mentioning "float gold"; the loose remark brought swarms of people to Montana, among them—us. And never in the annals of America was a place as wild, as lawless, as rough and brawling, as Montana when the miners came.

[2]

Beaverhead Valley, December 21:

After a nightmare of trouble, near-murder, and near-starvation, we are camped, through a kindly Providence, in southern Montana, where

*Scholars have not yet produced a convincing reason for the inaccurate name of "Flathead," which the tribe bore without complaint. Probably some person, a white, irritated by a trifle, burst out with some expletive as "you bloody flathead!" and the noun, at least, stuck.

game abounds and where peace, for the moment, is the chief of our blessings.

We left the Duncan cabin, or structure, in mid-August—with four strangers headed for Montana and "gold to play knuckles with, gold to waller in, gold to buy the U.S. Mint and turn it into a whorehouse." I quote the leader of this group, not able to mimic his atrocious speech, and, to be sure, deleting his loftier blasphemous peaks.

A council was held to decide if the season was too far advanced for this journey of 900 miles. It was Brother Grantly's contention, I'm afraid, that resolved the issue. The strangers, individually and in sum, proved ignoramuses about travel, gold, and every other line except, perhaps, theft and throat-slitting. In appearance they had an emphatic gallows complexion, being huge men with fierce features, their beards so black as to appear blue, their tattered buckskins greasy and badly burned here and there. (As to this last, I never saw one, at any time, without some kind of tobacco going.) Their slouch hats were torn and caved in, causing a flapping sound in a wind. What was recognizably an Indian scalp dangled from the leader's belt, and I gathered that the artifact, as it were, was a team effort; ownership had been settled by combat. One had a filthy old kerchief wrapped round his head beneath the hat; and the spokesman's right forearm bore a tattoo, showing a gibbet and a woman hanging beneath it, with the simple inscription: "Jane."

"There ain't no flar," said this individual with a leer. "We throwed down on two Chinks supposed to thieved some, then left them as flar for the buzzards, so to say, and I'll acknowledge, outright and open, that I've contracted a run-out case of the bow-wows."

"My brother and I, and Mr. Nickerson, will provide meat for the start, if a start *at this juncture* is advised," said Grantly Duncan, holding his chin as usual, looking as knowing as textbooks. "The gold is said to lie in profusion? And the news has not been widely spread?"

"Puke it up again, son. You sort of swallered your tongue down the home stretch."

"There's gold; you're sure?" inquired James, standing relaxed.

"Ain't I practically seed it with my own eyes? Ast Turk, ast Mose, don't bother to ast Bill; he ain't real bright in the head. A man told us—not two days back. He only pulled out to see his pore old dying mother in Frisker.[Here the scoundrel had the indecency to remove his hat.] Tell you what, if you ain't convinced, I'll show you where he's burried, not two mile from Balsein's Ranch—"

"That's where you got your grubstake?"

The leader thereupon clapped James on the back like a thunderbolt, and briefly I saw a look in his level gray eyes that made me shiver. I can't explain it, but the pupils changed color, to a shade somewhere between pink and purple. "Now you got it! For a minute there, by Jesus, I figured I was preaching to the squirrels!"

For all his crudeness, the stranger had noticed the symptoms, too, and made no reply when James said shortly, "We'll draw aside to consult."

"Opportunity," observed Grantly, "has seen fit to knock; better yet, to hammer on our door.

My opinion would be, in short, that hard times lie behind us. Frankly—"

"I don't like the skunks," said James. "Up, down, or sideways."

"We needn't like them; we needn't, in fact, trust them, or embrace them closer than rifle-length. Remain alert, I suggest, and keep a weather eye open, but travel in tandem as strength against Unfriendlies toward the Divide. In union, as someone states, there is—"

"You there," James called to the leader in a friendlier tone. "How do you feel about starting this late? You have horses, and pack mules; we've now acquired the same, no thanks to gold. But climb into one early big snow, just one—"

This was the longest address made thus far by James in my presence, and I judged that he considered Grantly (ever sanguine) unrealistic in this matter.

"I want you to lookee here, friend." The man thrust his face forward in a losing attempt to seem sincere. "I taken a liking to the three of you when we first met. I says to myself as follers: 'Luke'—name's Luke—'them three's tough; they're rugged; they're what we need round out this here party!' "

These remarks were much manifest guff that I thought James might burst into laughter, but Grantly only smiled, pleased.

"And I'll go a step furder. It galls me to confess it, but it ain't in me to lie. I'd choke like a mouse trying to swaller a woodchuck. Now what do you think of *that*?"

Since nobody replied, we began to sort out gear and were off in the morning. Our mules had been bought at a bargain, from Emigrants down on their luck, and our horses, while not fleet, had what they called here "bottom," meaning that they could maintain a good steady pace all day, graze on the skimpiest grass, and continue indefinitely.

It soon developed why the four had enlisted us. While they had firearms, of a sort, I'm convinced that none could have hit a giraffe at forty yards with a cannon. It was hard even to guess at their origins. As descendent of a ship-owning family, I detected a sea-tang in their speech, and I advised (aside) that all had classic piratical symptoms. Grantly thought they'd been "honest tillers of the soil, in some rougher section of Kentucky or Missouri"; but James considered their hands "tailored to cracking skulls."

Grantly left a note, addressed to the Indians and nailed to the new cabin door. It was carefully couched (with flourishes) in what he considered the region's "picture idiom"; probably it couldn't have been deciphered by the wisest chief since Squantum. I only hope they divined that the house, with the remainder of our traps, was theirs as a gift, together with our thanks.

To my surprise, we made good time. If they had no other skills, our partners knew how to pack mules, a tricky and exasperating task. Once I recall being in sight of snow-topped Mount Shasta; then, over the days (which remained bland) we struck the Lawson Emigrant Trail where it crossed the Pit River, and other place-names now forgotten, climbing slowly toward the Sierra Ridge. From time to time we saw Modoc and other Indians, who rode up to stand beyond rifle range, reluctant to press in and take casualties. It was to these knaves that we lost our

dog Watch, who ran out—too far—barking, and
was pierced by at least three arrows.

Both Grantly and James sat silent on their
mounts, and I could only guess at how they felt.
What the Indians wanted—what Unfriendlies
always wanted for the next twenty years of my
life—was horses. Still, less single-minded members of this tribe or that might settle for livestock,
or weapons and whiskey.

This last brings me to our developing trouble,
exceeding all others. If our companions had anything in their packs *except* whiskey, plus some
very odd pemmican, we never found what it
was. And as the trail became harder, the grass
leaner, the game scarcer, the loose rocks and
climbs more annoying, the handier they grew
with the bottle. This caused suspicious looks
cast our way, the forming of a separate clique,
with much whispering and derisive laughter at
night across the fire.

For our part, we established three night
watches, to avoid whatever the rogues planned,
and this lack of sleep, to be sure, took its toll.
Many a time I caught myself swaying in the
saddle, not asleep and not quite awake, either. At
length we found, in a declivity approaching the
summit, a sound (and empty) log cabin, with a
stable and a corral. Twilight approaching, and
the sky looking ominous, we stopped, entered,
and read on a notice at the chimney: "Welcome.
Replaice firewood. Bed-sprinklers sleep on
floor.—P. L. Smith."

"See here, sir," called Grantly as the four
waited outside, close in huddle; "I'm afraid I
don't know your last name, and what I frankly
regard as a mounting and inexcusable hostility

has made your first name stick in my throat. If it is your first name, which I doubt."

Stunned as I was, I heard James chuckle softly. Then the leader said, with a horrible look of grief, "Friend, are you seggesting I ain't got a Christian father and mother, same as other 'spectable folk?"

"If you have," Grantly replied stoutly, "I make no doubt that, at this minute, they are regretting their unfortunate decision to propagate."

I expected this careless answer to provoke gunplay, but all four doubled over in laughter, the leader being the noisiest and slumping, at last, against a tree for want of breath.

"Luke," said one, "you was propagated unfortunate; I knowed it all along. He got you that time, square in the bunghole. Own up, now."

James said, softly, "We three will look around for game; we're low on meat. When we return, we'll see a fire going, coffee or Evans Root brewing, and the nonsense finished. For good."

He was looking at the leader, who gave him a stare and changed countenance.

"I'll acknowledge—again outright and open—that things ain't been hopping along too sprightly. I claim my share, and willing to suck eggs for it. Men," he said, aiming at no particular group, "it's Montaner gold we're after; I'd durned near forgot. We'll lay aside the Tanglefoot and commence to pull double harness."

I suppose this was as close as he could approach to admitting guilt, and we three fanned out up the slope, hoping for a big-horned sheep but settling (with luck) for a deer not much larger than a dog.

The cabin, when we returned, looking inviting, with smoke rising from the chimney, horses and mules grazing in the corral— on rocks, I assumed—and all in order once more. It was a relief, and when we were inside, with the door shut tight behind us, those villians were divided against the walls, rifles cocked and aimed at our heads.

"Sit down easy, gents, without no sudden move or propagation, and you'll save I and my pards sweeping up your brains."

We were trussed to a split-log bunk, our money—several hundred dollars—removed, together with other usefuls, and out came the bottles again. They sat at a table, ignoring us, the deer still outside dripping, and drank a prodigious amount of liquor, belching, scratching, and cursing. Then they got out a greasy deck of cards and proceeded to dispute our funds. In half an hour a quarrel broke out, blows were exchanged, and patching this up, they broke into song. Of all the events of that evening, this last was by far the most painful. The song was incredibly foul, but I append a line or two in respect to frontier lore:

Oh, she ripped and she snorted
And she _____ on the floor,
And she wiped her _____ on the knob of the door,
And the moon shone down on the_____ of her_____,
And she brushed her teeth in jaybird _____.

Well, that stanza went on, and got worse, and became downright unprintable, and then it led into the next one, which stated the theme, and more, but I'll draw a curtain of charity over most of it.

Come on ye bastards, come on ye whores,
Up with your dresses, down with your drawers;
First lady forward and the second lady back,
And the third lady's finger _____ (etc., etc.)

There were additional lines, but I see no need to go into them, they were so raspy and ignorant.

Anyhow, the leader liked that song just fine; he said it was real music, and not many could compose it.

"I don't know," he said, seeming to cry; "all the great ones appear to have throwed in the towel. As a nipper knee-high to a hoppergrass, I attended a singing school—drug there behind a mule—and I ain't too happy about the present drift. Down on my luck in Frisker, I visited one of them opries, and had to knock down a floor-man to get out. Sounded like thirty-five cats penned up in a outhouse; what's more, a female woman was a-walking around wearing horns. No, I expect music—the true music, with beauty and all—to give a sneeze and a fart and disappear out."

Then he jumped on Mose for not staying on pitch. "I hope you don't take this personal," he said, "but you sound like a jackass eating briars, porest artist ever come my way."

While they were wrangling about this, Mose sticking bravely to his assertion that he'd been a choir-boy once, which gave him talent for songs like the above, two men slumped forward—asleep, or drunk. Shortly afterward the others fell heavily into bunks. From first to last, they'd never mentioned eating, and we had apparently slipped their minds.

Proceeding slowly, as if rehearsed a dozen times, Grantly freed James' clumsy knots; then we were loose within seconds. Grantly tiptoed over and recovered our belongings, adding their guns and even the wicked-looking knives at their belts. James, outside, had repacked our animals, and we made ready to move.

"Big snow coming on this side; I can smell it," and in future years I found this sense of his to be true. Brother James had some magic weather powers which were seldom, if ever, wrong.

"Frankly," said Grantly, "I don't regard the score here as even, and I try to make allowance for my fellow-man, including swine as deep in the mud as those—" gesturing inside toward the snoring and sodden four.

"Oh, I had a note to leave on," said James. "Better not touch their horses and mules—risky out here—but one good turn deserves another, as it says in the Book." He'd already made reciprocal preparations, with a log that he lodged against the door. Now, enlisting aid, he roped a broad slab, or slate, over a tree limb and onto the roof. This he carefully placed across nine-tenths of the chimney and performed a kind of acrobatic trick—just for fun—in getting down. Then we were off.

"Will they suffocate?"

"They'll come to, but I don't anticipate they'll feel like traveling soon. Then they'll have the snow."

Snow had started falling when we made our way—walking, leading the animals—upward through darkness relieved by old snow patches in gullies. But the trail was easy to follow. I have no idea when we reached the Pass, probably around midnight, where a wind was howling to take a person's hair off. It was bone-shaking cold, too, but during the descent the snow stopped, the temperature rose, and we were pretty soon comfortable again.

"They'll have five to fifteen feet of snow over there tonight," said James, nodding his head backward.

"In my considered opinion, then," replied his brother, "our friends will find themselves on short rations, especially since we took the deer. Yes, their diet will consist of, to wit: pemmican, and I think you know the pemmican I mean, Brother James. In these last three years," he continued with the musing look, "I've seen this gruesomeness often before. You'll recall the late, unwholesome episode of the Donners. The German who best survived was fat, even greasy, when the snow cleared and the party was found. Among other horrors, he'd eaten the brains out of children's heads. Now *that* monster was forgiven! He is today proprietor of a restaurant in Sacramento! A *restaurant*, if you please!"

"That's what they'd planned for us."

I wanted to ask what he meant, but the idea was so revolting that I held my tongue.

Presumably James sensed in me a certain concern, for he let his horse fall back abreast mine, put a hand on my shoulder, and said, "Chappie, don't waste any grief on those buzzards. Society would be better without them. They'll kill, and rob, and torture, and kill again. Nothing will change them. You see," he went on, "there *are* such things as criminals born. In this setting decent folk must realize it to live. In other hands, the scoundrels would have been shot without a thought."

I had occasion to remember those words later in Montana.

In course of time—days, weeks—we reached the Humboldt River and at Goose Creek saw camped the first Emigrant trains of our route. From these people we bought supplies—food, boots, heavier clothes. Then, at a prime fork of the trail, the right hand leading to Salt Lake, the left to the Hudspeth Cut-Off, we learned that further normal progress was blocked. Brigham Young, during a periodic tantrum, had formally declared war on the United States again, and his men lined the road to the Mormon capital. Countering, the Army was present to protect Emigrants en route to California. And now in winter, of course, the stand-still was worsened. We'd hoped, after cold-weather troubles, to proceed to Salt Lake—then to approach our target in the spring.

After consultations, notably with a man named Meek, who was rabidly fond of Montana and would be honored there, we decided to buck north for Beaverhead Valley, an amazingly temperate—and attractive—Montana refuge.

The Mormons were inconsistent. We saw many wagons selling stores to travelers, defying Young's edict, for the sect dearly loved to make money. But memory remained of the frightful Mormon massacre, when, in southern Utah, Mormon "militia" murdered in cold blood an entire Emigrant train—120 men, women, and children. Only seventeen infants were spared, for reasons best known to the Prophet. Young, under some slight criticism, at length condescended to give as "excuse" the fact that the train was from Arkansas, where one Parley P. Pratt, a member of the "Twelve Apostles," had himself been killed, by a Mr. McLean, whose wife Pratt had seduced. (McLean took an unreligious view of the act, implementing his peeve with a pistol.)

As I thought this over, the excuse seemed thin, and I concluded that Mormons, nearly all Mormons, and most religious fanatics, might to advantage be re-settled on some small, unhealthy atoll in Micronesia, preferably where food and drink were scarce and beri-beri flourished without medication.

But after we'd turned north toward Beaverhead, finding rough going and sparse game, now in deep winter, when sensible people and beasts dug into shelters, lo and behold, a Mormon bishop manning a small Mormon "fort," turned out to be kindness itself. Quite secretly he sold us flour, bacon, coffee, and sugar, at low prices and with evident alarm for our safety.

Reconsidering the whole problem, I resolved to make no further generalities for two or three weeks.

[3]

Game at Beaverhead abounded, to use the popular phrase. Especially were there antelope (lean), black-tailed deer, whole bands of elk, and big-horned (or mountain) sheep. But these last were wary and quick, and to shoot one was to be hailed with triumph. We camped by Blacktail Deer Creek, where Snake Indians provided us (by trade) an elk-skin lodge big enough for a family of ten. In this lodge we were comfortable, there was plenty of wood, and game was

everywhere. But the lack of other provisions
forced us to live on meat alone. Fat was prized
above all, badly needed for good health. By good
fortune the winter was unusually mild, with little snow; more often than not, we went hunting
without wearing coats.

The local Indians were Snakes and Bannocks,
with a few Flatheads. All were peaceable, not
seeming to crave liquor, as most tribes did. Fifteen miles distant, at the Stinking Water River,
lived a settlement of mountain men commanded
by a Captain Grant (also of Hudson's Bay origin)
and a mile beyond these were Jim and Ben
Simonds, very large men, weighing well over
two hundred pounds each, and both, to my surprise, Delaware Indians. This fact seems piquant
when one reflects that the name came, of course,
from that long-ago colonial, Lord de la Ware, just
as "Indian" sprang from Columbus' misconcep-
tion that India was the land he struck. In any
case, I had no idea what Delaware Indians, obviously native to the East, were doing in the Rockies.

All the mountain-men had Indian wives, or
"kept squaws." These ranged from "full-
blooded" on up, or down, to near-whiteness. So
far as I know there were no all-white women in
Montana then. Squaw-wives were not handsome
by white American standards, but many were far
from ugly, and they were well made—with deep
bosoms, marelike buttocks, and round thighs
that fitted close together. Indian "braves" were
beardless, and the women had little body hair.
Often (as a susceptible male) I deliberately
averted my eyes because here, too, except in
extreme cold weather, all went about nude. The

men, from the Duncan Journals that they kept "turn-about," "wore at most a 'fig-leaf,' and fig trees were at a premium in Beaverhead Valley . . ."

Captain Grant, a hardy Scotsman, rode the fifteen miles to invite us to Christmas dinner, which included buffalo meat, boiled smoked tongue, bread, dried fruit, a preserve made from choke-cherries, and real coffee. And in the afternoon we went to a lodge sixty feet wide to play the never-ceasing Indian game of "Hands." While our neighbor tribes disliked whiskey, they were prey to a mania perhaps worse. Of all the inveterate gamblers I was to meet in the years forthcoming—and I served my time in gaming halls—the Indians of southern Montana outstripped the pack.

When we arrived the game was in full cry, and "cry" is the correct word. I could hear the racket for a hundred yards before the lodge came into view. Inside was a circle of mountain men and Indians, these last singing and pounding on sticks, to attract genial nods from the Spirits. Offhand I could think of nothing better calculated to send a Spirit hiking toward home and the quiet life. The din was represented to be "music," but a concert of coyotes, by contrast, might have booked engagements for a tour. To borrow from another Journal, "the tent sounded as if the hounds of hell had suddenly been unleashed and were scrambling for the exit."

Participants were arranged around a lodge-pole, and each had his treasured small belongings in a pile before him. My success at gambling was slight; in college I'd separated (by dice) a dress suit from a student whose mother wrote in

some heat and demanded it back. I could remember no other peaks. Now I was amazed to see
the Duncans taking their place in the circle, with
avid looks and every sign of experience. I was
probably taken aback because of Grantly's frequent righteous reminders that neither he nor
James touched drink, the attitude suggesting
that they'd shaken off other sins as well.

I should have known better. Both were perfectly normal, whatever the term means, and
while Grantly's claim about alcohol was true,
they enjoyed many mountain pleasures not endorsed by churches.

"Hands," which had variations, was as block-
headed a game as a primitive people could de-
vise. Yet it had a hold on the mountain-men as
well. They thought it tricky and subtle, or in the
words of a squint-eyed old gas-bag who enjoyed
a strong reputation for lying, "Son, I throwed
dice with the crowned heads of Europe, thieved
gems from African chiefs, and outskinned the
heathen Chinee, but nothing's in it with Hands. I
hope you won't let this out, for I got a decent
father and mother, rich too [he could scarcely
have been less than seventy] in Philadelphyer,
but it's got a grip on me like a beaver-trap."

Despite his windy statement (and he seldom
made another kind), a certified idiot could have
played the game after five minutes' instruction.
Reduced to essentials, a gambler took a polished
stick or bone an inch long and an inch and a half
in diameter and flirted it back and forth—before
him, over his head, and behind him. Then, after a
series of such brilliancies, he inquired which
hand it was in. There, you may agree, was a
complexity to tax the powers of Aristotle.

Once the gymnastics ceased, the bone passed to the next man after a single exertion, win or lose. An astonishing amount of gold-dust and goods began to change ownership. The Indians stepped up their music (the Spirits apparently being sluggish), and all was confusion.

A fire burned in a raised earthen box, and everyone was smoking. The mountain-men (or miners) had tobacco, and the Indians used "Kinnikinick," which was shredded from the leaves of a red willow and softened with a plant known as "Larb."* Thus our air, though the roofhole struggled to help, was thick and blue, not only with smoke, but speech and music as well.

James had a good afternoon. When we got home he counted up and was ahead by $11.40 worth of dust, a fiddle-bow, what was advertised as a Blackfoot scalp, a bugle, an eaglebone whistle, a pair of opera glasses with one lens missing, four and a half pounds of bacon, a conch shell, and an infant raccoon that bit through his thumb and was tied up outside.

But the big loser had been a mountain-man who, item by item, peeled off every garment he wore, surrendered his pan and pick, risked and lost his horse, and then lost his wife, said to be a willing worker of about sixteen. These things accomplished, he sat looking around, without a stitch to cover him. "Well, she ain't been a bad old woman," he said, "but she's up the spout for sure." He seemed philosophic, as if he'd known similar straits. "Time I borry me a pan, I'll raise enough color to regain a costume, as well as a

---

*Larb—from the French "l'herbe," meaning "plant"—was used throughout the Rockies to sweeten Indian "tobacco."

nag and a squaw, but by Jeeters if it ain't cold to prospect pelt-raw!"

Several men expressed agreement, and even sympathy, and said what a pity it was to be naked on Christmas, but I noticed that nobody offered to lend him any clothes.

If this sounds harsh, even suicidal on the miner's part, with the temperature at twenty-eight degrees, I'll add that he kept his lodge, it being an unwritten law not to take a man's dwelling or his pipe and tobacco. With these he was thought able to survive under any conditions.

Mountain-men were tough in a way foreign to me. I learned that the cabin we'd recently used across the Sierra was the property of one Peg Leg Smith (hence "P. L." on the chimney sign). A chapter in this old fellow's history provides a picture of these "half-men, half alligators," as they liked to call themselves. Some years before, Smith and four companions were holed up against a storm, drinking whiskey to keep warm. But they drank too much for one member, who, after a series of blood-curdling yelps, raised his rifle and let off a shot at a trapper who'd "insulted" him.

Well, the shot missed and struck Smith's left leg below the knee. It became quickly evident that, to avoid gangrene and save his life, the leg must go. The carousing had ceased, of course, and the assailant had made a general apology, plus a handsome one to Smith, which failed to improve the wound. Smith thereupon begged each man to cut off the leg, but all refused, on grounds of surgical ignorance. They said they were afraid he might die in the process. Smith nodded, understanding, and stated that any man should be proud to have such friends. Then he set to work himself.

Suffering terribly (for the leg soon turned septic), he filed teeth on an edge of his knife, cut through and around the flesh, seared the arteries with a piece of red-hot iron, and finished by reversing the knife to saw the bone. He bandaged himself without assistance and lay back to await convalescence.

During this process, which required two days, the group (including Smith) saw it natural to resume drinking whiskey. Then they joined in a sentiment-filled but simple funeral for the leg. The five—with the former owner propped against a tree, participating—sang three or four hymns, and one man delivered a eulogy in which he praised Smith's leg for carrying him as far as it had, and for other good works, such as kicking dogs, and hoped that the other leg would "waltz in and take up the slack." There was some talk of carving a head-board, or foot-board, but nothing came of it.

Smith's companions ("pards") were further useful by insisting on sticking around to hunt and feed him for a while, claiming that he looked "pukey and run-down." But within a week or so, what remained of him was able to arise on his own and whittle a wooden leg, which he still wore at the time we used his cabin (one of several). Also, it seemed natural to mountain-men thenceforward to drop his original name (whatever it was) so that he was thenceforward known, simply, as Peg Leg Smith. He was a leading figure of his place and period.

(We had this account from one of those same

companions—elderly now—and, "insofar as you can believe anything a mountain-man says" [Grantly], I think it was true in its essentials.)

The case of Smith's friend and fellow-trapper, Hugh Glass, is doubtless more melodramatic, in the same tough sense, for Glass, in a hand-to-hand fight with a grizzly, lost most of his scalp, suffered a badly broken leg, had all his back ribs bared, and was generally chewed to rags. For a week he lay unconscious beside a stream. On awaking, he set his leg by placing the foot in a sapling-crotch, pulling, and splinting it; fashioned knee-pads from grizzly hide (the bear having died of knife wounds), and then crawled two hundred miles through Indian country to Fort Kiowa. He moved mainly by night, dining on grubs, mice, and berries. When the stripped back threatened infection, he found maggots to cover and cleanse it. Glass lived for many years after, a close friend of Smith and Jim Bridger, drifting into the Rockies when beaver finally played out. In this, he was one with the Montana mountain-men.

CHAPTER IV

SPRING CAME EARLY that year, and we removed to deer lodge valley, sixty miles north. We settled at a place we named American Fork. Placer (or panned) gold had been reported here, and besides, the Duncans were restless again. I think both brothers recognized their mining handicaps, and Grantly, at least, was ever alerted for sidelines that might free him for scholarly research. Once at the Valley, in a beautiful setting, the stream swarming with fish, good timber on the slopes, game everywhere, we set to work building a large cabin, with improved skill now. During our labors a "Chinook" blew steadily, this being a warm, gentle breeze from the Pacific northwest that tempered the area most of the year. Finished, the cabin was solidly packed round the bottom with sod, and sod was laid thick on the roof, to keep us cool in summer and warm in winter.

We also built a corral, since we planned to "accumulate stock," in Grantly's words, and go into that enterprise on a pretty large scale. No barn was needed, for Montana bunch grass was rich in nutriment. Animals could openly stray all winter and be as fat in spring as if stabled and fed on corn during the cold and snowy months. Southern Montana was, and is, a kind of paradise in that way.

Our stock business worked out as follows:
Emigrants and miners were frequent visitors—
again on the move—and from the Emigrants we
bought exhausted cattle and horses, fattened
these and re-sold them, the horses mainly to
Indians. The cattle meat, after a winter of bunch
grass, was so fat as to turn cherry-red, tender and
juicy, superior to any beef I ever bought in restaurants, either in New York or in Boston. We
ourselves often butchered, then sold choice cuts
for ten to twelve and a half cents a pound.

Familiar tribes—Bannocks and Snakes—lived
in this region, but some Nez Percés—amiable
and quick—had lately drifted down from the
north. Poor creatures, they'd contracted
smallpox from some unknown source, and we
often saw them riding trail in single file, their
faces scored with open sores. The Indians once
called our valley (thirty-five miles long) White-
Tailed Deer Lodge, from a low butte formation
near the center; and while I never fully grasped
the connection, the name (or part of it) remained
in perpetuity. Atop the butte was a boiling-hot
spring that rose and bubbled, never spilling
over, and many warm springs and marshes lay
below. It was a joy to bathe in these, even in brisk
weather, and to watch the Indians, principally
the young girls, cleanse themselves now and
again. In the roughest winters here, snow never
stayed on the ground more than a few days.

Now in late spring, our log-house complete,
new projects ahead, troubles behind us, and food
not a problem, the future seemed filled with
promise. Still, at our busiest—building, butchering, setting out garden seeds bought from

Emigrants—James and I noticed a new restlessness in Grantly. Many times he slipped off for an
afternoon, unanounced. Toward dark he returned with a heavy string of trout slung over
one shoulder. Then he made a strong point that
"from a dietary standpoint, fish is essential to
good health." But he looked a trifle sheepish all
the same. It was mysterious.

Assuming Grantly was right, we lived in a
dietary Garden of Eden. The streams, and the
lakes they flowed into, were a-boil with trout in
such numbers that nearly any cast, with a reed
pole and an insect, would bring a four- or five-
pounder thrashing in, mouth open and seining
the surface. Its bright hues and speckles made a
fisherman glad to be alive in such a place. And to
point things up, I quote from Grantly's Journal:
"A friend of mine, fishing, asserted that the trout
were so big and aggressive that one leaped out of
the stream, chased him into the pine woods and
bit off the end of his spurs . . . he may have been
joking—"

And then, after a while, Grantly began to return on the following mornings.

During an evening when the three of us were
busy at tasks inside, snug and cozy, a cheery fire
popping and blazing, he cleared his throat and I
gathered that a pronouncement impended.

"It has come to mind," he said as we looked
up, James with a smile, "that man—natural man,
and casting no aspersions on those present—was
not decreed by the Almighty to live alone, specifically, without a mate. In this connection, I
make scriptural reference to the joining of the
late Adam and Eve, not digressing to comment
on their offspring of Cain and Abel and the still

embarrassing question of how the race descended from the family without incest—"

(His own embarrassment was so plain, I thought, that he was having more than his usual problem coming to the point.)

"People are, to be sure, different. What seems to be a biological need in one is a trifle for another, worked off by different means—creating a great painting, writing Shakespeare's mighty works, composing a masterpiece of music (not, I hasten to say—the odious swamp gas of our friends across the Sierra) or [in deference to us] by hunting, herding, planting, prospecting—"

"I gather you're planning to buy a squaw," said James, but Grantly hastened to correct him.

"Your description of my carefully considered program is not precisely the manner in which I myself might have phrased it—and while I intend no criticism *at this time*, Brother James, I beg that you not allow your rhetoric to degenerate with our present reduced (though genial) surroundings—"

"What's she look like?" inquired James.

Grantly winced. "As you know, a settlement of Snakes, consisting of ten lodges, exists four miles down the Valley, or two miles past the Butte. The chief of this group has a daughter, issue of the third of his four wives, who has expressed a desire to unite herself matrimonially to your narrator. I wish to stress matrimony, Brother James, for I am taking unto myself a *wife*—not 'buying a squaw,' as you so crudely put it—"

"I know him. What's the old buzzard ask?"

"Forty dollars, but subject to barter," said

Grantly, holding his chin. "Frankly, I consider that cheap. The girl—my betrothed—is a wizard at tanning hides, and I've never seen a lighter touch with a trout line. She—"

"How old?"

"Rising fifteen, but in prime condition. Another, of only ten, helps round out a brood of twelve, but she lacks the skills [here he had the decency to look out of the window and cough] of my fiancée. And ten, besides, may be young even by the mores of our Montana brothers, than whom no finer breed—"

He would have rambled on, being rattled by now, but James brought him back to earth: "What's the kid's name?"

" 'Dó-pur-rah,' which means 'Apron' in the native Snake, or Shoshone, and when I say that this maiden—girl—has such inborn modesty and breeding that, almost alone of her sisterhood, she insists on wearing an apron *at all times*, you might get it through your head," he concluded, lapsing briefly from his lofty diction, "that I'm grabbing up one hell of a bargain."

"We're all three expected to go over and swap knives?"

"For some reason," said Grantly, back to normal but not offended, "you've seen fit to place this step in wedlock on an informal, or even humorous, base, but there's another point with which you're not familiar: *both the Chief and Apron* have offered to help with my dictionary of the Snake language!—for a consideration, of course."

(I should add that Grantly indeed went on to write his admirable dictionary of Shoshone, as he'd done with the Chinooks in California, and both works now enrich the shelves of libraries in colleges over the land.)

Next morning we put on our best clothes and set out down the Valley, carrying items thought suitable for barter. James had the bugle and defective opera glasses, Grantly carried a framed mirror with embossed cupids that he'd picked up on the trail, and I offered all I had left of interest—the faded Harvard blazer. Arrived at the camp, we were greeted without effusion. (Indians manage to conceal their camaraderie with trade in the offing.) So—we proceeded to the Chief's lodge, or wickiup, as miners called these dwellings. The old rogue, alerted, came out and touched hands, and we sat down in a circle, his wives inside, not on display. He wore some kind of headdress that included feathers, a necklace of bear teeth, surprisingly clean buckskins, and, hanging round his neck with the teeth, a letter from an Army general, alleging his comparative honesty and non-hostile status. This he showed us before we got down to business. His not displeasing face was wrinkled and lined like a sunburst; he could have been, as James remarked, "anywhere from seventy-five to a hundred and fifty, and slippery to match."

"Let's trot out the merchandise, have a look," James suggested briskly, causing distress to the groom. The girl propelled into view was shapely—but not wearing an apron. Grantly whispered into the Chief's ear, and she left to verify her name. To me (when she returned) the apron had little look of usage, but I felt disappointed that she'd put it on at all. The girl's features were a trifle heavy for whites accus-

tomed to delicacy, and her expression, while not
sullen, lacked that dewy-eyed eagerness of the
average bride. Here, for some reason, James saw
fit to unsheath his bugle, sounding a blast to
rattle the tent poles. Grantly began a protest, but
the horn attracted all who heard it; we collected
an audience. Showing little interest, the bride-
to-be wandered off toward her apron-less
friends.

I'll omit details of the haggling. I'm convinced
that Grantly might have forked over forty dollars, and the wedding train could have headed
home. But the tactic of preamble must be observed. To my dismay, the Chief fastened on to
my blazer as the choicest prize at hand; that and
the bugle. The garment being my last physical
link to home—with some abusive letters from
my father—I was saddened to see it go. College
can be a sentimental experience, and the garment represented what I was supposed to do
there.

In the end, or after two hours, the girl went for
$28.75 in dust, the bugle, the mirror, and my
blazer, which the Chief promptly threw over his
buckskins. He presented the most outrageous
sight I'd ever seen, and Brother James took the
same view. But I was soon resigned, and wished
I could have given him one of the new Harvard
skull caps, with a pennant to complete the mas-
querade.

Grantly was pleased. "Frankly," he stated,
aside, "I thought we'd have to ante up more dust.
I think it was the blazer that tilted the scales; I'm
grateful for it—" but James replied, looking serious, "Don't we have the usual ceremony of best
man, ushers, bridesmaids, and the like? And

what about a parson? Frankly," he said, bearing down on the word, "I don't consider you married."

Grantly fell into his musing pose. "I would deceive you if I said that the question had not occurred. But you can see plainly enough—one potential bridesmaid is busy boiling a dog, and the others have removed to bathe in the springs. As to the ushers, I doubt if they could be secured without a gift of buffalo, or bear, or, at least, an elk. Even then they'd have no idea what they were ushering. About preachers, I know of three in this general area. All sleep during the day in order to play poker at night. No, I've concluded that the smart plan is to have two best men and crown the ceremony with bride and groom jumping over a broomstick. You'll observe that I've brought one for the purpose."

But the girl flatly refused to make the jump. So we three followed the custom, and then the Chief, curious, insisted, but caught his right foot, falling on his neck. And after him other adults in the tribe jumped—everybody, as I say, except the bride.

When we started home, the Chief, upright and honest, put a rope around the girl and handed the other end to Grantly, adding a cottonwood switch. This seemed to augur poorly for future wedded bliss, but we got home all right, and that night James and I slept in an elk lodge, near the corral, that we used as a tool shed.

In the next days we'd added another room to the house, with a smaller chimney. During the interval, the girl tried twice to run off, scratched up Grantly's face, and declined to talk when he patiently tried to get on with his dictionary. Then, on an afternoon when Grantly, frustrated, went fishing, James unemotionally seized the girl's hair, dragged her to the lodge, draped her face-to around the center pole, and tied her hands and feet, while she kicked and yelled and tried to cut off his head with a scythe. After this, he gave her a thorough, deliberate thrashing with a harness strap, doing his best work on it. I figure she'd remember it for some time, and maybe murder us in our sleep.

But no; the punishment had a wonderfully soothing effect. It even gave her a kind of affection for us all. Her expression improved and she fell to work at all manner of chores, humming a Snake or Shoshone tune that (I supposed) had to do with scalping, or spreading over an anthill, or the like. I wasn't quite convinced, not with that wildcat.

Well, two or three weeks ran by, peaceful and pleasant. We got our seeds in, sold several dozen cattle—the usual exchange to Emigrants being one sound cow or ox to two half-dead ones of theirs—and panned a little gold from this stream or that. The big gold strikes were coming—nearby, too, with violence unsurpassed, and in amounts to make American fortunes. But that lay in the offing. If we lacked zeal for prospecting at the Lodge, it was from two main reasons. We had, really, no professional tools, and we hadn't much skill, either. But maybe a better excuse is that we enjoyed trading more.

A lot of this was with the Indian tribes that lived within ten or fifteen miles of us. Most of our trade goods were obtained from Emigrants who'd decided to settle here, dropping their original ideas about California. This is not a book about Indians, but they were present, and should be described now and then. Besides the Bannocks, Nez Percés, and Snakes (who so enriched Grantly's life), other tribes drifted through in this year—Yakimas, Coeur d'Alènes, and, later, Blackfeet. With all of these except the Blackfeet, we continually traded, their principal wants being calico, red cloth for female leggings, paint, beads, knives, powder, lead, percussion caps (for by now peaceful tribes owned firearms), combs, blankets, and—above all—vermillion. For these articles, James plied the Emigrant trails or went to settlements, with cattle and horses to trade.

What the Indians offered in return was mink and beaver hides, dried meat, dried tongues, buffalo robes, and an occasional nuisance like Apron.

Now—I've read much material calling western Indians low and thieving; I'll say here that many were absolutely honest, and less avaricious than whites we dealt with. It was the mechanics of trading that attracted Indians, mainly. From first to last, in those years, we never lost a cent from business trickery with our red neighbors. The Nez Percés, for example, knowing the value of gold and how to get it, usually had money, and paid cash on the spot. As to the others, if a buyer given credit fell dead or became sick, one of his wives or relations appeared to settle the debt.

Small bands of red visitors rode by now and then, and the frontier form was to ask the Chief inside to dine. The others camped nearby, and were gone early the next morning. They could

easily have stolen cows, oxen, horses, but they
never did—not once. All that came later, with
different tribes, and I'll admit, in sorrow, that it
more than offset the integrity of our first Indian
friends.

A Captain Higgins had formed a settlement,
with a store, several miles to the northwest, near
what became Missoula. They named it Hell Gate
(after the river), and it was from these gentlemen
that we'd bought our first seeds, and a plow. But,
all unawares, we planted those seeds in low de-
pressions where frost formed, sometimes even in
the summers. And since none of us knew how to
plow, our early venture in gardening came to
nothing, unlike successes of our neighbors a few
miles distant.

Here I can't resist quoting the Duncan Journals, because an understanding of the brothers'
near-triumphs may be grasped from the always
cheery account: ". . . Frost visited the low
spots every month in the year, and no sooner did
a vegetable poke its nose out of ground than it
immediately froze. The nights were cool, but the
sun turned the days into delights . . . Had we
selected a place on the bench *east* of the house,
we could have watered it from Gold Creek and
had a beautiful garden free of frost . . ."

(To Grantly, at least, the loss of produce was
merely a phenomenon that he, as an observer,
found more absorbing than tragic.)

Of greater interest (to him) was the population
influx, and a later Journal entry says, ". . . about
this time other people arrived, up the Missouri
River—made navigable by a new, low-draft
paddle-wheeler as far as Fort Benton (100 miles
north) . . . these intended to mine at Oro Fino,

on across the Divide, in Idaho, properly speaking, but they decided to stop near Deer Lodge . . . here they scattered out to prospect. Most remain in Montana, with a pocketful of rocks . . . still, they seem as robust as grizzlies, though some periodically suffer attacks of 'quartz on the brain,' which rages over the region. It seldom proves fatal, the victims usually recovering after bleeding freely from the pocket."

One morning a man from Higgins' rode up, his horse all a-lather. He had news of vital interest, in particular to Grantly. When Grantly stepped outdoors, puzzled, the fellow handed him a note and waited. Then both James and I went out, and Grantly recoiled—stepped back a pace—as if struck. He told the messenger, "Come in; my espoused will prepare your breakfast," and he pressed one of the new dollar bills on the man, who was a part-Indian clerk at Higgins' store.

"We haven't a minute to lose!" said Grantly hoarsely. I'd never seen his expression so grimly set.

"Blackfeet?" said James. "I've been expecting this." He turned to run into the cabin. "Loose the stock, Chappie. Give them a slap and start them moving."

"Books!" said Grantly. "On the highest authority—that is, Captain Higgins himself, wonderful man, educated, erudite"—he was practically babbling—"a white trader of gentle breeding passed through, refusing to stop, and among his affects—effects—was—yes, it's true—a *trunkful of books!* He's headed to establish camp in Bitter Root Valley—"

"Saddle up," said James in a weak voice.

"Two pack mules and our fastest horses. Let's see—over a hundred miles; we can make it in four days in this weather, *if* we push."

"You think the muzzle-loaders, Brother James? There may be others on the trail in a crisis of this kind—"

"Take all the guns. If it comes to a skirmish, we'll have an advantage atop Devil's Canyon, shooting down—"

I could barely believe my ears. No more peaceable men ever lived than these Duncans—I'd come to look on them as fathers, and they treated me as a son and an equal—and now, unless I'd mis-heard, they were talking about combat over a trunkful of—gold? Not at all; over a possible collection of *books!* Both were great readers, true, and I myself was starved for reading, but this! Then, quite suddenly, I realized that it wouldn't do to be outflanked. We might lose the books altogether, and I thrust my new Colts (birthday presents) into my belt.

When we left California we had about two dozen books, but most had been soaked when we crossed streams. There remained the Almanack, the Bible, and *Pilgrim's Progress*, and, frankly, these had worn thin. Grantly claimed that, with our minds on so many new things, Montana might "temporarily creep into the library," but that hadn't happened to me yet. Even so, the Almanack now seemed fuzzy, with an over-abundance of statistics. The truth is that I'd come to a point where I was never perfectly sure of my ground. I remembered, and was glad for it, that Niagara Falls was a mile and a half high, and that Aaron Burr had killed Benedict Arnold in a duel—shot him with a buffalo gun. The Bible stayed intact, with Moses climbing Mount Shasta and all, but *Pilgrim's Progress* had turned into a bore. It never came across why the fellow left home in the first place. Unless, of course, he'd gone after gold, which made sense, but I decided to quit worrying about it. I'd never liked the book in college and wondered why professors treated it like the Holy Grail.

"Here," said Grantly to our informant when we were ready to go, "I want you to have these," and he thrust forward a rusty old beaver trap and the conch shell, but the man declined them, for some reason.

We left at a pretty rapid gallop, then slowed for the horses' sakes, and took up a steady pace west toward the Bitter Root. Snow and all, canyons, climbing, drifts in the high places, marshes in the low, hard fords of the Blackfoot and Hell Gate, we made it in four days. And then, after inquiries, we found that the owner had gone to the low country leaving an Indian to guard his trunk.

This was a good, loyal Indian, who said that Mr. McArthur (a Hudson's Bay trader) had given him no authority to lend books. But after much palaver, we left a deposit to take several volumes on loan. Then we set off (at a brisk clip, lest he change his mind) with a Shakespeare, a Byron, Headley's *Napoleon and His Marshals,* and Adam Smith's *Wealth of Nations.* As parting generosity, for the Indian had lately been converted, and looked it, he fished up a Bible printed in French. But we ducked out of that and left.

And when we got back, Apron had vamoosed—jumped the stockade, so to speak.

Departed the premises for good. She'd also carried off some edibles, a lantern, a buffalo robe, several pieces of red cloth, and a horse.

I don't think anybody minded, and that included the groom. We made a fire, settled down to read, and didn't stir for a week except to eat.

But later on, true to his scholar's duty, Grantly wrote a thoughtful appraisal, in the Journal, of Indians' characteristics; those in our region, that is:

"The Bannocks and Flat-Heads are the bravest Indians in the mountains.

"The Snakes are the most gentle, tractable, and best dispositioned.

"The Bannocks are the finest-looking men, but the women are the ugliest of any.

"The Snake women, and part of the 'Tó-sawees,' are the best looking among the foregoing tribes.

"The Flat-Head and Nez Percé women are masculine in disposition. They are most intolerable termagents, and they generally wear the breeches.

"The Snake women have the characteristics of the men, being kind, gentle and tractable.

"The Bannock men are proud and quarrelsome, the women are stubborn and obstinate.

"The Flat-Head men are good-dispositioned, conceivably due to the efforts of Jesuit missionaries, who were among them for years.

"And I note that all Indians here, like the Algonquins, have a name for 'best men'; with them it means—hunters."

Reading these, I concluded that Grantly, with such information at hand, might have done a little research on individuals, too. Our Apron may have been (and was) handsome, but she was ornery enough to have a mixture of white blood. I hoped Grantly would dig harder on any future try.

It was eight days before he drew me aside (me having read all four books twice) and said, "Ross, my boy, I hope you apprehend that my remarks about rivals were spoken in jest. I am *not*," he emphasized, "a man of violence; surely you realize it by now. I don't know," he said, looking off, "there was something about the abrupt mention of new reading that appeared, well, to jangle the wits just briefly. I trust you'll forget what has passed," and James, later, offered a like sentiment, though pared down some. As for me, I didn't open my mouth. I wasn't too happy about the way I'd felt, either.

The Chief rode up to restore the stolen horse, and the lantern and the buffalo robe, and stated that Apron had gone east across the Divide with a buck. These were all he could recover. Nobody pressed him for the gold; it was worth that much to be rid of her. In fact, Grantly gave him back the horse (which was sway-backed and had fistula) and said he could keep it as long as Apron didn't return. And then, thinking it over, he added the lantern and robe and said if she did show up, tie her to a lodge pole if she talked of coming to us. James thought it might be better to break one of her legs, and the Chief agreed, but Grantly vetoed the idea, considering it "a trifle extreme."

Into the turbulent future, both Grantly and James had a succession of uniformly irksome squaws, like most Montana men. And then Grantly met the gentle Aubony, who enriched his life for many years, seeing him at last a leading man of the frontier. Apart from Journals, the Duncans had small, leatherbound "Accounts," and in these they faithfully kept records of all purchases and sales. Now, after a passage of time, they seem both sad and comic.

"Acquired [Indian name], short and well muscled; hog-eyes; about 15 years old. Paid $30 in merchandise; she lasted 3 weeks. *My decision this time—unable to stand her litter and filth; showed her the door. She was a son of a bitch!"*

"Acquired [idem]. Ten or twelve years old and the smallest piece of humanity I was ever in bed with. No virgin: I made sure first, not being a monster. Gay little girl; paid $36.50 for her; this broke down to 1 blanket, 50 lbs. flour, 6 lbs. sugar, 6 lbs. coffee, 6 yards of sheeting, ½ yard scarlet sheeting . . . She ran away, but was rather dear for four nights."

"Acquired [idem] . . . tall, well-built, formerly Dick Berry's woman; she had a high-toned old son-of-a-bitch for a Daddy . . . Paid: one Remington revolver, one Army blanket, 2 beds picked up on Emigrant trail; one yard red cloth; eight yards domestic muslin. She climbed over pickets after daylight, leaving me asleep in bed, and went to Baker's Fort. I followed, and got back most of the stuff. She was a son of a bitch!"

"Acquired [idem]. About 14 years old—well made. Not very tall, and has had three white men. She was a f____g machine, and that probably drove men off, for they left the region."

"Acquired [idem]. Plenty of hair, above and below. Understands English . . . Daddy is blind and has custom of begging around Forts. Rather poor pedigree, but paid $61.00. This was a horse, woolen blanket, ten pounds sugar and two pairs of scissors. She was mean, and I'm afraid I treated her so. She went back to camp."

"Bought a handsome girl, 14, a Santee, giving the Chief a gun and promised a horse in Spring if she suits. Afraid she won't suit. Is too independent and goes fishing and refuses household chores. Also won't wear stitch indoors; distracting to all. Shooed her out, after catching her in willows with other girl her age, locked in nude embrace. I called her disgusting; she cursed back. Much homosexuality among female Indians; said to be some among men. Cannot verify this . . . She was a son of a bitch!"

From the Accounts, written in tiny letters, there is no way to tell which entries are James' and which Grantly's. The handwriting is too small for differentiation, but I assume that the uncharacteristic "son-of-a-bitch" was used by one brother only.

All the squaws but one—the Santee—were Snakes, and I'll confirm that these girls—or women, for they matured very early here— would try the patience of Saint Sebastian. Neither Duncan was a saint, but both were gentlemen by breeding and instinct, and gave that impression. Indian girls were accustomed to Indian life, and, in general, took badly to the white man's ways.

CHAPTER V

Now I MUST consider the problems, the terrible happenings as miners, gamblers, and other drifted into southern Montana over the next two years. As a start, Blackfoot tribes migrated from the Badlands and began stealing horses and cattle, influencing the normally decent Bannocks. We maintained vigilance, but the skirmishes became more and more annoying. And since, besides, few of our seeds ever matured, dashing our hopes for crops, we considered moving to a new town called Bannack.* This lay at the mouth of Willard Creek, southward; reports of rich gold deposits had lately come from there. Perhaps the way to describe our life in this time of the 1860s is to choose at random from the Duncans' Deer Lodge Journals:

". . . will try to harrow such crops as rose tomorrow . . . killed three large wolves last night with strychnine, and probably more could be found . . . late yesterday John W. Powell and two other sports arrived for a poker game and we played all night. Powell lost $97.50 and another $65.00; I was the best winner . . .

*There exists no good explanation for this curiosity of spelling. The best guess is that some map-maker new to the region inscribed the word phonetically, and it passed into the language.

"Complexion of this area changing from peace to roistering, to our dismay . . . Went to Dempsey's ranch today, found everyone drunk and three strangers there with fifteen gallons of Minnie Rifle whiskey—this usually composed of one part alcohol and ten parts water, with considerable tobacco and cayenne pepper to strengthen. It also has effect of strengthening a drinker, so that he's apt to knock out a window or shoot holes in the roof, or a dog, to show he's a good fellow. *Oh! for a lodge in some vast wilderness where drunks would never come and whiskey was unknown!* . . . heard one man remark, 'I'm told they're having trouble back East—the North's fighting the South' . . . we have not kept current with news from those parts . . .

"We now have nineteen young calves, four yearlings, 33 cows, and three bulls, aside from horses and mules. But the Blackfeet causing much trouble . . . Some Flatheads passed in hot haste today after losing horses; we gave them bullets and percussion caps; when they returned, two days later, the Chief held aloft what purported to be a Blackfoot scalp . . . Tied our best horses at the cabin door and lay on porch all night with our rifles at our sides . . .

"Gold Tom* came to visit today and stayed overnight. He will never give up prospecting; though he's often near starvation. He says he's found 'strong color' up a gulch near Pioneer.

---

*"Gold Tom" was one Henry Thomas, a Montana fixture of the period.

Brother James and Ross and I rode over to see his 'dig' the following day . . . were amazed at the work he'd done. First off, he hewed by hand a wooden bucket, pinning it together with pegs; using this he hoisted dirt while sinking a shaft. He would slide down the rope, fill his bucket with gravel, then climb a notched pole, and dump the contents; he'd hewed boards eight inches wide and seven feet long, to make four sluice boxes; these he placed near the shaft and beside a ditch he'd dug to the stream . . . thus he washed the gravel. Even so, he seldom made more than a dollar and a half a day, and on many days, nothing . . .

"Brother James has returned from trip to Fort Benton after tools. Thanks to the rich American Fur Company (once formed by John Jacob Astor) and its broad-bottom paddle-wheelers that fight up-river now, often swiveled on sandbars, smashed by logs in fast water, beset always by Indians—persons of every degree pour into Montana from the East. In passing, I'll add that James nearly fell to a disaster typical of the Territory now. As the boat he meant to meet—the *Chippewa*—approached a wharf, it exploded like a rocket, raining down debris enough for all . . . on investigation learned that a deck-hand, carrying a candle, had entered the hold in search of alcohol.

"Today—Nov. 12, '62—held counsel and elected to start move to Bannack. Reports of gold there have grown, and our settlement has gone sadly downhill. Indians not only gaining in boldness, but a rougher element has taken up residence, and whiskey, gambling, and violence have replaced the peaceful pursuits of farming, cattle-raising and gold-seeking. Already we've bought (for a niggling sum) a cabin sight-unseen in new town and have arranged for a butcher-shop; wish to dispose of livestock. Bannack some ninety miles south.

"We completed drive without distress, thanks at one point to James and his markmanship. Proceeding through a low canyon, we were startled by a lone Indian, wearing feathers and paint, and mounted on a dappled horse. He appeared from nowhere and shook his coup-stick* angrily, then wheeled to ride off, obviously to collect help. He was perhaps 240 yards distant.

" 'Blackfoot,' said James, and coolly stretched out on ground to steady his rifle, an Adams' .40 calibre breech-loading Maynard. There came the sharp report, a puff of smoke, and the Indian dropped like a sack of wheat; no muscle twitched after he hit the ground.

" 'Wasn't that a head-shot, Brother James?' I said with a hint of reproach.

" 'Base of skull. I thought the gun could do it, and by the Great Sachem it did!' He seemed jubilant, and I said no more. Then I noticed friend Ross looking peaked, and put him to work, saying, 'My boy, can you catch that pony? He'll give us away if you don't.' "

Journal entry by James: "Bannack: Largest of new towns we've seen; don't care for it. Busy,

*Many Indians in fights counted the "touch" of an enemy with a coup-stick almost as important as hitting him with a weapon.

busy! . . . springing up like Jack's beanstalk
. . . Only two main streets, half a mile long . . .
'hotels,' restaurants, grog-shops aplenty. Everything confusion, much crime. Homicide nearly
every day . . . no churches, schools . . . buildings all of logs, pole roofs indifferently covered
with sod, as low as you could imagine a man to
live in . . . Most of town on Grasshopper Creek
between high canyons . . . we never see the sun
rise in this valley [and then, laconic and self
effacing] . . . Run-in with fellow named Slade;
turned out unimportant . . ."

I'll return to my own notes and describe what
James considered "unimportant" (though no
one in town did). After a morning of wandering
through ravines, we were in Fogle's Universal
Joint playing poker. That is, James and I were
watching Grantly, who, never drinking, had always an advantage, it seemed to me. After the
passage of years, I remember others of the
group—Whiskey Bill Graves, Hank Crawford,
Sam Hauser, Club-foot George, and, I believe,
one of Bannack's two fiddlers, whose name I've
forgotten.

(In the years to come, these men would follow
widely different courses, one or two advancing
to lead Montana, others choosing paths with
ends too awful to dwell on.)

Thus far the play had been quiet and orderly,
despite bottles on the table and rough-house at
the bar. Grantly was seventy dollars ahead and
reaching for a pot when several chilling war-
whoops were heard from outside, and a wild-
eyed young man astride a black horse burst

through the door and rode up to the bar. I heard someone say—I think it was Hauser—in a discouraged voice: "Slade!"

"Fill him with Tarantula Juice. He's loped without rest from Pike's Peak,* and tonight he smells blood!"

"Yes, sir, Mr. Slade; I certainly will do just that. Tarantula Juice for the horse coming up. Same for yourself, sir?"

Hearing this, Slade whipped out a Navy Colt, lightning fast, and addressed the bartender, who was shaking so badly he spilled half the horse's portion on the wood.

"I may have mistaken your words; I hope so. I drink nitric acid dosed with gunpowder, and, yes, by God, this hole needs a new swamper—" but before he could level his weapon the horse snorted, twisting away from the whiskey, and Slade found himself staring directly at me. He gazed me up and down, as if I were a new kind of insect in town, along with the black flies and mosquitoes. Then he laughed at some joke that I failed to comprehend.

"You, there, with the spanked-baby face. What's your name? Where'd you come from? You got an undertaker handy?"

Scared as I was, my mind had time to form an impression: a handsome fellow in the early thirties, raffish western hat, a broad but well-bred-seeming face (now hotly flushed), yellow hair down from his hat at the back, and wearing two bowie knives known here as "Arkansas tooth-

---

* At that time "Pike's Peak" was the generic term for what afterward became Colorado Territory.

picks." Dressed, further, in torn buckskins with a good many silver trappings for himself and his horse; and the blue eyes sizzling crazy, like a lunatic in an asylum.

I could think of nothing to say except "Which question first?" but the words stuck in my lower organs. An Indian girl lay asleep in a corner, one hand on a black and white dog, and now she stirred and the dog got up and stretched. This madman—there couldn't have been a second between—shot the dog in the head, and the girl bent over, crying and wailing and beating her fists on the floor. She was spattered with blood, head to foot. But that dog was a favorite of the place, and three or four men started from their chairs, inching down very deliberate when Slade glared at this one and that. Then he returned to me, but James stepped nimbly between, in his circus-acrobat's style.

"Who's this cricket? I take it he's running partners with the Devil, and trying to get back home. Speak up, Squatty."

"I'm unarmed," said James in his normal quiet voice.

Perhaps it was the easy tone—Slade appeared just perceptibly to rein himself in. But he braced up, eyes crazier than ever, and said, "You want it on your knees, like a Christian, or standing all spraddled out?"

"When you rammed through the doors," said James conversationally, "I figured it for another loud-mouthed rummy, but when you shot the girl's dog, I recognized you were a cowardly son of a bitch, and had a whipping due. Leave your pop-gun on the bar and step out in the street."

You could hear the gasp in that room halfway across town. And these weren't a breed of men to be spooked by much short of Hades. It was hard to understand, but I had it cleared up fast when told Slade's history. As to that wild-man, he sat on his horse the picture of shocked surprise— "like a grizzly knifed onexpected in the back at a social," as a miner put it later.

But when he'd recovered, he said slowly, leaning over, "Squatty, have you got a pig's notion who I am?" I somehow sensed he was trying to find a way out, but I was wrong; and James was far off in calling Slade a coward. I doubt, today, if he ever had a feeling of fear in his life—up to the end, that is.

James smiled. "In a general way. As you'd know a family of polecats taken up quarters in a barn. I do know this," he continued, while the shocks built up and up and up, "You've got a regular fancy-man's get-up there"—nodding toward the silver—"but you'd jangle better from a tree limb." Here I heard Grantly chuckle softly and saw Sam Hauser glance at Hank Crawford. It was over my head; I scarcely knew James, the gentle, relaxed companion of California, the trail, and Deer Lodge. But I saw that, for reasons of his own, he was bent on a show-down.

Slade cocked his gun but seemed uncertain. Then he gave another war-whoop, tossed the gun to the bartender, and said, "Hand up that bottle!" After he'd downed half the contents at a pull, he wiped his mouth, saying something like "*Yah!*" and threw the bottle at a mirror behind the bar. The glass was still splintering down, with a kind of Christmasy tinkle, when he rode outside, yelling louder now and daring James to step out and "face up, toe to toe, all free, nothing barred, throat bit, eyes gouged—mountain rules and the winner buy the funeral!"

He said some other things too, as James and the rest filed out in no haste. These remarks were descriptive of himself, though maybe overdrawn. Many emerged in halves; he was half-horse, half-crocodile, half-grizzly, half-rattlesnake, and half-blasting powder, accustomed to pulling up trees by the roots, biting through crowbars, eating Chinamen and Greasers for breakfast, and topping off with ground glass and dynamite.

According to this, James hadn't much chance, for the sum added up to at least two and a half men, and all above the average. I'd never shot anything worse than an elk, but I resolved to put a bullet through this zoo if things reached a danger point. (By and by, in Bannack, I found that such brags were routine mountain talk, trotted out for any occasion, especially if a bottle was going. Slade used them only in drink, perhaps imitating something he subconsciously admired.)

I don't mean to make the above sound absurd. This was serious trouble, and I noticed store keepers bolting their doors and boarding up windows. They'd had visits from Slade before, and suffered for it. They expected gunplay before the day was over, and so did everyone else.

Slade now stood in the street, stripped to the waist, and about a dozen scars stood out clear and ugly in the afternoon sun. Some, I learned, were from a running duel he'd had with a man called Old Jules—absorbing two frontal shotgun blasts before killing him at last, nailing him to a fence, and cutting off his ears for watch-fobs.

James handed his hat to Grantly, threw down a Chilean cigarillo, and moved into the street. He said, "You've needed hobbling for a long time, Slade. People've let this go on too long." Then he dodged a wicked kick and a roundhouse swing that might have taken his head off.

But there was no fight, not what the crowd hoped for. Slade's lunge sent him sprawling into the dirt, and when he got up, screaming and swinging wildly, James moved just enough to let the blows whistle by. This went on for three or four minutes, and several miners began to laugh. And sure enough, on all fours, panting, Slade whipped a knife out of his boot, and the finish came in a hurry.

James slipped beneath the slash and, behind him, hoisted this reckless maniac high overhead, one arm under the crotch, the other at his neck. It was done so quickly no one properly saw how he managed. Then he slammed him down so hard a number of tied-up horses shied and swiveled around, one breaking free and galloping off down the street, trailing its reins.

Dimly, as if far off, and the scene unreal, I heard somebody say, "By God, if he ain't forked lightning corked up and ready!"

Altogether (though I could have miscounted), Slade was picked up and slammed down three, four, five times, and then he was unable to stand any further. When James stepped back, waiting, not damaged, not breathing faster than normal, a group of Slade's friends dragged him to the walk. One said, "Don't kill him, partner. Take away drink, and he's different as night to day. Whiskey appears to poison him, like."

"I know his habits. It's a pity he forgot; we've met before, and apt to meet again."

But when Slade was washed off, and straightened out, and maybe several bones slipped back on location, he approached James and said, perfectly white-faced and seeming sober, "Stranger, you just died and went to hell. I'll be back at four o'clock tomorrow: I'll break custom and warn you, this once. Be gone. Be good and gone, and don't come back."

In the next twenty-four hours as many as fifty miners and others begged James—and Grantly and me—to leave town and lie low for two or three weeks; some suggested we vacate the Territory.

In explanation, a bearded miner said, "I've knowed him here, knowed him there, knowed him on the Overland Trail, and he predicts as easy as weather. Vamoose—that's my offer, unless you're partial to lead."

For myself, I wouldn't have balked at a trip to see some new country, but Grantly and James never mentioned leaving. If we'd known Slade's story in detail, Grantly and I might have begged James to withdraw. For one thing, nobody in the Rockies was considered his equal in a hand-gun duel. And if we could have looked forward to Slade's career when complete, we might have *dragged* James out of town. Of the human landmarks in Montana's early days, Slade was the most enigmatic, and the most tragic. All histories of the state now give him a chapter alone, but never quite explain him.

Next afternoon an uneasy quiet settled over Bannack. Business closed, with most places boarded up tight; and the citizens disappeared from the streets. James (chewing on a straw) stood on the plank walk—armed this time—and Grantly and I were behind posts, both with .40 calibre breechloaders. And then, on the stroke of four, here he came, alone in the street, an odd sight. No other sound, no movement except the cloppety-clop of his horse's hooves. But there was something different here; he cantered along as steady as rock, upright in the saddle—a serious and imposing figure with a purpose.

He dismounted in front of James, holding his reins, and said, "Sir, I don't know you, though your face seems familiar. I have in mind that I gravely offended you yesterday and received a thrashing. I beg that you accept my apology for conduct so rude a gentleman might hang himself for it. I wish you and your companions well in Bannack and hope that, in time, we can become friends."

James shrugged and said, "Forget it." Then he added, neither friendly nor unfriendly, "Slade, these sprees are getting worse. Surely a man like you—from a fine home and family—can find some means of improving life—"

"Sir," Slade repeated, "I value those words. But there's no turning back now. I'm as good as dead; I wish I were dead. Good day, the best of luck to you all."

Next day I noticed that the Indian girl had a new dog, and the saloon's mirror was replaced with one larger. The girl, by the way, was thirteen or fourteen, the property of a miner past seventy, who referred to her without exception as "my old woman."

Slade was born of gentle, affluent parents in Carlyle, Illinois, and during his youth was popular though rambunctious. Accounts of his early life vary, but all agree that at last, in a fit of temper, he killed a man, then joined an Emigrant train for California. One biography has him briefly in the Army, but details are fuzzy, and other stories of his wandering half-wild through the Rockies sound more credible. Even in this phase his infamy was beginning to spread. Once he provoked a quarrel then said, from his gentlemen's side, "It's silly to waste a life in heat; I suggest we throw down our guns." His antagonist, relieved, did so, and Slade promptly shot him dead.

Many of his murders were whimsical. He shot one man for trying to prevent a dog fight; then, filled with liquor, walked out of Goodrich's (a saloon) and killed an Indian "for luck." A bartender made the mistake of offering him a bottle of inferior whiskey and, told to "dig down and bring up your best," was shot the instant he turned his back.

This being a period without law in the Rockies, Holladay's Great Overland Stage Company (expanded from the original Jones and Russel Stage Company) was an easy traget for horse thieves at the stations and, on the trail, for highwaymen, desperadoes, and outlaw gangs. In the words of a writer at the scene: "There was absolutely no semblance of law there. Violence was

the rule. Force was the only recognized authority. The commonest misunderstandings were
settled on the spot with revolver or knife. Murders were done in open day, with sparkling fre-
quency, and nobody would have thought of inquiring into them. It was considered that the
parties who did the killing had their private
reasons. For people to meddle would have been
thought indelicate."

If the Overland Stage was to thrive, then, it
needed men who were half-everything. Slade
was a logical choice; he was hired and started on
the first, bland leg (Atchison) then quickly
moved west to the Rocky Ridge Division, where
thugs were thick as mosquitoes. Slade made an
overnight transformation and became "the
nemesis of the thief and the gunman." In no time
he was acknowledged to be the best, the most
gentlemanly, the most courteous division chief
on the line, "the man most solicitous of pas-
senger comfort, the employee remembered for
his exquisite manners."

But he showed another side, too, even in his
job for Overland. His official duty, he saw, was to
cleanse the route of crime, and he pursued this
career with zeal, based on experience of a general nature. A few station-keepers—isolate in
their setting—relieved the tedium by stealing
and selling company horses themselves, by custom blaming it on Indians. Two of these were led
to back yards and hanged by Slade in person, as a
warning (he stated) to others. Skeptics said that,
yes, his motive might have been what he
claimed, but there was a chance, they said, that
he was merely following a habit, hoping not to
get rusty.

"Slade's name soon became a terror to all evil-doers along the road," wrote a Diarist of the period. "Malefactions of all kinds were less frequent, and when one of magnitude was committed, Slade (and his friends) were early on the perpetrators' track, seldom failing to capture and punish them. The power he exercised as division agent was despotic." And another contemporary wrote that "Slade began a raid on the outlaws, and in a singularly short time completely stopped depredations on stage stock, recovered numbers of stolen horses, killed the worst desperadoes . . . and gained such dread ascendancy over the rest that they respected him, admired him, feared him, obeyed him!"

But Professor Thomas J. Dimsdale,* an English Oxonian scholar who sought improved health in Montana, observed that "Those who saw Slade in his natural state would describe him as a generous friend, a hospitable host, and a courteous gentleman. On the contrary, those who met him when maddened with liquor and surrounded by a gang of roughs would pronounce him a fiend incarnate."

This was the man whom James had whipped unconscious, and the above offers a fraction of his escapades to that date. Southern Montana's people were convinced that this puzzle of good and evil would bide his time (as he'd done before) and gun James down when he, Slade, had the advantage. Overland's load of complaint about Slade's erratic course had grown so heavy

---

*Professor Dimsdale was the first editor of the *Montana Post* (in Virginia City, Montana) and was appointed Superintendent of Public Education when Montana became a Territory.

that his career with the line was drawing to a close; and this visit to Montana, among others, was evidence that he knew it, and required greener fields for the future.

Now, in the years after, I see where a Samuel Clemens, known as Mark Twain, has described an encounter he had with Slade, in riding an Overland Stage then writing a book called *Roughing It*. Taking into account Mr. Clemens' hyperbole, I believe the anecdote to be true in its essentials.

"Here was romance," wrote Clemens, "and I sitting face to face with it!—looking upon it—touching it—hobnobbing with it, as it were! Here, right by my side, was the actual ogre who, in fights and brawls and various ways, *had taken the lives of twenty-six human beings,* or all men lied about him! I suppose I was the proudest stripling that ever traveled to see strange lands and wonderful people.

"He was so friendly and so gentle-spoken that I warmed to him in spite of his awful history. It was hardly possible to realize that this pleasant person was the pitiless scourge of the outlaws, the raw-head-and-bloody-bones that the nursing mothers of the mountains terrified their children with. And to this day I can remember nothing remarkable about Slade except that his face was rather broad across the cheekbones, and that the cheekbones were low and the lips peculiarly thin and straight. But that was enough to leave something of an effect upon me, for since then I seldom see a face possessing those characteristics without fancying that the owner of it is a dangerous man.

"The coffee ran out. At least it was reduced to one tincupful, and Slade was about to take it when he saw that my cup was empty. He politely offered to fill it, but although I wanted it, I politely declined. I was afraid he had not killed anybody that morning, and might be needing diversion. But still with firm politeness he insisted on filling my cup, and said I had traveled all night and better deserved it than he—and while he talked he placidly poured the fluid, to the last drop. I thanked him and drank it, but it gave me no comfort, for I could not feel sure that he would not be sorry, presently, that he had given it away, and proceed to kill me to distract his thoughts from the loss. But nothing of the kind occurred. We left him with only twenty-six dead people to account for, and I felt a tranquil satisfaction in the thought that in so judiciously taking care of No. 1 at that breakfast table I had pleasantly escaped being No. 27. Slade came out to the coach and saw us off, first ordering certain rearrangements of the mailbags for our comfort, and then we took leave of him, satisfied that we should hear of him again, someday, and wondering in what connection."

CHAPTER VI

Now WINTER CLOSED down in earnest, the worst winter southern Montana had known. Game disappeared, and Bannack streams were fished out. The cold, frozen gulches, the snow, made prospecting a torture, and miners from outlying valleys straggled into town. Under these conditions, amusement "parlors" boomed, and a new, dubious element joined the miners to swell the population. The stage was being set. Drifts blocked all trails to Salt Lake and Pike's Peak (Colorado), so that provisions getting through were sparse and infrequent. Grantly had expanded the butchering to be a general store, and James took turns running this and hunting. Occasionally he came back with an antelope, but an antelope's lack of fat and general meagreness offered next to nothing. For food, they were considered the least of the deer, and hunters of our region often passed them by in the hope of fatter game, able to back-pack a limited amount.

Then James and I, hunting in the mountains, had a strange experience. During that day, which was pretty far advanced, we'd seen no game whatever, when, standing belly-deep in a drift, were six or seven antelope, rigid, ears alerted, and making no effort to run. I saw James frown. and heard him say, "Take the one on the right flank, and I'll take the buck in the center—we've got no choice today."

We fired simultaneously, and not a member of the herd stirred. We fired again, and moved forward. But when we reached the poor beasts all were frozen to death—as James had guessed—exhausted by trying to free themselves from the snow. They froze standing up, and stayed that way.

Supplies at the store were spread thin. The Duncans were grieved to charge the prices needed even to pay costs. A hundred-weight of flour sold for $100 gold or $200 in "Lincolnskins" (greenbacks). Common hard tack, which generally required an amateur dentist after a few crunching bites, was $1.35 a pound, and a suggestion was made that the commodity be soaked in boiling water. But when it failed to dissolve in a day and a half, some mountain-men put forth that it was made out of wood, and hard-wood at that—on the order of mahogany or teak—so it never gained popularity. Beans (often wormy) went for $2 a pound, ten pounds of sugar was $15, and salt was listed as having no price. That is, it was so scarce that an entry could never be fixed with assurance. Instead, I see "1 paper saleratus—six dollars." Saleratus was in essence the alkali dust of the plains, containing, one gathers, a certain degree of saltiness, unless my Latin roots have failed me. And when I say that, a year before, flour sold for 12§ a pound, you may see that these present prices were high.

Unable to buy tobacco, the miners reverted to the Indian "Klinnikinick," and several old sourdoughs complained that it left a bitter taste "around the region of this chile's gums." But I'm convinced that those stringy fossils could have smoked poison gas without discomfort, and would have done so if pressed. They used a "green pipe," called "Póo-e-toy"—made from a rough green stone— which crumbled when exposed to air for a while and needed replacement often. The Indians had advanced from the Póo-e-toy to a transparent pipe, its fire visibly a-glow. This was also green in color, fashioned from an odd kind of rock that they rubbed over and over with grease, to prevent cracking.

Broadly speaking, my contribution had been hunting with James and digging coal—for the fireplace—in spots where low-grade deposits could be found beneath the snow. Fat—and greens—were what we wanted worst; a grizzly would have supplied the former, but non-hibernating bears, in this weather, strayed north toward Oregon and lived on salmon that swam the rivers there.

(It might be said that Oregon was never very popular with mountain-men or Emigrants, because of its long, heavy rains. The people who settled there were known, with some ill-deserved contempt, as "Web-footers.")

We scoured the gulches for stray moose, the edible parts being their huge, sagging noses— several pounds each—most of which was fat. But during our crisis the nearby Indians gave us pointers. Themselves suffering, they still had stored-up acorn-mash, grubs, grasshoppers, and similar foods, and they sent scouts to alert us about vegetables. It appeared that the common thistle had roots which tasted like turnips or cabbage, and these proved sufficient. James had complained that his teeth were "rattling in his

head," and, hopefully medical as always, diag-
nosed the noise as "scurvy." And I must say that
when a band of Snakes (prompted by miners'
wives) pressed handfuls of dried and frozen berries on us, the rattling ceased. So maybe he was a
born doctor after all. And the Indians here were
"gentry-born," as the Journals put it.

Our cattle had long ago been sold, and the few
saddle horses we kept were sheltered in a rear
addition to the store. Normally horses could be
loosed in a protected valley and thrive, even
grow fat, on the rich bunch grass. But horses,
now, would sicken and die from drinking the
near freezing water.

On an afternoon when I came in from a fruit-
less hunt, I found Grantly, alone in the store,
studying a note from James that said, simply,
"Gone for food, idea from an Indian. Back presently."

"Conditions," observed Grantly (glad, I
thought, for a chance to pontificate), "cannot be
sufficiently dire for Brother James to launch
forth with some quixotic notion of immolation
for the general weal. To me, such a notion verges
on lunacy, in a family noted for the strength of its
mental forces. My father, as I perhaps let slip
once or twice [upward of two or three hundred
times] was a man much given to reading, to the
detriment of his professional career—which, as
stressed, consisted of keeping on the move. And
my grandfather, his father, was said to have had
no peer in the field of poetic quotation—the only
field, I believe, that he ever ploughed with
success—"

"The temperature's just on thirty below zero,"
I interrupted, for he was good for half-an-hour

more, especially when worried. "Whatever he has in mind, he's running a strong chance of freezing. I'm tempted to go search." I made a motion toward the door, which the wind was shaking as if it meant to drive on through and finish us.

"My boy, what fate the Almighty holds for James—with, of course, a strong pull from Brother James himself, for he has experience not made privy to you—it is better, in sum, to have one man missing than two. Darkness is settling down. I beg that you take the advice of a much older man, and wait. We'll remain clothed, and see this out together. If nothing happens by dawn, well—"

(Grantly was, at this time, just on thirty, but his judicial manner, plus his lofty carriage and a sprinkling of gray hair, left the impression of a figure in his middle fifties. He was aware of this image, and nursed it to his advantage. I've seen him consent to give counsel to miners twice his age, who, grateful and jubilant, rushed off to do precisely the wrong thing.)

The night passed slowly—one of the most anxious of my life. Innumerable times we sprang to the door after a loud clap of boards, only to admit a choking blast of snow. And at dawn, the blizzard lifting, we prepared to put on snow-shoes and head off for—nowhere. But both pairs were missing from their place, and while we looked the building over, including the stable, they were not to be found.

"It should have occurred," said Grantly, seating himself near the fire, which I'd built high for a long absence, "that Brother James, with that cunning for which he has been remarkable, would have taken steps against foolish moves by his companions; what I mean is, precautions for our safety. Our situation, is—we're stuck."

And all that fiercely chilling day, no one approached the store. Bannack was bottled up tight, and, I assume, many miners, in their cabins or wickiups, were literally so.

Then, in the late afternoon, with a feeble sun struggling to work through, we heard a stomping of feet and sprang forward once again.

"Well, it was a rouser," said James, grinning through a face-mask of hoar-frost and snow. "For once, I was glad I took the compass."

At his feet was the crudest possible sledge, held together with limber strips of what I took to be willow. Later he told us the runners had been picked from cottonwood limbs having a curve at the base; these he had greased with melted jerky. He had his Arkansas toothpick—a weapon of multiple use—a hatchet stuck in his belt, and a breechloader over his shoulder, its magazine bound in bandages. Aside from home-made flies stuck here and there in his atrocious skin cap with the ear-flaps, these tools provided his armament.

On the sled was tied a sheet that covered a large, suspicious-looking bulge that I naturally took to be a corpse; shootings in Bannack's gambling saloons now took place at least once a day.

"I'm afraid I had to borrow a mercantile sheet, Grantly," he said, "and I see it's been ruined by blood—"

"Who is it, then? That is to say, is it anyone we know? While I dislike to lose a friend—be he red, white, or median—I'm convinced, Brother

James, that your motive was good. As to the sheet," Grantly went on, agitated beyond coherence, "we have yet to sell the first selection from our shelves. The fact is that a miner, standing inside our store, remarked to me as follows: 'I catch ary man a-sleeping twixt sheets and I'll perforate him to let in air. I ain't altogether calm about blankets either, when buffler were sufficient for my father, and *his* father likewise.' "

"Fish," said James, and ripped away the sheet.

Stacked in neat, shiny rows, gutted and frozen, were trout in the dozens, in the hundreds, fat and all of a size—four to five pounds.

"Exactly three hundred. I stopped there; no reason for gluttony; these should last out the winter."

"Then how—?"

"An Indian friend told me. A stream and little lake a few miles off—fed by warm springs. But I'll confess that the climb up and back was boisterous. Not to mention a night sleeping under a ledge and feeding a hungry fire."

"We must divide with your benefactor, of course. I only wish we could have him cast in bronze and placed beside the stream for future generations."

"This particular group spurns fish. They call it 'bear food,' and think it brings bad luck, evil spirits. No, we'll hoist the three hundred and show gratitude by another means."

This mention of "hoisting" requires explanation—of the fifteen-foot poles that stood behind most miners' "shebangs,"* as they called

*The word "shebang" was born in the Rockies, probably a corruption of several Indian syllables.

their lodges and claims. It sounds unlikely, but even in summer meat wapped in cheese-cloth and hauled to the top of these poles seldom if ever went bad. Scholars who examined the phenomenon agreed that the Montana air here was so pure, and the breeze so fresh at fifteen feet, that there was little chance for the development of whatever causes the rotting of meat.

But in the end, thinking of Bannack's present thievery and murder, and growing Blackfoot insolence, we stored the fish in boxes in the stable. We kept the door tightly locked, with a string attached to a warning bell aloft. There they sat, frozen stiff, slowly diminishing through that awful winter.

A natural disaster can raise an unhealthy yeast in the persons it affects, as decent people are apt to turn looters after a fire or an earthquake. This was the year Bannack erupted with violance. In a newspaper piece called "The Dark Days of Montana," that staunch, ailing Englishman, Professor Dimsdale, wrote, "It is probable that there never was a mining town of the same size containing more desperadoes and lawless characters than did Bannack during [this] winter . . . While the majority of citizens were of the sterling stock that has furnished the true American pioneers, there were great numbers of the most desperate class of roughs . . . Many of these last had fled misdeeds elsewhere, others had heard of rich pickings in Bannack, where much gold lay for those properly skilled and equipped, and more were corrupted by the degenerating tone of the town . . . Shooting, duelling and outrage were daily occurences, and many was the vile deed done of which no record was kept."

The population had grown to about a thousand, with the returning miners and new-comers. Many of these were strangers to each other. There was no resemblance to villages back home, where everyone knew the rest, what they did, what they had for breakfast, deplored it, wishing they'd had worse, and lived in the tradi-tionally mild ill-will and gossip. These new ar-rivals to Bannack were hard cases, using the local term. To ask one his name and origin was to provide quick business for the undertaker (a fur-niture maker who, it was said, hadn't produced a stick of furniture in his frenzy to keep abreast the coffin trade).

On any bland day I walked down town and nodded to persons whose faces were familiar but whose manners had yet to be tested. All—including the miners—wore guns, and usually a knife or two, and in the gambling saloons any harmless greeting might be misconstrued. Bar-tenders kept standing in a corner, as standard equipment, a mop for swamping up blood. A main trouble had to do with the atrocious liquids served at the bar; Tarantula Juice, Tanglefoot, Minnie Rifle Whiskey, Vally Tan, St. Vitus Bit-ters, and the like. As far as I'm aware, no real assay was made of these devil's brews, but most contained tobacco, pepper, and a sprinkling of black powder. They further contained, accord-ing to a squinty old miner with a stench to send foxes hiking: "poison ivy, wore-out socks, skunk-piss and dandruff"—but the man's vera-city was not of the highest, and his remarks were generally discounted.

Human life was held very cheap, and few of Bannack's happenings that winter conformed to a pattern. Two well-known men, George Ives and George Carrhart (the first of whom would make history) were talking in the street one morning when I passed. Their words were heated, and I stepped up my pace, along with some others. It was the custom for store-keepers to place barrels before their places, as protection for viewers; an omission of this would have been thought indelicate, and likely caused a ruckus. And a ruckus, as often as not, led uphill to the graveyard, which then had no single resident free of punctures, sickness being unknown in Bannack.

The voices were raised; Ives cried, "You son of a bitch, I'll shoot you!" and stepped into a grocery for his revolver. Carrhart ran into his cabin, returning with his pistol, and found Ives peering in the opposite direction. A man of honor, he waited till Ives swung round, and then fired, missing by inches. Carrhart's gun now misfired as he skipped nimbly behind a door. But his chance came when Ives futilely emptied his gun and started to walk off, disgusted. Following a fairly loose code, Carrhart thereupon shot Ives in the back, the bullet passing through to kick up mud in the street. Not much inconvenienced, for he'd acquired other holes along the way, Ives roared out, "I'll get another revolver, by God!" Carrhart seemed content, however, and left the scene. Later that day they resolved their quarrel and went together to have Carrhart's revolver mended; the misfiring had puzzled them both. Ives, at that time lacking a comfortable abode, lived at Carrhart's ranch* for the rest of the winter.

Bannack's viewpoint toward shootings came close to being humorous, and it was certainly offhand. There was even some effort to make them "stylish." Not long after the Ives' ventilation, with its happy reunion, three strangers rode into town, occupied a deserted but fragrant Snake lodge, and began showing up at the games. They seemed to have no lack of money, but one appeared to be amassing sizeable winnings while the other two saw their dust steadily dribble away. This fellow was described by a miner as having a "kindy tucked-in greedy look, like a coyote or a politician." He was also unusual, for he was tall, and portly, and clean-shaven.

Among themselves they were friendly but not warmly so, having met (it was shown at a preposterous "inquest") during a lucky, chance hold-up three weeks before. Commonly, by-passing monte and faro, they played seven-up at a table alone. At length the losers became alerted, and they searched the winner's room at a time when, drinking, he went to sleep in his chair.

Their findings included seventeen new decks of cards, wrapped and expertly notched for the "sand-tell," extra aces for emergencies, three pairs of no-seven dice, and further tools of the career gambler. But the two went to bed without protest, each owning something of the kind himself. Next day, however, the grievance grew on

---

*A "ranch," then in Montana, was any dwelling place well outside of town.

them like a fungus. After consultation, they headed for Bannack's single-rocker barbershop, where their friend was being shaved. One side of his face was finished when a call came from the door, "Stand back if you value your life!"

The barber, not greatly upset, for he'd lost five clients in the rocker, obligingly stepped aside, and the scoundrels pumped four shots into their companion's chest. Seeing him dead, they removed their hats, swabbed their eyes with filthy old kerchiefs, and one said sternly, "Now take care of our pard, hear me? And don't do no slipshod job of it, neither!"

"Certainly, gentlemen," replied the barber. "Leave everything to me," and he resumed work on the corpse, shaving the other side of its face, taking special care in the tricky underfolds of the chin, and routinely started to ask if the razor was all right but caught himself. Then, remembering the piratical look of the callers, he applied liberal hot cloths with scent and powder to top off on. During the process (which required a little time) his mind wandered off again, and he said, chuckling, "One of the boys was telling a rip-snorter of a joke this morning. Seems there was this farmer who—" then he looked down, disappointed. With the powder liberally dusted, he laid down a mirror he'd started to hold up, gave a professional whisk to the hair-cloth, and cried, "Next!" Then, recovering again, he went to fetch the undertaker. (He later offered all this poppycock as "evidence.")

A farcical inquest was held (the decent citizens absenting themselves), and a verdict of "justifiable homicide by virtue of being shook down and hornswoggled by a crook" was re-

turned by five miners, in a saloon, who couldn't
have risen from their chairs without assistance.
The "foreman" was congratulated on the skill of
his wording, and several straight-faced men
treated him from the bar. There was some
grumbling about it in town, but nothing happened.

Then Bannack's troubles were suddenly seen
as more serious than comic. A history later said,
"It required a succession of horrible outrages to
stimulate the citizens to their first feeble parody
of justice." For one thing, the lawful
residents—greatly in the majority—tired of the
town's system of settling debts. No documentary
proof exists that Shakespeare visited Montana,
but he appears to have anticipated the Bannack
method. "When the debt grows burdensome,
and cannot be discharged, a sponge will wipe
out all, and cost you nothing." One Hayes Lyons,
of whom a miner offered the lyric description
"No lowerdown polecat ever crawled out of a
hole," rode into Bannack and decided that he'd
found, at last, the Green Pastures. He announced
his habitat as "of the Rockies" and gave his profession as "Receiver-general of all moneys and
valuables not too hot or too heavy for transporta-
tion by man or horse at short notice."

In the saloons this news was received with
calm, since it fitted nicely into the regional
scheme and rhetoric. He boarded with a Bannack
landlord who delayed mentioning the touchy
matter of payment. But when he heard that
Lyons, during an evening, had won $400 play-
ing monte, he hinted that a settlement might be
due. Lyons went into a frothing rage, presented a

revolver at the man's throat, and cried, within hearing of people in the street, "You son of a bitch, you ask me that again and I'll make it damned unhealthy for you!" Then he shot out a lamp, started a leak in a handsome brass spittoon, and wobbled down the street, aiming at a dog here, an Indian there, and even a miner (out of range) on horseback. He was too drunk to hit these last and apologized for it next day.

But his actions launched a mass protest, the feeling being that they might be out of proportion to the cause. It was one thing, understood and normal, not to pay for rent, but it hardly required shooting up the town. And there was bitterness over a decision by the landlord. He said he seemed to be in the wrong business— there was no profit in it. Then he closed his place and left town, much regretted. The man had been popular. Finally the complaints took on an ominous tone at a senseless massacre of several Indians, with whom, in general, Bannack had previously lived in peace.

One Charley Reeves, widely considered of little account, bought a Sheep-Eater squaw, a young girl who refused to remain long in residence. Her grounds were that he'd settled into the domestic rut of kicking her when convenient. Reeves went to Yankee Flat, a small Indian encampment near town, for marital counseling with the Chief. But the two fell into a wrestling match instead. Reeves, not winning, thereupon tried to shoot the Chief at close range, "ploughing a furrer down the middle of his head-piece," as an onlooker noted.

Eventually Reeves succeeded in knocking the Chief unconscious with his pistol butt. Then he left for Goodrich's Saloon, picking up a friend named Moore on the way. Moore had no grievance against Indians, male or female, but expressed himself as being willing to "shoot anybody, any time, if there's enough sport in it."

En route to Goodrich's (one of Bannack's most popular spas of the moment) they collected two double-barreled shotguns and four revolvers and slapped these down on the bar, causing three tipplers to seek other parts of the room. According to several accounts, Reeves then said, "If the damned cowardly white people around Yankee Flat are afraid of Indians, we're not, and we aim to set the ball rolling!"

Each tossed off a quick, stiff drink and marched toward the offending Chief's teepee. There they fired several rounds into it without warning. (It was afterward shown that they'd wounded one Indian.) This triumph under their belts, they returned to Goodrich's and had three more drinks, added a confederate in the person of William Mitchell, a drifter, and advanced on the Chief again. Arrived, they stood pouring volley after volley into the teepee and, in an excess of alcoholic spirits, killed a bystander Frenchman named Brisette. (Mitchell claimed this trophy, proving that his gun was loaded with buckshot and an ounce ball. The point was a subtle one, but it made little difference. The blast was certainly too much for Brissette, who fell with a total of ten wounds.)

Altogether the toll broke down to two parts: Indians in the teepee and spectators who'd run up to investigate. The Chief was killed, and a lame Indian boy, and a papoose, while other Indians in the lodge, badly wounded, escaped from the opposite side. Among the white audience were, as mentioned, Brissette, plus John Burnes, who suffered a broken thumb, and a man named Woods, who took a charge in the groin. This last fellow was maddest of all, for two or three Bannack "doctors" examining him said he might "be out of whack for a year or more."

In any case, the slaughter was the final straw. Meetings were held among the "respectables," including the miners, who were, at worst, devilish, and agreement was general that something must be done. Bannack had reached its first point of no return.

Grantly drew me aside near the store and spoke in a low voice, since other people were talking along Main Street. He somehow seemed embarrassed. "A kind of inner-council is being formed by a few men of education—leaders—and the first meeting's called for tonight—midnight. Ordinarily, I'd—well," he sighed, "so be it. There's no other way. You're asked to join me; Brother James is off on a hunt. Place is the late Brissette's shack, now made available by Mitchell. It's solitary, up past the wood line. Don't mention the meeting to anyone else." Then he was off on some mysterious errand.

(In the town's beginning, low evergreens were scattered over the rolling hills, but these were shaved down as shacks went up, and, I figured, they'd likely stay that way.)

I loitered around town, listening to this group and that, staying in the background but absorbing what I could, too. The weather was bitter cold, the temperature maybe twenty to thirty degrees below zero again, and hundreds of breath-vapor plumes looked odd as arguments waxed and waned. The streets were a mixture of frozen snow and ice and mud. It required about five minutes to pick your way across Main Street. I saw three fistfights and one near-shooting, the man tripping in a rut before he could fire. One roughneck broke off to address me as a "dude" friend of Grantly and James, but others held him back. I've forgotten exactly how I spent those long next hours, but I remember going into Goodrich's, to see the women in the new dance addition, but when a bartender demanded, "What's your pleasure?"—convinced that I couldn't have any with my overyoung face—I mumbled something or other and slid out. It wouldn't do to turn up for a midnight council—any midnight council—with beer on the breath.

It wasn't safe, walking Main Street tonight, but I dodged trouble, and finally, consulting my Aunt Rachel's husband's watch, which he hadn't further use for when I left, being dead, I saw it was 11:45, and made toward Brissette's, keeping to the shadows, my hat pulled low.

No light showed from the shack, but since both oil-paper windows were in back, I stepped around, trying not to break through the crust, and sure enough, the meeting was about to start. The truth is that a noise of breaking through would have been drowned by the wind, which was roaring through the trees, making a high singing sound.

Grantly, sober-faced, let me in, and I nodded to eight or nine men I knew. All were in the forefront of Bannack's lawful life. A desk had been installed, and several rude chairs, with a lantern on a peg. A Bible lay on the desk. Behind this sat the chairman—a stranger to me. He wore a short beard and moustache, and I had the impression there was very little nonsense in him. He was introduced as Nathaniel Langford, and he'd been summoned from Beaverhead, where he ran a sawmill. He had been some kind of important figure back East. Right now he had a species of gavel, which I recognized as a Blackfoot tomahawk, but I refrained from inquiring how he got it.

This was the first real meeting of what later developed into the Montana Vigilance Committee, and there's no need to name all the men present; some never made themselves public.

Mr. Langford struck his gavel at the same time Brissette's chimney belched out a ball of black smoke, and I wondered if the deceased hadn't improved his situation. But this was a deadly earnest council, and, when we could see again, Mr. Langford began in a deeply resonant voice: "I—we all— regret the need for tonight's gathering, but I agree with the men here that, in the circumstances, steps should be taken and leadership provided by those best qualified.

"I think we're all sufficiently civilized to avoid composing some silly 'oath,' with recognition signals, symbols, and other claptrap. What we're after, if you concur, is simply the establishment of order in a region where we now have none. Regrettably we have no law; even so, we can certainly lay down rules for the future. Duncan?"

Grantly spoke up slowly. "My instinct is to proceed with moderation, use restraint always, gather and weigh all evidence impartially, hold public trial by jury, and—above all—to avoid any semblance of 'lynch law.' "

Three or four complained that Bannack had seen too much restraint already, and that our assembly was the result. Every man had his say. One, an Englishman, pointed out a reason or two for extraordinary troubles, saying that gold had an unsavory history, "attracting ugly parasites and changing all values." He gave several examples and predicted that conditions in southern Montana would worsen, "especially if a large gold strike is made somewhere near. Among other things," he added, "here we have nothing but rough-and-tumble outlets, and weather to make it worse. I doubt if any group ever faced a knottier problem. In a sense, we're trying to change human nature."

Most agreed, though the same three or four stuck to their notion that a good, hard example should be made, here and now (meaning next day or so), of Reeves, Moore, and Mitchell. "String 'em up and let 'em dangle for all to see," said one with an oath, a merchant whose place had been burglarized seven or eight times, after which the villains were seen on the streets wearing abstracted articles like boots and skin hats and gloves, and bragging about it.

"I know how you feel, Harvey," said Grantly mildly, "but burglary is not commonly regarded as a capital crime—"

"And what about the owner of this shanty we're sitting in? Wouldn't you call his case a capital crime? Shot down in cold blood, because he wanted to see some fun—"

"You can scarcely class the murder of several Indians as 'fun'; they have, or should have, rights—"

At this point, Mr. Langford tapped his gavel again, we struggled above another cyclone of smoke, and the chairman said, "We seem to be straying from the subject. The Indian problem is, I agree, difficult. Among other excuses for Bannack rascality is the absence of white women, and their generally softening influence. This is not meant to disparage 'squaws,' as we're apt to call them [at least half of the men present had Indian wives, and the subject was touchy], but only a fool could fail to admit the unequal advancement of Indian and white. The result is that Bannack's rougher element sees all Indians as inferiors, or even animals. The murder of Indians, to such as Reeves, Moore, and Mitchell, comes under the heading of sport. It's unhappy but true. What's that? By God, I believe—"

A crunching of snow behind the hut, a heavy fall with the inevitable picturesque oaths to follow, rose above the cabin voices, and Langford, snatching a rifle from a corner, kicked open the back door.

There was a pell-mell scramble down the hill. I heard, "It's that old nuisance Langford that operates the sawmill—he can knock the drawers off a mosquiter—hump it, Deke!"

I'd eased open the front door in time to hear the "crack! crack!" of Langford's rifle and see snow explode at the runner's feet. I thought he was aiming to scare rather than score.

Then all was quiet again. When everyone was seated, somebody said, "Seems one of us was followed," and his eyes looked suspicious—at me, I imagined, for no reason at all.

"Could any man here make them out?"

I said, "I could see well enough, and recognize the voice. It was Beaver Charlie Johnson and Deke Burns. Drunk and, I'd vote, harmless." [They were harmlessly frolicking, as it turned out, trying to light a corner of the shack with kerosene, but the wind was too high to make it work.]

Mr. Langford gazed at me steadily, as if at an unknown quantity and a pretty young one at that, and Grantly broke in quickly: "Neither of those has been in serious trouble; miners, both; limited so far to saloon frolics."

But the gaze was not interrupted, and I would remember it later.

In a unanimous vote, it was resolved (1) to consider banishment preferable to hanging; (2) to hold jury trials if enough veniremen were possible from miners so divided; (3) to provide counsel for all accused; (4) to hire trained investigators for major crimes of the future, and (5) to enlist some outdoor men as posses, should any be required.

These counsels would be kept secret and other Bannack leaders enfolded with care. One man present on that wild, windy, strangely moonlit night, whose name can be mentioned, was Hank Crawford, the butcher, who functioned as self-appointed Sheriff, mainly because he enjoyed dealing with violence. He promised to handle all arrests and "knock heads together when needed," and while I saw that neither Langford nor Grantly felt his wording fortunate, they let

this first meeting go at that. It was a beginning.
Much, much more was due to come.

I'll stress again that foremost in consideration
was the absence of all law. As Grantly said on the
way home, "Liberty without restraint can lead to
licence, as several groups have found to their
sorrow. And Montana's desperadoes, with no
fear of punishment, compete to see how far they
can go. They compete in deed and style, and
both are enriched by whiskey."

It was true, of course, and here I'll use Professor Dimsdale once again, the mildest and most
liberal-minded of men, whose notes perhaps
stress the point best: "The administration of
the *lex talionis* by self-constituted authority
is undoubtedly—*in civilized and settled
communities!*—an outrage on mankind . . . but
the sight of a few mangled corpses of beloved
friends and valued citizens, the whistle of a desperado's bullet, where civil law is powerless as a
palsied arm, will reverse that conclusion . . .
Let readers suppose that New York's police were
withdrawn for twelve months; then let them picture the wild saturnalia which would replace the
order that reigns there now."

Well, Bannack's citizens weighed the above
points and finally concluded to hold a "trial"—
the first of Montana's Popular Tribunals, as they
came to be called. Grantly made a number of
speeches that seemed to me pretty courageous,
in view of interruptions like, "Continey to prospect that vein, friend, and you'll find your head a
mooseholler up the gulch!" Splits in opinion

were frequent and noisy, but the dissidents were
sternly ordered, with the bulk of miners pointing
guns. Bannack life had grown familiar, and certain miners hated to see it go.

Noting the sentiment, Charley Reeves and Bill
Moore lit out on foot toward Rattlesnake Creek.
But after a cry for volunteers, four "sentries"
caught them at some distance from town, hiding
in the brush. The miners' inborn sauce could
scarcely change over night, and a sentry's af-
fidavit that the fugitives were trying to swim
under a beaver dam was given small credence.
Mitchell, believed sheltered at an outlying
ranch, was tried in absentia. When this last was
announced, of course, his friends made a howling point that they'd never heard of "Absentier,"
not in Montana anyway, and if he wasn't tried in
Bannack, with the others, "it wouldn't in no way
be legal, and by God—" etc, etc., But ribaldry of
the sort was put down quickly.

Next day more than six hundred men turned
out for the proceedings, which were held outdoors, there being no building large enough
to accommodate such a crowd. The two
prisoners—Reeves and Moore—were hauled
along wearing arm-and-leg chains and seemed
pleased to be the center of attention. I doubt if
they ever considered they were on trial for their
lives.

Now it's difficult to describe the following
mixups without seeming flippant. I'll simply
have to try—and sound a reminder that, if things
were not smooth, Montana had absolutely no
experience of such matters. The evening before,
a Mr. Rheem, claiming legal training, had volun-

teered to conduct the prosecution, and a "Judge"* Smith would conduct the defense. But at the meeting of 600, Rheem announced that he'd been retained by the *defense*, thus eliminating Judge Smith, and, too, leaving the people without prosecution.

Here a Mr. Copley stepped staunchly in "to press the people's case," but on reflection, he made the stunning observation, "I don't believe my talents lie in that direction; I was never successful as an advocate." At this point the miners grew restless. There was talk of hanging all the lawyers first, to warm up on, then to discuss Reeves, Moore, and Mitchell at leisure. Calmer heads prevailed, and messengers were sent to Beaverhead Canyon, to fetch Mr. Langford again. Not only the Council but everybody knew him to be absolutely forceful, honest, courageous, and even learned. His sawmill was booming, but when he heard about the muddle, he saddled up promptly. (Grantly, I believe, would have been solicited, but the truth is that, as uniformly admired as he was, people saw him more as a scholar than a man of action.)

Once Langford was present, a breakdown threatened over the question of trail-by-jury or a

---

*Many Montana newcomers laid claim to titles, or accomplishments, from other parts, and these, of course, were beyond checking. "Judge," "Colonel," "Attorney-at-law," "Doctor," and the like were common, and while any might be genuine, most were thought false, or flawed. There were, for example, many deserters from the Civil War, the preponderance appearing to be Confederates, and if even one announced himself as a private soldier, I never met him. Most such titled luminaries came to Montana for reasons which they kept to themselves.

judgement en masse. Every one conceded that
the chance of picking an unbiased jury in Bannack was risky, if not absurd. But this was the
system ordered, and that hurdle over, a Mr. Hoyt
was voted Judge and Hank Crawford "elected"
Sheriff, this time.

Mr Langford (who later would be the first
Superintendent of Yellowstone National Park)
was a member of the jury and insisted like iron
on hearing all evidence from persons anywhere
near the massacre. And he called in the
wounded Indians, too. There was never a question of guilt. "Done it?" cried Reeves, "Of course
we done it, and proud. Me, I wish there'd been
more skunks in that hole." Then, still in chains,
the villains fell into argument over who'd scored
the highest tally. "Judge" Hoyt thereupon
showed great restraint by instructing the jurors
that "if you find the prisoners guilty, you must
pronounce sentence yourselves." In short, he
washed his hands of all responsibility. Langford,
looking contemptuous, took a poll which on first
ballot stood—for death, one; against death,
eleven. Since these last jurors were friends of the
offenders, and since Langford was a man among
men, he simply took charge and pronounced
"Banishment plus forfeiture of goods" on all
three killers. He told Reeves and Moore that,
because of the season, they could remove to Deer
Lodge and "dig in till the weather allows passage across the Sierra."

Then Hank Crawford auctioned off the prisoners' guns, to defray expenses, and the trial was
over.

CHAPTER VII

THE SENTENCE—HAILED by the long-bulldozed miners—caused immense ill-feeling among Bannack's rougher groups. Up to the end, they'd seen it as some kind of game. And a number, visiting the saloons, emerged brushing their eyes and sobbing about "Pore ol' Charley and Bill! Treated like varmints in their own home town, wrenched loose from their hard-earned propity [several guns and some debts]— throwed out in the snow. Now if *that* ain't gratitude!" and the usual threats gathered force as the whiskey went down.

A burly man—complete stranger to me— stopped us on the way home; he blocked our course in the street, weaving slightly. "You," he said to Grantly, "I'd like it told, where'd *you* stand? You was real handy with speeches—spit it out!"

Grantly eyed him a moment, in no way disturbed. More scholar than fighter, maybe, but he was about as skittish as a badger.

"Were my remarks unclear? I have a certain rhetorical tendency, I admit."

"I didn't grab that proper."

"I can't vouch for your hearing, but your manner needs refining. I believe you're impeding our progress."

"Lookee here," said the man, putting his face almost against ours, so close we could smell his horrible breath. "I didn't relish that—it scraped me."

Several onlookers tittered, and this appeared to give him inspiration.

"Now I ain't no shoot-and-run specimen; I'm civilized, born to it, knowed for it—and that ain't no discredit to Charley Reeves and Bill Moore. You've heard of the Californy code dueller?"

"I take it, sir, you mean duello, or duelling, if I may improve your discourse."

"Now that done it!" the fellow roared. "Up to there you was sailing along comfortable and snug—you can name your weapon, by God!"

To my surprise, Grantly said in a conversational tone, as if his mind were elsewhere, "Rifles at fifty yards; we'll set it up for Goose Creek Canyon tomorrow. Don't bring more than three riffraff with you. I'll have Langford, my brother, and Ross, here."

The man staggered back, astonished.

"Now see here, friend, you *look* like a schoolmarm. You itching to be drug up to the marble-orchard?"

"Oh, there's not much chance of that. Say noon; don't be late. Good day to you, sir."

But the man was almost whining to back down. "Un-say it—humble yourself, with no disgrace attached. Jesus done it, and never regretted it, neither."

Someone in the crowd called, "Acquiring cold feet, Sweeny?" whereon the drunken bully—he was several inches over six feet, and heavy to match—lunged to bear-hug Grantly, but found a revolver pressed into his stomach. He stepped back, face chalk-white.

From a miner: "Shot any more Sheep Eaters, Sweeny?"—apparently referring to some habit, or hobby, of our friend.

"Tomorrow, then," said Grantly, and we were off.

In those Montana days, there were so many things I didn't understand that I'd given up asking questions. I had no way to know that my companion was a friend of the slain Indians, who'd helped him with his dictionary, and that a girl Grantly liked—handsome and sweet natured—had been bought by Sweeny, then humiliated and dragged about, and whipped, and kicked and beaten, and finally choked to death in a drunken fit of temper. He'd shot an unarmed Sheep Eater, too, for failing to give way in the street. He himself came near to raising a meeting before Reeves and Mitchell and Moore committed their cowardly crimes. I was scared; I'd never seen Grantly *looking* for trouble. But not for long. When we reached the store, James was there and, told of our encounter, laughed and said, "You'll use the Westly Richards?"

Grantly had recently bought, from a man named Jacobs, a most curious English rifle; the only one of its kind ever seen in those parts. It was made for "big-game hunting," so they said. It had a two-foot barrel of .65 calibre and chambered a one-ounce lead ball. There was a small back-action lock of beautiful finish, with brass fittings, as well as a spring to regulate the trigger-squeeze, and both ram-rod and screw for extracting balls. All this with a mould and a dull leather case, the whole weighing eight pounds.

Grantly liked that rifle and, before offering to trade, listened with sympathy to Jacobs' complaint that it was "mighty shiny and ornamental but it won't hit anything, unless you walk up close and use the butt." And the curious fact was that, in a miners' competition shoot, Grantly had not only missed the bull but after three tries had missed the target altogether. He good-naturedly took a lot of ragging; he was considered the best rifle shot around, better even than James, who was known to be quick and sure with a pistol.

But was Grantly crushed by the shoot? Not at all. He saw the problem as a study in physics. Taking various equipment, he went out in the woods and spent all of one afternoon. Then he came back looking satisfied and cheery.

"Well?" said James.

"First off, it was my opinion that the gun, per se, was capable of the task for which it was ordained—specifically, shooting tigers in India. Plainly enough, a tiger—fully mobile—is a challenge worth three deer, with perhaps a moose and a bear thrown in. The fault," he went on, lacking only a pointer and a blackboard, "was an under-use of powder, with some careless adjustments. As matters stand, I have every confidence that I made a worthwhile, if not brilliant, exchange."

"Somebody got a fine Kentucky rifle," James reminded him drily.

"*Weighing fifteen pounds!*" and they let the subject drop.

At noon next day we trudged—Mr. Langford, Grantly, James, and I—up Goose Creek Canyon, making very little talk on the way. Langford ob-

served at one point, "I was the only juror voting
for death. Banishment will come back to haunt
us, wait and see. The fact is," he added, "those
animals shouldn't be permitted to use firearms at
all."

"I have certain limited hopes," replied
Grantly.

It would be incorrect to say that Sweeny and
his cronies were sober. They set up a little chorus
of jeers, until they saw Mr. Langford; then they
muttered among themselves, plainly hoping to
hit on a Plan. In the years to come, Langford and
his family would be threatened over and over for
his staunchness at the trial, but when James
drew and cocked his revolver, letting it dangle
beside his leg, all whispers broke off.

"Back to back, men," said Langford briskly.
"Walk till I cry 'Halt!'—one shot only."

Here Sweeny reinforced his fierceness with a
pull from a bottle and said, "I hope to God you've
left a Will, for the way I hear it, you ain't apt to
leave much else."

Grantly nodded, as if business had indeed
been bad, and then moved out relaxed at the
count. At the cry of "Face round and shoot!" he
turned to his left, to take the ball away from the
heart, but in no special hurry and holding the
gun lightly in one hand.

As for Sweeny, he wasted no time. He whirled
and got off a shot that whistled through the
pines, loosing a fine cloud of snow. Grantly
waited, very deliberate, until the target angle
suited him; then he shot off Sweeney's trigger
finger. It was cleft clean at the first knuckle.

He fell down screaming and rolling over and
over in the slush, and his friends shifted their

rifles but found themselves facing James again. He said, "Easy. Move easy, and no widows tomorrow."

"Pick him up," said Langford shortly. "There's one scoundrel out of business. Now tramp! And—keep clear of honest men."

"We'll get you, brother. We'll get you all, and not clean and quick, besides. You'll wish your mother'd never give birth."

"Very likely. But be sure it's dark, and sneak up from behind."

Sure enough, supporting Mr. Langford's words, Bill Mitchell was back in Bannack a week later, acting as frisky as usual. People made a practice of asking how he liked banishment, then nodded, straight-faced and sympathetic, when he complained that it was "like laying in hell with your back broke." He said he wished he'd been hung, and blamed Langford for not hanging him, out of spite, and would square the account later. It was the loneliness that got him, he added, reaching for a bottle in a saloon, him that had always lived sociable, trying to take his place in the community. He said it was in his mind to start a Sunday School, soon as he'd killed off the remaining Indians, but now he couldn't do it, being banished, and added he wouldn't give a fig for that Jury's chances at Judgment Day.

This kind of nonsense got to be a regular Bannack joke, until Mitchell started organizing dog fights, and then it wore off a little.

Reeves and Moore never left the Territory either. There was no means of forcing them out, no organization yet, no police, no officials of any

kind, and no jail. More accurately, there were
federal prisons, the nearest in Detroit, and federal marshals at each. So that, if Montana citizens raised enough money, a marshal could be
summoned to place the outlaws under arrest.
But this plan offered drawbacks. Montana had
no detention centers, as stated, and no fund for
expenses, and the chances of any marshal suc-
cessfully herding killers like Reeves and Moore
and Mitchell as far as Detroit were remote. The
best guess is that, somehow, they'd manage to
cut his throat and be home a few weeks later. But
even if Detroit *was* reached, how could the three
be convicted? There remained problems of witnesses, prosecution, lawyer-trickery, the usual
courtroom charade, and little hopes of justice.

Thus the stage was set for positive solutions to
Montana's violence. Banishment, following
predictions, had fallen down on the job. Viewed
in cold blood, execution would have been simpler, cleansing the territory of some very dirty
ruffians. But I'll repeat, now, at the start of reprisals, the keynotes were caution and restraint.

Then the miners decided to draw up rules for
staking out and settling disputes over claims.
Thus far, the region's richest gold-seeking had
been by claim-jumpers, hold-up men, and professional gamblers in saloons. This innovation
was good news for Grantly and James and me, for
we'd hoped to try, at last, some serious mining,
now with winter broken.

Grantly helped the organization compose its
Code, and if an educated miner or two came
along behind and removed some multi-jointed
words, it was to be expected, and no offense

taken. These Bannack "mines" were easily worked, being mainly gold-bearing bars of gravel in creeks. The custom was for prospectors first to pull up sagebrush growing in banks, shake the dirt off roots into pans, and, adding water, swirl until tiny flecks of yellow settled heavily to the bottom. A good many workers, waggish to the end, maintained that sagebrush alone was sufficient for them, so that they never bothered with creek beds. "Where you located, Jake, generally speaking?" and "Prospecting the sagebrush along Dog-ear Gulch at the present time," was a typical exchange between Bannack miners in the streets.

But as Montana mining would evolve, with huge fortunes made in the dozens, these were meagre pickings. On many days, a miner might quit with a dollar or two in his sack. And if one happened to pick up a nugget, worth sixty or seventy dollars, like as not he heard an insinuating voice from the brush. "Now, say, partner, why don't you toss that bauble up here? You haven't got any use for it, you know, at your age, and I can't vouch to keep this old muzzle-loader quiet much longer."

All miners went armed to their digs, but since they could scarcely pan while holding a gun, they were continuously vulnerable. Still, these fellows were anything but timid, and gunfights were common in all gulches.

And if a man, or group, chanced onto a rich area and let out the news, strangers were usually there the next day. Argument was futile, unless the first owner had superior guns and wished to shoot it out. "Now lookee here, you jumping coyotes, this here's our works. So claimed and so stated—on a note stuck upright on a stick in a bottle. You saw it!"

"No bottle around here; you see a bottle— Slats? Skeeter? You better check your geography, friend, and be mighty cautious heaving accusations at honest men!"

So the episodes went, daily, at Bannack. A case could be made that the outcome had small meaning, since nine miners out of ten, "raising the color," knocked off promptly and hiked in to saloons, where they lost it, happy and content, like miners everywhere then. At the same time, their resentment of outlawry, of the haphazard system at large, was rising.

It was hoped that the Code, and the organization of miners banded together, might reduce the friction. First, a Miner's Court was formed, to settle disputes about claims. At a meeting, B.B. Burchett was elected Judge, and Hank Crawford was named Sheriff again, though bad feeling lingered about his sale of the late prisoners' guns. The Court was far from perfect, all claimants had their coteries of friends, and many pressures were applied.

But it was better than nothing, and its findings were accepted as absolute. Most of all these miners were men of integrity, and while they might grumble at this decision or that, they never held grudges, and certainly they stopped short of violence.

In the beginning, the rules were simple. A single claim was 100 feet up or down a creek, and as broad as pay dirt existed, on both sides. Title to a claim was established by staking it, and posting a notice, and having it recorded with the Court. This was easy enough, but to prevent the saloon gangs from prowling creeks and staking everything in sight, the rules also ordered that an owner had to work his claim every day water was available. An absence of three days constituted a forfeiture, whereon that claim could be "jumped." There was a sickness clause, too, which stated that a sick miner's claim was protected until he felt fit to work.

The Court did not, of course, have punitive powers. But the miners outnumbered the rowdies, and, as feeble as it turned out, the trial remained fresh in the minds of all. It was so shocking that no one knew what another crisis might bring. Nothing like it had happened before. Violence, in the gambling halls, in the town at large, continued its merry pace, but the miners at their claims found peace.

Here a word should be said about the difference in markmanship among the cliques. In the broad sense, most prospectors were mountain-men whose beaver plew had played out here in Montana. This after their solitary lives of trapping from Iowa across the Dakotas through the years. Since nothing could woo them back to civilization—all would have died first—they turned to the desultory, unskilled mining that kept them alive. As a rule, each was warmed (or exacerbated) by a bought Indian girl, and each saw his rifle as his most cherished possession. It was his chief means of finding food in a hard and primitive setting. The Kentucky rifle was the staple gun of the breed—a long, heavy piece of accuracy admired to this day. The owners were dead-shots, their lives depending on the felling of game at astonishing distances. Usually each had a pet name for his gun, such as "Old Bull-thrower," the rifle of Hugh Glass, mountain-man who'd been ripped apart by the grizzly.

Grantly's precision in removing the bully's trigger finger was not extraordinary. He could probably have done the same thing at a hundred yards. In his private Journals, he speaks of downing small antelope at more than twice that. And while he and James were scarcely mountain-men, in the term's strict sense, both had studied marksmanship and practised it hour after hour. A freighter of the period noted in his Journal that "Only mountain men and trappers shoot worth a damn. Tenderfeet put up with fish and piddling game killed near camp with shot-guns . . ."

Now all this was in contrast to the hit-or-miss gunplay of the outlaws. Not being professional hunters, but gamblers, or highwaymen, or worse, they had no great dependence on guns, excepting quick-draw pistol shots that usually went wild. The fuss, as related, between George Ives and George Carrhart was a case in point. As I look back, a droll concept remains that the Texas cowboy (nineteen or twenty years old) driving his herds to railheads in Kansas was expert with both hand-weapons and rifles. To lean on an old phrase, most would have had difficulty hitting a barn at any reasonable range.

Even such celebrities as Wyatt Earp, Billy the Kid, Bat Masterson, the Daltons, were mediocre shots at best. Their fame was based on courage, or meanness, or a taste for killing, and had little to do with ability to shoot a gun, or even draw it quickly. In a much-sung "battle" held in a corral between two sides totaling nine men, more than thirty shots were exchanged at a range of twenty yards. Five men only were hit, though one participant carried a double-barreled shotgun. Hero of that spree was Mr. Earp, every child's god, who, after his dubious service as marshal, spent his remaining years as a professional gambler.

Among Bannack's men of violence were two revolver shots of uncanny competence, and I—and Montana—will deal with them soon.

CHAPTER VIII

"Ross, my boy," said Grantly one evening as we sat at the hearth, "Brother James and I have been, if you'll excuse us, discussing your future. And I hope you won't take this amiss, we've agreed that the time has come for some planning, a bit of fatherly counsel, a direction that will not, to recall a Scotsman presently deceased, 'gang a-gley.' To be explicit, your life lies before you. What do you aim to do with it? Have you considered, ah, wedlock—a social blessing under certain conditions!" Here he coughed, looked briefly distracted; then he continued, shaking himself to clear the cobwebs. "How should a young man of birth and, I sense, of expectations—how, I say, should this person structure what we see as an indefinite, if not permanent residence in Montana—"

Grantly was warming up again but James broke in.

"Chappie, you're one of the family; I needn't say it. A helper through good times and bad, with no thought of yourself. Now here we'd better be blunt. You've seen that Grantly and I suffer from restlessness, or wanderlust. No, Grantly, it's true on your part as well as mine and likely won't lead to anything much. I doubt if either of us really lusts for gold. I think we'd be dismayed if we found it and had to settle down.

"Your case is different, as Grantly was tuning up to say. With your education, you have a career to think about, marriage, something all your own—"

"If I may interject without" (glancing in pique at James) "suffering an imputation of prolixity, this mercantile triumph with rooms upstairs (the whole decorated with a variety of hides not wholly free of stench)—"

"You were saying, Grantly?"

"My boy, this wretched dwelling is your home, for as long as you wish. I could hope that such a condition were understood. Do with your chambers as you will. Choose, or buy, a bride, if your taste runs to that dusky segment of our citizenry known—possibly in jest—as 'the gentler sex.' But if you'll take the advice of a man nearing middle-age [Grantly was, as suggested, not long past thirty] be cautious in your selection. Give thought to disposition, number and probable greed of kinsmen—"

I said, "I hadn't thought of marriage, among either the Indians or the whites coming along. I've visited the Indians, of course, and have a friend"—here I flushed—"in the new dance hall. But I hadn't felt the need of a wife 'in situ,' as Grantly might say. To tell the truth, we've had such jolly good times, the three of us, that I never considered branching out."

"I believe you spoke of a letter from your father, somewhat positive, or warm, in tone—"

In the uproar of the trial, it had slipped my mind. During my time in Montana, I'd kept up a regular correspondence with Boston—a letter like clockwork every six months, or maybe eight—and had received replies that occasionally became lost, or unopened. But only the week before I paid five dollars in dust when the Stage rolled in with mail from the East, via Salt Lake City. We had a spur, now, of the Great Overland Stage Company, that was known as the Overland Mail. You lined up at a shacky little "Post Office," to see what annoyances were on an incoming Stage. Rather, all the bums in town lined up and refused to move until you bribed one for his place. Then you paid for the letters, which worked out at so much per ounce, depending on how far they'd traveled.

Anyhow, my father sent along a bulky envelope, which was written in what I took to be his angry hand. The words were black and upright and the sentiments thrustful. He seemed displeased with my letterwriting and said—perhaps joking—that my younger sister had more family feeling in her little finger than I had in my entire body. It was one thing to sow a few wild oats, and another to loiter and skulk and avoid the responsibilities for which you'd been trained. Since I hadn't chosen to answer his past questions—but had "substituted slippery evasions and lies"—he was thinking of visiting me in Montana, to see if I looked competent to take over the third largest shipping line in New England, when the time came. He knew my sister could do it, and deserved the chance, and he wondered if I was in jail.

My father was a whopping big man, with a reddish face and arms like belaying pins, and had worked his way up—with his fists, mainly, I

judged—from the lowest junior officer on an
uncle's ship to be a power in trade. Now he was a
rich and a prominent, not to say domineering,
figure in Boston. But when he got mad—really
mad—he was a kind of human typhoon, and he
asked the extent of my gambling debts at the
present moment, wanting them "set down to the
penny." He pointed out that my sister had never
been in jail, nor arrested for gambling, nor stolen
bric-a-brac from an aunt, and, yes, the only thing
for it was to come to Montana on the first available "paddleboat." If necessary, he'd take one of
his own ships to connect with the line being run
by Garrison up the San Juan River and across
Lake Nicaragua to the West Coast. (The Garri-
sons avoided transferring to land at Panama or
going round the Horn; many California Emigrants were proceeding by this safe, quick
route.)

Well, I couldn't have my father here, of course.
So that night I wrote a long letter home, and told
the truth, that I was working with two foremost
Montana citizens—pioneers—with wide and
profitable interests, including gold-mining,
cattle-raising, clapboarding, squirrel-bagging,
wheat farming and dry goods retailing. And
then I couldn't help getting off the track a little,
saying I could scarcely be in jail, since Montana
hadn't got a jail, or any plans to build one, and I
neither gambled nor drank but belonged, in fact,
to Bannack's "Sons of Temperence."

There was such an organization, but it was
composed of roughnecks and sots—mostly too
old to mine much—who held meetings now and
then, mocky serious and sober, and took on like
hyenas about the evils of drink and the pitfalls of

mining camps and saloons. They even got up,
one by one, to tell the stories of their downfalls,
whilst the others cried and mopped at their eyes,
and then they pronounced the benediction,
Amen, and scampered as fast as their wobbly old
legs would take them for Goodrich's or someplace and held contests to see who could drink
the most in the briefest period of time. It was
aimed to ruffle the decent folk, who wouldn't
have thrown a dog into a meeting, let alone enter
themselves. Grantly and James and I went to one
and agreed that it was disgusting but comical.
These roisterers had what Grantly called "a local
school of humor."

They even stopped genuine temperance
people on the street, and handed them cards
they'd printed up, and begged them to pull
themselves together and mend their ways. Several members were "preachers," and they
worked up into an authentic nuisance around
town.

Well, I thought about that letter to my father,
who could sniff out humbug like a detective, and
decided to let it drop. I was about to write it over,
and be more careful, but James began telling us
about an expedition he'd consented to lead to the
Yellowstone, and I forgot. James said there was
gold in that wild fairyland—full of hot springs
and geysers, and canyons, and lakes, and water-
falls. But the Crows and Sioux had made it a
winter camp, and massacred all whites who ventured near. Yellowstone remained mild during
the severest winters, and game flocked to its
valleys in numbers too vast to count. James and
his group would reconnoitre, and wait for rein-

forcements led by Bill Fairweather, and together
"open it up" for passage and settlement.

The mission sounded dangerous. The Crows
and Sioux were mean and foxy fighters and
would grow worse later, and they had tribes
enough, it was said, to advance on Washington,
which people around us, being southerners
mostly, thought was a very good idea. I wanted
to go, but James considered it and decided not to
take the responsibility.

"You'll get your chance, Chappie," he said,
smiling. "Right now we'd best scout it first."

He was on fire to get started, and we told him
and his band goodbye three days later. Then
Grantly elected to check our ranch at Deer
Lodge, leaving the store to his off-and-on partner, Mr. Spence, and, in a lesser degree, to me.

Placing a hand on my shoulder, he said, "Now
look around you, Ross. Be in no hurry. But give
every thought to a line of endeavor that may,
avoiding those vicissitudes which have
thwarted James and me, bring you fame and fortune. Fortune, as you've observed, is elusive,
and means to be so. Seize it! Show it no mercy!
Place its head in chancery, and hold fast! There,
now. That's advice from one who has ever tried
to play fair but has, in brief, overdone it."

He turned aside, in some emotion, collected
his mounts, and left. It was puzzling; I'd never
seen him so. I laid it to the winter.

Mr. Spence was a dried-up little prune wearing goggles and a look of suspicion; and since he
appeared to be more interested in counting merchandise than in me, I left to stroll around. I
guessed that he was more an investor, or lender,

than an active partner, and I think he received a
fair return for his money, in lean times and good.
That store was successful, in the main. The Duncans gave full value to all, Indian and white, and
maybe more than that, and perhaps that's what
Grantly meant. The Indians—going downhill,
now—had taken to shoplifting anything handy,
and some of the whites were worse. When James
caught one man trying to get out with a wagon-
tongue and another with three shovels and a
ladder, he came close to losing his temper.

The weather had finally turned mild. It was a
nice day for figuring out your future. Bannack
had two main streets, each half a mile long, and
some ramshackle buildings marked "Grog
Shop," or "Hotel," or "Restaurant," or something like, but these came and went so fast that
half were empty, or maybe a "Hotel" of two
weeks ago was a grocery now. Hank Crawford,
who acted as Sheriff, still ran the butcher shop,
and I passed Davenport's Boarding House, and
the Peabody Express Office, where the Overland
Stage stopped, and Frenchy Le Grau's Bakery,
which actually baked something every month or
so but served as a gambling den (in back) mostly.

As I say, few places held on long. An owner
went prospecting, or had his life threatened and
sold out, or maybe got shot. The Universal Joint
lasted a few weeks, or until a bunch of rowdies
decided to make a formal call and put it out of
commission. They did a good job, breaking all
the windows, chopping up fixtures, except an
ignorant painting of several naked and forthright men and a lady stretched out on a divan—
imported from San Francisco, so they said—and
even sawed up the floor to be taken home and

used for clapboards. But the loafers never found
the energy to use these, of course. I saw them
piled up, rotting, here and there.

James told me the men had a sound grievance.
At least two had been poisoned to death by the
Universal's whiskey, and two or three more were
"under treatment" by doctors trying to fit their
stomachs back together. It was shown (in a hearing) that the drink was mixed in a dirty old vat
back in the woods and contained, besides rotten
alcohol bought from the Mormons, testing acid,
a box of dynamite fuses, and, to give it flavor, a
number of skunk pelts. I learned later that skunk
odor was effective in producing French per-
fume, but it appeared to miss fire here in Montana. The visitors had a mind to ride Captain
Fogle out of town on a rail, and brought tar and
feathers for the purpose, but he was absent when
they arrived; he'd left a sign saying "Called to
California on Business." This last seemed to
plague the men worse than anything. Several
stated, out on the wooden walk, holding
brushes, that the act was both cowardly and immoral.

I passed Skinner's Saloon, which had a bad
reputation, even as saloons went here, and the
owner, Cyrus Skinner, was headed for trouble
soon. The streets were mud, mainly, with some
snow mashed in, but there were wooden walks
in front of most stores, and besides, wearing
boots, you became used to this kind of travel. It's
hard to convey an impression of a mining camp
like Bannack then, with no churches or schools
and the streets full of drunks and brawlers and
pimps and gamblers—the refuse of humanity.
Hardly an hour went by without trouble, and a

shooting occurred nearly every day, and two or three on Sundays, when the town knocked off to rest. A mere case of two men falling out, with one shot and killed, was considered upright and proper—their own private concern—but a massacre like the one that raised the trial was seen as excessive, entirely out of bounds.

Everyone walked about armed, as stated, and probably this prevented more shootings; I never could tell. Nobody *wanted* to be shot, of course, so that many disputes trailed off into threats so meaty and vivid and full of mountain speech that a stranger might assume those men were enemies till death and would kill each other at last. Then you were surprised, and a trifle disappointed, to see the braying jackasses embraced in a saloon shortly after, sharing a bottle, so thick and harmonious you'd take them for brothers. Perhaps the best way to sum up Bannack is to say that it gave off an air of noisy, wild confusion that scarcely let up day or night.

Built in a canyon, it often remained warmish when the temperature on top might be twenty below zero. The sun was best seen at midday, or now, as I passed Meninghall's Store and turned into Goodrich's. This was a saloon and gambling hall of the better type, that is, not very good, and Goodrich was considered a tolerably decent fellow who insisted, always, on paying the burial expenses of anybody shot there. He took no sides, of course, and on each occasion stood a round of drinks to everybody present, including the killer and loafers who never bought anything at all, but only came in to watch and get warm.

Goodrich had lately built an addition—"for dancing"—at the back of his place, and had white girls who'd arrived by stage from Salt Lake, where they'd been shamefully treated. They weren't wanted there at all; so it was said by a woman of about forty, with bronze hair and a pretty large shelf at back, who'd taken pity on them and consented to act as manager.

The reasons, as she explained to a group of men who understood it, and deplored it, were entirely religious. Brigham Young wanted them to be Mormons, you see, especially a very young, plump one, with what was described as "an uncommonly religious bust," and a man with a patch over one eye told the woman after she'd descended from the Stage, "If a person's been squashed down, and hasn't got freedom of religion in this country, well, he ain't got a pot to piss in, and they might as well have scuttled the Mayflar shortly after it pushed out from Sweden."

He had the allusion wrong, of course, probably on purpose, but his comment was well received. Several of the ladies thanked him.

Goodrich's had a number of rude tables and chairs, as many as a dozen beautifully polished spittoons, a mahogany bar from a paddlewheeler that blew up, and a mirror saying "God Bless Our Home." The dance hall in back was spacious, and heated by a pot-bellied stove bought from some starving Emigrants, who got enough money for food that way, and then went ahead and froze. There were little bedrooms upstairs, too, for the dancers. Mr. Goodrich was always friendly to me, though I seemed to amuse him somehow. He explained that dancing was exhausting, and dancers like his needed lots of rest, often going up for "cat naps" in the middle of the evening. He was accommodating and gallant, and sent a male escort in each case. It didn't take me long to figure out that these girls were more than dancers, of course, but I was convinced that Dixie—she appeared to have no other name—was upright in every way.

Back in Boston, my family were strait-laced, frowning on things like dancing, and reading novels, and playing cards, even when a game was honest. And there was a municipal ordinance where you couldn't play a violin, or spit on the sidewalk, or scratch in church, or kiss your wife on Sunday, and I believe those laws remain on the books to this day. They all came down from the Puritans, of course, and a pretty good part of Boston never worked out from under. The other part tried to make it up.

In college I was shy of girls, and usually slid out of parties when girls were present. That's why my friendship with Dixie was so all-round satisfactory. She was an accomplished dancer, with more movement than employed back East, and so hospitable that even my aunts might have approved. On three separate occasions she'd asked me up to her room, for tea, and I'd refused, not wishing to embarrass her in the daytime. She seemed puzzled. Then her manner changed to a kind of motherly, half-humorous camaraderie. For some reason, I never felt shy around her.

Most days she rose late, being tired out from dancing, but here she was—the only girl down at Goodrich's bar, having a drink at noon. Now I might as well confess that, by some standards, this girl wasn't perfect. Because of a childhood disease, her blood had been thinned, and the doctors told her to build it back up with spirits.

She had courage, all right, because she told me she hated all forms of strong drink, but she was gaining on it. Goodrich himself said so, but it didn't seem to please him.

The day being fine, only two miners were at the bar, and Dixie was standing apart. She saw me and said, "Well, here comes Little Boy Blue."

Goodrich said hopefully, "Eye-opener, Mr. Nickerson?"

Since the Duncans were absent, I said, "Glass of beer, strongest in the house." (They had very good beer here, made at the brewery in Salt Lake.)

"Large glass, small glass?"

"Largest you've got," and then, trying to show off, I addressed the two miners. "Gentlemen join us in a drink?" One looked around to see if there was somebody else present, the other said, "Chaw it again, son, and throw it into English, if it wouldn't place any strain." (I'd taken some ribbing about my "accent," which some thought peculiar, but you never knew if they were joking.)

"Tanglefoot? Tarantula Juice?"

"Now that's right-down handsome, especially when a person's cleaned out and dry," and he made a sign to Goodrich, after which, confound the luck, he said, "Leave the bottle lay."

"Up your leg, Ma'am," he added politely.

This struck me as cheeky, so I turned my back.

"Drinks for miners, nothing for little Dixie?"

"Well, you've got a drink, but have another by all means," and I plunked down a coin.

"For the blood."

"How is your blood today, Miss Dixie? You don't look quite as chipper as usual."

"Just ignore the 'Miss'; someone might over-
hear. Blood? Well, I had a tiresome night. I got
stuck dancing with two or three *old* miners, and
each insisted on telling me his life story. They
worked at it so strenuous and hard and long that
I almost got up to a point of enjoying it, but I
never quite did. Dixie's worn out—and jumpy."

I said, "I'm sorry to hear it. Would some more
medicine help?"

"Not down here. For some reason, it does more
good taken in my room where I can measure it
and all."

I wasn't absolutely sure what to do. Here it was
mid-day; yet I didn't care to be responsible for
somebody's health, particularly Dixie's. I'd
drunk my beer, so I stiffened my spine and said,
"All right—would you care to have some
medicine in your room?"

She looked me up and down in her sweet way,
smiling but friendly and grateful and interested,
too.

"How old are you, Little Boy Blue?"

I didn't care for the name, and feeling stronger
for some reason, said, "Ross."

"Now I declare. How old?"

"Twenty-three next birthday."

In a playful way, she felt the muscle of my
right arm and said, "My goodness *gracious!*"
Then she gave a sigh, and sort of shivered, as if
her blood was working again. She said, "Come
along. And bring my bottle. I've always placed
my faith in *young* doctors. Old doctors—old
miners—should know when to quit. They don't
do much for a girl."

Her room was more ornamented than customary; different, too. But she explained, making an

apologetic joke, that she was a "Roaming
Catholic," and I figured that this accounted for a
good deal. The bed was large and had a lavender
satin counterpane, with any number of bright
silk pillows strewn about the head. Over the bed
was a monstrous big crucifix that showed Jesus
bleeding from a number of punctures, and additional crucifixes hung on the walls, with a nice
last-year's calendar from Meninghall's that
showed the Virgin Mary holding the Infant, intact, and a religious sampler over what looked
like a small water-closet, right out in the open.

There was a dresser with a collection of objects
on it; I thought some of these might be gifts: a
Teddy Bear, and a big doll that said "Ba-a-a" if
you pressed on the bottom, and a quartz blossom
containing considerable gold, and a solid-gold
toothpick in a shiny wood holder, and a tray
from Niagara Falls, with several cigar butts and a
pair of brass knuckles. There was a round chalk
statuette that appeared to be a bald-headed man
in front but something else if you picked it up
and wrapped your hand around. It was curious,
but I decided a miner had presented it to her,
being frolicsome like all the breed, and she
didn't know what it was. Still, I was embarrassed, and off-set it by going to the window and
peering out. And when I turned back, she was
lying on the bed entirely naked and not too se-
cretive about it either.

Well, in the next hour or so I became
convinced that she'd worked her blood back up,
and maybe two or three times, and I worked
mine up, and then down, as happened when I'd
gone to the Indians. But this was different. When

she recovered her breath, and quieted down, and was less sweaty, she said in a shaky voice, "I scarcely know what came over me; I really and truly don't. You must have set out to mesmerize me, right from the start, you wicked young scamp. And here I'd been thinking you were a gentleman, too."

Well, I could hardly remind her about sprawling out in the bed before I'd opened my mouth, so she went on to say, "You must think I'm *that* kind of girl!"

"Now, you know better, Miss Dixie. If I thought so for a minute, I'd have to offer you money and—"

She sat up, her eyes blazing. "Don't you *dare!*" and then, by George, if she didn't burst into tears. I felt bad, having hinted at such a thing, but she said, "Oh, it isn't your fault; I purely provoked you, whether I was rightly conscious or not. It's something else—and there's no help for it, none whatever. Her that worked and worked like a nigra and raised me from a baby." She rocked back and forth with her head on her knees.

I said, "Hold on now, Miss Dixie, *anything* can be helped, or nearly anything. And whatever I can do, you tell me. After all, what we've been to each other, right here in this room—"

Then she told me the story, about how her mother ("the sweetest Mama a girl ever had") lay prostrate in New Orleans, at death's door and requiring repairs, the way I understood it. Her gall bladder had refused to continue, and one kidney had quit without notice, and both legs were troubled with varicose veins. And there was something wrong underneath. I couldn't make out what.

It occurred that she might be happier in a nice, comfortable graveyard, but I didn't say so, and I got as indignant as Dixie when she broke out with, "And all because those mean old doctors won't operate, or even touch my precious Mama, unless I put up forty dollars as a down payment—"

It nearly cleaned me out, but I made it. Then we got dressed, with me being very skillfully "attended to"—a new experience—and I found out the meaning of the water-closet. It had worried me previously, because a regulation commode was placed as usual under the bed.

Downstairs a few more men were gathered at the bar, and a big brawny miner was making things howl—buying drinks here and there and yelling about what he was planning to do in the future. And when he saw Dixie, he grabbed her waist and swung her around in two or three circles. Her skirts billowed up and you could see her legs, practically indecent; and he roared out, "Now you lookee *here!*"—holding up a nugget the size of a walnut. "There ain't a thing can stop me now. All staked out and recorded. To start off, I'm fixing to buy London Bridge and knock it down with a maul! Whoo-ee, Yankee Doodle! I'm on a rampage and two-dozen grizzlies couldn't stop me!"

"Now Big Jake, you know you can't spend all that by yourself."

"Little lady," he said, removing his wolfskin cap, "this here pretty's for you, to warm up on. There's plenty more where that sprung from. Where?" He became confidential to a man drinking whiskey. "Don't spread this, but go out just a *leetle* mite past town, take the first road branching off toward Hades, and commence digging when you strike Brimstone. If you don't hit nothing, call for the Proprietor."

This struck him so funny that he choked on his drink, spewing up a portion; then he swung Dixie off the floor again, shoved a glass in her hand, and headed for the stairs.

"Miss Dixie," I called, following after, "what about us? I thought—"

"I'm perfectly helpless, Little Boy Blue—all you big strong men! My Mamma surely will be obliged," and she laughed about as hearty as Big Jake, showing a gold tooth I hadn't noticed before. "Come back and see me, hear?"

I left feeling like the worst fool since Balaam, and I was mad, too. In the next half-hour I probably grew up about ten years. I wondered if I hadn't slid briefly out of my mind. Traditionally mining camps—especially in a bad winter and without the presence of women—can affect people that way. Nobody, ever, had heard of two sourdoughs bottling themselves up for a winter, away from all other contacts, who came out on speaking terms in the spring. There was no single case on record. That's why mountain-men, each autumn over the years, headed north on the beaver trail alone. One man in a cabin could make it; two meant trouble.

Needing to cool off, I decided to take my rifle and walk up to the hills in the afternoon. Mr. Spence gave me a hard look when I entered and left, as if I had a keg of shingle nails under my coat, but my good humor was revived and I replied civilly when he said sharply, "See here, young man, aren't you supposed to be on the job in this store?"

"Geezum, or omnia gallia in escrow?"

"What's that you said? I don't believe I quite—"

It was necessary to be patient with Mr. Spence. His mind was slow in some ways, being snarled in inventories, and you often had to overexplain.

"*Quantus!*—using the hexameter ferris winch, or boggled into happy. No, no!" (for I could see he was off on the wrong track) "epicenter the oxygenetic valance on litmus, and then? Sulphic apse—all you can drink."

He turned a kind of brick red and said, "Let me warn you, Nickerson. The Duncans may play teacher's pet here, but I have an interest in this—"

I cried "Shush! Grizzle! Behind the crocus!" and, pointing, cocked my rifle. He jumped clear off the floor to turn around, and before he got back I was gone, and feeling better. It's amazing what a little horseplay will do to lift the spirits when you're down. A miner named Foss was teaching me that kind of speech, which he called "duck quack," but I appeared to enjoy it more than Mr. Spence did.

CHAPTER IX

IT WAS STILL weeks before "run-off," when the mountains gave up their snows, but the streams gurgled in their beds, the pines showed more green than white, and the weather was brisk and bracing.

Animal tracks were everywhere, and atop the canyon I saw two of the little black deer whose hind feet leave no scent. It's an odd quirk of nature, in the way of self-protection. Their front feet (or hooves) leave scent like all other deer. But in moments of danger, these frisky little fellows run with such precision that the hoofmarks are superimposed, staving off predators—lynxes, cougars, wolves, even bears in a surly humor. I let them go, not trying a shot. They were clipping along, and besides, they always seemed friendly. They were my brothers.

Prowling around in Montana then was delightful. The range was forever. You could descend into hidden green valleys, with cottonwoods thick along streams, or climb rocks that looked like people or animals, or run into animals in variety to take your breath away. What I wanted, now, was a big-horn sheep, which is rare and aloof and skips nimbly through the high places, making a shot difficult. Of all the trophies that hunters collected here, these lofty white ghosts were most sought after. And near the end of a valley I knew, I saw one, standing high on an outcrop, looking proud and disdainful. He was the sentinel ram they keep, and I knew that, at any suspicion of lifting my rifle, he'd whisk off and vanish.

I laughed out loud. It was a grand day to see humans of the kind I'd met lately as inferior to the beasts that lived here sensibly, without emotion, not needing saloons, or gambling, or even Dixie.

Then I decided to seek out an old Emigrant trail I'd once found. The route was by-passed now, leaving its valley still warmed by bubbling springs, some blistering while others ranged on down to bearable-hot and tepid. For some reason I craved a bath; and besides, these springs were fun, unless a grizzly came lumbering along. And then you could move to the deep-water middle and call him names, as Indians did. Air temperature was about fifty, and if this seems odd, before winter entirely folded its tents for the year, you might consider that Deer Lodge, for example, has the same latitude as Venice.

I found a place that suited, stripped off, waded out in the sand, and sat down. Nothing could have felt better. I reflected that I hadn't properly had a bath in five or six weeks. It may have been why the little black deer had swished off pretty fast (being downwind, you know).

The water swirled round and round, caressingly, and this brought to mind one of Grantly's theories. At any time he had more theories than a lodge has graybacks, but most worked out after experiment. As to swirling pools like this, he

stated that the rotary, or whirling, motion of the
water, if brisk, had a pronounced healing effect,
and I quote his Journal: ". . . good for muscula-
ture strain or fatigue, affections of the joints,
unless fractured, rheumatism, arthritis, hemor-
rhoids, sprains, tension, many lesser complaints, and even the aging process. One must
practise patience, not an identifying mark of
homo-sappy-ones [this was a prime joke of his]
and remain immersed until the waters pum-
mel, un-twist, accomplish their medicinal
chore . . ."

At Deer Lodge he'd sat in one of these warm
pools, holding a watch, and detected a marked
slowing of the pulse, which, as he walked out
with satisfaction, he said was "exceedingly
hopeful for heart patients." The fact that several
persons, curious, had gathered at the pool, including an Emigrant's white wife, and that he
was naked except for the aging tall hat,* had
slipped his mind until too late; then he dove
back in the pool, and didn't waste time about it
either. He was funny that way.

In any event, the above is what he said about
whirling baths, and I wouldn't be surprised to
see it taken up, for he was seldom wrong. That is,
after observing and doing experiments, he often
sat thinking for hours, "laying the groundwork"
(as someone wrote) "while strangers later reaped
the rewards." He might not make a dime out
of something—probably wouldn't—but he'd
suggest how others could get rich. That was his
style during most of his life.

---

*Grantly's folding hat, during the severe winter, finally
went to an Indian in exchange for a more practical wolfskin.

"You—young man—you'd better explain what you're at!"

A young girl, no more than seventeen, with black hair and soft features and a body so swaddled in a linsey-woolsey frock that even her feet were hidden.

She was lugging an old Hawken rifle, bound round with wire. It was much too heavy, and I wondered if she could get it up to her shoulder.

"We heard somebody singing. Pa said it might be part of a Celestial Choir, but Ma said go investigate."

"I'm taking a bath. Come on in," I said, in a jolly good humor.

She looked indignant, and then, I'm a baboon if she didn't drop to her knees, clasp her hands and gaze at the sky. "Most merciful Lord, take pity on this poor benighted soul and lead him out of wickedness, for Thy name's sake—"

"Now hold on—I'm taking a bath. I told you." The day was so fine and this creature so crazy that I added, "It would be wicked not to, the condition I was in."

"—cover his nakedness, even as Thou covered the Israelites in the Wilderness, and cure his tongue of Blasphemy!"

Suddenly I felt suspicious. I said, "Look here, you haven't come from Brigham Young's Angel Works, have you?"

"Oh, Whore of Babylon!"

I'd begun to enjoy myself and cried, in alarm, half rising. "Where? Which way did she go? See if you can get her back. Now be a good girl!"

My father, in church, made an impressive pretense, singing like a foghorn and clearing his throat in an ecclesiastical sort of way. Then, after

the hymns, he usually went to sleep and snored,
undoing everything, it seemed to me. Actually
he hadn't much religion, if any, so that we often
mimicked the pastor during Sunday dinner.
(Though of course I went too far and got
punished for it.) It was my aunts who laid it on
thick, but I noticed that some of them, after
checking what the other ladies wore, frequently
dozed off themselves. So—I had some experience of religious nuts, and appreciated them.

But this girl gave a shriek, putting her hands to
her eyes, and said, "Cover his nakedness, Lord!"
(this with a plaintive sniffle) "and help him ease
our dilemma. Moses struck the rock—"

"What dilemma? Turn around," I said, "you
won't be hurt," and I walked out to the bank.
"Where's your camp? How many are you? Let's
have the whole story."

I whipped on my clothes as she stood looking
away, frightened but chin up, and now I saw
that, beneath the awning, she was thin as a slat. I
placed a hand on her bony shoulder, and she
trembled but stood without moving.

"What's the trouble here, girl? You're starving, aren't you?"

"Pa and Ma have our ox-cart behind those
cottonwoods. The oxen were slaughtered time
past, but Indians stole most of the meat. *But
we're not complaining!* Our blessed Lord tried
Job and—"

"Job's boils!" I said, annoyed. "He should
have consulted a doctor. Lead me to your folks,
and don't hesitate about it, understand?"

She looked shocked, but after searching my
face, she marched off toward a thick tree-clump a

few hundred feet up the stream. I hadn't noticed it before.

Bending over a grill was a sweet-faced woman as gaunt as the daughter. She'd made preparations to cook two puny fish of a sort called here "false trout"—a whitefish that resembles the Eastern sucker. From a covered wagon a quavering voice called, "Now, Harriet, you and Daisy divide those fish. I don't seem in no-wise hungry today. You bear in mind that Jesus handed out the fish; I'm unaware he ate any himself."

"You'll be fed, without palaver, share and share alike," she said before seeing me. "I'll just tell the truth and say it now—I don't give a hairpin how Jesus handled the case. This time I'll have my way!" She looked as full of purpose as a commander; then she glanced up, not in the least afraid.

"Now what?"

"Good afternoon, Ma'am. Your daughter happened on me at the springs. My name's Nickerson, and intending no offense, I apprehend that you need food."

"Ma, he was sitting in the warm spring, purely naked. I'd be stunned to hear he'd been Saved. But he never laid hands on me."

"How'd you think he'd be setting, in a overcoat? Or maybe holding an umbrella? His noodle's on straight, if I'm any judge. And I misdoubt he'd break a leg rolling down a preacher's aisle!

"Yes, sir, we need food, and done so since the Indians come. The flar ran out three weeks past, and our Army bacon, together with beans and other bought rations—greens and such. The

oxen, poor beasts, went when we bogged down
lost, and I and my daughter have held ribs off
backbone by fishing. If you could rightly call it
so. I'm a lame hand at it, and Daisy couldn't
catch a cold. Poor child, she's scarcely able to
stand."

"Ma'am, you're only six miles from Bannack.
But you're off the trail, way off."

"I declare! It's no wonder Christians didn't
come."

"Your husband's in there?" I pointed to the
wagon.

"That's him. Rather, the remainders of him."
She wiped her hands on her apron, giving a
worn-out sigh that had lots of fight left in it.

"He hasn't got smallpox or cholera?" (You had
to be careful of Emigrants coming in; it sounds
hard, but many were turned back.)

The wagon voice quavered again: "Harriet, is
that a man? I was laying here thinking of the
Return of our Blessed Lord Jesus, who sees the
sparrer fall, and I hoped—"

"Sparrer fall, and you'll eat it, Ewing
Smithers. No sir, my husband's got a broken leg,
from religion."

I was set back abruptly. "Religion? You mean
he's a minister and the congregation rose up and
broke his leg? It's no wonder you moved,
Ma'am." I was perfectly serious, you had to be
with people in so sorry a plight. But I couldn't
imagine any other way; things came close to that
pass back in Boston, when sermons got too frisky
or dull.

"No, sir, we're Pentecostal Rollers. Or were
before our group split off from the one that had

split off before. My man got Took at a meeting, and jammed his leg betwixt two benches while rolling toward Salvation. It was broke bad, but people wrenched it into place, near-abouts. Now he's frost-caught in the chest—"

Here she stumbled and would have fallen across the fire if I hadn't stepped in. She'd fainted dead away. Very clearly she was starving to death, and I said to the girl, "Take your Ma and prop her against a wheel. Throw a blanket down, and feed her this—little bites at a time. No, don't argue, and try to get your mind off Jesus." ·

I'd removed the string of jerky that all hunters carried round their necks, against becoming blizzard-bound or the like, and handed it over. "Eat some yourself, and give the rest to your father—your Pa. Now hand me those fishhooks and twine. I'll be back in an hour, two at the most."

But it wasn't fish I was after, except as a last resort. These people needed fat, and there's about as much fat on a trout as there is on a maul. I examined the specimens the woman was trying to fry, but they'd turned black, for lack of grease in the skillet. The afternoon had moved on, so I knew I had to hurry.

I moved up the stream-bank, silent, bending low under willows and cottonwoods, as the Duncans had taught me. I trusted Providence to throw something my way, Him having such support back at the wagon. There was snow under the bank, and a scattering of snow on top, though bunch grass showed through here and there. Below a bend—farther than I'd been in this valley—was a spring-clear pool maybe sixty feet across, and trout, real trout, were rising to gnats and mosquitoes and flies. The place was boiling with fish.

Said I to myself: In case game continues scarce, I'll lay up something, at least, to hold till tomorrow. Then I slid down and had a handful of worms and grubs in no time. All nature seemed to be moving now that spring was near. I cradled the worms in my cap, since nothing else was handy. And after this I cut a pole and began swinging out trout like a metronome.

In fifteen minutes I had a dozen, all good sized, speckled and shiny, the color fading soon out of water. I gutted them, and shucked out the gills, and breaking off some twine hung them on a limb. But not where crows could spot them.

Busy doing that, I didn't see him coming. It was a flash of silver prickles, and Providence must have been there somewhere, for he was after fish, not me, only knocking me flat while streaking by to smash at the limb. But his humor was foul, like any grizzy is after hibernating. (Or near hibernation, for there's no telling whether they will or won't, here.) For a minute he worried the string, slapping it back and forth, amidst growls that sounded crazy, but chilling, too. Then he fixed his attention on me.

I was crouched there, practically paralyzed, when Providence stepped in again. I'd seen this before, and Grantly had notes on it: The bear stood upright and began stripping all the leaves and small twigs off a cottonwood, snapping and biting as they fell. He looked ten feet high, and his noise might have reached to Bannack. But it gave me time to haul the rifle waist-high and fire directly into his chest.

He seemed startled, or shocked, as if he had no idea what happened. Then he went into a lunatic frenzy, and this time he moved on me like a tornado. I had my revolver out and backed into the pool. It was ice-cold and had the effect of making me mad at last; my coat was torn and one shoulder knocked out of plumb. And I was sore about those stolen fish.

The fact is that Grantly and James and I liked animals and enjoyed watching them, but grizzlies were dropped from our list. They were mean, born mean, intended to be mean, and killed small game out of meanness rather than hunger. You could never tell, sleeping in a tent, whether one, in a fit, might turn and rip everything to shreds, including you—for recreation. There were others we disliked—wolverines, for instance—but grizzlies topped them all.

He rushed to the pool's edge—a big ball of silver, with sound to match. But he hung up long enough for me to put a revolver shot in his forehead, and another through the right eye, and others in that region. Standing chest-high in near-frozen water, I held the gun with both hands and felt good about it, and maybe about myself a little. I'm not sure about the revolver, but that rifle slug—a full lead ounce—had begun to take hold. He slumped, sitting, then stretched out on one side, looked me in the face. When I started up the bank, filled with brag and bounce, he wrenched himself up and started on the trees again. But it was his last gasp; he toppled sideways, and this time he stayed there.

And then, all at once, I found myself out of wind. My legs shook so I had trouble getting up the bank, and my heart was going like a bass drum. I was drenched in sweat everywhere, too; it even dripped off my nose. The scene round about? Well, the ground was strewn with debris, and the tree was bare, and all in all you'd have thought the horriblest windstorm on record had passed this way.

I sat for a space, resting up, mopping sweat from my hair and face. But it wouldn't do to dally; twilight would be here soon. So I tackled the painful job of skinning. At Deer Lodge I'd watched a grizzly skinned, as well as other bears, but I wasn't quite certain about the best meat. All bear meat I'd eaten was stringy, tasting of fish, unless they'd been feeding on berries. But this was no time to be finicky. The idea was to get food down those starvelings.

Light snow had started falling, and I hadn't much patience with that grizzly any more. I was so tired the glitter had rubbed off. Still and all Providence (or a colleague) had presented me the best possible game in the circumstance. Deer and antelope and even elk were lean as buffalo hide this winter and wouldn't have served half so well.

Then, sharpening my bowie on a stone, I noticed that the fish were intact—only strewn around. Giddy as I was, it struck me as a prime joke on the grizzly, and I addressed him aloud. "You ugly devil, your tantrum got you in a mess, now, didn't it? You failed to steal a single trout and wound up dead besides. It ought to be a good lesson, but don't look for sympathy."

Realizing that I wasn't making sense, I bent to the task, slitting, or haggling, the thick hide from the throat down belly to rump, laying it open to reach inside. Now a dull bowie, or Arkansas toothpick, isn't exactly a skinning knife; it was designed (a miner told me) by the former Congressman for "puncturing humans, as well as politicians," and this was mean work.

I wanted to keep the skin whole, as a trophy. But snow had begun to thicken, falling in small, warningful flakes, so I hastened my pace. I took some fat parts from the neck, and the heart and liver, plus additional organs, and some tenderish meat from the thighs. With the trout, this was all I could carry. Especially since my shoulder had begun to throb.

Finished, I shook out my cap and covered the carcass with twigs, and even sand and gravel, hoping to stave off the wolves. There was a good chance, for the snow was settling straight down. Not the faintest breeze stirred; all around was silence, pure and wintry.

When I'd staggered two miles back—coat full of meat—dark had almost come, with the snow building up little by little. It was the kind your boots make dry skreeky sounds on, and meant to stay. They had a big fire going—reckless the way Indians behaved—but the woman was heavily dressed and oiling up the Hawken. From the wagon came "Harriet, if you're aiming to help that young man, I'm blessed if I'm not coming along, cough or no cough," and I saw an old Maynard breechloader poke its way out of the canvas.

"You'll lay back in that wagon, and without lip-sass. We've got enough on our hands without you pulling another fool stunt, Ewing Smithers."

I walked up into the firelight, then sank down on a three-legged stool they had. My heart seemed apt to pound out of my breast, and I was swimming in sweat. Worse, my trousers had commenced to freeze with pond water. Unshucking my load, I said a little weakly, "You weren't planning to follow me, were you, Mrs. Smithers?" Apparently her husband failed to hear, for he called, "That young feller's been set on by Indians, and no white woman short of the Pearly Gates is apt to stop me, once I've made up my mind." He sounded downright testy, or as testy as he could get.

Seeing the bear meat and the fish, the woman put her gloves to her face and wept. These people were so decent they'd been ready to push out in a blizzard to do what they saw as God's given duty, and it made the whole venture worthwhile, somehow.

"Ma'am," I said, "Rub your skillet with bear grease and start cooking. Without meaning to give directions, maybe the fish first. They're easy on hollow stomachs."

"Ma, is he Jesus?"

"He's Jesus enough for you, you impudent whelp! Now set to work, without further palaver." She'd got her spunk back, and started laying about with pots and pans and I don't know what all, to contain the bear meat. But first she went to the wagon and said, "I was cross, Ewing, and beg pardon for it."

"You're always and unvariable cross when you're afeard, Harriet. I might mention—He was cross in the Temple. Now keep clear! I'm coming out, and I'll give warning—I'm armed head to foot!" As down as he was, he could still make a joke. And sure enough, he started climbing out, in sections.

The woman noticed my torn coat and blood that I'd overlooked, and said, "Why, you're hurt, you poor thing! And we'd been thinking only of ourselves!"

"We'd better Drop, Harriet. It's time to give thanks to our Savior and to a young man that I'd be proud to own-up as a son, Saved or otherside."

He'd emerged now, about six feet three inches high, or more, and weighing around a hundred pounds but stringy and knotty-looking, as if he'd been much bigger once. His expression was so open and easy I realized that not much could upset him seriously, ever, not in this world. He held on to the wagon to stand, then lowered himself to his knees like the others, and gave a rambling kind of prayer that was to the point, mostly, and not too long, besides. Jesus only got into it six or seven times, but briefly, not intrusive.

The woman propped him back up and gave him a hug, then hugged Daisy, and was about to pounce on me but changed her mind; so she set to work on my shoulder.

"It's disrelocated. I'll ask one and all to stand aside." Then the old stringbean seized me in a grip like a gorilla's, starved or not, and after a quick wrench, I was almost comfortable. She rubbed me with bear grease and pinned up my coat.

By now four trout sizzled in the skillet, which looked home-wrought, I thought, and above the ordinary. The girl tended them with a long black fork with a carved wooden handle.

If I hadn't held them back, that family would have eaten everything in sight. First off, eight of the trout disappeared, handed down like mailing parcels. How anybody could eat two four-pound trout was a puzzle, in their shape, with their stomachs shrunk. But they faced up to it, winning without trouble. The fattest bear meat followed after, without a hitch except that the girl Daisy became queasy, midway. So we took her off in the snow and emptied her. But she was made of tough material, like the rest, and reappeared a few minutes later.

When I came to look at the bear meat, a good deal was gone, and I congratulated them, about half-sarcastic.

"It came in the nick of time," said Mr. Smithers, digging at his mouth with an ivory toothpick attached to his vest. "And I'll own up that I myself go unaccustomed. I'm a sparse feeder, widely speaking, and have been so since birth."

"Now, Ewing Smithers, a fib for larking's one thing, and a downright lie's another. I misrecollect ever getting you filled, not entirely. You ought to be ashamed!"

"Son, I was guilty of a weakness that's plagued me always. Feeling better, I tossed out a pleasantry, and apologize if it struck the wrong note."

"What's more," said his wife, whose face, in the firelight, shone with grease, "your Pappy et like a hog, as you've openly confessed, and your Grandpa was a beer-barrel on stilts. Yes, it's true; we'd be a sorry three to have secrets from this young man, who's saved our hides."

"Son"—he limped over, able to stand now, and seeming filled out all over—"I was out of line, and acknowledge it." He took my hand, and after I got it back, hoping it would straighten up later, they thanked me as handsome as could be, and the woman cried again.

"Ma, I've aimed to ask since the Meeting after Salt Lake. What did Jesus eat at the Last Supper? What did they have for dessert?"

The woman boxed her ears. Then they put things away, scrubbing the pans with snow, which had begun to blow, and started arranging the wagon for the night.

"That's all right, Ma'am. If you can spare a blanket, I'll sleep underneath; I can ward off cold if I keep the fire going."

"You'll do no such thing!" she said, eyes ablaze. "That wagon's big enough for four, and you'll burrow in along of the rest. Besides, the temperature's dropping. The idea!"

It was true. Winter had wound up to deliver its final punch. The wind was howling as we climbed in, one by one. We slept forward of the cargo, and they had a number of blankets and a buffalo robe. Mr. Smithers, before turning over to let the food gurgle and digest, explained that he'd been a tanner once, "amongst scattered trades." He mentioned the "sweet aroma" of the robe, which he'd shot—I mean its owner—and tanned himself. The hide being remindful of a pig-sty, I figured this as another pleasantry and started to work on it but fell asleep like a dead man.

CHAPTER X

AND IN THE MORNING, when I looked out, we were in a kind of wonderland. Everyplace solid white. No sign of green or even trees, with the snow still falling. And dozens of criss-crossed tracks beneath the wagon. Wolves had been there during the night, and foxes, and, I thought, a lynx, but I'd taken the precaution of tying our remaining fodder in a bag and securing it on top. I'd heard nothing except, once or twice, Mr. Smithers coughing, from far off and with no force in it, as if his problems were receding away like a barrel rolling down steps, the sound growing fainter and fainter toward the bottom.

But when I sat up, that shoulder said don't take liberties, and at breakfast they removed my coat and woolen shirt to examine it. There was a blue-black bruise from top to thighbone. The girl seemed concerned, but was told to "Turn your head away, you fresh thing!" And afterward they applied Dr. T. Figley Entwhistle's Warranteed Anodyne for Warts, Cancer, Sprains, Heart Failure, and Female Complaints—massaging it in "to bring out the scent," which was interesting and ripe. Altogether, I doubt if the salve delayed healing more than three or four days at the most.

After breakfast I was stumped how to drag that bear's remains to the wagon, but the woman said she and the girl were now in tiptop shape (untrue) and would go along and help. And Mr. Smithers descended nimbly from the wagon, stating that he could do it alone, if need be. I noticed, in daylight, however, that he used an oak stick for a crutch, with a crosspiece on top, so he was useless here. He believed, he went on, that the people who set his leg had taken the wrong turn with it, and made it heal crooked, producing uneven lengths. But it was a mistake he understood, and he thanked them—some Brazilians and two Chinamen—and viewed it as the best possible sample of Brotherhood.

Still, in the end it was Smithers that figured things out. He was presently a blacksmith by trade, and had his equipment stored in one end of the wagon, which was the main reason it bogged down. He said he was "real sprightly" with his hands, and by George if he didn't haul out some barrel staves, knock them together in the snow, and apply sandpaper and wax on one side. It made a very workable sledge. Tying on a rope, he said, "Now there's no reason I can't hippety-hop alongside and help heave back with the load. If Jesus carried the Cross, the least I can do is tote a bear."

Frankly, I missed the connection, but didn't say so, and the three of us made our way slowly—the woman and the girl and I—upstream and across several big drifts of snow. During the night it had snowed at least a foot and a half, and the grizzly was covered—no scent there for prowlers.

I cut some limbs, and after an hour of so we prized him onto the sled. Then I caught some

more trout out of open places, to show them
how, and we headed for home. It was slightly
downhill, and what with the wax, we slid right
along, the women riding part-way. I would have
finished skinning the carcass but it was frozen
like iron. So I told the Smithers I'd tramp the six
or seven miles into Bannack, get some oxen, and
haul them to town. All in the same day, I hoped.

But I stayed overnight in the town before I
could borrow six oxen from Mr. Langford and
start back the next morning. The snow was already beginning to melt, with the streams just
rushing it, and a "swoosh" now and then when
pines released a shower; and all would have
been fine except for those pesky oxen. I'd tied
them tail to head, of course, but I had one set of
ideas and the leader had another. And the ones
behind him strung out in file this minute and
strolled up abreast the next. And where the wind
had blown snow off, letting bunch grass show,
they stopped for a snack. Hauling that bear was
blind man's buff compared to moving those oxen
to travel. A prospector had drawn me a map, so I
could circle around the ridges, and I finally
made it, sweaty and out of sorts, by noon or
thereabouts.

After this, things marched forward briskly,
thanks to old Smithers. (During my bad humor,
I'd demoted him from Mr. Smithers to old
Smithers, but it didn't last. A person might as
well get annoyed at the Twelve Apostles.) He
said they'd eaten a trifle heartier than that first
big supper, and he felt "as strong as the Lord's
right arm, now." That was his stock phrase, to be
used whether he felt strong or not, to show he
was not complaining. If he cut off his foot with

an axe, and a mule kicked him in the face, and a
tree fell on him, and lightning scorched off all
his clothes and broke his neck, he'd maintain the
same disposition.

He hitched up the oxen, after I'd fallen down
on the job. Then he gave me all the credit, tied
the toboggan on back, and produced a black bull
whip. This he used to crack like pistol-shots over
the oxen's heads, saying it would be a sin to flay
the Lord's own creatures. I offered to borrow the
whip and take the job off his hands, but he
seemed not to hear. Lurching through the snow,
with the women riding the seats, he told me their
story, and I'll condense it, having dallied with
too much detail.

The Smithers came from a mountain area of
West Kentucky, where people were unusually
religious and often showed it by gunplay. They
had a single denomination, once, but split-offs
had occurred over this point and that—whether
Salvation required total immersion or if foot-
washing might fill the bill. Some (I believe they
were Methodists) even held that a minister's
flinging water in a baby's face was as satisfactory
as soaking, and since there was no means to
check, they sailed along as brassy as anybody,
though shot at more than most.

Anyhow, the Smithers, seeing religion as less
violent in nature, finally moved with fifty
friends to southern Illinois. There they set up
business and started over. Their group had fixed
on shouting and singing and falling prey to
"Seizures" as the highway to Heaven. But the
Illinois town became peeved about their shouting on the Courthouse steps—said all civic business came to a stop—and gave them a week to be

religious someplace else. (The Mayor made a
public statement, Mr. Smithers told me, that the
town wouldn't have an eardrum intact within
six months if they stayed.) The event was not
unlike the Mormons' trouble in Nauvoo, Illinois,
where two men with the ecclesiastical ranks of
Head Prophet and Patriarch were shot while taking religious dives through windows at the
County Jail.

In the meantime, Mr. Smithers' friends had got
onto Holy Rolling, from Negroes in the area that
appeared to backslide and then roll again soon.
And they'd studied where the Mormons went
wrong, too. In the end they decided to follow the
Mormon trail and set up a city as fine and effi-
cient and holy as Brigham Young had done,
somewhere near. They planned to be good
neighbors, if the Mormons consented to roll.

They had a variety of troubles on the way.
Many split oft, as in Kentucky, while others
joined, and they arrived at last under the name of
Apostolic Pillars of God in Jesus, the Holy Ghost,
and Zion. (They'd previously been known, at
one time or another, as the Brethren of God and
the Saints in Christ; the Baptismal Fire in God's
Celestial Furnace; and the Free Will Salvation
Army of the Seventh Day Alliance.)

Well, it was the old story. Young treated them
with his frequent Old World courtesy, and suspicion, with some threats, and gave them advice
about a place to locate, which he seemed to think
could be California. But when the Pillars hung
back and set out gardens, and began to practice
little odd jobs, such as blacksmithing and
house-painting, and opened a small store,

Young called a meeting of the Elders and laid down an Edict. The Pillars could "quit trying to sneak in like thieves in the night," and become Mormons immediately, or head free of the City and be lucky to get out alive. It was a ringing Christian Edict, typically Mormon. But first, to join the Deseret Church, such girls as Daisy would be "sealed" to the Elders as extra wives, to help around the house, do washing, sit with babies, listen to the other wives complain— things like that, as I got it.

This wouldn't do, of course, so the Pillars packed up to leave for Montana, where they'd heard of the booming gold mines. First though, they decided to hold one last meeting, out of defiance, I suppose. Somewhere along the way they'd picked up a fully ordained preacher who had a whopping big tent in his wagon—bought it from a circus. He was doing well until citizens in Missouri, with shotguns, urged him to marry an eleven-year-old girl who sang in the choir. He left after dark, and had been, Mr. Smithers assured me solemnly, as "upright on God's Sanctified path" as anybody in the train.

It was during this meeting that Mr. Smithers broke his leg. His close friends pressed him to stay in Salt Lake for treatment. But he refused, and some foreigners amongst them—the Brazilians and Chinese I mentioned—undertook to put him back in repair. From that point, one clique after another fell into quarrels and split off, taking ornamental and convincing names, until the Smithers were left on their own. They had very bad luck. Winter was coming—a terrible winter. His leg wouldn't heal, one ox sick-

ened and died in the face of sustained prayers
that I privately thought might have hastened the
end, and a group of Crows ran off their cow one
night. After a big snowfall, they bogged down,
their food shrinking and shrinking, and it was
there that I found them.

On delivering this recital, Mr. Smithers admitted to being ("slightly") tired, and I persuaded
him to climb up to the wagon. He'd been sweating along with that stick, occasionally falling
into ravines but getting up smiling, and it was
only when he commenced to cough again that I
realized he was taking a chance with his life.

Alone, leading the oxen, I began to think about
that blacksmithing gear and review what I knew
of the trade. Mr. Smithers would never be a full
blacksmith again; that much was certain. Indeed, he hinted that, in Bannack, he hoped to
make a profession of spreading the true gospel,
under their new name of Pentecostal Rollers.
When I asked him what the true gospel was, I
never understood it entirely. It seemed to hinge
on a kind of dunce named Uriah the Hittite—that
and rolling. I'd heard of him, of course, but was
hazy about his actions, especially in the field of
rolling. Even so, I said they couldn't have picked
a better man; Uriah suited me all right, then
spent the rest of the journey feeling guilty.

You couldn't take these people entirely seriously. They were so hipped on religion that it
warped their outlook; it addled their brains now
and then. All but Mrs. Smithers. She'd seen
enough hardship and had spent such lively
times keeping Daisy away from the preacher's
clutches (as she told me later but never told her

husband) that she'd developed some downright practical good sense. She was a fine wife, and Montana would be lucky to add her to the decent white women now starting to sift in.

CHAPTER XI

I FOUND THE Smithers a one-story cabin, for ten dollars a week. I tried to remove them from dance halls and saloons, and did—there wasn't a "palace of sin," as people called them, within half a block. Such tasks weren't easy in Bannack then. When they were settled in, with provisions to spare and firewood bought from a peddler, I awaited my chance and, one day, caught Mr. Smithers at home alone.

I said: "Sir, I've been thinking about that blacksmithing set, and your bad leg, and your knowledge, and began to wonder if—"

"Son," he interrupted, "my old noggin was working along them self-same lines, lately. I know you'll grant pardon, but you don't appear to have any trade, or none to suit: You've informed me about Mr. Grantly Duncan and Mr. James Duncan, but their store seems scarcely fitted, if we're speaking of Clerks. Now a man without a pursuit is a lonely man, sooner or later. If I'm speaking up too candid, call a halt—"

"Will you teach me the blacksmithing trade?" I asked quickly, to ward off references to Uriah the Hittite, or Leviticus, or another of those bores; and added, "I don't wish to sound forward, but I can afford to *buy* your outfit, if it comes to that—"

"Son, I expect you never laid eyes on a more plain-appearing pauper than Ewing T. Smithers, as you cast your glance around. It's a kind of trade-mark. Now step here, sir, if it wouldn't discompose you." (He had an annoying habit of calling me "sir" as often as I did him, and I hadn't figured out a good way to stop it.)

Using his stick, he crutch-hopped to a corner of the room, and, with some difficulty, prized up a section of plank. An iron box lay there, as snug as a nugget in a stream bed.

"I wish I could represent that box as containing rocks!"—he tapped it with his crutch—"but it don't. I'd be lying before Jesus." (I looked around the room, but we were alone.) "No, sir," stooping to lift the lid, "not a solitary rock's mixed in yet. Not to shilly-shally, it's gold, and it come chiefly and direct from my wife's father, a man, if you'll excuse it, that could squeeze a pence till the head appeared opposite. Dead now"—making a heavenward sign—"and content in one of the Lord's counting houses."

"I'd still like to buy the equipment, Mr. Smithers. A man without a pursuit, and having no tools for trade, is a lonely man. You said so yourself."

He sighed. "Those are English smithy grapples. Come down from my male parent, and, previous, from his, who carted them across the water in time to join the Revolutionaries and receive an English ball in the chest. English to the end, you might say."

"Will you sell them?"

He sighed again. "No sir, I won't. But look here," he said briskly, "we'll sign articles, you and me, in spite of dissimilars." He hopped to a table and took up a sheaf of paper and a pen.

"Now—if you'll lay your name to that, I'll undertake to make you the best blacksmith since Tubalcain in the Good Book—a man I presume you know by repute."

I looked the paper over. "Now, Mr. Smithers, this says you'll rent me all your equipment, for a dollar, for a period of two hundred years—"

"Say fifty cents, and split the difference."

"That's not what I meant."

He threw on his coat and beaver hat and said, "Blacksmithing looks easy but comes hard. Now there couldn't hardly be a better time for Lesson Number One than the current. That is to remark—now. We'll step around to the rear and seize those tools one by one, know them, get the feel of them, and head them toward their Dooty.

"Son," he concluded, his face lighting up like a forge, "taken together, we'll make the sparks fly upward, as the Bible seggests."

In the next few weeks, while a stone-mason worked on a forge, I learned so many things my head gave off a buzzing sound. I walked around in a trance. In the teaching line, Mr. Smithers believed in thoroughness. He led off with the anvil, on which blacksmiths pound iron into shape, and has a punching hole, and other irritations. Then he went on to beam drills; punch drills, flatters (convex-faced hammers); the farrier—a box for making shoes; pincers; sledge-hammers; buffers; boxes of chest-hardware; the bellows, to be sure; and such a further variety of implements and programs that

I began to wish I'd tackled something easy, like train robbing or opera singing.

Mr. Smithers would give me a pretty deep look and say, "I'm satisfied you understand, son, that a blacksmith is, all at once, and simultaneous, a shoer of animals, a gunsmith, and a wheel-wright, to mention three branches. And—what was that? I don't believe I under—you'd like the side-hinges explained again? I had in mind you'd grasped it like a snapping turtle with a frog. Like as not, I come across fuzzy."

Nobody could have been more patient and kindly, but he had a mild little sarcastic vein, too. And in my case, with my record as a scholar, I'm surprised he didn't explain things on my head with the anvil.

But we were progressing very well, and I was taking real interest in what I'd started to see as a noble trade. Without it, as he said, civilization would long have sat helpless, and we wouldn't be in Montana, to use a specific. And then, of a sudden, Bannack exploded. I can't think of a better way to say it. What happened ended our plans for a smithy there, and came close to ending Bannack itself.

Now I'll get right to the point and tell things in order, for they could hardly be more important. It might even be said that they formed Montana.

Everything began with James' expedition to the Yellowstone, where he and his men hoped to drive off Indians and open the region for settlement (and prospecting). As stated before, I think, Bill Fairweather and a group took the trail shortly after, hoping to join him for the finish. But the Indians—Crows and Blackfeet and

Sioux—were too strong, and James, briefly, was taken captive. He broke free and escaped, after ripping a lodge from top to bottom. When some fleeing men reached Fairweather, he turned his squad homeward, like an army retreating from a field of defeat. This time they went by a different route—along the Stinking Water River into Alder Gulch, as the latter came to be known through the world.

I'll quote from a Journal of the party; it gives an accurate and lurid description of what followed: "Early in June 1863 Alder Gulch was discovered by sheer accident. When we and Bill [Fairweather] failed to reinforce the remnants of Duncan's Expedition, we started drooping home to Bannack, and Bill said, 'Boys, we've seen the one passage, let's trail back along the Stinking Water.' Before camping that first night, he set out with his pan—'just for luck'—and two hours later came back a-burst with excitement. Without the least trouble, he'd panned $7.75 and could have gone on but was boiling over with the news. He said—he shouted—'By God, boys, the Stinking Water's paved with gold!—bed, sides and gravel. Now mind—not a word when we reach home! Mum's the word, and we're rich men all!' Grievous to relate, the first bunch entering a saloon let fly the tidings, and the Stampede was on . . ."

"Stampede" was the word. By now, I'd been around diggings a long while, and had heard rumors, false rumors, had watched rushes here and there—most ending in failure—and I genuinely doubt if such a wild, pell-mell, slam-bang madness ever before seized a community

searching for gold. And, yes, I mean to include
Sutter's Mill in California. Every mobile person
near Bannack lit out helter-skelter toward the
"color." The streets were filled with galloping
riders, lurching wagons, miners on foot dragging what tools they could manage; and the dust,
and yells, and banging of pans and hardware
cookery raised a storm so deafening that to hail a
friend across the way was hopeless.

It was as if the town had lost its sanity all in a
twinkling. Unhappy and comic incidents occurred one after the other. Toward twilight of the
first day's riot, one man, shakily erecting a tent,
mistook his partner for a beaver and shot him as
he stood knee-deep in the water. The victim
lingered for several days, cursing the luck that
cut him down only hours from Elysium.

The Stinking Water had gained its name, by
one account, from the fact that local Indians
buried their dead above ground. They placed
them in alders that lined the river's banks up and
down from Fairweather's find. Well, decomposi-
tion lent such frangrance to the stream that an
inventive mountaineer, working within his vo-
cabulary (always able) thereupon produced the
unlovely term. Grantly, of course, had a different
theory, based on his usual research. He thought
the stream was fed by sulphurous springs whose
vapors gave off the acrid stench in question.

Whichever was correct, the alders were superb
in appearance, or were until another man, careless in his rattled state, ignored a wind that
howled toward the East. Making camp, he set
fire to the growth, which burned to the ground
along its length. Nobody appeared to care. Typically, the sluice was merely rechristened after

the alders, which weren't present any more, and Alder Gulch it remained in the tumultuous times ahead.

Some understandable yowling arose from Indians who complained that their deceased appeared to be missing, but it died out in the uproar.

I was afire to join the Stampede, even if it meant a delay in blacksmithing, and I discussed it with Mr. Smithers. He said, "Go along, son. Purge it from your system. When the shine wears off, come back and we'll resume. No offense intended or took," and he hobbled toward his boarded cache. "As for the family of Ewing T. Smithers, *they'll* survive—don't fret."

When I stopped by the store, Grantly was home from Deer Lodge. I found him alone, seated near the fireplace, watching the flicker, hiss, and sputter of the half-green wood that burned without zest. He was musing again, and this time, seeing me, he motioned toward another chair. "My boy, for perhaps the first time in my life I find myself, not to deceive you, on the horns of a dilemma, or, as it might emerge in Boston—in a pickle."

And then, of course, he strayed on the track, one idea leading to another more remote, as was usual with that mind.

"I'll confess here," he said, "that the origin is obscure. I've never *shot* a dilemma and can't vouch for the length or shape of its horns. I'm not certain that, as a horned species, it exists in Montana—"

"You mentioned trouble?"

"When I left Bannack, as you recall, I carried a sum of money; more than suspected. Traveling

alone by horseback, I suddenly felt a curious
floating apprehension. It was one of the few
times in memory. I think we can agree that
Bannack"—looking out at the hullabaloo—
"with its cutthroats, bushwackers, card-sharps,
pimps, and assorted riffraff, could presently set
up as an outskirt of hell. Even so, if you'll forgive
an immodesty, my skill with guns long and short
(and occasionally multiple-barreled) had thus
far erased the sense of insecurity with which
most people tread these streets. James (I speak in
his absence) feels the same, for he is both boxer
and wrestler; no man to trifle with, despite his
good nature.

"But riding along, somewhere near Rattlesnake Creek, I sensed, through some indistinct
force not yet known to science, that I was, in
short, being trailed—"

(Here, to my relief, he abandoned his flowery
style and resumed in straightaway narration.)

"By one ruse or another—dismounting to
tighten a cinch or look to the pack mule—I kept
close watch on the trees and undergrowth behind. Flirting in and out were three men who hid
themselves instantly I looked back. Now I'd like
you to harken with care: *All were wearing
masks!* In other words, they were persons I
would recognize on sight. Nevertheless, in the
case of one, from the nicety and grace of his
movements, effeminate and hard to disguise, I
positively spotted that recent arrival and,
now—ousting Hank Crawford—self-appointed
'Sheriff'—Mr. Henry Plummer."

(This Plummer had drifted into town,
foppishly dressed, courtly of speech, and in no
time picked a fight with Crawford. Nobody knew

much about it, but Plummer was shot in the hand
and Crawford left town for Wisconsin. As soon
as he'd gone, Plummer stepped into office. Since
the job amounted to nothing, nobody paid much
attention.)

"Well, sir, when that thrustful gentleman became aware that I was looking him over, all three
pursuers faded behind and vanished. Now—
let's be certain. Who knew the nature of my trip?
You, of course. Spence—we can dismiss him; no
more honest man ever lived. James. And—I
grieve to say—Plummer himself. I recall discussing with him, on the street, in his official role,
my reasons for visiting the Lodge. In doing so I
succumbed to that absurd vanity which has cost
many a man his fortune. Like a fool, I hinted that
there was more here than met the eye.

"Very well, then. How to perform my duty? I
have no firm evidence. The man thus far has
stayed pretty well within bounds. Worse yet, we
have no valid law, no courts, and he's the un-
crowned Sheriff!"

"I have an idea, Grantly," I said. "Tell your
suspicions to a few trusted friends—Langford,
Professor Dimsdale, James when he returns—
and wait for some slip, a brag during a card
game, any suggestion of where he came from.
Then send a man to check him out. Let's see what
he did before. His 'record,' as they call it."

Grantly slapped his knee. "By George, my boy,
you've hit it! We need a dossier. And, to be sure,
'X' Beidler's* the very man! If ever mortal was
born to the detective's mantle, he's the one. Beidler came out here as a miner, but he's made

_____
*"X" was the name that Beidler preferred, and he used it
from start to finish.

himself a watchdog for law and order, as a kind of hobby. The fact is, he's uncanny. When he looks me in the eye, I'm convinced he knows I stole a squash pie, cooling in a window, from my mother when I was seven. Knows it, and is waiting for a recurrence—a local outbreak of squash-pie thefts—"

"There aren't any squashes around here, so you may be in the clear. You understand I'd take this job myself, if you and James said so. But to tell the truth, I've got a pretty bad itch to—"

"Yes, yes. So I've heard. Oh, things get around town, which I now see as one of the world's garden spots. *Everything*, if you follow me."

I turned a little pink, and tried to stop it by concentration but failed. Grantly stood up and placed a hand on my shoulder. "My boy, you've learned some useful facts having to do with women. File them, store them up to serve as shield and buckler—which reminds me that, while 'shield' is, of course, familiar, I'm in the dark concerning the employment of 'buckler'—"

He'd switched back again, so I left.

Taking the belongings needed, I traveled the sixty miles by horseback, with two pack mules, and reached the smoking ruin of a once handsome tree-line toward nightfall. Runty little evergreens had been mixed amongst the alders, and with the wind, all had gone up like fireworks. Many seasoned campers, blinded by bonanza, had lost their entire store. Half-burned wagons stood here and there, and sluice boxes, and cradles; and the ground was strewn with charred remnants of tools and household effects. All in all, the scene was enough to wring tears from a mummy. But there was no time to brood about it.

The trail was still jammed by people trying to catch up before the yellow metal played out. Their frenzy was wasted. As stated in the Journal of a miner named Dickson, "In the rush that followed, more than sixty thousand people gathered $100,000,000 in the next few years," and the Stuart Journals, which Montana considers among the best, state flatly that, "The Alder Gulch diggings were the richest gold placer diggings ever discovered in the world . . . the bed of the creek and the bars on both sides were uniformly rich; the bed rock being literally paved with gold." But the two appraisals, taken together, require amplification.

While it's true that, for a long time, nearly every miner who prospected that stream took gold in abundance, these were not the founders of fortunes. It was the same old story. From the Stuart Journals: "The miner who indulged in gambling usually worked six days, then cleaned up his dust. Placing it in a buckskin sack, he hied himself to the nearest gambling house, where he remained till he'd transferred the contents to professional gamblers. If he played in luck he might stay in the game twenty-four hours. Then he returned to his 'diggins' without money and often with little grub. He was a sadder but no wiser man, for he would repeat the same thing over and over as long as his claim lasted . . ."

Meanwhile I got caught in the hoopla and jamboree. I arrived to find such another bedlam as was perhaps never seen before. Certainly not of its kind. Hundreds of men, and some women, were trying with desperation to erect a town, in

the hours stolen from panning gold. Among
these, of course, were fools and knaves, but
mainly it was men of vision who directed progress. A "town" had not, however, been built in
the brief time since the discovery. There were
no real houses, and few materials with which to
construct them. Every sort of shelter was used.
Men threw up brush wickiups; others made
dugouts; some sought refuge beneath overhanging rocks. And the majority spread their blankets
beneath tall trees of dense foliage, to endure
night-cold and storms. The nearest sawmill was
seventy miles distant, so that the ring of axes
daily made music on the slopes.

Still, log cabins sprang up pretty fast. The first
was built by a prudent fellow, a baker; and a
saloon followed by a few axe swings. This
alignment gave rise to the first staple town joke.
"It marks the sole and solitary time," wrote one
Thomas Hardin in a "Day-book," "that a bakery
got in ahead of a saloon."

I walked my horse and mules in, the animals
fagged, for people ahead had stripped the trail of
grass. After some disheartening tries for lodging,
I paid two dollars a night to a wizened old buzzard with a youngish squaw and three
daughters. They had a workable, un-smelly elk
lodge. I was given a corner and advised that
"Concerning the nether generation—and two's
maids simon pure—I've been vexed with my
trigger finger. It's fixed, like, in a curl. And it
don't take nothing to make it grip."

I emphasized that I had no designs on his
daughters, and feeling out of sorts, added, "And
that goes for your wife, and you, and your relations, and all the Indian tribes in Montana!"

I regretted my rudeness, but he seemed not at all offended. He was merely surprised. "Why, son, I didn't in no way intend to put you out. More proper, I aimed to convey that the sprigs was available for companionship, decent and hospitable, at a price that appears to suit. The one that got reamed knocks down to half, make it, and that's three dollars. Gold—smack on the nose."

Revolted, I assured him his "sprigs" were not required. Then I turned in beneath the buffalo robe given me by Grantly and James, at Christmas. There was plenty of room. The lodge was sixty feet across, like most Snake lodges. It had sixteen poles, fastened at the bottom with wooden pegs, a hole at the top—for smoke, of course—and a raised frame of earth for the fire. Commonly the women sleep and work to the right of the entrance—which is part of the hide and pins down at night. The floor is covered by rye grass or willow twigs, with tanned pelts placed on top. Hanging from this pole or that are 'parflashes'* containing pemmican, dried roots and berries, newly-dressed skins, and other possessions of the family. A ditch is dug round the outside, for rain, and altogether such lodges make very good dwellings.

I stretched out, lazy and content, with an ice-cold wind screeching outside, snug as a bear in its winter hole. But around midnight, I judged, there came a rustle, and one of the girls slipped in beside me. She was naked and felt silky and smooth to the touch. Well, the predicament was

---

*From the French (again) "parflèche," having originally to do with arrows, or quivers, as I got it.

awkward, because, for one thing, I hadn't any idea which it was; I hoped it was the sprig who'd tumbled from grace, so to speak.

Not inclined to raise a rumpus, I had a lively night's sleep, and next morning she was gone. But the old man was up and devising what I took to be a scoreboard, with some twigs fixed to a sinew. The wife was seated sewing, and all the daughters were asleep. Embarrassed, I had trouble looking the old devil in the eye. But he was in a crackling good humor.

"Now don't fret yourself, son," he told me. "I ain't the one to demand sudden payment. I don't hold with it, commercial. Moreover, I know a gent by cut and palaver. We'll keep tally; and I'd ruther have my gullet slit than cheat."

I suggested moving, so as not to concern his wife, but he practically forced me back down. He said, "Her? Concern? Why, cock an ear and listen to her singing!" And indeed she was making a kind of clucking sound. "She ain't the one to go against natur, and those sprigs have leaned heavy on her mind. Overcome by itch, what if they took and skedaddled? We'd be pore as Job's turkey hen."

He said the girls had turned sulky of late. Or since he'd changed their names. Indians are given baby names at birth and then, as characteristics form, a mature name that's meant to be permanent—Swift Arrow, Sitting Bull, and the like. Until the Stampede, these three had gone by tribal words that, as he rolled them off his tongue, seemed soft and euphonious: "Timpa-a;" "Pish-ip;" "Ó-nim." When the family pulled up from Bannack, heading for the gold, he swapped things around "to bring luck."

He renamed the youngest sister "Alder," and the next "Gulch," but when he tried to change the non-maid to "Stinking Water," his wife blew sky-high. She "raised so much dust" about it that he backed down and they settled on "Reamed." The wife said that was satisfactory, and fitted the case, and it was thus that the poor girl was called.

Next day I tried panning, but a Miners' Court like Bannack's was still being organized, and someone or other, usually with a gun, laid claim to every place I tried. Eventually I gave up. It made no difference; I felt tired, somehow, and my back hurt.

In the next few days, I entertained every night, and I'm convinced that the three were being rotated. There was no way to tell—"simon-pure" or not. (I doubted this last, by the way, and figured it was a means of jacking up the price.) And then, after a week, with me peaked but still game, one crawled in like a starved-down mink, and I figured I was through. I didn't properly get any sleep at all that night. It was curious but sapping. The I saw it all—these females were gaining in strength while I was hobbling around town like a cripple. But when dawn came, I looked down, and by jings it was his wife!

As usual, he was up and poking the fire. He was trying to put an aggrieved look on his face, but it failed to come over.

"Now, that'll be ten dollars," he said, moving some twigs along the counter. "You take and another chile might toss a conniption, but that's never been my way. Ain't she frisky? Ain't she spry? I'll tell you this, boy—she's wore me down to a nub. Make it eight dollars and call it a steal."

(I was not greatly surprised. I'd seen one chief sell his prettiest daughter outright for six dollars and a moth-eaten blanket. And another old mountain-man I knew "rented out" his women when his "rheumatiz stunned him," leaving him unable to work, which was generally, if business was good in the lodge.)

Disgorging this rubbish, my landlord looked as pious as a bishop. But around noon, having settled the "tally," which I thought had been fattened, I arranged to sleep in the bakery. Then I spent two days getting back on my feet. Thus refreshed, I struck out again to pan, and this time wore two Navy revolvers. No one bothered me. Perhaps by now I'd lost some of my boyish look; I shaved when it suited me; and the Duncans had given me the best possible lessons in firearms. I was, by now, a very good shot.

And, like the brothers, I remained generally ignorant about prospecting. Still, at some distance up-creek, I managed to pan six or seven dollars' worth of dust. All in the space of three hours. I suppose I had some notion that, try as I might, the East would eventually haul me back, with the fun all gone, so I meant to delay things as long as I could. Meantime I was more interested in absorbing the sights than in getting rich.

The town was rising like a beanstalk, and people—mostly miners—continued to flock in. The prevailing mental state was hysteria, and suddenly the populace fell prey to additional rumor-fever. The period became known as the Stampede Craze. A man rode in, eyes wild and horse lathered up, and cried, "There's a strike on the Gallatin that makes this look like toss-penny!"

You'd scarcely believe it, but half the miners saddled up, left Alder Gulch behind, and, as shortly before, hit the trail in a spirit of pell-mell, slam-bang, stand aside, don't block my way! None of the fools even bothered to ask a question. It was the Bannack bedlam over, and when they arrived at Gallatin, what happened? Well, there wasn't enough gold there to stuff a tooth with, and a few settlers, advised to point out the diggings and be quick about it, merely looked puzzled and made replies along the lines of "Said what, partner?"

So—the miners turned around and galloped back to Alder. Then, after a short breather, word came from Wisconsin Creek, thirty miles distant, that a miner had stumbled onto gold so thick it probably reached down to China. Saddle up, grab some pemmican, and light out again—not having learned as much as a Sunday School lesson from the fiasco at Gallatin. And, of course, the same old story. Wisconsin Creek contained pebbles for throwing at birds, if you needed exercise, and a bed of solid rock, and not much else except willows along the banks, and bunch grass, and old fallen trees, with maybe a bewildered beaver or two, wondering if the end of the world had come. It was ludicrous, and this time they trooped back a trifle sheepish.

The chagrin failed at last, and a third rumor was ripest of all. These miners were taking respectable panfulls every day from the stream, but they climbed out as if snake-bit when someone flashed forth that the mother lode, the *real*

gold, was located in the town itself! By now,
streets had been lined, many structures were up,
and a committee formed to settle on a municipal
name. But nothing much changed. The Miners'
Court still pended, so the settlement continued
to have no popular rules.

The miners swarmed over everything—front
yards, back yards, middle of a street, anywhere at
all. I saw a man thrust his head out of a doorway
and complain, "Here, now, Lafe Buckner, you
and them rummies are in my yard, and
a-choking off my front door! You didn't expect
us to climb in and out of the chimbly, did you?"
There being no answer, the picks kept flying, but
when the hole was down ten or fifteen feet, with
nothing to show except rocks and old tangled
roots, they "opined" that they must be "a mite
south-southwest of the precise exact spot." So
they shifted to create a similar nuisance at a
neighbor's.

A fight almost started over the business of
naming the town. As stated, the bulk of these
Emigrants were Southerners, not remarkable
when one considers that nearly all wagon trains
started from Missouri, a slave state and a main
spot for collecting men sick of the War. On June
16, 1863, the Townsite Committee recorded a
claim of 320 acres of land, and a Colonel Butler
jumped up to propose the name of Varina, in
honor of Mrs. Jefferson Davis.

Well, that set off a pow-wow that nearly
wrecked the building. Another leading citizen,
Judge Bissel, arose to say he'd "be damned" if
he'd use Jeff Davis's wife on any document he
prepared; they'd have to scrounge further. In the
end, the miners—wonderfully lazy about

names—reminded the group that down in Nevada they had a smooth-working town named Virginia City, and they saw no reason to grind harder.

So they named the new find Virginia City, and when a sister-town sprouted alongside, they simply whacked on an inspired "Nevada." The solutions led to confusion, off and on, but nobody took it very hard. At the worst, they could drop into one of the several saloons, have a drink, and jaw about something else.

CHAPTER XII

VIRGINIA CITY, SUMMER, 1863. After the stampede from Bannack, the crowds poured in from all points of the compass. Houses, stores, restaurants, bakeries, saloons, nearly every establishment possible now lined the streets, which were filled with a wild tumult of humanity. In its best days, to choose a poor figure, Bannack had not remotely approached such sights and sounds. To watch a town leap up suddenly and overflow is a rare curiosity. Here I'll add some notes of my own.

"Within weeks we had a population of ten thousand buckskin-clad miners with beards and flowing hair who moved in and out with supplies; these they carried in huge back-packs . . . donkeys were loaded with assortments from groceries to lumber to Tanglefoot and tobacco and bright-colored clothes with which to buy a squaw . . . many Indian wives took in washing, and Chinese often supplied household work for the whites; they also built laundries, restaurants, and 'hotels,' which were little more than eating and storage centers, furnishing no lodging except a bare floor where one could roll up in a blanket unless he preferred the privacy of the trees . . . All structures were built of pine logs with clay for mortar and sapling roofs thatched with layers of long swamp grass, there covered thickly with sod—the rude houses were good and sound, cool in summer, warm in winter, tight against rain . . .

"Freight lines from Salt Lake and Fort Benton via the Missouri were busy hauling all articles used—provisions, lumber, carpentry and mining tools, furniture, ornaments for saloons, even imported wines for the new dance halls or 'Hurdy-Gurdies' . . . Gold dust served for currency; merchants and saloon owners kept scales and a 'blower' prominently displayed on their counters . . . a miner's sackful went into the blower, which was meant to emit pure gold and sift out impurities . . . most were dishonestly rigged, so that the buyer lost about five per cent on any transaction.

"Every miner's dust was contained in small antelope bags, these carried inside very heavy imported shirts of curious quality, being woven of wool so tight it could keep a man warm in sub-zero weather without an outer garment; thus the shirts ideal for freedom in panning . . . they sold for upward of fifteen dollars, or whatever an unscrupulous merchant could pry . . . In theory gold now was worth $18 an ounce; practically miners cheerfully settled for somewhat less—there was always more where that came from . . . greenbacks went for about half that . . . Never have I seen men so heedless of money . . ."

Few Journals dwelt long on the "Hurdy-Gurdies." The omission seems odd, for these recreations made a strong pretense of respectability. The truth is, I'm afraid, that the town's majority felt embarrassed over the ambiguity of the frolics. The name, in this context, was believed peculiar to Montana, a region as richly creative as the mountaineer's speech itself.

All Hurdy-Gurdies were large rooms off the backs of saloons, with partitions of lattice work, and gates for passage back and forth. There was a gate-keeper; benches round the walls for the drunk or exhausted; a corner where the girls waited to dance. "Musicians" occupied another corner—two fiddlers, a jug-blower, and a harmonica or so. The mixture of artists varied. One Hurdy-Gurdy had a man who extracted noises from a musical saw, until his body was found in the creek several miles above town. Nobody expressed concern; his death was seen as musical criticism. Besides, in drink he made himself a continual nuisance to the girls. The Bale of Hay, a popular pub (and Hurdy-Gurdy) had an Iowan who played the nose-whistle, and the California Exchange was perhaps most successful of all, with the possessor of a concertina that leaked slightly and occasionally refused jumps in the upper register, emitting nothing but wind. The chief object, however, was noise, and this increased as the whiskey went down and the evening wore on.

The females who danced for fifty cents a ticket were a study. How and why they'd arrived in southern Montana was never firmly established. All were known as "Teutons," the bulk handled by a manager who in sterner circles might have been described as a pimp. Most persons assumed they'd come from the large German section of St. Louis. They were, in the words of one Journal, ". . . large, buxom, flaxenhaired, and tireless."

And, further, it struck me, very agreeable

types, good-humored, poised to laugh at the smallest joke, stronger than many men. For his ticket, a miner was entitled, with the Hurdy of his choice, to a "Cotillion," that is to say, three short tunes. Then he was expected to march his partner to the bar and treat her. Her mission was to coax him into buying an expensive bottle of wine; his, often, was to maneuver her out of this. If he refused, she was unruffled but settled, as a rule, for a soft drink or oddly, a cigar. Their ambiguity lay in this: they'd been trained to arouse male lust, subtly, by wearing a dress so low that their bulging bosoms were exposed, and upon sensing a likely subject, dancing with pelvic contiguity aimed at warmer acquaintance after the close.

There was some show of keeping these assignments secret, and to this day I have no firm idea where the over-ripe Hurdies took their gold-laden lovers. Buildings being chiefly single story, it was supposed that the managers kept outlying rooms to accommodate the post-dance rites. No miner complained of failing to get his money's worth, and some, past their first youth, appeared to walk stooped for days. Those exuberant Teutons were fashioned for love, and they enjoyed their work—that of dancing both upright and prone.

Around this time an effort was made to start a newspaper (later to be called the *Montana Post*), and the editor carelessly referred to the strapping Venuses as "our lovely members of the Demimonde."

Well, a miner carrying a rifle burst into the office in a fit of drunken indignation. He said, as I had the story second hand, "Now you ain't

agoing to insult our female women thataway.
You fail to print a reetraction, and pretty damned
fast, or your front side'll be pumped fuller of
holes than a riffle-box!"

But he'd misjudged his man. The editor, a
young newcomer, carried two holstered revolvers, even when at work on an article, and had
been known to flash them.

He said, "Just how do you see the word 'demimonde,' Mr. Throgmorton? That is, what does
it mean, exactly?"

"How! You seggest I'm some species of
dictionary-worm and there'll be further trouble,
rest on it." Then he leaned over the desk and
added, in an injured tone, "You've set there and
disappointed we all, Oliver. I never figured you
for no slander-merchant. Fact is, I taken a liking
to you. I'll say it out loud now—demimonde
ain't up to expectations."

"Well, well, Mr. Throgmorton, we'll see
what's possible. This office aims to please."

And in the next issue, printed on butcher's
paper as usual, the editor ran a praising piece
about the Teutons, and called them "soiled
doves" and "frail Cyprians." The miner thanked
him personally, wiping his eyes, and
acknowledged that it was a "beautiful tribute,
beautiful," and he'd cut it out to "send back to
my old woman."

It should be noted that these dance-hall
women (and, of course, their managers) collected huge sums in dust, after paying the
saloon-keeper's rental. Ticket prices varied from
place to place, fifty cents being the cheapest. But
that basic sum was niggling. A miner in high
fettle was apt to hand a favorite dancer a bag of

gold worth hundreds, even thousands, if he rounded off the night on her pallet. At a time when an expert might be averaging twenty dollars a pan, gold was flung right and left as a sport, with no thought of tomorrow, or a possible fading of the rainbow. It became common for the Hurdies to appear in the richest kind of cosstume, imported from Eastern cities, and many had the foresight to deposit fortunes with the first merchants—of tried integrity—who functioned then as bankers.

The baker where I stayed (taking my meals at restaurants) had incomprehensibly named his concern "The Mechanical Bakery," and this remained the chief such establishment in town for years. He was a curious man, the proprietor, seldom if ever speaking and doing all the work himself. Like many then in Virginia City, he'd plainly suffered some mind-jarring jolt in the past, and he functioned, on the human level, largely by means of facial expressions, with explanatory sounds. When I asked about the name—for it was the least mechanical enterprise of my experience—he shook his head, crossed his wrists, as if for shackles, and gave forth a kind of growl and whistle that did, indeed sound vaguely like a machine. From this I deduced that he considered himself a drowning serf in an age fast turning mechanized, and that he would hold out to the end. At one point, I recall, I mentioned the steamers calling at Fort Benton, and he turned a bright pink, ignoring me for two or three days.

And then one evening I came home from pan-

ning and found him departed—sold out to
people who promptly installed those alien aids
that apparently drove him across the earth. The
Mechanical Bakery now had a series of pulleys
and runners for moving bread in and out of
ovens, and more of the accursed machines followed. Since the new owners, a man and his wife
from Louisville, both the color of the bread they
baked, felt that my buffalo robe might be infested
with vermin, to the detriment of their loaves, I
looked for other quarters.

It was all right. The bakery business, to have
bread warm and ready in the mornings, required
a noisy bustle at night; and the smell of heating
dough, as chemistry changes, in the historic business of keeping man alive, is un-conducive to
sleep. I could have gone back to the lodge, with
its ravening females, but I felt in robust health
and decided to keep aloof. In the end, I rolled up
on one of the hotel floors for a few nights; I was
dickering about renting a cabin of my own.

Meanwhile, the town continued its wild,
rackety growth. More than ever, the streets were
jammed with bull-trains and pack-animals, and
even these were insufficient to keep supplies
flowing. Then a man named Gates, hearing of an
experiment in Arizona, rode down lickety-split.
Before long he came back leading five camels
that he mistakenly called dromedaries. (I
thought it elementary for anyone to know that a
camel has two humps, while a dromedary is
blessed, or cursed, with one.) There was a hullabaloo about it, many asserting that the beasts
were savage, and probably man-eaters. Indians

in the area, after scrutinizing the newcomers, struck their lodges, packed up, and left, lodge poles trailing behind the horses' sidestraps.

But was Gates put out? Not in the least. He was a flamboyant fellow, with loud, checked clothes, a gray derby hat, and a voice that was said, in sobriety (or the kind of sobriety then in Virginia) to peel bark off trees at a hundred yards. So— Gates got the paper to print up some posters announcing a "Gargantuan Exhibition" on Idaho Street for the following Sunday. He would prove that his dromedaries were docile and "could carry ten or more children as if on a featherbed!" He threw in further lies and promised to revolutionize freighting in the Rockies, since his animals had "twenty-two stomachs and only drank every other leap-year." This part was supposed to be humorous, being followed by a parenthetical "Ha, ha!" And after that, "Seriously, folks—" reducing the stomachs by fifteen or so but leaving everybody in the dark, too.

You may be certain that Idaho Street, in front of Gibson's Hotel, was solidly, noisily packed for the demonstration. Sunday, of course, was the great day of the week. The miners all came to town, the Hurdy-Gurdies, saloons, and gambling halls ran wide open and roaring (to celebrate the Sabbath), and the streets were choked with peddlers and auctioneers. These last were new here. Each had a bell and sold off oxen, horses, mules, and supplies, usually on commission for freighters. Gambling houses and the like did more business on Sundays than during the rest of the week combined. And it's equally true that most miners returned to their claims flat broke and often in debt to merchants who grub-staked them by custom.

But on this Sunday, Gates and his zoo were the attraction. He piled up some boxes at Gibson's and held forth with a speaking-trumpet, starting around noon. He had a shifty look of circus about him, and I figured he'd slammed out just in time. The dromedaries were tied to a railing, and seemed in a medium-poor humor, which I afterward learned was their normal state. There was a fair amount of heckling. A miner held up one of the super-eloquent dodgers and mentioned the phrase "Gargantuan exhibition!"—asking, "Now I can see drodemaries [sic] plain and clear, but what I'm coming at is this: Where do you keep them Garganty-ones? They ain't on hand, leastaways not visible."

Gates gave a hearty laugh and said the word "sprang from Greek mythology" and meant something else entirely. He said it was "allusive;" there were no Gargantuans.

"Then it's a swindle!" cried the miner, and threw down his bill and stamped on it. He said he was "going back to the Exchange and get cheated according to rules." But he never did—he wanted to see the fun. Here another man offered a "drodemary" a drink from his bottle, but the animal bit him across the knuckles. This caused some trumped-up feeling, naturally, with threats to drive them all, with Gates, back where they came from. He absorbed it with good humor and calmed the crowd by cracking a few jokes.

Then he trotted forth a string of very pretty maids all dolled up in their Sunday bonnets and ribbons. Every child in town, I heard, wanted a ride on the "funny, hump-backed horses," and Gates promised to "satisfy all." Things turned out slightly less than planned. Clearing a space in the street, and using a homemade ladder, he actually did seat ten girls on one beast, which switched around pretty brisk and indicated a dislike of Virginia City, including the girls and Gates. But he knocked it on the nose and started off leading the squealing youngsters down toward Coleman and Loeb's.

Now a camel's gait is notoriously rocky and jarring, and three of the girls got seasick and threw up, and "a handsome lass of sixteen summers," as a Diarist put it, "slid off on her plump round bottoms and was taken back to Gibson's for an application of Herkimer's All-Purpose External and Internal Balm." They had to expose her to do it, or said they did, and a number of people—mostly men, including me—looked on, interested and concerned. Several expressed a willingness to help by rubbing more salve, but the victim's parents arrived and angrily led her off home.

Eventually the camels, being too cussed for use, were staked in Snow Shoe Gulch, several miles from Virginia, but they broke loose and wandered off into the hills. A year later, an eccentric hermit-hunter shot what he thought was an elk; after he'd examined it, however, never having seen such a thing before, he turned mentally woozy and was infrequently seen again, shaking his head and muttering to himself.

CHAPTER XIII

THE DUNCANS ARRIVED soon after "The Great Camel Farce" (*Montana Post*), with two Conestoga wagons crammed full of gear, and some stock trailing behind. They'd been preceded by most of the old crowd from Bannack—the Smithers, Sam Hauser, Professor Dimsdale, and others. Practically no one stayed behind. All were moving bag and baggage, closing out interests there. Grantly was physically below normal, from chasing and recovering a twelve-year-old Indian he'd bought at a bargain. She'd made a practise of running away every day, and after three or four weeks, he'd given up and rested in bed for a while.

They rented a log dwelling, on Jackson Street, while James arranged to build a bigger place to serve principally as a store. Once we'd settled in (and I was happy to get off the Chinaman's board floors), the brothers were afire to prospect. It was the first time they'd showed zeal for such a venture. I was surprised.

We set out on a crisp blue morning, horseback, and went up Alder Gulch as far as twenty miles, till the miners thinned out. The Miners' Court had now been established, thank goodness, so that the chance of a fuss was slight. Many of this floating population had left during the Stampedes and had never returned, for one reason or another. But the influx of merchants, artisans, hangers-on, and others made up for their loss. And plenty of miners remained, with more coming in. They lined the banks and filled the stream for fifteen miles or so and prospected little tributary gulches and other regional hopefuls.

We found a likely spot—nobody in sight up or down—and Grantly held forth on gold-mining as an Art. This struck me as pretty good, considering he'd been in the Rockies for several years and, thus far, had lifted maybe two hundred dollars.

He consulted a notebook—his constant attendant, the contents aimed to enrich posterity.

"I've taken the liberty of probing secrets of gold extraction," he said, "thanks to material presently available. There is much to know; more (in local practice) to be discarded."

He seated himself on a stump, while James chewed a straw and looked off into the distance, as if he wished he were back at Yellowstone.

"The simplest, least fruitful, method of wrenching gold from its nest is that which we are here beginning: i.e., the panning of placer or gulch deposits. The required tools, I needn't remind you, are the pick, the spade, and the pan. Up to this point"—he cleared his throat—"our conquests have been, in a sense, Pyrrhic; that is, while we've won skirmishes, most have proved costly out of proportion.

"To date, I learn, Montana gulch miners have attacked their work imperfectly. No finer breed of men ever lived—but *they are heedless and impatient!* It's a safe conclusion that they leave as much as they extract. These careless methods we hope to avoid today. Now I shall descend to specifics." (I heard James mutter what sounded like "Thank God!") "Among them are the following, or *sequelant*, and I quote: 'Much, very much too often pans overly freighted with iron are tossed aside in disgust, as being a nuisance to work.'

"To offset this, I availed myself of a small but powerful magnet"—holding it up. "We shall draw forth these particles of iron, salvaging the gold for its worthier purpose. Number two: My informant, though today confined with delirium tremens, has stated that the prime oversight—in what he loosely describes as 'the insane profligacy of Montana'—concerns old driftwood, or watersoaked logs. These, he says, contain gold in such quantity as may often be absent in the gravel itself. We shall, if you please, attack all fallen sentinels of an earlier age with gusto (and pick).

"As to Montana's larger search for gold—the quartz operations which may expect to build fortunes—well, let us consider those another day. A day when, in brief, we are provided with the funds needed to assume our place beside the Astors and the Rothschilds. Frankly, I regard every bluff and ravine north of here as auriferous in some degree—perhaps a bonanza beneath every lodge . . ."

He made some other pronouncements, touching on Long Toms and cradles used in California, as compared to our Montana sluice boxes. But James and I were in the water by then, picking, spading, and panning. For much-sung Alder Gulch, our start seemed pretty thin to me. Still, Grantly was right. By drawing out iron with the magnet, and by removing gray drift logs that looked like drowned corpses, we took some respectable panfulls. But we had to work like slaves. We'd staked our claims, of course; described them, then thrust the papers in reversed bottles on sticks.

I'd been told by a dozen miners, and had read in a Salt Lake paper, that Alder's bed was "paved with gold," and I'd believed it, more or less. But this particular stretch bore a suspicious resemblance to rock, and pretty hard rock at that. Then something stirred in my mind; it had lain there all day. It was that stump! Grantly had sat on a fresh stump, and I had trouble deciding why it was there. Virginia City had plenty of timber closer at hand. I climbed out on the opposite side and walked up and down for several hundred yards, parting new shoots here and there. And on the way back, I found what I sought—a claim bottle hidden in the weeds grown out since June. Altogether, in the next half hour, we uncovered four more, or enough to span our range, with some to spare. Weeks before, this claim had been picked, spaded, and panned, and the owners moved on to richer digs, leaving the usual behind.

Grantly re-assumed the stump, after wringing out his socks. For once he appeared just slightly defeated.

"I believe it was the senior Duke in *As You Like It* who remarked in a forestial glade not unlike our own: 'Sweet are the uses of adversity.' To the best of my knowledge, he was not prospecting at the time. In that I must applaud him, though he may have caught fire later in life. I've noticed that nearly everybody does. From time to time I've received hints that the pursuit of gold is not my natural métier.

"I'm not even convinced," he continued, musing as usual, "that gold in itself is a good thing. A mere metal, though heavy, scarce, and shiny, is not important enough to direct the course of human-kind. I can call to mind a number of grossly undesirable uses to which, over the years, men have put it. As a lone, revolting sample, it forms ad majorum the substance from which crowns are made—symbolic of Governments subordinate to those of the baboon. I allude, in one case, to the late George Third, a dribbling half-wit barely able to sit erect. There have been others, worse—"

James interrupted, following his habit.

"Well, Grantly, thanks to your magnet and the stuff about drift-logs, we've taken fair pay today. In the circumstance, I see nothing to moon about, and I'm not a miner by taste. My suggestion is this: we rig a sluice box and give it one more whack. Surely we can find, in all this wilderness—"

There came a second interruption, in the shape of several shots. Gunfire from downstream, a mile or so distant.

"Trouble," said James, abruptly, and we loaded and saddled up. Both Duncans looked as if they expected something of the kind. Unsheathing rifles from holsters, we prepared to sprint toward the commotion. But our horses had only just switched round when three riders came crashing up the trail at a gallop. All wore masks and all were gleefully yelling, one swaying as if he might tumble off. Seeing us, they reined up slightly, exchanged a few words, and veered off to circle under the trees. James and Grantly sat stolidly in their saddles, waiting. Neither seemed disturbed. Their manner, rather, was studious, as if storing up facts for the future.

The man swaying pulled out a revolver as they flashed by, but Grantly brought his rifle up smartly, and I heard another say, "Don't be a fool; that piss-ant could hit a gnat's ass in Bannack!" And then they were gone. We could hear their jubilation for several minutes as they pounded up the trail. After that, all was silent, save for the gurgling stream and a bird or two chirping angrily, I thought, in the pines.

"Well?" said James.

"I think so; I'm not sure. A good guess would be Lyons, Yeager, and Stinson. But guesses are weak props for order. My boy, you can put up that gun—the play here is finished." He sighed, his heels nibbling at his horse's flanks, all hope of gold gone.

"Well, then, face up and do our duty."

We walked slowly down-gulch toward Virginia, most miners now gone from their claims. At three or four points the stream was covered in growth. James, at last, dismounted and led his horse by the bridle, knocking weeds aside with a stick, now peering at the opposite bank, now examining the soft turf for prints. This was his proper sphere, I thought, the probe for the unknown, a pursuit of adventure. Not dully picking for gold in which he had no interest, and certainly not trapped in a store. For me, with no grasp of what had happened, the march proceeded at an aggravating pace. And the setting, with its stream, great rocks, and evergreens high overhead, had turned from beauty to something ominous and evil, too quiet, unnaturally empty.

"Here, I believe," cried James over his shoulder. He'd moved in front, excitement burning in his face. "They rode up—two men—then crossed to keep clear of travelers."

I was hot, the mosquitoes and black flies had left welts on my neck, and I asked with a tinge of irritation, "How do you know? Hoofprints are hoofprints; one's like another. What makes you think two men waded horses into this sewer?"

"Because one of them's lying there, across that log."

I started to say I was sorry, but he clapped me on the shoulder, and we tied up our horses for the unpleasant task ahead.

The miner a-sprawl over the log lay face down, shot twice in the back. He was thoroughly dead, and, as Grantly observed, "He neither heard them ride up nor felt the lead that struck him." The stream fell at a gradient here, making what before had been a merry plashing. The man was dressed in the common uniform of the miner— kneeboots, rough jeans, and the heavy shirt that all wore winter and summer. He must have had a hat, James said, but we never found it though we searched both banks downstream. His partner, a grizzled old fellow who might have been his father, lay staring upward, eyes open, against the opposite bank some fifty feet up toward Bannack.

There was evidence that, after the first fusillade that ended prospecting, and hope for his son's future, this second old gamecock had scrambled quick toward his rifle, which rested

against a charred sprout, not a yard from his
hand. But a soft, heavy bullet, as large as' .50
calibre, had struck the side of his head and spun
him round—a terrible wound, with fragments of
skull nearby and brains still oozing onto the
ground. Like the other, he wore a red neckerchief, against the insects. And here, too, we
never found his hat. In the case of both, tools lay
in the stream, and others were on the bank
nearby. Needless to say, we found no antelope
bags. Thongs by which two, at least, had hung
from neck into shirt were cut or rudely ripped
free of the bodies.

"Goddamn the goddamned swine!" exclaimed Grantly in a voice that rang out like a
shot, echoing in the ravine. "Murdered, plucked
like chickens, and—mark this—*even their hats
stolen!*" His rage appeared to settle on this last
fact, and to this day I have no notion why it
bothered him. After we'd dragged the men
across to inspect them, James returned for their
horses. But these were skittish and wary, their
eyes wide with fright. Grantly, meanwhile, continued to mutter about the hats, saying, ". . .
stripped of dignity . . . blazing sun . . . leave
them decently covered . . . kill a man and steal
his hat! . . ." etc. It was the first time I'd seen
him angry out of hand, and I wouldn't have
given a used cartridge case for those trash if
they'd ridden back.

We laid them out on the ground, and Grantly
went through their pockets. Neither had possessions of value—a claspknife, some tobacco and
two cob pipes, a buck-eye (for luck) that looked
shiny enough to be waxed, a bottled nostrum

thrust down the old gentleman's shirt that said
"Dr. E. Moses Quinly's Omnibus Specific for
Catarrh, Piles, Lockjaw and Tuberculosis," and
was 78% alcohol with the rest "secret Choctaw
herbs." And, finally, a water-soaked, still read-
able letter that the young man was writing home.
It was about half finished, I judged; it said: "Dear
Lucy we made it all right but nothing to brag
about (ha, ha). Your father good now but contracted griping of bowel from salt pork so had to
rest (and I) in Salt Lake. I complained to train-
master about food and received black eye. Three
people died of dysentery en route two of which
were women. Changed stage line in Salt Lake in
charge of man named Slade who broke his back
near about to make Emigrants comfortable look
after all needs keep cheerful and etc. I think the
best man of good heart as well as handsome I
ever met. When he saw my eye he sought bully
out and thrashed him bad in the street. Man still
unconscious when we left but expected to probably live.

"I know you know how I crave you and children and your father asks to say likewise. Our
delay missed first big Montana gold rush at place
called Aldar Gulch [he made the common mis-
spelling of 'Alder'] and think anyways to clean
up soon and be back with my Dear Ones—"

Here the letter ended, on a note that sent
Grantly off in another tantrum about hats, but we
got him quieted down. Then we bound up the
elder man's head, which leaked. Preparing to
lash the bodies to horses, we found bills of sale in
both saddle-bags. These were made out to T.
Eskew (the younger) and Abe Stricklin (the

other) and their address was given as Olympus, Mississippi. Grantly said he would write the widow.

It was after dark when we arrived, and the Duncans decided the first thing to do was leave the murdered men at the undertaker's. There was only one in town then, for a short space before he was urged to move to California. Grantly claimed he knew less about embalming than "an educated gorilla" and that he was, simply, in the business of selling pine boxes. He called him a fugitive carpenter who, bright though eccentric, cast one look at Virginia City and saw where the profits lay. I made no response, for the man—tall, sallow, very sad-faced (which Grantly described as "a false look of professional bereavement")—had been courteous to me in the street, though I'd never fully understood a word he said after the opening "Good day!"

Riding toward his lighted sign, I heard Grantly snort in contempt, and here, at least, he was on solid ground. For that sign, like all of Virginia City, and miners, and maybe most of Montana then, could scarcely have been serious, or not entirely so.

" 'O. I. Bledsoe—Mortuary and Sundries' "—Grantly spelled it out. "Likely, isn't it? And what a tasteful pun. The imbecile's probably named Jones, if he has a name at all, and what, pray tell, are 'sundries'? There should be limits to nonsense, even in a mining camp."

We knocked, and knocked again louder, and waited awhile till a light showed inside. Then the door opened and Mr. Bledsoe (or Jones) stood barefoot in the doorway holding a coal-oil lamp. He had on a flannel nightgown, with a tasseled nightcap, and his expression indicated he might break down altogether. In the aggregate he was about the worst-looking outrage I ever saw, and I wasn't convinced he was sober.

"I'm so very, very sorry," he said, with a moist glint in his eye.

"You blithering jackass, do I look dead?" inquired Grantly with the only snappish rudeness he'd showed in my presence. "We've got two dead miners on the hind horses. Murder's been done up the Gulch. Is that your squaw?" pointing to a large, muscular Nez Percé not dressed at all. "Tell her to throw on some clothes and clear your work-place. No, don't argue about it. We're not in the humor for humbug."

At this the undertaker shook out brisker, put a hand on Grantly's shoulder, and gave a sympathetic nod. We undid the lashings, slid the bodies off, and, helped by the woman (who was probably stronger than all of us combined), carried them into a room off the back. There they were laid face-up on a porcelain slab. (I thought it might have been something from a doctor's office—picked up on the trail.) Three or four deal chairs were in the room, a pile of black plumes and hatbands, a sampler "Oath of Hippocrates," which struck me as odd, and a vase full of strong smelling flowers. Maybe it was the flowers that made the room entirely horrible. When I glanced down at those poor useless men, filled with life and hope a few hours ago, then smelled the flowers, I had an urge to wheel and bolt.

But that idiot of an undertaker brought us back to earth. "So young!" he said in the mournfulest possible tone, gazing down. "So young to go!"

"That's the father-in-law, you fool! He's seventy if he's a day. You're looking at the wrong one! For two cents—"

I'd never seen Grantly in this kind of humor, and wondered what might come of it. Then the undertaker brushed his shoulder again and said, "A grave oversight. I acknowledge it."

But the wonders of that day refused to end. James had stood by, with one foot on a chair, chewing at a straw. Now his revolver flashed out like a snake—it was so fast I couldn't properly see it—and the muzzle touched the undertaker's throat. In an undisturbed voice, he said, "You have one more joke, one more 'oversight.' Then you'll join these miners on the hill. Understand?"

The fellow never batted an eye. With the woman, he pulled the still wet boots from the bodies, and when she started skillfully undressing both, we returned to the front room. Clearing his throat, Mr. Bledsoe inquired softly, "Was there, ah, an estate?"

"What the hell do you mean, was there an estate? What business is it of yours?"

I'm convinced that the lunatic had never before worn a more stricken and disinterested look.

"In these matters, sad though events may be for the family, and I assume they were relations, there are certain professional levies. Costs of materials, shrouds of course, my services, those of my registered aide, coffins, room rental for perhaps two nights—"

"Would you repeat that last?" asked Grantly, starting to remove his coat.

"I have a poverty-struck miner, with insomnia, who sleeps there when business is slack. He states that it eases his problem. Two dollars a night, cheaper with weekly rate—"

"If the miner shows up, or lodging charges are added," said James conversationally, "I'll cure his insomnia, and yours." And Grantly added, somewhat cooled down, "Your bill, a reasonable bill, will be settled promptly. Don't bring it up again."

The man half-bowed, as if impressed, removed his tasseled cap, and replaced it with an offensive black derby from a peg on the wall. It was a hat such as politicians and pawnbrokers wear. He said, "If you gentlemen will step to the rear, we can select suitable coffins, after I measure. We have on hand several Specials—this week only, because of the typhoid scare that regrettably came to nothing."

"Do you wish to remove that hat, or shall I knock it off?" asked Grantly.

Bowing again, the man said only "Service!" which came out worse than nothing, hung up the hat, and we went round behind the office, or work-room. A pile of raw-pine coffins lay piled up higgledy-piggledy; there must have been ten or twelve altogether.

"Rough or smooth, gentlemen?"

"Meaning what?"

"Some, as you'll note"—holding up a curious kind of lantern that James said was commonly employed by burglars—"some, as I say, are left in their native, sawed state—fifty dollars, screws and handles extra. Others have been planed and sanded to a beautiful finish. How's that item, sir,

as Departure for the *haut monde*?" He pointed to
a box not much different from the rest.

"They all look pretty damned ratty to me,"
remarked James, and gave the nearest a kick,
causing the lid to fly off and reveal an elderly
Indian woman with arms crossed over her
breast.

"Sorry, gentlemen—that's occupied. Funeral
tomorrow at ten; family only—"

"Exactly what I meant," James told him, and
unholstered his gun again.

Even today I'm not sure he would have used it,
but there came an interruption that, to my relief,
and surprising us all, finally squelched this pes-
tiferous ass. The squaw had stepped quietly after
us, and like a thunderbolt out of the blue,
slapped him literally head over heels. She spat
out a number of remarks that sounded uncom-
plimentary, or in the nature of threats, and he
scrambled up and ran—he didn't walk—around
the building and dove through the first door.
Then she and Grantly held a chat in her tongue,
and we left, exhausted.

At our cabin he turned to me and said, "My
boy, we're going to Hauser's for a meeting that
I'd rather you stayed free of—or any such meeting for the present." Then, his old self, he added,
"I'm afraid you've had a pretty shocking day for
an Eastern younker."

"I'm not as young as I was, and 'East' seems a
long way behind."

He sighed. "God lad. Because worse days lie
ahead, shocking days, I'm afraid. There's no way
to avoid them now." Turning aside, he said, "I
hate it, hate it *per se*, hate what it stands for.

Good night. Put it out of your mind. Get some sleep."

I watched them walk down Main Street toward Sam Hauser's Bank, Store, and General Emporium—establishment run, and run fairly, by a future Governor of Montana. The moon was up, and the figures seemed to cast long shadows before them. I was worn out, at the edge of tears, and somehow I saw the scene as unreal but promising, like the flicker of summer lightning, with thunder that rumbled past the horizon.

CHAPTER XIV

THOSE KILLINGS CAUSED a furor. The town had seen worse, but these snapped something, as Reeves' slaughter of Indians ended a chapter in Bannack. Once again, all miners came in from their claims, standing on corners, in the streets, in saloons, and talked quietly. They had pretty grim faces, too. But the worst omen of next day was the absence of saloon quarrel and horseplay. For once, there wasn't a single fight.

Then the Hurdy-Gurdies opened that night— an hour late—the liquor began to take hold, and the town soon roared again. But not in the same old way. Some felt sheepish about the lack of fights and tried to make it up by improving things in the evening. A rough element that included George Ives, Boone Helm, Frank Parish, and Ned Ray demolished Morier's place on Cover Street, and for the first time there were mutters about action. Then a handsome pot was collected to "defray damages," including some done to Morier, who required a splint, and the turmoil finally simmered down. Still, everyone remained edgy, until the day after, when that undertaker came through with as little nonsense as possible, in his case. He'd arranged a funeral for the victims. People were astonished and relieved; something unusual had been needed to reduce tension.

Heretofore most persons had simply been hauled up Cemetery Hill and dumped. At this time, with Virginia City young and without serious illness, all residents of the Hill had met violent deaths, as in Bannack. Without one exception. Some graves had head-boards, with the carved essential facts. Name, date of death, and the like. A few boards, done by friends bolstered by bottles, added an embellishment or two, such as crossed pistols, or rifles, or a knife with blood dripping. The birth dates of drifters were unknown, of course, so the habit spread of making these up. Thus one man—"a established skunk," as an acquaintance said in toasting him at a saloon—was put down, with nice work, as having been born in 1376, and another was inscribed as "1858-1863," which would have made him five years old when he had the street-fight near Dick Hamilton's Store.

But the undertaker, now on the second day, was all a-bustle. Grantly said invitations existed for him to re-locate, and he was trying to offset his "whiskeyfied impudence." Few found fault with this first formal interment in Virginia, now lost to history except in a diary or two. Aside from those, it's mentioned only in a water-stained letter to people back in Ohio, as far as I know.

I should say, in Bledsoe's defense, that his lack of embalming materials was explainable, and justified. As said before, southern Montana's air was so crystal-pure that meat wrapped in sacking and hauled atop poles rarely spoiled. So when Grantly (who was biased) contended that "the stringbean couldn't embalm a woodchuck if a group stood by with a halter," he over-simplified the case. Probably Mr. Bledsoe never had embalmed a corpse, and couldn't, but there was no need, not here, and the Indian lying out behind was unremarkable. There was no hurry and nothing to bother her, if the screws had been properly set.

Well, Bledsoe had some bills printed that morning announcing a "melancholy Event" for that afternoon at 2:30. They went on to list a "Eulogy" by a "Reverend Thomas Whistler, D.D.," whom I'd never heard of (there being no churches in town then, religious writers to the contrary); "Hymns;" "Voluntary Tributes"—whatever that meant (the deceased had arrived five days previously); "Capacious seating for all!"; a choir; and, if you please, "Collection for the families Back Home."

"I haven't the least doubt the blackguard means a collection for Bledsoe in Virginia City," said Grantly, but he was wrong. Several men saw that money through to the Post Office.

Mr. Bledsoe had tried to organize what he called a "Processional." The participants were supposed to wear black arm-bands and start from the Bale of Hay, then file up the Hill to a dirge played by the Hurdy-Gurdies' concertina. But citizens like Langford, Colonel Sanders, Hauser, J.E. McClurg, and the Duncans blocked this, saying it was undignified, especially originating at a saloon. Then two or three took Bledsoe aside and warned him that "even a semblance of buffoonery" would see him and his business headed toward the Divide by sunset.

If the funeral failed to shape up as planned, it was not the undertaker's fault; not entirely. I'm

convinced he did the best he could; *he* thought
he'd performed all right, as mining camps went.

Me, I enjoyed the program, which was out of
the common run. Cemetary Hill was a grand and
lofty place, the day was fine, with a bottomless
sky and a soft breeze that stirred pines to rustle
and sigh, suiting the occasion. People dressed in
whatever black they could scrounge began arriv-
ing before time, and sure enough, Bledsoe had
managed to find enough chairs and benches to
make five or six rows near some yawning holes,
not fresh, that he "kept open for emergencies."
The coffins had been placed side by side and
criss-crossed with tape. I wondered if the bodies,
now, were clothed in the usual integuments of
the tomb, and doubted it, though I figured a
charge would appear on the bill.

I went alone and took a seat toward the front.
Shortly before 2:30, Bledsoe and his wife appeared, both decently dressed, the former without his derby. Beside them was an oldish,
saintly-looking gentleman wearing what I took
to be a croupier's black coat with a white collar
turned around. Directly behind these came a file
of Hurdy-Gurdies—the "Choir"—but they were
modestly attired and they lined up, with the
concertina man, facing the crowd. Then Mr.
Bledsoe stepped foward to announce, in unctuous tones, the singing of "those two comforts to
the soul, 'Rock of Ages' and 'The Arkansas
Traveler.'" He asked the audience to join in. The
first was probably all the choir had heard of, in
the religious line, and with the second he'd tried
for the miners' home state but found the supply
bare and settled for a state across the river.

Anyhow, the Hurdies, helped in a sense by the

concertina, took aim at "Rock of Ages" and did it
tolerably well, considering they had no hymnals
and weren't fully acquainted with either words
or tune. Then they pitched in to square accounts
on "Arkansas Traveler." Oddly enough, for a
lively, frivolous folk-jig, it appeared to fit in
well, up here in the trees. It cleared the air, funeral or not. But toward the end a commotion
broke out on the rear bench. And when everyone
turned to look, I'm scraped (as miners said) if it
wasn't Hayes Lyons, Red Yeagers, and Buck
Stinson—the men who'd made the function possible. They were trying to sing, but broke down
repeatedly. There was no tomfoolery in it, either.
They were as honestly distressed, being half
drunk and sentimental besides, as if their
mothers had walked into a buzz-saw. Others
were with them, and these had caught the infection, but in differing degrees. Their "singing"
was apt to rise up high, high, high in quavering
falsettos, and they made too much of red ban-
dannas they'd brought to contain their grief. A
more troublesome breed of cockroaches never
plagued a town struggling to right itself.

Then the bench turned over, and some men in
front got up, and those devils scattered downhill, fanning themselves with their hats. They
didn't waste any time about it. After this, Mr.
Bledsoe restored order by shifting around here
and there, righting the bench and the like. Next,
he introduced the Reverend Mr. Whistler, who
got up from his chair, clutching a Bible. He
started off in a pleasing voice, mentioning, first,
the departed miners by name, getting both
wrong, and affirmed the "dastardly fashion" in

which they'd passed away and hoped, he said, that that sort of thing could be kept to a minimum in future. His statement, to my ears, suggested that it needn't quite be eliminated but could be reduced some. As this rubbish emerged, Bledsoe nodded and smiled, reinforcing the man's remarks, glancing happily at the crowd.

Well, it made little difference, really. The sun shone through the Reverend's silvery hair, and the quality of his voice, if not his remarks, was musical, and even uplifting. That is to say, things held together till he sailed off on the Bible. His book was marked here and there with slips, and he explained that these were "precedents" and bore on the case.

Now I'd studied the Bible in school—forced to; my aunts encouraged it with a hair-brush—and if Mr. Whistler got a solitary reference right, or if any bore on the deceased, it missed my notice. What he did, or tried to do, was give a kind of chronology of Biblical events, but they came out scrambled. He told about the Lord creating the earth, breaking down toward sundown of the sixth day, since the job was too much for one man. He cautioned about "overwork" and waved toward the coffins, while Bledsoe practically nodded his head off, the point was so clear. The Flood was mentioned as good and proper, to wash man's sins away, and he said it was natural for Noah to appear on deck every morning, with an animal or two, to see if things were letting up. But wouldn't it have been better if the rains had continued for a year and a half? They'd only begun nibbling at the problem

after forty days, and he waved at the coffins
again. I noticed Grantly's face turning red, and
Reverend Whistler was in the midst of reminding us that Jesus, too, was a carpenter, and had
likely made many a coffin in his time—when
there came a skull-jarring racket in the trees and
a group of dogs crashed directly through Mr.
Whistler chasing a deer. That is, they, not Mr.
Whistler, were chasing the deer.

Well, Mr. Bledsoe and one or two others
picked him up and brushed him off, and he made
a feeble attempt to continue, but the sermon ran
out of steam. He closed his book, after advising
everybody to straighten up, said "Amen!" and,
relieved, sank back to his chair, but it wasn't
there any longer—the dogs had seen to that. So
this time he sprained something beneath his
back, and seemed hopping mad. He came very
close to falling in a grave. Mr. Bledsoe moved in
to help, of course, and his men commenced with
the coffins. But both holes were a foot short, so
he announced they'd correct the situation later,
and we filed out, while the Hurdies sang "The
Arkansas Traveler" again. It hadn't been much
of a funeral, if you think it over, but it was all
Virginia City offered then, and I suppose people
were satisfied, and some (stifling laughter) appeared downright refreshed.

That night I dropped into Coleman and Loeb's,
as being the quietest place to drink beer, and saw
the Reverend Whistler dressed in rough clothes,
smoking a cigar, with a bottle beside him and
playing poker. One or two men addressed him as
"Peahead" and when he lost a pot (skip-straight
to a pair of deuces), he ripped loose a non-

religious statement that might have skinned paint off a signboard.

As usual with humans, Grantly said, the funeral was widely discussed, the reaction being favorable at first, then turning critical, of course, everybody throwing the blame on Bledsoe. They said he did it all on purpose. So he sold out soon, to O'Neill and Courtwaite, and left town with his squaw. We found out later he was a man of education and upbringing, but had gone off the track, you might say. There were many such cases in Montana.

But even the new owners, who ran a mortuary a long time in Virginia City, were unable to keep a whimsical note out of their ads, which appeared in the *Montana Post*. "Ready-made Coffins for the Miners, and Ready-made Graves for the Coffins," they said, and you can look it up and check it today, if you're interested.

CHAPTER XV

WE HAD AN INDIAN helper do most of the shoeing preliminaries, but the new boy, Páh-ta-se, was slow, and with a horse-and-customer of this kind, it was best to put on a show. By tradition, the apprentice cuts off all old nails with a metal piece called a buffer and removes the shoe with pincers. Then he cleans and smoothes the hoof, with knife, rasp, and hoofparers, until it's flat and ready. Mr. Smithers was home, sick, after the move from Bannack and our setting up of the Forge.

I congratulated myself that I tackled these functions with flourish, stepping back now and then to survey the work, run my hand over the hoof, and mutter something that I hoped sounded like the trade. After six weeks' work, I felt less self-conscious before people, and Mr. Smithers, as an authenticated member of the Worshipful Company of Farriers, was a marvel of style, bad leg and all. What with good food and rest, his leg had healed till he threw down the crutch and only walked with a limp, now. But his lungs were still weak, and over-exertion was apt to bring on coughing and fever.

So far, I'd done nothing more complicated than farrier work—that is, shoeing horses and oxen. But Mr. Smithers promised he'd have me "handy" with ox-yokes, tire irons, hinges, chest hardware, and even locks and guns by and by. I believed about half of it, and asked him how he made a rifle barrel. I could see him struggling, with friendship and Christianity on one side and blacksmith-secrecy on the other. Then, finally, he said, "Well, son, you take and fashion a barrel in two halves, join them with a round rod of high-melt in the center, and that's all you need to know for the present. Over and above which, guns are instruments of Beelzebub; shun them!"

"Even when used on grizzlies?" I asked with an innocent look, but he merely chuckled, being good-humored to the marrow, as well as shrewd about human hypocrisies, including the few of his own.

"Son, there's an old saying: 'Needs must when the Devil drives,' and if that don't cover the case, I couldn't play farrier to a rocking-horse."

The term "Farrier" has to do only with shoeing, and for the process a blacksmith keeps a separate set of tools in a "shoe-box," eighteen inches by ten. They aren't used for anything else. And a strict law is that they stay neatly tucked in the box when idle. Horseshoeing can be a quick, emergency act, and you don't want to start sifting around for implements when a man's waiting, impatient, and his horse stamping round even worse.

Our box contained pincers, hoof-parers, buffers, a very hard rasp, a hoof-cleaning knife, a catshead hammer, a shoeing hammer, and a nail-heading tool, besides some other things of no great interest to laymen. I'd begun to acquire superior airs, as I settled in, enjoying myself

more than I ever remember, and Mr. Smithers
and Grantly agreed that this was good unless the
airs went too far. Mr. Smithers, of course, hauled
in the Bible, mentioning "Vanity of vanities!"
Then he knocked everything down, I thought, by
remarking to Grantly, aside, that I might make a
fair blacksmith in ten or fifteen years; he was
practically sure of it. So he'd got even about the
grizzly.

Right now, with him home, I wished that the
job had been simpler. It's one thing for a horse to
develop shoe trouble—loose, or a nail missing
and pebbles picked up—and another to throw a
shoe completely. Mainly this is caused by galloping too fast on rocks, or by hard-sucking mud.
The condition presents a smithy with tasks of
two separate classes. For the last, a farrier—that
is to say, me—had to make a whole new shoe.
And that's what Páh-ta-se and I were doing, or
trying to do.

The customer was Mr. Henry Plummer, the
new Sheriff. He was now Sheriff of both Virginia
City and Bannack, where he'd slid similarly into
office, edging out Crawford. It wasn't his position that placed me on my mettle; it was the man
himself, the most stylish, dapper, and genial fellow alive, with a gift of making you feel he was
aware of you. And, at that moment, you alone in
the world. In short, as I summon various small
scraps from college, his manner was simpático.
Within ten minutes after he'd arrived, leading
his glossy black horse, he'd treated me like one
of his closest, most trusted, and most worthwhile friends. It was, and is, a rare trait, and it
took him a long way.

At the moment, he stood leaning against a

post, smiling when he caught my eye, nodding in admiration, amused, in no hurry when Páh-ta-se (as usual) loafed on the long bellows handle, having spotted something more absorbing down the street. Whenever he did so, the coals quickly lost their bright-hot glow.

At first, we'd tried making charcoal for fuel, Mr. Smithers and I, assisted (and instructed) by Grantly and James. Mr. Smithers had employed charcoal in his professional life, but he had no knowledge of local timbers. It was Grantly, first, who stepped in to say that ash was best, here, and that he, Grantly, had fired more charcoal kilns that he could count. So we tramped to a nearby ravine, half broke our backs cutting five cords of ash, shaping it into a cone and covering it over with grass, plus sand from a stream-bed. It was perfectly air-tight, Grantly alleged, except for the vent at the top, and small openings around the bottom, thus to create a draft and drive gases through the vent. He said it was satisfactory now, and we could light it. So we did, and a stiff north wind howled in, and the ash burst into bloom and burned up without wasting time.

Grantly said he couldn't understand it. He'd copied that material out of a book and failed to see where we went wrong.

"Then you haven't, or rather have not, 'fired more kilns than you can count'?" asked James.

Reflecting, Grantly finally said he believed that to be correct. He'd intended his remark as a figure of speech, put forth, as he recalled, to give us "that sense of confidence so vital to the performing charcoal artist."

"One, then. Say one."

"No, I don't think I could say that, not to deceive you."

James snorted in disgust (his hands being badly blistered, like ours), and we cut some ash stakes and dug coal, which showed in places hereabouts. And the combination, with somebody ambitious to pump the bellows, served very well. But you had to keep the bellows busy. Properly speaking, it was a job for two grown men.

Finishing the hoof, I cut one of our long iron rods with a cold-set hammer-and-chisel to the length needed. Then, after some threats aimed at Páh-ta-se, I heated the piece to a deep cherry red. Lying in the coals, it appeared to breathe, or pulsate. Now I could have stopped here and worked it into a "V," but I went on and heated it white-hot, mainly to show that this was a genuine professional shop and took no half-measures. Red-hot iron can be bent and twisted, which is sufficient for shoeing, while white-hot metal may be beaten to any shape. Mr. Smithers would have bawled me out, in his roundabout way, but since he was absent, I figured he'd find it awkward.

So I charged ahead, cocky as a rooster. But I'd overdone it, the piece having changed bulk here and there. I had to spend a little time drawing down (or fullering) which means to reduce thickness by pounding with a sledge on the anvil. And after this, I wasted more time in upsetting, which is approximately the reverse, or pounding to get more metal at one place than another. The boy Páh-ta-se looked on, startled (he was far from stupid), and Mr. Plummer seemed amused, too. The flourishes getting out of hand, I dropped the brag-and-bounce and tucked in to finish the job.

Using the catshead, or shoe-turning, hammer, I turned the piece to a "V," then applied more heat and shaped it like the horse's hoof. Mr. Smithers' way, now, was to hold the hot shoe briefly against the hoof, to leave a charred curve and wipe out irregularities. But this black stud of Plummer's had ideas of its own about shoeing (and blacksmiths), and though I'd fettered the hind feet, it kicked up a fuss. Then Mr. Plummer, understanding and gracious, gentled it down so I could lift the hoof without getting my head chewed off. Studying the charred shape, I heated and made refinements, then went about punching nailholes. We used eight nails; most blacksmiths used six. And it's here that slipshod blacksmiths (so to speak) have caused the majority of horseshoe problems.

People generally assume that a shoe is held to a horse's hoof, after which some dunce takes a hammer and drives nails straight in. I've watched this, shuddering. *That poor horse is headed for trouble.* Mr. Smithers' system, the correct one, was to place the shoe on his anvil and punch holes through and out at an angle. (He had an "English pattern" anvil, of steel, with holes for holding this and that and a softer "end table," where chisels would never break.) Thus the shoe, nailed on, had no single nail pointing in, with a chance of probing the horse's foot. Our eight could only emerge at the sides. Sweating, I got them in then smoothed down the heads, and the fit was as snug as hide on a deer.

I stepped back, mighty self-satisfied, and almost asked, "Pair for yourself, sir?" but caught myself and in the style of a barber whisking off the cloth, said, "Smithers and Nickerson at your service. Anything else, sir? Stew-pan, strap-hinges, spur, axe-head, cow-bell?"—and then, brightening—"Sheriff's shackles for hands or feet, Mr. Plummer?" (There wasn't one of those things I could have made in fifty years, and even Mr. Smithers avoided rowel spurs when he could; in fact, for some reason, they were the bane of his life.)

As Plummer studied me, curious, I began to get rattled and thought of suggesting a thumb-screw or a pike. Then he interrupted to ask, polite and friendly, "Mr. Nickerson, I don't mean to pry, but what's a young man like yourself—with expectations, I hear—doing out here learning to blacksmith?"

I didn't much care for "learning," so I said, "I *like* being a blacksmith," and then, because of his friendliness, "To tell you the truth, it's the first time I ever had anything of my own. I like it. Everything about it suits me, especially working half-outdoors."

"Well, sir, it's a noble profession, and goes back—with dignity and respect—for a very long way." He looked off in the distance, thoughtful. "You'd probably be surprised to hear that I was once apprenticed to a butcher, as a youngster Abroad."

A small red light flashed in his eyes. "Now *that* was a fine profession! Hack, hack, hack!— three raw chunks of meat with blood spilling down to the gutters!" Then he seemed to regain control and said, "You asked if I required anything else; the fact is, I do. Does your boss—Mr.

Smithers, and appropriate-named he is—tend teeth, as smiths once did by tradition?"

"Yes, sir," I replied, not really knowing. "He's able with both teeth *and* iron. What appears to be the trouble?"

"The trouble is, I have a toothache, and need a tooth removed, or so I believe. The problem is this: it's a jawtooth, and pretty far back. The imposter briefly in Bannack had the effrontery to tell me he specialized only in incisors and bicuspids, and that his license forbade him to go deeper. I'll say, in confidence, that a good, sound horse-whipping might have mended his impudence." But Mr. Plummer appreciated him well enough to laugh, all the same. When he did, I saw that his left jaw was, indeed, badly swollen.

"Mr. Smithers is sick in bed, Sheriff. We can walk up and see what he thinks. He's a religious man, as no doubt you've heard, and Samaritan to the bone."

Mr. Plummer said, "If a visit would in any degree endanger his health, I'll withdraw and endure the pain till he's well."

I said, "Mr. Smithers would be hurt, sir. A moment while I leave instructions and hang out a card."

I undid the horse's hind fetters, dodging a kick aimed to remove my head. Mr. Plummer apologized and we walked up and around the corner. I knocked, expecting to see Mrs. Smithers or her religion-addled daughter. But Mr. Smithers himself came to the door, wearing a long flannel shirt. (The women had left for

Pfout's Store, Mrs. Smithers carrying a stick with nails driven through.)

"Well, now, son, this is kindly," he sang out. "It's kindly; it's like you. It's—well, Biblical, but"—he gave me a sharp look—"I hope you're not losing heart. I'll tell you true; I'm improved to that point where a doctor out of college wouldn't believe it. Tomorrow, if the sun still climbs from the east—"

"Mr. Smithers," I interrupted, for Mr. Plummer was obscured behind me, "this is our new Sheriff, Mr. Henry Plummer. I shoed his horse, but he himself has a toothache—a bad one. I don't—"

"You'll step in, gentlemen, and not loiter further on my doorstep! Mr. Plummer, sir"—pumping his hand—"you honor our house, and we'll just cast an eye over this said tooth. Seat yourself there, sir, on that high stool. Ross, my boy, perhaps you'll hold a lantern, for our windeys[he said "windeys"] here in Montaner ain't of the best, being waxed muslin, you see, laid in small. So, so, if you'll look up, sir—" He wrinkled his forehead and appeared puzzled, as I was, for Mr. Plummer made no motion to take off his high squarish black hat.

"It ain't my nature, sir, to offer offense to a guest, and I mean none, but we might probe this easier if you'd see clear to removing that hat. Thankee—we'll place it without damage on that peg. Now, sir"—peering into Plummer's opened mouth—"as we come to the forge, so to say, the first thing to mention is—which tooth are we at?"

(When the Sheriff reluctantly lifted his hat, I began to understand something that writers everywhere, all reporters and papers, then and later, remarked on. With the hat, Mr. Plummer's face seemed normally shaped, even pleasing when expression lit its features. But the hat concealed what approached disfigurement of the forehead and crown, which splayed out and up from the hairline. The head had a mushroom shape, and its cranial capacity must have been huge. Still, a person seeing him uncovered* might think, as I did, that the Sheriff had great potential for either good or evil, with the scales tipped toward the second.)

"We'll just go tap-tapping with this midgety chisel—up with the lantern, son; we can't snooze on a job like this, and, yes, sir—hurt there, did it? That's the enemy right enough, second tooth from rear, and we must corner him, place his head in chancery, and make him crawl out begging. So to do, we'll employ our smallest flywheel-bit and test him, sir, for softness in the pulp; I'll confess I'd take pleasure in saving that tooth. Pain again?—customary and expected." (Mr. Plummer had risen half off his stool.) "In the trade, sir, we commonly scrape and gouge, removing all detritus, then fill with the client's choice—iron, which chances to rust and flake with age; silver, a favorite with the gentry; or molten gold, sir, at which Smithers and Nickerson is experimentering, there being plenty around.

"No, sir—it aggravates me to confide that that

---

* A Special Edition of the *Helena Herald* later observed that "—Plummer knew he had a bad forehead, and therefore kept it jealously covered with his hat . . . his politeness was notable, and he understood the formulas of courtesy, but the one of uncovering he failed to observe."

tooth's come to maturity, done his job faithful,
fell prey to a flaw, or fissure, and looks ready for
the boneyard. In brief, we'll have to snatch him."

Here Mr. Plummer's eyes were goggling
slightly, though he'd made no real complaint.
He said, as courteous as possible, "Mr. Smithers,
I hope you won't take umbrage, but are you sure
your, ah, present health is up to this task?"

"Spry, spry's the word for Ewing T. Smithers
today. And a contest between I and that tooth
seems to have throwed spirit into this carcass.
Now the forge is aglowing and ready, Journeyman's here with the lantern, and we'll just rig
a contraption-lever to save knocking out your
front teeth when she blows." (He hewed to custom by calling me "Journeyman" at the shop,
while addressing me as "son" or "my boy" at all
other times. The Indians, he said, were "apprentices"; we had Páh-ta-se, now, and another
scouting Emigrant roads for discarded iron.)

"Mr. Smithers, I'm not jumpier about pain
than most, but isn't it usual to offer, say, a swig of
something soothing?"

Here I could see my boss in a muddle, embarrassed; then he spoke up with a faint film of
moisture on his brow. "Sir, I know what you're
coming at, but this is a temperance house.
Spirits, to date, have not seized the proprietor's
coattails, for reason that father—bless his memory, whichever road he took—drank enough for
four. And the Bible—"

" 'Take a little wine for thy stomach's
sake?' "

At this, I saw Mr. Smithers sweating worse,
but he suggested lamely, "Times past, I've taken

and used a rap on the head with a ball-peen hammer—"

"I think we'll forgo the hammer, if it wouldn't grieve you."

In a convulsion of soul-wrestling, Mr. Smithers now limped to a far wall, where he appeared to have sawed out a corner log, neat and removable, and came back with a partly-filled quart of whiskey with a scrolled label that mentioned Kentucky.

"You've heard, sir, of snakes?"

Mr. Plummer replied with an admirably straight face, "I have indeed, Mr. Smithers."

"Montaner snakes, with rattles on their tails?"

"The place crawls with them."

"You'll recall it was a snake that done mischief in the Garden? So. We'll combat those same snakes, if you're content I brought the anecdote for the purpose."

"Entirely satisfied. For what other?"

"Right as rain"—as Mr. Plummer, tilting the bottle, let perhaps a quarter-pint gurgle down his throat. "Now we'll tuck into this tooth without further pumping of the bellows."

"You're certain, Mr. Smithers, that you recall precisely the right tooth?"

"I marked her, sir, using a piece of yellow keel. We won't go wrong on that score! Now—slap together a couple of planks for a steady on the lever. Lantern high, Journeyman; keep it lofty with light enough for all—and yes, sir, if you'll hold patient, we'll hobble that serpent afore he mentions Apples."

Here Mr. Smithers up-ended the bottle himself and bit off enough to clear the Garden for several years. I could hardly have been more stunned if Judas had walked in carrying his rope. But my boss was refreshing to watch, all the same. He was a chief of nimbleness, and whatever he did made sense. The crossed planks offered a rest for his arm; and of the tools lying around the house—some awaiting repairs, others used domestically—he laid his hand on each without looking.

"Now, sir, if you'll open just a *leetle* mite wider, we'll lay this Suffolk over-lip tong inside, grasp that devil right down to the gum, and gently, gently but firmly—and I dislike to brag, but I'm blessed with sturdy grip—and, yes, sir, here she comes! She's responding beautiful, if I say so myself. There! *Out!* Now I ask you, gentlemen both, on your rambles here and there, have you laid eyes on a finer sight?"

I could hear the slow squulch of the tooth as it rose from the bone, and Mr. Smithers' arm, where he'd rolled up his sleeve, was a ribbed board of sinews as he exerted more and more pressure. Sick as he'd been, that bean-pole was stronger than iron itself. He knew it, and felt guilty about it, considering that the Lord had favored him above others. At the forge he wore, besides his leathern apron, a jersey to cover his arms, for he disliked to display "on-seemly cords and knots and fibers that might appear braggy or contentious."

He held the tooth up, bloody and dripping and with a long jagged root—like pictures of cypress knees, I thought.

"She failed rapid, sir, when aware that tongs was there on purpose. Handsome, would you say? As fine a tooth as ever I met, and if Sheriff

Plummer twitched an eyebrow, I neglected to note it. Brave as a lion, in the view of this blacksmith! We couldn't have did it otherwise. Congratulations, sir!"

Mr. Plummer had not, indeed flinched. But now, when he started to rise, gingerly feeling his jaw, Mr. Smithers cried, "Hold on, sir! Remain seated for post-attentions. There'll be no putrefactions in *this* office!" and he hopped to a shelf, removed a bottle, and said, "We'll cleanse it, using No. 3 hollow-mouthed pincers, with cotton wool and a dab of whiskey, then numb it down with laudanum. There now, and if presently you don't feel like a stud horse at the County Fair, this office, sir, has fell flat as a hoe-cake."

Mr. Plummer got up and shook his hand. "Mr. Smithers, I recognize an artist when I see one. I'm grateful, and I'm not apt to forget. What, sir, is my bill?"

"Bill for shoeing unknown. Dental? Let's call it a deed done Biblical, in the nature of good works. In brief, zero, and happy to serve Jesus."

Mr. Plummer laid down a minted fifty-dollar gold piece. "I'm not a religious man, sir. And I hope you won't mistake me when I remark that Jesus was not the patient at hand. *I* was, and a trifling gold bit is nothing compared to the relief you've brought. Take it, and use it in any cause you like."

Mr. Smithers stood frowning, the bloody tooth still in his tongs. Then, solving his indecision, he brightened and said, "In the past, sir, with a tooth of this size, and dealing with gentry, I've been accustomed to wash it, gild it, then hammer-and-clink a nice iron chain, for weskit or neck. Thrown in, as I hasten to say, without charge—"

"Excellent!" said Mr. Plummer drily. "I'll drop by the forge and pick it up later. Good day to you, Mr. Smithers, and my thanks once again."

We shook hands all around, and the Sheriff and I left.

Returning to town, or the center of town—for it was growing like a toadstool—I became aware that Mr. Plummer had something on his mind and was groping for a way to bring it up.

"Tooth hurt pretty bad, Sheriff?" I said, trying to help, and he replied no, the laudanum had numbed it, though he expected it to report in soon. Then he said, "Mr. Nickerson, what I have to relate is delicate, and can be of use only if you're careful not to repeat it."

My reply, of course, was that all the devils in hell could never force a confidence out of me. He, in turn, answered with an admiring smile and a polite clap on my back. "I thought as much. I won't mislead you, my friend. I've knocked about in life, tried to shed as much grace as Blacksmith Smithers, and have not always succeeded. I confess it. My desire at present is to contribute what I can to Harmony. Virginia needs it. Now I dislike to sound fulsome, but when I first laid eyes on you, I said to myself, 'There's a young man who can help. If ever I saw a person in Montana with background, education, integrity, and, altogether, those components which added together mean Character—that young man is the one.' I hope you aren't embarrassed?"

On the contrary I was, in my idiot's immaturity, as flattered as possible. I virtually writhed with pleasure under these compliments. The fact is, I'd always suspected I had hidden graces, but it took Mr. Plummer's silky assurance to drag them out in the open. I gave a deprecatory cough and started to murmur some routine insincerities, but he broke in to say, "No, I mean every word of it. There's no occasion to be modest. We in the Sheriff's office can only hope you will elect to stay and grow with Montana when it becomes a Territory,* and then, eventually, a state."

By this point, I was hoping to be able to vote for Mr. Plummer for President soon and wondered why he wasn't in Washington where he belonged. (I hadn't forgotten Grantly's story, but it was fading from my mind.)

"I'm sure you know that the office of Sheriff is both arduous and complex. We try, within our limits, for we are gravely understaffed, Mr. Nickerson, to keep our streets safe for all, including our swelling and fortuitous number of white women—"

"And do a fine job of it, Mr. Plummer!" I burst out, not quite hearing a rattle of gunfire from the direction of Van Buren Street. I'd forgotten, too, the recent burlesque perpetrated by that con-

---

*Idaho Territory was formed in 1863 as separate from Washington Territory and included not only the regions known as Idaho and Montana, but Wyoming and parts of Nebraska and the Dakotas. The area called Montana was declared a separate Territory on May 26, 1864. It became a state in 1889. Samuel T. Hauser was a Governor of the Territory, and Col. Wilbur Fiske Sanders was later the state's first Senator.

summate ass, O. I. Bledsoe ("Mortuary and Sundries"). The fact is, I'd swelled up like a peacock, and blush to think of it now.

"Chief concern of the Sheriff's office is to keep track of—and guard—the constant heavy outgo of gold, by Stage, from those miners prudent enough to bank, save, send funds home to their loved ones—"

Here it fleetingly occurred to me that I'd seen this same Plummer, with some shady cronies like George Ives and Whiskey Bill Graves, relieving those woebegone miners of whopping big sums in dust at the tables. But I dismissed the thought as unworthy, realizing again that Virginia City had few recreations for strong, red-blooded men like the Sheriff.

"More specifically, the miners *will* make shipments without notifying our office. I needn't remind you that Stage holdups have been greatly on the rise. Not only those of Wells Fargo, lately established in our town (to our pride), but others along Overland routes. The key here is secrecy, Mr. Nickerson, the normal reluctance to divulge facts about gold movements. This is the trait that sends Stages in and out unprotected. Result is that all Stages, always, lie vulnerable to attack. The truth is, I suspect, that outlaws merely strike at random, on the theory that by attacking nearly every Stage they are bound to raise color, as we say, sooner or later."

"Precisely, Sheriff! And I've heard approximately the same sentiments from the Duncans and oth—"

"Right!"—his voice rang out too high, but his next words fell into the controlled tones that I heard one man (unfairly) describe as "unctu-

ous." "You are friends, young fellow, with most
leading men here in Virginia—a clique, and a
clique, I say, for the good. But they make the
common mistake of not enfolding Protectors
into their conversations.

"We've seen this," he said, reflecting, "in
every pioneer settlement with sudden wealth
and no official law. Those men—your friends—
are justly close-mouthed in such a situation.
Now what if one of their number—the *outstand-
ing* member, of high intelligence and *faith in the
Sheriff!*—what, I say, if this person should inform our office of rich shipments that come to his
knowledge? Why, that gives a chance to guardians of this slaved-for property. *My* guardians,
good men and true. Sufficiently brave, you ask?
Well, lions aren't braver. My bloodhounds could
provide the one thing most wanted in Virginia
City—*safety!* With an easy mind and safe passage for all."

"Sheriff, I want you to know, and wish you to
count on it: I believe in you, heart and soul! And
there's my hand on it!"

"Well, you're a man, Mr. Nickerson! I knew it
when first I watched you handling the Hurdies."
(The figure struck me as odd—I failed to recall
any special handling—but not too odd, either.)
"Now as between ourselves; as between men of
the world, let's agree that there's no need to tell
your friends and alarm them. Can we say that?"

"Nothing!" I said with emphasis. "Nothing
could be better calculated to fuss them and leave
them more private and mute. You're absolutely
right and you have my hand on that, too!"

Mr. Plummer gave me a solemn look as we
neared the Forge and his newly-shod horse. "I

suppose you realize, young man, that little stands between you and the first governorship of Montana, when it comes. Nothing, when we consider the power of your old friends and your new." He looked into the future and sighed. "I was imagining the jubilance, the glee. Yes, the celebrations back in Boston and the pride of your family. A statue, both there and here, and, shall we say—struck off in bronze? Ah, to be young again, and have your advantages!"

He saluted, once mounted, then turned and cantered in his graceful style toward home and office. As for me, I stood glowing at a brighter flush than the hearth-fire.

CHAPTER XVI

EVENTS MOVED ALONG at a pretty fast clip. Reviewing the Sheriff's words, I could see the odds that faced him. He had no legal standing, of course, since we were part of Idaho Territory, with its capital at Lewiston, several hundred miles distant. And the Governor there had no law machinery at all. In that line, Idaho was helpless—"a typical oversight by boneheaded federal politicians," as Grantly pointed out.

No day passed now that went unmarked by large or small crimes. But Virginia's decent citizens seemed reluctant to bring it to a head. Men disliked traveling between towns after nightfall. Even in mid-day they carried only enough gold dust for current needs. If a miner visited a neighboring claim, he was lucky to escape robbery on the way. And if the amount on his person was small, he was threatened with death unless he brought more next time. Often mere wayfarers were shot at, and sometimes killed.

So you see, the state of things had worsened in a hurry. I may have stressed Virginia's reckless-comic aspects at the expense of the horrifying. When Mrs. Smithers carried her nail-studded stick, there was every chance she might have to use it, to protect herself and Daisy. And now, I was convinced, Sheriff Plummer did need help. I felt disappointed that Grantly and James, Hauser, Langford, and the like appeared unwilling to pitch in. I resolved to try and make this up, whenever free of the smithy. And by good luck an opportunity came the very next week.

A miner named Jenkins, whose white wife and two small children waited in Arkansas, had decided to leave brawling Virginia City and move to Deer Lodge. There he hoped to ranch, or start a small lumber mill. He was a conscientious fellow, bright and eager to succeed, and had already done well, panning alone for gold. He and I chatted in the streets; he never wasted time in saloons. The fact is we were friends. He had, he confided, amassed the rather startling sum of twenty thousand dollars in dust, and with this he meant to launch a new life. His "poke," he said, was on deposit at Hauser's, which I thought sensible, but he was making an exploratory trip with these savings. Once set, and the money banked at Deer Lodge, he would send for his family.*

Well, the smithy being closed while the Indians scrounged for iron, I offered to join him. I had a good excuse—Grantly and James had asked me to perform an errand. Their store was prospering, now, but they lacked supplies. Unlimited replenishment was available, they thought, at Worden and Company's, not far from the ranch we still owned jointly. The main things mentioned were two dozen long-handled shovels and twenty pounds of chewing

*Jenkins was the miner who, in the first Stampede, took a nugget from the Gulch that weighed two pounds, five ounces—believed to be the largest of pure gold found in the vicinity.

tobacco—which last sold in Virginia for eighteen dollars a pound. Nearly all miners now chewed tobacco, because the chore of keeping pipes lit while digging annoyed them. Moreover, they'd taken a fancy to marksmanship spitting and had worked it into a sport.

As with everything else, they'd overdone it, naturally, and on Sundays held contests, with pompous "Judges," dressed in tall gray hats and shiny frock coats, showing a hole or two. Favorite game, involving four or five men, was to scuff a wide circle in the street, place a cockroach in the center, and, after the "Gentlemen, choose your positions!"—and "Spit freely!"—try and douse the poor, bewildered insect, which probably thought the town had lost its mind.

Altogether it was as ignorant a "game" as ever devised, I suppose, but it grew in popularity until the miners got careless and took to spitting unsupervised, in any old direction. The one finally spat on a roughneck's boots in the Exchange and was shot through the shoulder for it. After that the competition slackened up some.

Anyhow, the Duncans' list of supplies had swelled to a point where (when I'd explained about Jenkins) Grantly said their needs called for an ox-wagon. He gave me three thousand dollars, partly for supplies and the rest for the Nez Percé who ran the ranch. Jenkins was excited when I told him, and we resolved to start first thing the next morning—at dawn, before the majority of thieves had got up, rinsed their mouths with whiskey, maybe eaten a chunk of cold bear-meat with eight or nine eggs, and begun to shop around.

But that evening, worried a little myself,

mainly for Jenkins and his hard-earned hoard, I
dropped into Sheriff Plummer's office—a mean,
dingy place with a desk, some chairs, and several "Wanted" dodgers pinned to one wall with
a Confederate bayonet. The Sheriff was in residence, hat firmly planted, feet on the desktop,
and a bottle beside him. Others of his group
lounged in chairs, tilted back against the walls. I
knew most, but not very favorably. In general
they were a bunch of troublemakers. They nodded, one or two saying "Howdy." And Mr.
Plummer was at his courteous best, not tipsy but
as officious as a Mayor the moment he saw me
enter.

He came round to shake hands, and when he
heard me out, said, "Mr. Nickerson, let me
repeat—you're a man, and as for courage, well,
you could knock *their* heads together!"—
waving toward the "deputies." One, I think it
was Buck Stinson, said, "He could do it, there
ain't no doubt in my mind! I only hope he reins
in and takes pity, without flying off the handle."
And Ned Ray added, solemn as an owl, "It ain't
my nature to back down, but there—this'll show
and demonstrate how *I* feel!" and he jerked out
his revolver and placed it on the desk.

I was accustomed to such bilge, and paid no
mind, and Mr. Plummer said, with a look of deep
pride, "They're rough, Mr. Nickerson, but
they're ready! You won't believe it—I've heard
them criticized as being *too* rough! But what
does it take to catch a thief, as the adage goes?
(That's a joke, sir.) Enough said! Now, what time
were you and Mr. Jenkins departing? Dawn, was
it? Well, this office suggests a precaution or two,
detective-fashion, according to the book. There's

comings and goings on that trail, and I, for one, regard the route as risky. These days you don't know one crawler from another. Let's take this yellow scarf—pretty as a picture and bold to stand out—and tell Mr. Jenkins to drape it round his arm. I'll have one of my deputies light out now and inform my boys up the way. They'll maintain a watch; bank on it. No—don't thank me. It's part of the job."

When I got up, not wholly at ease, Ned Ray rose and opened the door, saying, "If it won't gall you, I'll replace my hog-leg. But give a man a chance and don't draw down sudden. I've got a widdered old mother, and I'm her sole and only support."

The preposterous notion that Ned Ray, or Buck Stinson either, had ever had a mother was too much for the average person's stomach. But I didn't say so, and left.

The sun was not quite up when we rode out of town heading along the Stinking Water. This was the first leg, at that time, of a trip to Deer Lodge, which was 120 miles distant, more or less. (We hadn't good maps, then, and no sure way of measuring distance, either.) I say "rode," but I was on the wagon-seat while Jenkins had a good saddlehorse, a spotted Indian pony, that stood up to the country. Also, he was leading a pack mule that somebody might have sold him as a joke. Jenkins was from the Ozarks, in Arkansas, and knew livestock, but he said the mules down there "were broke to the plough," and this was a new specimen on *him*. It was new to me, too.

Now a mule isn't the noblest breed of animal,

having an odd set of parents; that is, a jackass and a mare. And when you add the fact that he's sexless, unable to reproduce, or have any fun along that line, maybe he (or it) has an excuse to be grouchy. But this customer was in a class apart. If you tried to steer him left, he went right, and if you struck right, he went left. And he had a neat trick of wrinkling up his hide to shuck off packs. Allowing that he carried, among travel gear, twenty thousand dollars in dust, you can see we had a problem. But if you argued, explaining the need for cooperation, he looked as meek as a missionary. He rolled his marble eyes and nodded in sympathy, or so we thought for a while.

"Now look here, friend," said Jenkins at one point, standing face to face, pack on the ground, "you'd better understand that we're moving to Deer Lodge, or I am, and we have to hurry. My wife—that would be Mary Ann—and the children—Bub, the eldest, and the girls, Martha and Betty Jean—are coming along later. So you see, we require all the help you can provide; we'd appreciate it." The mule nodded and tried to bite off his ear.

Jenkins had been to Mexico with his father and favored the ariero's system of packing—slinging over an aparejo, or big leather pad stuffed with hay and secured with a long-grass bandage. But it was no use—the mule had never been to Mexico, so he tossed off the aparejo and ate it, while we sat under a bull pine, defeated. In the end, we placed Jenkins' goods in the wagon and turned the mule loose, hoping to replace it 'at Beaverhead. For the first time in history, perhaps, an owner had the high pleasure of kicking a mule in the rump, rather than vice versa. But he only wandered off, shaking his head, as if *we* were crazy. I lodged a heavy-booted whack on his right ham, and Jenkins topped me. He took a little run and, sailing his body horizontal, gave that nuisance about a thirty-foot start toward Colorado. Afterward we felt refreshed and had a smoke. Jenkins transferred his dust to a "cantina," or kind of Spanish-California bag used by all miners traveling hereabouts; then we resumed our trip, having lost no more than an hour or so.

Here we switched to the Beaverhead and followed it north to the Big Hole. We had to cross the Divide of course, using Deer Lodge Pass, about 6000 feet high. But the road was simple, now in early fall, and we looked forward to easing down the slope and pushing through beautiful country to the Lodge. We would pass the Warm Springs, where I met the Smithers' girl, and then the ones where I'd enjoyed some Snake maidens when we lived at our ranch. (It was past Deer Lodge a few miles, near Gold Creek.)

The day was splendid, now with the mule gone. And when the sun breasted a hill behind us, it almost exploded in glory. There wasn't a puffball cloud in all that blue emptiness. It felt good to be free of Virginia and its violence, and I rode along convinced that Jenkins was making the right move. He was a fresh-faced fellow of twenty-seven or eight, and had performed a curious service for me; he and Sheriff Plummer. I being younger, the Sheriff, with his humbuggy compliments, had lifted me out of the "son" and "my boy" class.

So—I was just slightly patronizing to Jenkins,

calling him "young fellow" now and then. It
made no difference. I'd been to Deer Lodge before, many times, and he hadn't. But there was
no pettiness or softness about him. That tanned
jaw had a line that gave the stupidest observer a
warning not to take liberties. He'd made acquaintance with me long ago, as time went in
pell-mell Virginia, and would likely have
stepped forward to save my life. It's a strange set
of men, those Arkansas hillbillies; once you're
lucky to win one, you've got a friend for life. And
they're hard, strong stock, slow to anger or
panic, even by Virginia City standards.

With such companionship our trip was more
an outing than a chore. After we'd turned north,
the country grew wild again. No more miners in
sight, or anybody else. The road was tolerable,
once you got accustomed to oxen stumbling and
an occasional boulder that jarred your spine.
Jenkins rode along, whistling and relaxed, and I
would have preferred a horse, too, though I had
points in my favor. A Pennsylvania wagon-seat's
backed, and the bed is well sprung, and with my
buffalo robe folded beneath me, I was content.

By and by we began to spot game, and we saw
(without shooting) the little black-tailed, scent-
less deer; cat-owls; antelope in flocks, plenty of
ground-hogs, prairie dogs, deer mice—shaped
like kangaroos, larger than ordinary mice—and
dozens of squirrels scolding in trees. And then,
in a marshy valley, two black elk, which we
stopped to watch as they crunched on willows. It
was Indians that called them black elk, or "Tó-
pár-ree-ah,"—biggest of the deer family. But
most whites called them moose. In the spring,
when they "shed off," they turn nearly coal-

black, and at any time they were the ugliest animals on earth.

We kept at safe distance. Emigrants were killed by these creatures, whose overhanging noses
and sad faces make them seem harmless. But if
pressed, they'll charge and fight with the fierceness of grizzlies. And I recall that, years later,
when Langford became Yellowstone's first
Superintendent, he wrote that "There appears to
be no way to convince sightseers that a moose is
a wild animal, and a huge one, and that his looks
betray his disposition. We've had, alas, many
accidents, despite signs that are everywhere
posted on trees."

Skirting this browsing pair, we lumbered on
north toward Beaverhead. Jenkins wanted the
male's rack of horn, but I persuaded him, from
experience, that to kill a moose required an instantly fatal shot. Critically wounded, they gallop (their gait resembled galloping) for miles
and miles, and remain as tricky as foxes.

Some time after noon we stopped, half-
starved, for we'd left at five without breakfast,
and made a fire on the bank of a stream. Jenkins
ate bacon and beans, but during my stay in
California and Montana, I'd been overdosed by
those rations, and was glad to catch three trout to
fry in corn meal. The change was nourishing.
Trout in the Stinking Water reeked of sulphur, or
alkali, or maybe dead Indians; and besides,
when the Stampede started, any self-respecting
trout packed up in a hurry.

While we ate, a party of four "braves" and two
squaws, with a trim girl-child, appeared on the
scene. All three females were afoot and the men
were wretchedly mounted. I was startled, and a

little scared, for they resembled Sioux, or a poor
mixture of Sioux and Crows. Both tribes strayed
here now, and nobody liked them. They were
arrogant thieves, and most had guns and knew
how to fight. Jenkins rose up and I said softly,
"Pay no attention; pretend to ignore them. We'll
sound out what they want."

Well, the leader walked his horse back and
forth across the trail, which meant we were to
approach—typical Crow cheek—but we continued to scrub our pans in the stream. Then he
shot his rifle up in the air, to signal friendliness.
Curious, I fired mine, partly to show it was a
much better gun. They walked slowly forward,
as miserable a set of rogues as possible. I figured
they'd been cast out and were scrounging for
whatever came along.

When they were thirty yards distant, I stood
up and gazed them over, drawing my revolver
and twirling the cylinders in an absent sort of
way. The leader had his ribs outlined in red and
his face solid black; he was wearing (thrown
open) a bob-tailed military coat with brass
buttons—nothing else. Another male, colored
just as hideous, had a government blanket over
one shoulder, and his organ, of which he seemed
vain, was painted black with a crimson, over-
sized glans. He rode in such a manner as to make
this flop back and forth, not fully quiescent, and
his gestures, I thought, were girlish. So it was
easy to see why this group was expelled. The
girl, no more than eleven or twelve, was the only
member not pigmented and was, in fact, beaded
to make her attractive.

When they'd closed half the space, I held up a
hand and cried, "Halt—far enough!"—in, I ex-

pect, the worst Indianese they'd heard to date.
But they stopped, and, not surprisingly, the
leader thrust forward the girl, whom he iden-
tified as his daughter. He offered her for sale, at a
price which I took to be "two bottles of whiskey."

"What's the ugly devil want?" Jenkins asked,
and when I told him, he flushed and said, "Do
we start shooting now, or give them a chance to
run?" Having two daughters of his own, he was
affronted. The "Chief," meanwhile, sensing a
snag in negotiations, put forth the nude squaws
and said either could go for a single bottle of
whiskey; take our choice. He addressed us as
"Mastachulees"—or white men—and called the
oxen "Woo-haws," meaning "Whoa-has," the
only word most Indians heard whites hurl at the
beasts. (But they had no interest in oxen. I never
saw an Indian use one, not for years into the
future. Like Mexicans, they liked horses and
would keep a family impoverished for the simple fact of owning them.)

At this point, trying to look fierce, the Chief
trotted out his best bargain—all three females for
Jenkins' horse and ten pounds of coffee. He
explained, reasonably, that they could steal
more women but that horses were hard to come
by.

I restrained Jenkins from further decorating
his ribs (which looked like spare-ribs newly
butchered for the spit). Then I pondered the offer. It was a good one, for it provided inspiration
how to bid them goodbye. By now I saw the
encounter as amusing rather than dangerous.
Among them they had two old muskets, stocks
wired to barrels. One's breech had a quarter-inch

gap, and the other's sight was knocked off. Besides these they had two bows-and-arrows, of the size used here for squirrels and gophers. The infrequent slaying of a deer probably set off a two-day fiesta, featuring their dismal dances, which (like most folk dances) took the form of hopping on one foot then hopping on the other while grunting as if suffering internal distress. These were testaments to imagined valor and usually caused a sexual spree.

To return to the point, which got lost, we both had Kentucky rifles, two repeating Colts—of .45 calibre—and could have wiped out this group in five minutes, making their expulsion permanent. But we hadn't much taste for killing. So I told the Chief, with a generous look, "Coffee? Of course, but we have no need for your squaws, lovely as they are. We're traveling light, you see, and in a hurry. Seat yourselves over there"—pointing to a grassy mound. "We'll fill you up pronto."

I imagine that, considering my command of the tongue, he absorbed about a third of this, but they spread scruffy old robes to sit down, nonetheless. Before he did so, the Chief, with familiar mongrel-Indian manners, said, "Shug?"

"Quite so. There'll be sugar enough for all. Now sit back and rest, and think up some unlikely phrases for Fenimore Cooper." To Jenkins, I said, "Get out the big pot and load it up. Heap her full. It's a peculiarity of these skunks that they think they like coffee. But it sits hard on their bellies, especially when dosed with sweetening. They aren't used to it."

We shortly had the pot boiling, if solid coffee-

and-sugar can boil. Then I plopped it down, with a tin cup, halfway between us. The man with the two-colored exhibit (now bobbing in extension) darted forward, burning his hand, of course, but paying little heed. The males passed the cup round and round, gulping in their filthy fashion, and I waited in something like Grantly's scientific style.

It was about fifteen minutes before our first success reported in. The Chief, declining a fourth offer, seemed thoughtful, and sat gazing off toward the hills. The others put the cup down and appeared abstracted as well, the giggler's wagon-tongue wonderfully retracted. Then the Chief moved to the next phase. Holding his stomach, he staggered off to the willows and threw up. He did so several times, and when he crawled out—I say crawled—he appeared lighter in color, or pale, and his military jacket was bespotted. His fellows were close on his heels, whereupon the squaws lit in on what coffee was left. The girl sat holding her dimpled knees, looking unhappy. When I caught her eye, she tried a failure of a smile and then—her heart not in it, I thought—made an obscene gesture, parting her legs. It was simply an act of obeying former training. I had the impression she wished to leave this collection behind.

"She wants out," I said to Jenkins. "Probably she's never been used. In the beginning, they hoped to get a big price."

Jenkins turned red again. For his age, he was the easiest fellow to blush I'd ever known. "She's a child, and needs civilized care. And you're right, of course. We have to do something."

"All packed but the pot and cup? Then

whoa-ha!" I yelled at the oxen, cracking a whip, and we bumped over the mound, the squaws having joined the males at the stream. The girl remained silent. She'd abandoned her seductions and watched us, imploring. For the first time, I noticed she was nearly white, with yellowish hair, and it struck me, at last, that she'd been snatched from Emigrants.

"Hey, you," I called to the Chief, who was still at work shedding coffee. "Here!—payment for the girl!" and I threw down a fifty-dollar gold piece. Grabbing our tinware, I swung the girl up beside me, where she sat erect as a spear.

"That was a fine deed," said Jenkins, riding near. "Unless, and I beg your pardon for saying it, you plan—"

"Put it out of your mind. With a child this age? Besides, I have a young lady, a fiancée, in Bannack." This was certainly stretching the truth, but I couldn't resist it. "We can get her settled with a decent family, maybe in Deer Lodge."

The Arkansan seemed overcome. He blurted out, "I committed a blunder, with my best friend. I never knew any school-taught people before, though my Pa made us read books, and I hope you'll excuse—"

It was here that a rifle cracked from behind some rocks and blew off the top of his head. He dropped from his horse like a stone, finished, finished with all his plans. He'd become a memory, all in a second, to the family waiting in Arkansas. The last I saw was that bright yellow scarf, still tied to his right arm.

Indians weren't responsible for this. The over-coffeed group lay behind us; and besides, I couldn't mistake the sound of that white man's rifle, or its accuracy, either.

I swiped the girl backward into the bed and hunched down myself, rising only to yell and whip the oxen. Glancing over my shoulder I saw them—four murdering scoundrels bending at Jenkins' body and going through his packs. I heard one cry out as he lifted the cantina. Then he rose to hold up a bloody scalp. If there were mongrel Indians in Montana, there were more mongrel whites, and it was common for these last to scalp Indians, and wear the grisly trophies on their belts until they stank so bad people refused to come near.

Now they struck out for us, whipping right and left. All wore masks, and while we had a good start, I knew they'd catch us soon. Oxen are willing but slow, and those villains were mounted. In a frenzy, I pointed my rifle back, taking as careful aim as I could, with the wagon humping along, and fired. I heard a shout: "I'm hit, Neddy! [with an oath] He got me in the shoulder! By God, I'll slaughter that sprig!"

Rounding a bend, I saw a beaver dam; then I remembered that report of the ruffians trying to hide out. I dragged the girl down, slashed at the oxen, flung the reins forward, and flung us both into the stream. The girl was white-faced but nodded when I made a gesture to hold her nose, and we disappeared from view. Trying not to breathe, I groped from stick to stick, feeling all around, and then things opened up. We were inside, hoping for the best.

There was a strong stink of musk but after my eyes pierced the dark, I saw that the owners were absent. The structure was abandoned, probably for one up-stream where shoots and saplings hadn't played out. It's the pesky system of beavers, and, likely, if beaver hats hadn't come into fashion, the varmints would have chewed up the whole countryside. It was the first law I learned in the Rockies. Don't feel sorry for a beaver; his instincts are entirely selfish and destructive. And there's no peaceful way to move him from a project. It's either you or him.

We crouched, silent, and waited, me holding the girl's hand. Presently I heard someone yell, the sound near at hand. "Let up, George. Why go chasing an empty ox-cart? We've got the gold." Then a grumbled reply I couldn't catch, and after that a flurried drum-beat of hooves fading off in the distance. Even so, I gripped the girl's hand, and we sat without stirring for upward of an hour. I was taking no chances with those thugs, with no more answer than a drowned Navy revolver.

When we emerged, swimming as before, it was harder going, for the current was against us. But we made it at last, creeping into willows on the opposite bank. Nothing in sight or sound. I maneuvered out to look, and they were gone. So we crossed over, and, as I'd expected, the oxen were quietly grazing about a mile upstream.

Our traveling gear intact, even to my rifle, we started back toward Virginia, still silent, but my insides boiled with rage. We stopped beside Jenkins' body, and, taking a deep breath, then binding the head with a kerchief, I hoisted him into the wagon and covered him with blankets. A moment later we came to those Indians. All had been killed and scalped and what they call "mutilated" besides. They were sprawled out around that mound every which way. It was plain that the men had been killed first, and plainer still that the women had been made sport of before dying. Most were still bleeding.

I glanced aside at the girl. She was gazing straight ahead, showing no emotion at all. She seemed neither happy nor sad, and I thought that, for some reason, this might be a good omen. If so, it was the only boon of that day as we rode down-stream toward Alder Gulch and home.

CHAPTER XVII

"YOU'VE PLACED YOURSELF in a delicate position," said Grantly. He sat at his hearth, as did I, myself slumped in dejection. James was nearby, listening, making no comment as yet. "We were aware, to be sure, of your acquaintance with Plummer, but I'll confess that the agreement in his office exceeds imagination. At the least, you must have realized the character of the scoundrels surrounding him. I regret having to say this, but you appear to have a *very poor judgment of people!*" It was the first real criticism he'd ever made to my face.

"I've been a complete fool," I cried, at the end of my tether. "I can see now, too late for Jenkins, how tying that yellow scarf on his arm was a sign for murder, as surely as if I'd pulled the trigger!"

James finally spoke up, sprawled in his chair. "There are those in town who think you *did*— pull the trigger. According to them, you killed the boy, hid his gold, and brought him back to throw off suspicion. Such people exist in every town," he added to remove the sting.

"And the girl?" asked Grantly.

"Indian girls can be picked up at a dime a dozen."

"But her story bears him out exactly, as far as it goes."

"A girl, well, besotted, can be coached—"

I turned to James, anger beginning to creep past my shirt. "Now don't tell me *you*—"

"Quiet down. We two, and the decent folk of Virginia, know you couldn't shoot a weasel. Or steal, or do anything except perhaps be stupid." He pondered this, much in the style of Grantly. "I really do believe," he said at length, "that you're the most immature specimen for your age I ever met." Then he smiled. "Cheer up—time cures it. Meanwhile, as I see things, we might turn this to good account—"

"I was thinking along the same lines, Brother James."

"To tell you the truth, Chappie, we'll have to share some guilt here. Grantly and I, with some others, haven't been candid about recent events in Virginia. We decided against it, you're so confoundedly impulsive!"

"He came sneaking and complimenting and telling me what a great man I was, and I fell for it like a nine-year-old!"

"Yes, we talked you over, and it was Dimsdale, I recall, who mentioned the poet Browning, and '—she had a heart, how shall I say?—too soon made glad—' "

"You can rely on the English," observed Grantly, diverting his ire, "to prove all with quotations from their poets, relieving these with Latin when stuck. I consider the practice a national vice. Our father, by the way, was a foremost victim of the habit, though his remarks frequently came out scrambled."

It sounds unkind, but I am convinced that Grantly was piqued that the quotation hadn't occurred to *him*, in which case he would have switched things around, of course, and "vice" would have become the greatest virtue of man.

"However, it's time to be frank. You recall the meeting in Bannack; well, a Vigilance Committee is nearly completed here now. I needn't tell you that these are sensitive matters, deep waters indeed. Vigilantes, the business of taking the law into one's own hands, is morally wrong, and dangerous in practice. But unchecked violence, with no law yet in sight, can't be permitted to continue. That is, if we're to have a city at all. Now then—you say you recognized the voice of George Ives? And heard him call out 'Ned'?"

"I'll swear it in court! I *know* that gravel-throat, and Ned Ray was in the Sheriff's office—not three feet from my side."

"The precise measurement is probably not requisite at this time. A few inches here, a few there—"

"Beidler's had the run-down on Plummer from a friend in California. Perhaps Grantly would care to read it—*boiled down!*"

"To be sure; nothing could give me greater pleasure. A profile of that head, until the original is available—"

"Just read it," said James.

Grantly arose, with a reproachful look at his brother, withdrew a document from his pocket, and adjusted his steel spectacles. I had a notion that these were without correction for poor vision; they were part of his system for seeming older.

"Henry Plummer—Henry J. Plummer, middle name unknown at this juncture." (Since Grantly was, physically, unable to avoid paraphrasing,

I'll let him ramble on, his voice rising and falling, handsomely inflected.) "Subject born in England, in 1830, on a day to illumine that country's history of lopping off heads for recreation. Parentage respectable, of the lower middle class. At the age of eleven, Subject fittingly apprenticed to a butcher [here I heard James groan], a connection the boy severed as rapidly as possible. Thus"—and Grantly lifted his gaze, pleased with his point—"we see him breaking indentures, his first brush with Crime, unless, of course, there had been earlier, precocious thefts from the cradle—blocks, dolls, monkeys-on-sticks—"

"All right, Grantly."

"Shortly thereafter he departed the shores of Albion—'this Sceptred Isle'—to wash up in New York City, where he remained for two years. We, or rather the California police, have no record of his prowl through the dark streets of that hive, but we may suspect the worst.

"Subject's public trail resumes in Nevada City, California, when in his mid-teens. There he became partner in a bakery, if you please! Thus, again, we must assume that a subtle vinculum exists between the arts of butchering and baking, though I, for one, am not aware of its nature. Nature of the Subject, however, becomes evident when, resting from the ovens, he murdered a German named Vedder, with whose wife he was found coupled in flagrante delicto," and Grantly glanced round in satisfaction, having squared all accounts with Dimsdale.

"Yes, delicto indeed [savoring the word], and since the wrong man was very plainly shot, young Plummer entered the penitentiary. For

California had Territorial law then, even as we
lack it today in Montana. Now I'll ask that you
attend—and wake James if you can, my boy;
thank you. The following lays down a pattern
easy to read. *Concurrent with baking, Subject
had named himself town Marshal!* And it was in
the dual role that he heard the prison gates clang
behind him. Promptly pardoned, by Governor
Weller, an ass, on 'grounds of ill-health'—real
cause believed Subject's silken and persuasive
tongue—he joined a second bakery in Nevada
City. This enriched by numerous small and
medium offenses, since Subject, contrary to
Governor Weller, appeared in bursting spirits.
But this time at last he relieved tension by cracking the skull of a man in a whorehouse. (I'll ask
you to note, that, first to last, a main trouble of
Subject has been—women! He had a Mexican
mistress in Nevada City, hence the numerous
returns to that oasis.) *However,* he now fled to
Washoe and joined a band, yes, of Road Agents!

"So—we creep closer to the present scene
here. Subject failing, with associate scum, in an
attempted robbery of a bullion express, he returned, little daunted, to *Nevada City* where,
almost on the instant, he shot and this time
killed another man in a brothel of lesser repute.
Despite its low estate, Mr. Plummer resumed
Territorial confinement. By means of several
well-placed bribes, he walked out a free man
soon, leaving for Walla Walla with a fellow jail-
bird who'd lately murdered the Sheriff.

"You know," said Grantly, looking up, bewildered, "this scoundrel's slippery feats are almost
past believing. And the police terms strike me as
confusing. We must presume that the terms

'marshal,' 'sheriff,' and the like have no more standing than here, and that the Territorial force prevailed over all—"

"Let's wind it up."

"Yes, as Brother James so politely suggests—there's more to come. But, I thank God, not much. The records now fail us slightly. The best account says that, apparently for practise, Plummer caused the escape from jail of a murderer named Mayfield, a kindred spirit; then, he robbed a stage, bringing a federal charge on which he was somehow acquitted, to Washington's shame. And finally, having made his mark on the far-western slopes, he wended his way—no doubt thieving, seducing, killing—to our once-picturesque center of Bannack. To avoid pursuit at the source, he ingeniously mailed announcements of his death to all California and Washington newspapers. These were dutifully printed, minus the usual black border. I have one here, from the Sacramento Union—of historic value some day. The rest, or some of the rest, we know." He looked up again and removed his glasses, pleased.

"The foregoing depicts in a nut-shell, as I believe you'll agree, the fragrant young history of Henry J. Plummer. Dominus illuminatio mea, or, loosely translated—God will lead us out of this mess."

James murmured something to do with "nut-shell," not wholly flattering.

"Now, Chappie," he continued with unusual detail, "here's what we want you to do. Cosy up to Plummer. Pretend deep grief—perhaps you won't have to—assume all the blame yourself. Ingratiate yourself. Ask for assignments. Promise further information. In other words, get to be one of the boys.

"And hear this. Never let them suspect that you're even close to their game. You'll have to play actor here, and play *well*. These are ruffians—worse, if there's a name for it—and we'd have no way on earth to save you.

"Finally, we're sorry—all of us." Using his curious leverage, he half picked me off the floor with an arm across my back. "It's easy, when you're young, to believe in people. And when you lose that, a good part of life's gone with it."

Releasing me, he said, "I'm afraid complete happiness doesn't exist. In my case, I don't believe in many Indians, including the 'wives' that flit in and out. And since most white women scare me, well, you see, I'm sometimes lonely; I find release in adventure."

He smiled. "I shouldn't have told you that, I suppose. Only Grantly knew, as he knows a great deal, and worries for other people only, often to his injury."

I'd never heard James speak so, and Grantly, fussed, cleared his throat several times. "I see," he observed at length, "that Brother James has fallen into the habit of babbling. He *will* surmount his, let us say, reticence about women of his class. He'll marry, have children, and, to sum up, find peace and contentment. I mention these embarrassments," he said, peering at James, "because you chose, at last, to bring them out into the open."

James chuckled, back to earth. "Consider them withdrawn; I'll see that they stay that way."

Walking to my dismal shack, I somehow felt better. But I was puzzled why he'd dragged up things that men usually conceal from birth to grave. I thought of Mr. Thoreau's "*quiet desperation*" and laughed aloud. My mind was no longer on me and my troubles. Headed down the moonlit street, a noise of carousing in the distance, I was worrying about—James. That was his purpose, and I wondered what it had cost him.

"It was slackness on my part. It must have been, Mr. Plummer. The scarf was still tied to his arm, but I—well, I'm afriad I failed to keep proper look-out. Riding a horse is one thing; sitting half-asleep on a wagon's another."

"Now see here!" said the Sheriff severely. "You'll put those thoughts out of your mind. I doubt if anyone, the fastest gunman, the roughest hand, perhaps a platoon of guardians, could have prevented this tragic occurrence. That route is much traveled by Emigrants, Indians of every character, thieves, and murderers. Some say these last are organized! Road Agents, my young friend! Yes, I dislike to repeat that, but a band of bloodthirsty Road Agents."

"This is terrible news, Sheriff. Are you sure?"

"Not sure, sir, but alerted. This office—and I don't mind your spreading the word—is alerted and ready for eventualities. *Road Agents!*— that's the term."

(The monster himself, somewhere along the way, doubtless during his early promise in California, is believed to have put the name into circulation. Historians have weighed the question whether Plummer disliked "Highway Robber" as being a social stigma. In that malignant brain any Highway Robber was in a class below

Road Agent, and, no matter if he invented the lofty phrase, its constant repetition helped get him into trouble.)

He sat at his mahogany desk (another relic of the trail) which seemed to suit him. The slender figure (called "withy" in news stories) was clothed in a long black coat, with an embroidered vest, the trousers tucked into fancy boots, and a ring on the finger of his left hand. The whole would have been effeminate in another man. But that face darkened by the ugly black hat meant danger for anyone but a fool—and that fool was me. I saw him, now, as evil and, the office empty excepting us, I had a sudden urge to shoot him down. I may have given this away when beads of sweat appeared on my forehead.

Mr. Plummer leaned forward, interested.

"Are you ill, Mr. Nickerson? Your face has gone pale as bleach. Maybe a dose of calomel—" and he pulled a drawer part way out.

"No, no. It's just that guilt, and Jenkins, have upset me."

I wasn't mistaken in his looks. As the *Helena Herald* said later, "One might as well have probed the eyes of the dead for some token of a human soul as to seek it in the light gray orbs of Plummer." But for me those "orbs" had a quick glitter of understanding.

"To be sure. The reaction is normal and will pass in time. Now, while you reclaim your feelings, I wonder if you'd just mind the office while I step down to Hauser's Bank? Back in five minutes. After all," he said, rising and shaking my hand, "you are a deputy here, in a manner of speaking. And you have the sympathy of us all. I

want to repeat that":—and I saw mockery there,
or thought I did—"of us *all*. Every good man and
true on my staff!"

I was curious who these were, and thought
about means of finding out; perhaps I might
undo some damage.

I watched him walk down the street, bowing,
but never removing that coffin-lid over the bulging cranium. And when I turned back, I noticed
his "medicine drawer" remained open and that a
sealed paper was visible there. Suddenly I was
seized with purpose, but how to break the
monogrammed blue wafer of wax? It was
pressed from his ring, and I wondered which
corpse in his past had given this up.

After another quick glance down the street, I
warmed my pocketknife and slowly, carefully,
slid the blade under the seal and—it worked.
The wax came up in a piece, without leaving a
mark.

This was a trap, plain enough; the Sheriff, or
his men, knew where I'd spent the evening.
Plummer had affixed that seal, and hoped I
would carry the paper off intact. And here I'll
quote James, who'd been some mysterious kind
of lawman once, before I knew him. But he didn't
care to discuss it. "Just remember, laddy, a criminal's mind's an *inferior* mind. The breed leaves
mistakes that a child could spot, and that's why
prisons are bulging."

Well, I opened the paper, and Mr. Plummer
had indeed made a mistake. That paper could
have held a rhyme from Mother Goose and
served his purpose just as well. But it had, instead, the whole guilty list, with each one's job

described, and I copied it into my notebook as fast as my shaking hands allowed.

"Henry Plummer, chief; Bill Bunton, stool pigeon and second in command; George Brown, secretary; Sam Bunton, roadster; Cyrus Skinner, fence, spy, and roadster; George Shears, horse thief and roadster; Frank Parish, horse thief and roadster; Hayes Lyons, telegraph man and roadster: Ned Ray, councilroom keeper at Bannack. Additional roadsters: George Ives, Stephen Marshland, Dutch John (Wagner), Alex Carter, Whiskey Bill Graves, Johnny Cooper, Buck Stinson, Mexican Frank, Bob Zachary, Boone Helm, Clubfoot George (Lane), Billy Terwilliger, Gad Moore."

Before inscribing the last names in my notes (which I now have before me, the pencil loops faded), I returned to the door, and this time the genial Sheriff was no farther than a hundred yards distant. He was chatting with a bosomy wife who seemed flattered, and I wondered at the allure this man had for women.

But I needed to hurry, now, so I scribbled down the remainder, using abbreviations; then I re-heated the seal, placed it over the edges, pressed lightly, and blew hard. I aimed to have that document, seal and all, cool before an examination was made. I left things precisely as I found them, and, choosing a chair against the wall, tilted back like Stinson and Ray, when I visited first.

"Well, deputy," said Plummer on entering, with his imitation smile (I'd thought it very compelling during our earlier conference), "any business? No shootings, knifings, complaints about sharpers or drunks?" Then he tried what once might have sounded like a pretty fair joke: "Anyone walk in to give himself up?"

I managed a hollow laugh, and saw Plummer casting those restless gray eyes over the desk, the drawer, and its contents.

"You should have taken the comfortable chair. I'm afraid my errand consumed more time than planned. I'm obliged to you, sir, but in the exchange of courtesies with our townsmen—"

Here I had the inspiration to kill two birds with one stone—to stall, and to return some of the humbug.

"Sheriff," I said, plopping down, "I've noticed this, and so have others. You must be the most popular man in Virginia City. I've heard it spoken often." And then, maliciously, "How is it, for example, that all women make excuses to stop you on the street? Surely it can't be your handsome costume alone, or even your face and figure." I sighed. "Nobody seems to notice me at all."

He looked up sharply, pleased all the same, and I could imagine how his fingers itched to examine that paper. But he collected himself and said in a modest sort of way, "It's the office, Mr. Nickerson. People feel obliged to speak to their Sheriff; that, to my regret, is the sole reason." And he started after the paper as Whiskey Bill Graves walked in and slumped heavily down, legs a-sprawl.

"Well?"

"We had a Chinawoman for breakfast."

This was a usual way of saying that, as dawn

broke and the deputies searched out the streets, they'd turned up a dead Chinese woman, probably in an alley with her throat cut.

Chinese occupied a unique niche through the Rockies. These people had made the long, long trip after Alder Gulch gold, often sent by overlords as said before. The women were comely, more attractive than Indians to most miners. They were also, as a Journalist say it, "Strangers to virtue." For a while after the Stampede, all Chinese returned their dead to China for burial, at some expense; sometimes, in bad weather, they buried them here on the Hill, later exhuming and shipping the bodies home. It was an odd practice. If an excuse exists for early resentments of Chinese, it was that they themselves made no single attempt to blend into the local population. For a long time, they preferred to remain aloof, and were treated so.

Sheriff Plummer ordered Whiskey Bill to take the Chinawoman's body to the undertaker's for an "inquest," and I got up to leave.

I knew better than head directly to the Duncans, so I walked around the corner to Smithers'. On the way I was astonished to get hard looks from acquaintances and to be openly snubbed by others. There was no doubt—many persons *did* think I'd killed Jenkins for his dust. The feeling was uncomfortable, and, stupidly, I became anxious about my reception at the blacksmith's.

But the door opened to my knock, and Mrs. Smithers gave me a motherly peck, dabbing at her eyes with an apron. Shortly thereafter my boss emerged from a little room, dressing, and boomed out, "Heared of it? Yes, sir, we've heared, and maybe you'd forgot the lass?"

I *had* forgotten. I'd stashed the child with these people, as being the best family I knew, and now she came out, grave-faced and silent, her blue eyes staring up into mine when she sat on the floor.

"Now, sir, I'll make no bones about the trash-gobble abroad, and if I hadn't been rendered gimpy, as well as troublous in the lungs, well"—he scratched his head, hoping for something Biblical, I judged—"I'd fettered some back in the trees."

"Ewing!"

But he was mad and stamped around the room. Since we hadn't enough iron yet, Mr. Smithers had taken to his bed again, except for walking outside to cock an ear.

"No, throttling won't serve, Harriet. I mean to have my say, and I'll just leave the door hang open (them hinges, sir, was done by an amatchur; note the sway) so anyone can hear as wishes. I'll remind you the Philistines bore false witness, and look how they throwed off into bankrupt."

"You needn't call me 'sir,' Mr. Smithers," I said wearily. I didn't remember his allusion quite in that way, but he often mixed up the Bible, and besides, he was off and rampaging now and nothing could stop him.

As for Mrs. Smithers, at any stress she fell back to a fixed line: She made a Yorkshire pudding, and now she started one, raising a clatter.

"—you'll scarcely absorb, sir, what a self-righteous, one-eyed religious spouter relayed to me in front of Coleman and Loeb's. Stuffed with oyster-pie, he was, and spiritous liquors as well—"

"Ewing!"

"Oh, I know the breed, sir! When he drawed himself aloft, swoll up with pomp, he said, 'Smithers'—foregoing the 'Mister,' you'll notice—'if that whelp worked for me, the least I'd administer was horsewhip!'

"Now you know me for a peace-loving man, follering rules printed up by Jesus. On top of which, the Lord never seen fit to equip me with muscles and framework." (This last was a self-conscious fib; Mr. Smithers could have bent any man in town over his knee, and that included James.) "But I spoke up brisk. I said 'If you'll come to the Forge, sir, I'll cast a iron helmet to case your head in. Your tongue waggles too much for me!' "

"Ewing!"

"Them were my words, and I defensed for punishment, for he's six feet five and brawling. But you'd scarcely accept that he gazed me up and down, snorted, sir, and left." (I reflected that I could scarcely blame him; Mr. Smithers in rage was a very rare sight.)

"Now I acknowledge being riled, like the Israelites at Waterloo; I prefer to see all God's creatures as Good, as we're told in the Book. But there's backbiting and sin in this town, worse than the Wilderness. Sometimes my toes grope at the brink of Faith—"

"Ewing!"

He subsided at a table, seeming thoughtful. "Occasions arise, sir, when I wonder why Providence laid down his fullers and swages at the close of Sixth Day. What if He'd tucked in for another week, and filed off the edges? Yes, sir, it's struck this old ruin that He fell to snoozing on the job, or joined a game of pinochle. I dislike to speak so in the open, and I've not this far been galled by Doubts, but—"

"Ewing, that's enough!" But she was trying to conceal a smile, I thought.

"Altering subject, you inquire about the lass here. Well, she ain't one to complain—sits there like a graven image. But she can't weld one word to another. Not since the first night. We've tried and we've failed, and we don't know Indian—"

"For me," said Mrs. Smithers, checking her Yorkshire pudding in the oven, "I think she'd speak English, with coaxing. Don't you feel the same, Diasy?"

"Is she Saved, Ma? Or is she heathen?"

"Saved, my granny!" snapped Mrs. Smithers. "Now I mean to rebel right here at the oven!" She held up a pretty formidable spoon, leaking gravy. "It's time, and more, that Daisy removed her mind from the Bible! She's a girl twisted; that's my view—and twisted by Religion. She's growing to be right pretty; soon she'll be a female woman. To tell you the God's truth, I've had a stomach full of Gospel. There! Now—it's out—in the interest of my only begotten daughter." (It wasn't quite out, I noticed from the last sentence.)

Mr. Smithers looked the very spirit of meekness. "Why Mother, I hold the same. I thought it was you—"

" 'You,' as you call it, means your Pa and Ma,

rest their oversanctified souls. Give a trifle more, and we'll have a half-wit idiot on our hands. Let me hear another word about Religion!—"

"Things can be undid," said Mr. Smithers, sagging into his clothes. "But I misdoubt we could recover water employed for dunking or sprinkling—"

"Ewing Smithers," she said, banging the pots, "make sense! You *can* make sense, though it comes hard. There's too many Moabites, and Leviticuses, and Uriah the Hittites wandering through. Now let one more try to creep into *my* kitchen! All of a heap, I've had my fill!—and I'm as Christian as the next. Come to table!"

The last was hurled at us, and nobody argued. As for me, I tucked with relish into that pudding, and deer meat, and brambleberries, and the pickles and piccalilli that went with it. For I'd not felt like eating since the murder and was half-starved.

"Now, Ross," she said, "you talk to this girl, the poor peaked thing."

So between mouthfuls, I tried some pretty fair Snake, and what Chinook I knew, and then some English, asking her name. But it was no use, and I left.

"Most we know already. But you've given us direct material on the *assignment* of each, and we can agree"—glancing at James—"that this is Evidence, for when and if the time comes. My boy, you took your life in your hands, gathering information, and that should weigh with the Committee."

"You mean *they* think I'm guilty?"

He frowned and considered. "I only wish," he

said finally, "you hadn't been so thick with
Plummer beforehand. That, with the scarf, puz-
zles our best men—despite what Brother James
and I relate. But all will come right"—he
smiled—"I'm sure of it."

"That makes me very happy," I said. "I'd like
to see them prying off that seal, with a murderer
walking head-on toward me. Even your Mr.
Beidler."

James stirred in his chair. "Our 'Mr. Beidler,'
as you put it, is probably the most dedicated
insister on order in town. He's five foot six, and
more feared by those scoundrels than anyone in
Virginia."

Well, it was true. "X"—he may have had a first
name but nobody used it—was the busiest fellow
around. He was on the go all the time, and if you
asked him, "What's up, X?" or "What are you
doing?" he never answered more than "After
tracks!" or the feebler response of "Don't know."
(Several merchants paid him, I think, to face
down bullies, and while I didn't know for sure,
he was gathering material for the Committee.)

Whatever saloon he was in, things quieted
down in a hurry. And if he told the meanest
outlaw, courteously, to behave himself, that man
didn't talk back. He was a curiosity; no one quite
understood the influence he had. And later,
when he became United States Marshal, he
worked just as hard, and spoke just as little. He
was liked and trusted by all, including the criminals he brought to justice.

CHAPTER XVIII

THE DETERIORATION NOW stepped up faster. Many times, wounded men lay unattended in the streets, hardly noticed by passersby. Bullet holes pocked the walls of stores next to saloons; shootings and knife fights occurred almost on the hour. After dark, no one dared to go even as far as Nevada, the burgeoning sister city.

Things would have gone from bad to worse except for Hauser's and Langford's famous wagon-ride to Deer Lodge. (Miners, though courageous, had no gift for organization.) The two spoke openly of transporting dust, while carrying a sick friend to the Baths, and Plummer's gang made a mistake. Here they were dealing, not with miners, but with future Montana leaders, and these were ready to put the Gulch in order. The men were bent on a show-down; and they needed personal identifications to complete dossiers being compiled.

Both men loading double guns with twelve balls to a barrel, they headed north toward Beaverhead, while keeping the closest lookout. Not far from Big Hole Junction, Hauser said, "We're being followed, but let's not hurry. We can outshoot them in the open." Staying apart from the trees, they rode along, watching blanketed figures that sifted in and out behind the rocks. Langford surmised that the party would be jumped after dark, and they made camp in scrub pines before sunset. They built a huge campfire and gave every show of feeling secure.

Hauser and the sick companion spread robes for sleep, in shadows away from the fire. But Langford, with the thunderously loaded gun, paced round the group in a silent, widening circle. When at length he heard low voices, down near a stream, he crouched in willows to watch. Four Agents had a fire hidden behind a rock, and were preparing to strike. He heard them say, "When that son of a bitch moon slides off behind the ledge, we'll make our play."

Cocking his gun, Langford stepped out of the bushes and said, "Good evening, boys. Were you looking for us?"

There followed a noisy scramble as the men sprang onto their horses, bucked and slipped their way across the stream, and headed in the direction of Bannack to a whirlwind of hooves.

"Could you recognize all four?" asked Hauser a few minutes later.

"Easily. They were Plummer, Buck Stinson, Ned Ray, and George Ives."

Plummer and his Agents had made the common criminal error of flaunting their deeds. Even when robbing stages on roads out from Virginia, they seldom bothered with disguises. They were, in fact, fatally careless. Each member, when professionally engaged, wore a green and blue blanket covering most of his body. Whiskey Bill sported a "plug hat" and kept his sleeves rolled to the elbows, showing a recognizable tattoo. And the hat he wore made his black silk mask ineffective. George Ives rode an identifiable dappled gray horse with a "roached" mane, and Bill Zachary, when he remembered, covered his face with a mask of jersey shirting. Making the charade more absurd, the fools, while letting the disguises slip and laughing about it, addressed one another by name.

Ives in particular had become a town burden. He was known to be absolutely fearless, riding roughshod (no fault of Smithers and Nickerson) through the streets, now yelling threats, again shooting some lonely miner's dog—his favorite show of marksmanship. Worse was his growing habit of backing his horse into a saloon, tossing an antelope bag onto the bar, and gun in hand, crying, "Boys, I need a loan. Fill her up and be damned quick about it!"

Ives rode thus into the Exchange on an afternoon when I was there, the horse sending two men sprawling. Three or four miners lounged at the bar, finished panning for the day, which for them had started before dawn. Others sat at tables playing cards.

I'll delete the profanity, for Ives' speech was atrocious, but he observed his rite with the bag, damned and blasted everyone, and threatened to burn the place down. First the bartender (Cleve Yancey) contributed, then the customers one by one walked up to add as little dust as possible and stay alive. From some perversity (probably caused by Jenkins) I continued drinking my beer.

"You there! Shake a leg, or maybe you're hankering for two bellybuttons?"

I turned slowly to face him. Thoughts of the murder and of the snake-like Plummer tortured my mind, and I'd foolishly lost any feeling for safety.

I said, "Fill it yourself."

Ives looked bewildered; I suppose it was the only time he'd ever been refused. His own indifference to danger was notorious, and this reckless spirit had made him the terror of the Gulch.

James had patiently worked at teaching me to draw and shoot, and I'd become a tolerable quick and accurate shot. But I was hardly up to this, and knew it. Still, for the first time I felt a rage to kill someone, and that man was Ives. Heart thumping away, I stood waiting.

Then, surprising us all, he burst out laughing.

"Why," he cried with an oath, "it's Deputy! Collect loans from Deputy? No sirree, you don't catch George Ives taking chances like that! Exempt, and welcome!"

Bartenders in Virginia City were not chosen for their manners alone. They were expected to keep order, generally using a black-oak club. Yancey, for example, was suspected of enjoying, once, an eventful career "on the other side," or across the Divide; and now he made a leap for a sawed-off gun leaning against the wall. But faster yet, Ives whirled and fired two shots into the mirror, not a hand's span from his head.

"Now, Cleve, we've been friends, both here and across, and I'd dislike to bury you." Then, his good humor restored, he scooped up the bag, gave a shout, and spurred his horse in a bound to the sidewalk.

I was relieved, but set up, too. I said, "Well, maybe we've seen the end of that!"

A miner with whom I'd been on friendly terms said "Shucks!" and turned his back. The others attended their drinks without comment.

It occurred to me—late, as usual—that I'd been called a "deputy," meaning Agent, and that men in this room believed it. There being nothing to say, I emptied my glass and left. But the scene would return like a reproachful ghost.

By now it was known that Plummer had a thieves' headquarters at Rattlesnake Ranch, as well as "stations" along all routes from Bannack and Virginia City. Precisely how far his tentacles spread was never firmly established. But from confessions—made by arrested Agents—he was proved directly or indirectly responsible for 102 murders, besides countless stage robberies, beatings, whippings, and other violence. This last including scalping, rapes, and mutilations, the favors tilted slightly toward Indians. He was, as Grantly wrote, "an undisputed organizational genius, and the foremost genuine monster produced in the bloody early history of the Rockies."

But Ives now struck on his own, not able to let twenty-four hours pass without wreaking some kind of havoc, wherever he was. Near Cold Spring Ranch, between Virginia and Bannack, he met an independent thief who, lashed for larceny in one of Plummer's official moments, had vowed to tell "all I know of the Road Agents." It would be his last threat of gossip. Ives, from his horse, fired two shotgun charges into the man's chest, with was so thickly clothed that he merely swayed, not falling. "He was a mite heavier, by God," bragged the killer, (ac-

cording to confessions) "but not heavy enough."
Ives thereupon walked around and shot the man
in the head with a revolver.

The added lead tipped the scales, to complete
Ives' figure, and the man toppled to the ground.
Cold Spring Ranch being in a settlement, and the
shooting taking place around noon, there were
witnesses, including the occupants of two
wagon teams. But all stood so terrified of the
killer and his friends that they crept out only to
bury the unfortunate, as Ives, whistling, led his
horse off toward the hills.

Though he felt triumphant, his blood-lust was
far from spent. To collect a span of mules, a
trader named Tibalt had traveled to Dempsey's
Cottonwood Ranch, a gathering place for both
the lawful and the lawless. The ranch was large
and prosperous, but gambling for high stakes
was its chief attraction. Tibalt, with his occasionally mobile beasts, was headed toward Virginia City, presumably enjoying the Montana
scene, content with life. He was engaged to be
married, to a Hurdy-Gurdy, and doubtless
looked forward to brisk connubial tussles at his
cabin. Then he met Ives, flushed with drink and
victory. That is, the murder and pillage of a de-
fenseless man. Without preamble, Ives shot and
killed Tibalt on the spot, relieving him of two
sacks of dust and the mules.

Here, apparently, Ives felt a certain uneasi-
ness, since both murders were unauthorized by
Plummer. He thought it prudent to hole up in the
nearby wickiup of two friends and associates.
These were Long John Franck and George Hilderman, the latter colloquially known as the
Great American Pie-eater. This nickname was

due to a malformation of Hilderman's jaw,
which seemed hinged, like that of a reticulated
python. When opened, it could accommodate
eight pieces of pie stacked one a-top the other; I
saw him do it, in the bakery. Hilderman was
modest about his gift, and demonstrated only
under pressure—usually at pistol point by some
drunk or other.

For once, news of Ives' killings spread fast,
and the still-incomplete Committee enlisted
twenty-five men, at Nevada, who set out riding
hard for Dempsey's. "We went round by the
bluff, so as to keep clear of Cottonwood and its
people," a member of the band was to write. A
testament to the toughness of these Montana
men in the Sixties may be found in Diary details
of the pursuit.

"We crossed Wisconsin Creek at half past
three in the morning, and came to a stop about
seven miles below Dempsey's; but thin ice
coated the Creek and every man emerged with
his clothes frozen tight to his body." As if this
were not enough, on the opposite bank they decided to dismount and wait, each man holding
his horse, until daybreak.

It was common knowledge (somehow) that
Ives had sought refuge in the wickiup, and the
posse comitatus heard a dog bark shortly after
dawn. "Breaking to the right and left, they
formed the surround," say records of the Vigilance Committee. The occupants were called out
one by one, with a cry that soon would cause
even the innocent to shiver, a summons to ring
down the decades in mining camps of the region: "You're wanted in Virginia City!"

Ives, at his turn, made a "laconic reply"; he

said, "All right. I expect I have to go." Then, during the ride back, he spurred his fast mare and broke for freedom, near Daley's Ranch. But two posse members rode him down, finding him crouched behind a rock. "When ordered to come forth, he did so with a light and careless laugh," according to one captor's notes.

News of the arrest rolled like a prairie fire. Throughout southern Montana riders carried the details to neighbors and settlements, and a great many people now joined the gathering crowds. So far, no organized group of horsemen had ever before taken up such pursuit on these roads, and the action was infectious. They were still pouring in during the forenoon of December 19 (next day); I stood outside Pfout's and watched, amazed. Miners, merchants, and artisans were galloping into town, and the streets were turned into mush. In the official line, the morning was spent in examination of the prisoners, in private consultations, and in considering the best methods of trial.

I believe everyone in Virginia and Nevada was there, standing knee-deep in slush or under store eaves. For now there was a solemn feeling that an important milestone lay in the offing. Faces were grim and tempers ran high as these proceedings continued. The prisoners—Ives, Hilderman, and Long John Franck—were chained with the lightest logging chain available, and the links fastened with padlocks. Then discussions began whether the trials would be held in Nevada or Virginia City.

It was an eerie scene that night in Nevada. Partisans for and against stood in cliquey knots;

flares flickered in the wind, causing the shadows to shift. Arguments, and even fights, got under way as the talks went on, unseen, unheard, behind closed doors. Perhaps I should say that, friend of the Duncans or not, and despite my theft of Plummer's list, I was not among the councils.

"A sight like this will ne'er be seen again in Montana," a man went home and wrote, but he was wrong. It was decided at length that the accused should be separated. Ives—leading malefactor of the occasion—would be tried alone. He was surrounded by as determined a group of riders as the region had ever assembled; there would be no more "break-outs."

Next day, Colonel Sanders was persuaded to conduct the prosecution, with the Hon. Charles S. Bagg as his assistant. Sanders was a Bannack lawyer, recently arrived from Ohio, the nephew of Idaho Terrotory's new Chief Justice. (Bagg was a miner, and the origin of his honorific is obscure.) Twelve men from each town were selected as jurors, and so cautious were the extraordinary moves that two Virginia men were named "amanuenses." The defense was principally conducted by Colonel J. M. Wood and Judge Thurmond, who'd been attorneys somewhere in the South; they were assisted by Messrs. Smith, Ritchie, and Davis, comparative newcomers to the area.

Professor Dimsdale, not uniquely, cared little for the farcical byplay of courtrooms, and wrote, "Among the lawyers, there was the usual amount of brow-beating and technical insolence, intermingled with displays of eloquence and learning, but not the rhetoric of Blair, the learning of Coke, the metaphysics of Alexander, the wit of Jerrold, or the odor of Oberlin could dull the perceptions of those hardy mountaineers, or . . . forbid them safety from all persons of the community, and to guarantee like protection to those who cast their future lot in Montana."

(I use this quote—which appeared in the *Post* and kicked up mild argument—because it shows so clearly the restrained element's feeling.)

When I said, before, that the miners lacked decision, I scarcely meant that their attitude was tolerant. They'd needed leaders. Now they had them, and the uproar as these hundreds of armed men marched toward Nevada was deafening. Working in conditions of grinding privation, they'd borne all they could stand. Yet they were, taken all around, a sentimental breed, and there were those to whom Ives, at his worst, had seemed a friend and a neighbor. These—many of them—grumbled and protested this final threat to his person.

The trial was held outdoors, since Nevada had no building for the purpose; and a wagon was drawn up where Judge Byam, a well-known jurist back East, could monitor the proceedings. But the *Post* claimed that "the hero of the hour was Colonel W.F. Sanders; not a desperado present but would have felt honored by becoming his murderer, and yet, fearless as a lion, he stood there confronting and defying the malice of his armed adversaries."

This certainly requires explanation. Facing the miners were, of course, most of Plummer's band as well as other thieves, brawlers, gamblers, and outlaws, who saw Ives' cause as their own. These, with a scattering of hysterically drunk derelicts, tried but failed to shout down the majority. Increasing the tension was a rumor that Plummer had sent for outlying Agents who would momentarily swoop down and effect a Delivery. (This last was false; Plummer, alerted at last, lay low.)

As sober Tribunals went, Ives' had a certain offhand charm, odd as the phrase sounds. It was inevitable, rooted deep in the character of men to whom danger was a steady companion. The five defense lawyers opened by trying to prove (on Ives' word) that he had the customary "ironclad" alibi. This was based on assurances by a pair of palpable rogues: George Brown, cardsharp and Road Agent, and Honest Whiskey Joe, whose name might have raised doubts per se. When it was shown that Brown was in Bannack, gambling, and that Honest Whiskey was asleep in a whorehouse, their alibis, as an onlooker noted—"blowed apart." A hiatus now occurred when a lawyer, not conversant with mining camps, called Colonel Sanders a name that inaccurately involved his mother. Sanders promptly slapped him with a glove and, with seconds, marched off to duel. The Eastern defense man, having gained Western tutelage in a moment, promptly apologized, and Sanders cooled down.

After hours of fevered argument—"employing all the sharp quillets of the law"—the jury retired to some trees then returned with a verdict of "Guilty!" Twenty-three had voted Yes, while a miner named Spivey declined to give a finding, for reasons unknown. Ives, through his attorneys, thereupon begged an extension of time, and a miner sang out, "Ask him how much time he give Tibalt!"

In a roundabout way, Ives then made a sort of confession. "Well," he said—and nobody noticed a suggestion of remorse—"I wasn't guilty of *this* murder!"

Without delay, Sanders mounted the wagon to call out Judge Byam's ruling that "George Ives be forthwith hung by the neck until he is dead!" A pale sun lit what I thought was a very sad countenance.

Many outlaw friends, persons who scarcely knew him, and complete strangers now pressed forward to bid Ives farewell, with loud lamentations, and even tears. Of these last, the *Post*, maintaining its usual cheery tone, said that "The vision of a long and scaly creature, inhabiting the Nile, rises before us in connection with this aqueous sympathy for an assassin."

The prisoner was quickly marched to an unfinished house whose walls alone stood firm; and a perfect Babel of cries saluted the movement. Every nearby roof was covered, and shouts of "Hang him!", "Don't hang him!", and the like were heard all around. The butt of a forty-foot pole was planted inside the building, at the foot of one wall, and a spar fashioned for a crossbeam. With a noose adjusted round his neck, Ives was asked if he had a last wish. "I've always said I would never die in my boots," was his debonair reply, and someone supplied him a pair of moccasins. Then he demanded to dictate his will, in which he left his property to his attorneys and fellow Agents, excluding his impoverished mother and sisters in Wisconsin.

A surge now rose to rescue him—"but six-hundred miners smartly leveled their rifles." Ives stepped up on a box; a cry rang out from the wagon: "Men, do your duty!" and the box was kicked from beneath his feet. Judge Byam, standing on the ground, presently called, "His neck is broken! He is dead!" Fifty-eight minutes had elapsed from verdict to execution.

Ives' body was left hanging for an hour. After this it was cut down, carried into a wheelbarrow shop, and laid out on a workbench. A guard was placed over it; then his friends carried him up the Hill to be buried. By coincidence, he was placed next to Virginia City's most recent grave—that of Nicholas Tibalt, the man he had murdered. "Assassin and victim lay side by side, their rewards in Eternity doubtless proving vastly different," wrote a Journalist.

As to George Hilderman and Long John Franck, charged as accessories, their cases were reviewed with care. After long deliberation, and conceding that neither was guilty of murder now—the prosecution let them down lightly. The Great American Pie-eater, shaking with nerves, was declared banished from Montana. "My God," he exclaimed, dropping to his knees, "is it so?" Before leaving, within the ten days alloted him, he made a statement in which he not only reaffirmed Ives' guilt, while admitting some uninspired thefts of his own, but supplied fresh facts about Plummer's Road Agents. There remain no records of his further feats with pastry.

Long John Franck was acquitted outright; and being a careless fellow, he was seen off and on in Montana for years.

Now it was hoped by all lawful citizens that Ives' fate would be a warning, and establish law and order in that region. People could walk the streets unmolested, miners could mine, and southern Montana would prosper in peace. The notion proved fallacious. Ives' trial was the beginning.

CHAPTER XIX

"Now, son, this is an informal chat—no more. Some of the members have a few questions; pray don't feel that these men are hostile. You have good friends here, advocates, as you know. But this Vigilance group is pledged to weigh everything bearing on Henry Plummer's actions and associates, and you appear to have made yourself one of the latter. Perhaps in innocence. But we shall see, carefully, jumping to no conclusions. So, in this room, as traditional in American justice, you are certainly innocent until proved guilty. I speak as an attorney with, I hope, a fair-minded history of practise."

Colonel Sanders was the man who spoke; he sat behind a rough table in this loft—a tall, slender, very dark-complexioned man with jet-black hair and neatly trimmed beard. His level dark eyes held about the same timidity, I thought, as a side-winder's, though his expression was neither harsh nor unpleasing.

Nonetheless, I felt the old dark-red flush creeping up, and I was aware that I resented everything about this meeting. The hour was midnight, the place an unheated, unfinished upper story of a new hotel-restaurant. It had a hastily-built access up a rear stairway that seemed apt to tumble down at one of the meetings soon.

James had dropped by the Forge and said, in his casual way, "You're still bunking in Jenkins' empty cabin, Chappie?"

Mr. Smithers laid down his tools, gently, not looking up, and I replied, "Yes, I thought his family might use the rent; I've set it at a hundred dollars a month."

"—which he would do, ever open-fisted with them as has less," put in my boss. "This smithy can vouch—"

"Of course," said James. "You needn't remind me," but failed to smile, as he usually did at Mr. Smithers, and went on to say, still in the same easy tones, "Why don't I drop by tonight, late. I'd like a word or two, if you aren't busy."

"Come when you please; I'll be home."

"Arrive when you please, sir," sang out my boss to his back. "You'll find all shipshape and stowed, with no occasion to strike off fetters. And if it comes to a muss-up, Ewing T. Smithers ain't exactly the man to—"

James turned, smiling at last, and waved a hand.

"Now, son Ross, I hadn't ought to have did that. But they's something riling about them messages: 'You're wanted in Virginia City!'— Oh, I've heared. They're, well, what to say?— over-pompeous and sanctimonial. There! I struck it smack on the smeller! I couldn't have did it better—not with my eddication."

"Don't worry," I said. "It had to come sometime. I'll be glad to get it over."

I followed James out of the cabin, neither of us trying to make conversation. After a detour or

two, not very confusing, we disappeared from
Wallace Street and climbed the rickety steps to
the loft.

Behind Colonel Sanders, someone had tacked
up an American flag, and, to be sure, another
member had pinned a Confederate flag
alongside. Colonel Sanders' face suggested that
this kind of by-play was unimportant, and beside the point. In one corner was an old-
fashioned safe, with a padlock, and I wondered
how it got there. Also, a thin, bespectacled fellow, stranger to me, bent, pencil in hand, over a
thick, lined notebook.

I looked around slowly, recognizing all twelve
men present. Mr. Hauser, of the bank, was on
hand, wearing a solemn countenance; and Mr.
Meninghall, who ran the store, seeming sunk in
dejection; and Mr. Beidler, the detective, with no
expression at all; and Grantly and James, of
course; Nathaniel Langford; and a Thomas
Baume—a newcomer—and others. Neil Howie,
a fellow detective with Beidler, sat sprawled in a
chair pushed back, gazing thoughtfully at his
feet.

Colonel Sanders coughed—a contrived
cough—and asked, "Did you hear me quite
clearly, son? That is, I've made these procedures
familiar; you know your rights under the law?"

"Rights?" I said in a controlled voice. "I didn't
know a prisoner had 'rights' at such a meeting.
The meeting itself has no 'rights,' to the best of
my knowledge."

The chairman seemed unoffended, in his best
courtroom fashion. His face was unchanged as
he said, "I can understand that you might be

annoyed at being dragged out of bed at
midnight—"

"He was up, reading a book," said James, and
I figured it was the best he could do in these
conditions.

"You aren't a prisoner here," said Sanders
mildly. "You can leave if you prefer. We merely
thought you might help us tie a few ends. And
what you say is true—the meeting has no legal
standing at all, beyond morality, but"—and here
he managed a wintry smile—"nothing has legal
status in Montana at the moment."

"Yes," I said, thinking I'd gone too far; "I remember the first session in Bannack, and understood the need. I was there, but my role was
different."

"Are you sure about that?" said this man
Baume. He had a nasty face, I thought then, and I
put down an urge to improve it with the heel of
my hand.

"Ross," said Grantly, "why don't you go over,
again, your journey with Jenkins? From start to
finish, and try to include any detail you remember."

Starting off slowly, trying to keep out sarcasm,
I did so, and worked my way up to the girl and
our refuge beneath the dam.

"Very likely," said Baume. "Especially in
water that cold. You jest swum under and set up
housekeeping, is that right?"

I flushed hotter and almost lost my temper, but
Beidler interrupted. "It can be done. Howie and I
rode up to the spot; it can be done."

"Well, now—Ross—that account hangs together; it's plausible to me, at least," said Colo-

nel Sanders in what then I considered a soothery, shyster sort of way. "But you certainly appear to have made yourself agreeable to Mr. Plummer. Speaking figuratively, you've been as thick as thieves. Why?"

This time I spoke up hotly. "Perhaps you forgot—I stole a pretty valuable list from his office, at some risk, I'll add."

Colonel Sanders nodded, but the egregious Baume said, "The point has risen—is the list correct? Or is it merely a net full of herring to destroy the credence of this Committee?"

I halfway rose from my chair, but James pushed me down, none too gently.

The chairman eyed me with what I later recognized as amusement; long afterward I realized he'd seen in me some qualities similar to his own at my age.

Blandly again, he said, "You have a warm temper, my friend. It's a trait I know pretty well, and it's never, to date, advanced my fortunes. In your position—"

"What position?"

"—it might be well"—he was unruffleable—"it might be well to give us what help you can. These gentlemen wish to be fair."

"Yes," I said, not much chastened, "I remember the first Vigilance meeting decided that—always—banishment would be preferable to execution, and that full evidence was required for either. Well, George Ives wasn't banished and—"

"That's enough! The evidence against him would stand up in any legal court of the land. He was, as you impertinently remind us, while we sit here doing our best, hanged, to the greater

glory of Montana. I'll add that a broad benefit of
doubt was given to Hilderman and Franck. The
former was acquitted, and the second banished;
probably," he said, "to plague innocent residents of some other region.

"Now let's cool down here. I'm sure the other
members have questions. We can go around
clockwise."

On which side of Jenkins was I riding?

Did I *find* the ball that blew off the top of his
head?

Was I *positive* that the murderers, if plural, got
the gold?

("If Nickerson hid it"—this from Beidler—
"neither Howie or I could track it down. Let the
record show that.")

Could the Indian girl speak English, or did I
coach, or threaten, her to stay silent—this, again,
from the odious Baume.

Had I ever visited Plummer at Rattlesnake
Ranch?

Had I known Plummer before these events in
Virginia City? (Baume.)

"Oh come," said Grantly, annoyed. "Ross has
been with Brother James and me since California. I regard that question as offensive."

"I only wanted to know," said Baume with
caution, knowing Grantly's skill with guns; but
there was malice in his answer.

Why did Ives address me as "deputy" in a
saloon, or, as the case might have been, outside
it?

I was bombarded (in my view) by further
queries, but none—and I took cheer from this—
by Mr. Hauser, or by Beidler or Howie, the real
detectives here.

"Son, if you'll go over once more your acquaintance with Plummer and his Agents—*all* of it, for we'll spot omissions—I'll consider this phase covered, at least for the moment."

I watched Mr. Sanders' face, and for some reason divined that this man would never suggest an impetuous action, personal insult aside, and in that case, I didn't envy the offender.

So—I rambled on, trying to remember everything, calmed down at last, and when I finished, the chairman banged his gavel and said, "We stand adjourned." I could see Baume's dissatisfaction, wishing to continue yapping, but he never had a chance. I don't believe I ever hated a man as I did him at that moment, and when we descended the flimsy exit, I maneuvered myself behind him, the last in line.

Somehow, at about the third rung from the bottom, I lurched forward, and he tumbled head foremost into the snow. Nobody—not even a saint—could have been more solicitous than myself in picking him up, brushing off snow, plucking mud from his face, and the like. But I was surprised that he seemed ungrateful, stamping off with a series of oaths to do credit to a miner. They almost, but not quite, drowned out what I'm certain was a low chuckle from a retreating Colonel Sanders.

CHAPTER XX

SOUTHERN MONTANA STAYED in a state of boiling ferment for weeks after Ives' trial and execution. The chief reason was that neither side stood still for a moment. "All the prominent friends of justice were dogged, threatened and watched," wrote a resident, "but the Roughs' day was passing and the dawn of a better state of things was . . . enlivening the gloom which over-spread society like a funeral pall."

The "threatening" developed quickly. On the night of Ives' hanging, Colonel Sanders sat quietly reading in John Creighton's store (his main office still in Bannack) when a "desperado" named Harvey Meade walked into the room, a revolver prominently stuck in his belt. He began pelting Sanders with a string of obscenities (and threats) that might have caused a lesser man to complain. Sanders continued reading for a space, then removed an over-and-under derringer from his pocket, cocked it, and laid it on a table beside him.

Looking up, Sanders observed, "Harvey, I should feel hurt if some men said this, but from such a dog as you it is not worth noticing."

Several persons were in the store, discussing events, and a doctor, alarmed for Sanders' safety, put his hand on a pick handle. At the same moment, Creighton (the proprietor) bravely approached the ruffian and said, "Now you get out of here, and be damned quick about it!" Meade lost color and backed out of the doorway, his courage only briefly strengthened by liquor. Next day he tried to apologize in the street, and received a curt nod and a smile.

Soon after, when the now-solidified Vigilance Committee checked Meade's background, they uncovered the most bizarre crime they were to consider. It was not of local origin. Meade, it seemed, had recently left California at top speed, having been the prime mover in an attempt to seize and make off with a Federal gunboat at San Francisco. He had some notion of selling the unlikely package in Chile. Since he and his confederates had never so much as rowed a skiff across a river, as far as police determined, the try was viewed as hilarious. For a while, it was the best joke in California. The Committee (and Sanders) dismissed him as a harmless lunatic, and he was seen no more at Virginia City.

Then, as the strangely obtuse Plummer accelerated the offenses of his Agents, the Vigilantes voted to round the gang up. A "Flying Squadron" of horsemen again took to the trail, equipped with all confessions, dossiers, and certain knowledge to date. Their more physical equipment consisted of two revolvers each, a rifle, a shotgun, blankets, bacon and beans, and rope (emphasis supplied by a Journalist). This grim-faced party left Virginia City, riding in a snowstorm.

Their quick departure was triggered by a murder that Plummer must have known would raise a hue and cry. His conduct now seemed suicidal. It reminded me, and Mr. Smithers—both back at the smithy, with iron to spare—of highlights in his California history made known to a trusted few. Even Plummer's mother, if any, would have seen his actions as self-destructive. He purposefully concentrated on the most esteemed residents of the area. He even abandoned the hit-or-miss slaughter of stranger-travelers and the robbing of gold-laden coaches. What he wanted—clearly—was revenge.

Mr. Smithers "opined," while re-shoeing an ox (different from horseshoeing since two pieces must be made for an ox's cloven hoof), that Plummer had lost what little sanity the Lord provided him, and he dragged in a Biblical precedent so inappropriate that even he puzzled it over awhile.

Lloyd Magruder was one of Virginia City's most respected merchants, an honest, kindly fellow who'd first come from Lewiston, capital of Idaho Territory. He'd arrived in a wagon with his family and a load of trade goods, opened a store, and become a town favorite. But as Ives' trial left its rumble of warfare coming, he'd decided to deposit $14,000 back in Lewiston, several hundred miles distant across the Divide. Plummer promptly held what he called a "Tribunal" at Rattlesnake Ranch and delivered a verdict of his own. "Rob and kill Magruder!"

Now my relation to the Agents (who daily walked our streets) and to Plummer himself had degenerated to a sarcastic pretense that I was a main strategist. I might be accosted in full view of friends and told by some jackass, "Don't forget—Rattlesnake. Planning Session—Midnight tonight!" And then, with finger to lips, mock-furtive looks right and left, and other senseless contortions, the dunce would make off, crying "Shush!", "Not a word!", "Bottle it!", and the like. This expanding joke refreshed them, but did me little good. I was in enough trouble as matters stood.

Well, one of their number, Red Yeager— probably as wild an Agent as developed in Plummer's school for scoundrels—remained, I'm convinced, in the dark whether I was or was not one of the band. The murderous buffoon stopped me near the Sheriff's office one noon to say, "Likely you've heard the news—Magruder's up for wholesale."

I paid no attention, for he was leaning from his horse, leaking tobacco juice from the walnut-sized cud that swelled his be-whiskered features. But later, the advice irked me and I told Mr. Smithers, who promptly advised, "Lay down them tongs, sir, and relay it immedjit to Professor Duncan. Do so without loitering, if I may seggest." (Mr. Smithers often confused Grantly's name with that of Professor Dimsdale, owing to the former's more scholarly mien.)

When I hiked down Wallace Street, I found that Grantly (and others) already had wind of the council. After Plummer issued the death warrant, several Agents rebelled for the first time. One told him it meant "certain hanging," to which the enigmatic leader replied, "Those who don't hang together will assuredly hang separately"—an allusion doubtless lost on the majority. Specifically (as the Vigilantes learned) Steve Marshland declined in ringing, risky terms, in view of Plummer's volatile nature. "I'm on the rob but not on the kill," and he left the council intact for the moment.

"Magruder has a good start, I'm afraid," Grantly told me, "but we've dispatched a fast scout to the Squadron." (As stated, names of active Vigilantes were never made public, though they were not quite secret, either. To this day I'm unaware what part the Duncans played, or even Hauser and Langford; Colonel Sanders was certainly the active head. And the term "Flying Squadron" was interchanged with "Troopers" and others. All in all, the Vigilante operation was a study in strategic and tactical security. Perhaps Beidler and Neil Howie, who openly did detective work, were the sole members known positively to residents. The detectives, supported by citizen contributions, were the only members paid.)

On Marshland's defection, Plummer increased to five the number to be slaughtered, having heard that Magruder was traveling with four other men and some cattle. Red Yeager, in his absent-minded niche as "letter-carrier," rode to alert outlying Agents, and Magruder was found grazing his stock near the Clearwater.

He'd strayed a mile from his companions, who lay sleeping in camp, exhausted from night watches. The reports were inexplicit about the Agents involved in the following, but what took place was this: Magruder was murdered—in the common phrase of "cold blood"—by an Agent he took to be a friend, and all four others were shot and killed in their sleep.

Hearing the news, the Squadron was as coldly enraged as Plummer ever had been, and, not sure of the culprits, went at full gallop after any known Agents on those northwest routes. They followed up all reports and rumors, and at last seized Red Yeager and George Brown ("secretary"), the first at Rattlesnake Ranch, the second toward Deer Lodge. Both confessed to warning several Agents near Dempsey's and elsewhere, using a code message: "Get up and dust, and lie low for black ducks." The quaint advice had doubtless been composed by Plummer, its exact meaning lost to Montana history.

The Squadron's ensuing actions were brisk and unemotional. At first they sang out the summons: "You're wanted in Virginia City!" but the weather being treacherous, with a threat of deep snow, they changed plans. At the "shebang," or ranch, owned by a man named Loraine, the charges were jointly read to the prisoners, and Yeager, in the final hours of his life, flashed out like a hero.

He said, in effect, according to witnesses, "Of course I'm guilty, and I'll die happy to know that some others will get it, too." Assured that, on this score at least, he could rest in peace, he sat at a table and drew up a full list of Plummer's men, giving their titles, duties, and deeds. (Part was a duplicate of the list I found in Plummer's office.) Then, his memory further refreshed, he recalled a long, grisly string of slayings, robberies, beatings, stage hold-ups, and other crimes that a student in villainy must admire. For all bore the inspirational stamp of Plummer, the arch planner and rogue.

In short, Yeager confessed everything in detail, and expressed remorse at the dreadful life he'd lived. He felt, he said, that he merited hanging, and he mentioned, offhand, that his companion, George Brown, did, too; he specified that Brown had participated in several previous murders.

Brown took exception to Yeager's remarks. He admitted only to carrying Plummer's curious letters of warning to several Agents as the Troopers advanced. Also, he verified Yeager's absurd tales of ritual. All Agents used the password, "Innocent," which even the prisoners thought incongruous; their neckerchiefs were tied in sailor knots, for no good reason; and they were required, by Plummer, to wear moustaches and "chin whiskers." It seemed that Plummer often had little to do, and as he sat in his office, brooding, these small, lunatic scraps crossed his mind. It would be hard to hit on identifying marks more quickly recognizable, unless the men had worn sandwich signs saying "Road Agent."

"Men," the Squadron's captain called, after all evidence, and confessions, had been offered, "you've heard what these rogues had to say. Vote according to your conscience. If you think they deserve punishment, say so. If they should go free—vote for that. We've had long rides in terrible weather, and endured grinding hardship. But that's no matter. Be careful to do the right thing—for yourselves and the prisoners. All those in favor of hanging, step to the right; those for letting them go, step to the left."

Without hesitation, every man present moved to the right. Night had fallen, the ground was white, the cold bitter. Nevertheless it was decided to take Brown and Yeager to a clump of cottonwoods, on a curve of the Pas-sam-a-ri River. A light sifting of snow still fell, and a

Trooper inscribed in his Diary how odd Yeager's fiery red whiskers looked with "their Christmas mantle at this reluctant and unholy moment."

Two lanterns were held high, and a Trooper trimmed a tree of low branches with an axe. Then stools from the ranch-house were placed side by side. Brown was first to mount, but once on the stool, the knot beneath his left ear, he pleaded piteously for his Indian wife. He swore to leave and start a decent life elsewhere. His cries so unnerved a man handling the rope and stool that both he and Brown tumbled clumsily into the snow.

"You'll have to do better than that," observed Yeager cheerfully. A minute later all was made fast. Brown's stool was kicked away, his neck audibly cracked, and his body hung loosely; he was dead.

When the final seconds came for Yeager, he added to his former recital, standing on the stool. A dossier says that "No sign of trepidation was visible. His voice was as calm and quiet as if conversing with old friends." He spoke up to say, "Boys, you've treated me like a gentleman. I know I'm going to die, and I've got it coming."

"Yes, Red," a Trooper replied in a low voice, "it's hard. It's pretty rough."

"I deserved this years ago," the prisoner went on. "Now I want to say goodbye. God bless you, boys! You're on a good undertaking." After these words, the stool was yanked free, and Yeager's body swung beside Brown's in the ghostly lantern light.

Standing in the half-dark, Troopers prepared labels to pin to the suspended bodies. Yeager's said, "RED—ROAD AGENT AND MESSENGER!" Brown's read, "BROWN—CORRESPONDING SECRETARY!"

The tree was blazed, and it still may be seen, near Loraine's Ranch, an unhappy reminder of two lives wasted.

A footnote to Magruder's murder and the executions was seen in the spring, when the snows melted, "run-off" started from the peaks, and wild flowers began their annual struggle upward. Women near the Clearwater River found a few bones, several buttons from someone's coat, and the rusty remains of a rifle and pistol. The winter had been hard, with small game scarce, and coyotes had finished the work begun by the merchant's killers.

"You'll be surprised at what I have to say," said Grantly, when he and James and I met again in their cabin. "It has to do with Red Yeager, and I've never discussed this even with James—"

"Erastus Yeager?" asked his brother.

"You've known then? You're a curious fellow, James."

"No more than yourself. I'd hoped he wasn't the same person. But the letters taken from his pocket make it clear. Pity."

Grantly sat looking through the fire, back into the past. "The letters were addressed to kinfolk in the small town of West Liberty, Iowa. I may have said, in the past, that my first recollections were of Virginia. But our father had such an adventurous turn that he soon began the hippety-hops that saw us, finally, in land the government bought from the Musquawkee Indians. An area now known as Iowa. We took up a claim, as was the custom then—"

"Claim number sixteen," said James.

"You remember that? Odd—you never mention Iowa, and I've avoided the subject, feeling there was something—"

"You needn't analyze it. Just go on."

"Yes. Well, it was a lovely land, there were a few other settlers, and the Musquawkee were good and helpful neighbors. You'll recall that they used to offer us nostrums against the ague. Nearby we had two broad, winding creeks that, in warm weather, swarmed with mosquitoes in such numbers that their larvae—known as wiggletails—made the water undrinkable till Mother strained it through cotton cloth—"

"Not 'creeks'—'runs,' the name we'd used in Virginia. People laughed at us. I whipped a kid for it."

"We had the ague, badly; all the whites did. I remember how the cup rattled when I tried to drink, and my spleen—called the 'melt' in those days—swelled up as hard as iron beneath my ribs. The trouble recurred years after we'd moved out of those bottoms."

"It still plagues me," said James. "Called malaria, now. I've had it this winter. Not only chill weather brings it on; it seems to go hand-in-hand with bad times like these."

"You, too? You've never said so."

"Maybe stick to Iowa."

Grantly started to ask a question, then decided to continue. "The Indians were good to us. We played with the Indian children, and their mothers gave us maple sugar. They lived, as I remember, in decent bark huts—"

"—while the whites pushed in to take their lands and kill off the game."

"It was around 1840—am I right?—that our father moved to higher ground. And a better house, where the prairie began. Fine timber lay behind us—walnut, elm, hackberry, oak, hard maple, of course, butternut, and hickory. And in front the prairie rolled on, I thought, to the end of the world. Oceans of waving grass, and scrub bush, and the steady danger of roaring fires that frequently swept across. Started by lightning, I suppose. But our house was never caught, not once.

"Altogether we were four or five white families, and it was my father's notion to build a schoolhouse. I may have mentioned that he was an ardent reader of books—too steep for a child's understanding, though I tried. The school's logs were not even hewed or peeled. For windows, for light, we had a space cut lengthwise and covered with greased paper, and nearly one whole end was a huge stone fireplace. The floor was earth, solid packed, and nothing else.

"At first, summer was the school season. We sat barefoot on slab benches without backs and listened to a young woman of the neighborhood. She was paid, I believe, six dollars a month, and was worth two hundred. For texts we had Webster's Speller and Pike's, Dobolt's, Colbert's, and then McGuffey's readers.

"When children grew large enough to help at home—gardening, hunting, tending horses and mules—sessions were held in winter, the room not quite heated by the smoky fireplace. Between us and the timber ran a beautiful clear river, and when it froze, every year, James and I skated to school with some fine Dutch skates that our father traded game for—"

"Brother James did the skating, especially when the wind blew," said James, "and Brother Grantly held on to his coattails."

"I hadn't planned to bring that up, but let it stand. Father often worked as a surveyor, and he was a really famous shot. He owned two guns—a Virginia flintlock for big game, and a small-bore rifle for hunting birds in the prairie. We had venison, wild turkey, prairie chickens, beaver, squirrels in abundance, and—odd to think of now, in Iowa—dried elk meat hanging always from the beams. Then there was the river—it swirled and splashed with trout; you seldom cast a hook without bringing in a fish weighing several pounds. Father made a walnut canoe so steady that two men could stand on a rail, and, with someone holding a quart of lard with a lighted rag-wick, we cruised the river at night, gigging trout attracted by the flare. A normal night's take was upward of fifteen large fish, but some of these were gars, too bony to clean and eat. Mother somehow cooked all game in a Dutch oven. We ate well, even during the terrible winter of 1843.

"Now—the word 'Dutch' brings me to a red-haired schoolmate, bright, quick, maybe over-rambunctious, but as good a companion as a boy could wish. His name was Erastus Yeager, of a decent German family, and we called him, as the custom was, 'Dutch.' In a year or so his parents moved into town, and I never thought to meet him again. I was wrong. Here in Montana he's always been known as 'Red,' and I rode out to see him today, hanging from a tree-limb near

Loraine's. I'd recognized him when we first lit in Bannack, but he didn't know me—these gray hairs! And for some reason I never told him who I was. The company he kept, I suppose, and the rampages with Plummer. But when I stood near that tree, all I could see was a feisty youngster of twelve or thirteen, skating, wrestling, hunting, struggling with his lessons. I—" Grantly subsided, and James poked thoughtfully at the fire.

Grantly said finally, "Of all our schoolmates, I remember Dutch best. Dutch and the most ravishing, flaxen-haired creature God ever made. Ann? Well, Ann what? Yes, Ann Beecher. She married, I believe; some sort of scandal—ran off with a slick, smooth-talking charlatan who—"

We looked up. James had risen abruptly and gone to his room.

Walking home, I thought suddenly that Grantly hadn't spoken in the ornate diction of his usual style. It was curious; his writing was not in that vein, either. On the contrary, it was simple, objective journalism. Retreating into Iowa, into childhood, I supposed, had meant talking in different terms. Then it struck me that the learned pose had been the gift of that father, the scholar who made a show of reading great books, who taught Grantly a "smattering of Latin" (as he told me once) and, probably, flaunted his erudition, with enough contempt to scar at least one son.

With only a few years of schooling, Grantly felt constrained to an emulation of that insensitive parent. James, too, had been scarred, but in another way—driven into thoughtful silence and the need to be often alone. And, I surmised, the empty-headed Miss Beecher had added the telling blow. But I doubted if that story would ever be told by the victim, and it never was. Plainly enough, it was a place of pain, its aftermath kept quiet. I remembered from an earlier confidence that James had disappeared, when nearing his twenties, and lived a reckless life for two or three years. There was even trouble with the law, a shooting, and then he'd returned to the prairie, subtly changed.

What hurts children are given by self-absorbed parents! I thought with relief that I'd escaped all these, and was wrong. Ours was a family of generosity, concern, discipline. But no warmth or affection existed there; no single motherly hug, no fatherly pat on the back. Nothing but secret talks with my sister, who, I suddenly realized, would never be married, ever. She'd been treated, by my father, as a second son, and now shrank from any show of softness. I'd become aware of the reason I valued an occasional embrace by the Duncans. James, in lifting me off the floor, once brought a stab to my chest, and I'd never understood till now.

Oh, well, I said aloud to the stars, Heaven save us from the curse of self-pity!

CHAPTER XXI

As THE COMMITTEE stepped up its drive, Plummer refined his swagger. Rules and intent of the Vigilantes now were circularized, but his Agents seemed firmly under the spell of their leader. The Vigilante Oath had been posted on walls for all to read: "We, the undersigned, uniting ourselves in a Party for the purpose of arresting thieves and murderers, and recovering stolen property, do pledge ourselves upon our sacred honor, each to all others, and solemnly swear that we will reveal no secrets, violate no laws of Right, and not desert each other or our standards of justice. So help me God as witness our hand and seal this 23rd day of December, 1863."

Despite the phrase "We, the undersigned—," no signatures were affixed to the public notices. I thought the document carelessly drawn, in the emotion of the moment, and might better have gone un-displayed. Word of mouth would have served equally well.

A humane touch was added to information made public, and was widely admired. The length of rope used for hangings would be thirty inches—this considered long enough to break a man's neck rather than leave him strangling. I heard a miner say, near the new barber shop, "Now I regard that as handsome. Some of them skunks ort to strangle, and do it all night, and the

most of them, they know it, like Red's penitentiary aboard the stool."

If my version sounds frivolous, I make apology. But there *was* a wide variance in the methods
of hanging. A snapped neck meant instant death,
without suffering; the punishment endured,
with benefit of law, for decades thereafter. It was
endorsed and directed by the nation's highest
citizens, like Governors and other dignitaries.
But strangulation was slow torture, worthy of a
Church Inquisition.

Plummer's immediate response to the posted
compacts was to organize target-shoots at his
Rattlesnake Ranch. Aside from the office in Virginia, he had dozens of additional roosts. But the
chief of these was Rattlesnake, some miles up the
Gulch. Historians have worked hard to unravel
Plummer's skein of hideouts; they extended
throughout the Rockies. He, certainly, posted no
plans, place-names. For years after the Vigilantes, efforts were continued to trace even an
outline of his operations, and count the men at
his command. Stage coach robberies in Colorado, others far West across the Divide, were laid
to his cunning and to outlaws he trained. It was
concluded—based on confessions and detec-
tions of Beidler and Howie—that besides the 102
authenticated murders directed by Plummer, as
many more were committed without discovery.

"Who would miss the lone, stranger-miner
waylaid, robbed of his gold, and his throat cut?"
asked a Committee-member's Journal. "And, if
he were buried, who was to find his body? The
Gulch was littered with bones; animals dug
them up in all ravines. What group of miners,
avid after riches, felt disposed to attend human

bones? They lay everywhere then in southern Montana."

Many literate men made notes, wrote Diaries, or kept Journals, sent descriptive letters home, or, like Professor Dimsdale, dashed off articles about events as they happened. All these writers were frustrated how to place each detail in accurate sequence, especially so laboring in a terrible winter, placed without communications in a region with no jails, police, or official records. About the Magruder murders, for instance, a notebook hints that several men—Plummer's —were hanged in Idaho Territory's capital of Lewiston afterward. But the report is blurred and unconvincing. As for Yeager and Brown, in their roles as "letter-carriers," they were indirectly, at least, responsible for many murders and robberies, and other crimes. And Yeager himself, standing on the fatal stool, with no hope of reprieve, admitted, among other things, that "I've had this coming for years." The words that night of a Trooper, or Vigilante, should influence the most suspicious legal purist. He said, not enjoying his role: "You know, Red, that men have been shot down in broad daylight—not for money, or even for hatred, but for *luck!* And it must be put a stop to!" The assertion was transcribed by several for posterity.

With the Vigilantes firmly resolved, and no thought of retreating, the egregious Plummer displayed the fatal flaw of history's power-mad tyrants; he pathetically tried to keep step.

At Rattlesnake he increased his shooting, erecting a sign-post two rods in front of the ranch house. He had his Agents whirl, draw, and fire—over and over again. And so greatly did

they fear him that they gained in accuracy and
speed even when they weren't much interested,
preferring to be indoors beating back the chill
with Tanglefoot.

They were all capital shots. Plummer was
supposed to be the quickest revolver hand of any
man in the mountains. He could draw his pistol
and discharge its five loads in three seconds, a
man told me. The post was riddled with holes,
and was looked on as a curiosity, until it was cut
down the next summer.

And into the midst of this strife rode—Slade.
Discharged from his job with Overland, he
brought an Eastern wife to a spread he established on the Madison River, not far from Virginia. There he settled in to pursue his old trade
of freighting—alone, now. From every standpoint, he'd picked the worst of all possible
moments to visit his ungovernable habits on a
district whose patience with violence was gone.

Mr Smithers and I were making an ox-yoke,
while rumors gathered that Plummer personally
was under discussion by Vigilantes. There was
no specific outrage of the instant; the reason, as a
miner wrote, "If you're aiming to kill a snake,
you'd better take and lop off its head."

I suppose that, with improved rhetoric, the
Vigilantes proceeded on about that line. The
Road Agents were to be removed, cautiously,
justly, and completely. The limit had been
reached, as stated, but no Vigilante felt an urge to
haste or errors in judgment.

At the forge, Mr. Smithers and I conducted a
running dialogue of banter, philosophy, and

(I'm afraid) idiotic questions about religion. Religion had diminished in him, but it was hardly deceased. Most times, with the fire pumped to white-glow by Páh-ta-se, our attention was too preoccupied for speech. For Mr. Smithers, these, I expect, were the good times. Even so, he remained the best-natured boss conceivable. And often he was sharply entertaining as well. His chief trouble, if he had un-physical troubles, came from confusion about the Bible (which I privately thought he'd never read through) and, to be sure, his speech from the Kentucky hills and his near-cockney forebears. The truth is that I liked him as well as anyone I ever met, and his fellow townsmen held him in awed esteem. He was a master artisan, and no mistake.

The ox-yoke had presented some small problems, one being that our iron strap appeared partly crystallized. Mr. Smithers tossed it away, to resume with a piece from the eighteen-foot rods now possible to buy, off and on (when the Missouri was high) from Fort Benton. Here I tried to persuade him that a bad ox-yoke was better than no yoke at all, and it seemed a pity to waste iron. But he replied, clinking and hammering, "Son, the day Ewing T. Smithers offers a hand-flawed article to a God-fearing client will be Judgment Day Eve! Place that in your sneezer, my boy, and bank on it."

"Well," I said, downcast, "that's a yoke on me. And it's a yoke on the oxen, too. They don't know how bad a yoke they're carrying, and don't care. They'd likely be content with no yoke at all."

"Now, son, you're only trying to place an itch

betwixt my shoulders. You know we've contracted for an ox-yoke, and a stout yoke we'll
deliver; kindly swaller the news.''

"And there's another thing. How do you
know, how do we ever know, whether a client's
God-fearing or not? It never shows on them, the
condition they're in. I'll tell you what," I said
briskly, "and intending respect for all. I'd make a
wager that if Providence was sitting here, whit-
tling or passing the time, while waiting for a
stew-pan or a round of carbuncle spurs, and encountered one of these tobacco-chewing, gun-
toting miners, He'd light out up the hill like a
cougar. It'd make good sense. He doesn't wear a
gun, as you know. In other words, where's your
God-fearing client then?''

Mr. Smithers sighed. "Ross, son, I believe
you'd try the patience of forty saints—make that
forty-one for luck. Now you're aware you mean
sacrilegious, and it don't become you." He laid
down a beech-burl mallet and said, "I'll ankle up
home for the mid-dayer. You're welcome to
come, un-Godly statements or not.''

Feeling guilty as usual, I said, "I brought a
sandwich, Mr. Smithers, I thank you all the
same." And when he hung up his burn-spotted
apron, "I was only funning; it's a poor habit. I'll
try to get over it.''

"When the day comes that you—one of our
own—can disturb Ewing T. Smithers, he'll lay
aside his princers and tongs and take to hanging
drapes." And then, getting back some of his
own, "I regard you, son, as my share of Job's
boils. They gall at the forge, and they scrape
when I set. But I'd be bereft without them." And
smiling, he stumped up the street.

"I'll finish the yoke!" I shouted after him.
"And I'll do a good job—that's a promise." He
only waved, chuckling, and I set to work, hoping
to make up my nonsense.

Then there rode into our place, stopping with
a scramble and sliding of hooves, the person
who would change many things for me. A woman, or girl, of so reckless and bold a manner
that I dropped Mr. Smithers' grandfather's an-
tique "snitzel," or drawing knife (for an ox-yoke
is mainly wood, with iron laid on for support),
and straightened up, cold as ice.

Not once before, ever, had I seen a creature
similar in style, flair—whatever the words are.
For the moment I was struck dumb, forced back
to school days, and what came to mind lacked
meaning, for it was daylight now, though we
were shadowed in the Forge; and it was something like, "Her beauty lay on the cheek of night
like a jewel in an Ethiope's ear"—maybe from
reading in college.

Then I recovered myself slightly and said,
"Yes, Ma'am. Smithers and Nickerson at your
service." But I must have stared, or perhaps
seemed stupid, for she burst into laughter.

She slid expertly off the horse (a mean-looking
stud), a slender but filled-out girl in a careless
blouse, wide leather belt, and tight, worn jeans,
with boots and silver rowel spurs. But she hadn't
the look of caring whether the spurs were silver
or not; she looked, in fact, as if she cared about
very little in this lifetime. How little I would
learn, and live with, and live without, and never
be less confused than I was at this moment.

Her horse had an English saddle and bit, and
single reins, and yet she'd flown down the street

like a Comanche, coming to stop like the wildest
horseman in Plummer's band. She gave a half-
heeding sweep-back to her hair, which was
raven-black, parted in the middle, and tied in
back with a piece of ordinary twine. I'd lived
once amidst people of fortune, and somehow she
gave the impression of wealth—and indifference
to her station.

"Smithers? Or is it Nickerson?"

"Smithers," I said, as tense as a boy at his first
party. "That is, I mean—Nickerson."

"It doesn't matter much, does it, young fellow?"

It was a saving observation for me, since I'd
long smarted from youthful looks. So I felt my
spunk rising.

"Not younger than yourself, Ma'am. It only
matters because I'm the town youngster. All decided, and cut to measure. It might be worthwhile once, before I'm buried, to be seen as fully
grown."

Her clear blue eys changed to violet, or so it
seemed. She said, "I stand rebuked." Then she
added, as if it explained everything, "You look
like my brother. This devil's horse has a loose
shoe, maybe two—can you mend them?"

"Seat yourself, Ma'am, and I'll cast my eye
over the problem."

"I'll watch."

"It's lunch-time, or mid-dayer, as we say here.
The Virginia Hotel, new, clean, safe for single
ladies—"

"I prefer to watch."

The last thing I wanted was to work under that
probing stare. But I took a deep breath and prepared to fetter the stud's hind feet.

"One front shoe off. The other off soon—if you go on racing through loose stones and mud." The comment was aimed to regain my maturity. Besides, I now felt a certain confidence.

Meanwhile, she'd flung herself into our split-bottom chair, one leg indecorously draped over an arm. After (apparently) some amused thought, she said: "New England."

"You come from New England, Ma'am?

"Speech, accent, quickness to resent. What's a man—an elderly man—like you doing out here shoeing horses?"

"I'm in it for the money, Ma'am." (The question had begun to gall me.) "It's a noble profession. You're acquainted with the late Tubalcain? Vulcan?"

"Never heard of 'em. Friends of yours?"

I looked up sharply.

"Quick to resent that, too."

I returned to work, cutting the old nails with a buffer and removing the shoe with pincers. After I'd become adjusted to the eyes on my back, I added some extra flourishes, humming offhand as if this were routine and might lead, later, to the hammering out of a steam locomotive.

Then a second horse came sliding up, in about the same style as the first, and I turned to see, dismounting, Slade. I recognized him well enough from his fight with James in Bannack. In dress he was an raffish as the girl was slack, and finally I understood that I had here the legendary and passionately devoted wife, whose beauty people talked about but seldom saw. The fit mate, as Professor Dimsdale would write, for the man "who should have lived in feudal times, and been the companion of Front de Boeufs, De Lacys, and Bois Guilberts—"

He'd been drinking, but when he saw me, the gaze fixed for a moment, he touched his hat, and said, "I believe you saw me take a whipping, sir."

I wished him good health, and said I hadn't relished it. He'd drunk just enough to make the gray eyes glow, and I figured he'd shoot me when he got around to it. He generally shot much of what he saw when drinking, but he remained polite and courteous.

"Could I ask how much longer you'll be?"

I estimated the job to require twenty minutes more, and he said to the girl, "I'll step back to the Exchange."

"Why don't you wait here? Mr. Smithers was telling me about his friends. He has some wonderful friends, right here in town. Man named Tubular Cane. That's more than we've got."

"*Tubal* cain, a Biblical smith now living in Deer Lodge," and I took a prefessional whack at Mr. Smithers' new buckle, breaking it into three or four pieces.

"You've annoyed Mr. Nickerson," said Slade mildly. "Why can't you control your speech?"

"*I!*"

He turned gravely to me and said, "We see few people, sir, but we'd be honored to have you ride out for dinner. My wife wants for company of her own kind."

"Whoever said so? And what kind would that be?"

"I'm told the Devil, too, has his Twelve Apostles; no disrespect, sir," and he mounted, wheeled, and leaped into a gallop down the street, just perceptibly swaying.

I stood waiting.

"Oh, come if you like. But don't expect anything. There'll be trouble today," she said, reflecting. She took her handsomely tapered leg off the chair-arm, somewhat to my relief. I wondered how she'd got into the pants. "Who cares?"

I said, "I'll come another time."

"Do or don't."

When the job was finished, she asked, "How much?"

I was prepared to offer the work free, and throw in Mr. Smithers' tools, and the hearth, and maybe the Indian. But I had an obligation to my boss and to my labor as well. "A dollar, Ma'am, by going scales."

She tossed two notes onto the chair and said, "One's for you."

I picked it up with tongs and placed it on the coals. For a second I thought she might strike me with her quirt. But she burst into laughter instead, mounted the horse by throwing herself over its back like an Indian, and sprang away with a single spurred leap. Still, the encounter was not quite finished. In a couple of minutes she trotted back, slapped her horse's head down when it reared, and said, "Come Wednesday week. But remember—it wasn't my idea."

Some time past noon, Slade rode into a new saloon, bought his horse a bottle of expensive wine, and tried to make him drink it. The animal refusing, Slade swept the saloon's scales out of doors, broke up the bar, and cursed everyone in the place. People stood aside as the freighter rode up and down Wallace Street, yelling and firing two revolvers, with two stranger-companions mounted behind him on his lathered-up stallion.

Miner friends I talked to, when we'd closed the Forge, said Slade wreaked damage on several store-fronts but hesitated, finally backing off, at Lott Brothers' Emporium, newly established in the Virginia-Nevada district. The elder Lott was a man of indefinite reputation; he'd once advised Slade, in the street, that he and his brother would "hunt you down and kill you if you cause us the slightest trouble again."

Slade stopped at Lotts' and blinked at the sign, while his fellow drunks urged him on. Then he jerked the horse's head around and trotted slowly back into Virginia. "He was not frightened," wrote Grantly long afterward. "He knew in his heart that his time was growing short, and he hoped to prolong the Jekyll-Hyde existence."

A few minutes after this, swiping both men from the mount into the dirt, Slade made off whooping in the direction of home. Probably it's as well he did; I heard later that both Lotts were behind their counter, hopeful looks on their faces, with short double shotguns pointed at the door.

One of the strangest aspects of Alder Gulch violence was the separation as between Slade and Plummer's Road Agents. There was never a hint that Slade and Plummer ever met, though surely their paths must often have crossed. I myself never saw Slade talking to Plummer or any of his band; I think, now, that all were afraid of Slade. There was something about those maniacal rages that put the toughest of them off. Certainly none ever stepped forward during one of his sprees or was known to have accosted him during their own rampages around town.

The truth is that Slade, though he killed and destroyed in temper, had never robbed, stolen, cheated, or distinguished himself in the Plummer style. Plummer's band murdered for gain, and occasionally for fun, or luck. But the basic aim was gold. Also, Slade had never killed in the Alder Gulch region. Many a witness, however, described his crazed disposition of thieves or, even, incompetents when with Overland. His background of personal fury was so awesome that everyone, including Plummer, was content to leave him alone.

CHAPTER XXII

MEANWHILE THE STALKING of Plummer's certified offenders continued. The situation was curious. These men passed freely in and out of town, like respectable folk. Yet each knew he was a hair's breadth from ignominious death. It was their code to take all things mortal very lightly. A result was, naturally, that it endeared many to persons who still might have voted to hang them. Excepting two or three—monsters beyond Dante's nightmares—they were at once admired and deplored, sources of entertainment, providing jokes in the saloons. Some of their bloodiest feats were seen with a kind of pride. Words like, "You hear what old Whiskey Bill done over at Beaverhead last week?" were not uncommon, the implication being that he somehow represented Virginia City.

And if these outlaws dismissed their fates, exchanged pleasantries while committing crimes and even at their executions, the newspapers fell into the same vein. This was a hard land, and the slightest show of softness would have been treated with scorn. This being so, the papers strove with phrases to suit the mood and occasion. Happy predictions often emerged before the fact, and the villains mentioned, instead of horsewhipping the editor, showed the paper around, happy to have made the news.

The paragraphs irked Grantly, who said they were "tasteless," and inscribed this (with dilations) in his Journal. But I found them funny and, I think, James did, too. Each citizen probably had his favorite. The *Bannack Press* (it was thought) achieved rare heights with "A Vigilante hints that So-and-so may soon be a candidate for Hempen Honors." Well, the author of that inspiration liked it fine, and the *Press* used it over and over. "Hempen honors" was an undeniable favorite, on every tongue, but our own *Montana Post*, while reeling from the journalist peak, righted itself with "Strangulation Jig." (This last was written *after* the fact, the *Post* publishing in Virginia, within easy access if a band-member unaccountably took offense.) Even the *Sacramento Union*, to which former Californians wrote from this swarming hive, made its feebler attempt to join the competition. "Necktie party" is believed to have been its conception, and the paper took credit without protest. Other terms were equally jolly and macabre. "Neckerchief waltz," "tree-limb tarantella," and "suspended animation" were in the van of these. Since most doomed Agents met their end pushed (or leaping) from a dry-goods box, the ever-alert press fell into a habit of keeping "the box score," then continued to dig for further inventions.

The miner's reference to "Old" Whiskey Bill was a standby, a mark of affection, not limited to Road Agents. Any male of whatever age was "Old" Somebody-or-other, if he'd somehow established his identity. Many southern Montana terms passed into the language, and remain there. Some were noted in the Journal of an Alexander McClure, a traveling Pennsylvanian. If a man was "embarrassed"—financially or physically—he was also "corraled," McClure felt. Thus "Indians corraled men on the Plains; storms corraled Emigrants in the mountains; tender swains are corraled by crinoline"—etc. The most popular advice to vacate was "You git!"; an "outfit" was "everything from a plains-train to a pocket-knife to a wife, a horse a dog, a cat, or a row of pins"; a "layout" was "any proposed enterprise, from organizing a State to digging out a prairie dog"; and "anything that had been tried, from proposing Congressmen to bumming a drink, had been 'prospected' or 'panned out.' "

Mr. McClure visited us briefly, and as quick as his ear could be, he often missed, or got an expression half-right. "Outfit," for instance, was frequently used, but a real outfit, such as a claim or a ranch or even a wickiup, was mostly known as a "shebang," and I can't recall hearing "outfit" directed at a row of pins. "The man in the wagon," to do McClure justice, was for a while "an author of all sayings and doings which can find no responsible source"; but his "bilk," as being "a man who never misses a meal and never pays a cent," was foreign to me, though perhaps I luckily missed the type, in my work as blacksmith and later. (To be "bilked," of course, meant to be cheated.)

The Vigilantes were meeting every night now, and Grantly usually told me what went on. He knew my concern, and I think resented the reasons for it.

"We're finding it hard to agree on procedure,"

he said. "The hanging of Ives was the inevitable course after a particularly monstrous act. As to Plummer and his Agents, no special one, really, is guiltier than the next, on the record."

"Maybe you'll have to wait for another murder, with witnesses on hand taking notes. Is that the idea?" I still felt bitter about this oracular Committee. No word had come about my own fate; I supposed I wasn't important enough.

Grantly sighed. "Well, that's the theory most support, in effect. Others, of course, want action *now.* I can't even guess at the next move. No doubt our hand will be forced soon."

He was right. An explosive new issue rose a day later.

Dutch John Wagner, whose dossier contained several murders, with familiar accompanying crimes, elected to add another to the list. Outline of the attack was probably Plummer's, but Dutch provided gracenotes. Near a dell called Horse Prairie, he overtook a small wagon-train, and presumably for "luck," shot and killed its owner, a man named Lank Forbes, who gave in exchange a crippling hand-wound. A posse led by Neil Howie took up pursuit when the news reached Virginia City.

At Wagner's trial, it was shown that Plummer had sent the killer a warning "to leave the Territory at once," but Wagner's half-failure seemed to have gone to his head. His horse having collapsed, he stole a mule from Barret and Shineberger's Ranch and pointed toward Salt Lake, alert for easier pickings. Somewhere along the way, under-gunned with a disabled hand, he impressed into service a bewildered Indian who

carried a small bow and a quiver full of arrows
for partridge, gopher, and squirrel. Wagner expressed himself as content with this addition.
Regrettably (since the Indian vanished at the
first scent of trouble), the pair were sighted by
Howie's men near a station of the Latter Day
Saints.

The posse waiting in council, Howie rode
alone up to Wagner, resolved but wary. It was
just as well. The Dutchman's reputation was
fearsome. "Let it not be imagined that this man
was any ordinary felon," wrote a Vigilante
whose account I have before me. "He stood up-
wards of six feet; was well and most powerfully
built, being immensely strong, active and
ferociously brave . . . He traveled with a rifle
always in his hand, a heart of stone, a will of iron,
and the frame of a Hercules . . . For cool daring
and self-reliant courage, the singlehanded capture of Dutch John, by Neil Howie, has always
appeared to our judgment as the most remarkable action of this campaign against crime." Then
was added a strange remark, the afterthought of a
man of education and conscience: "Physical
courage we share with the brutes; moral courage
is the stature of manhood."

The encounter was not, however, lop-sided.
Howie, who with Beidler would become one of
Montana's highest lawmen, was himself something of a roughneck. "Those who have seen the
machine-like action and instantaneous motion
with which Howie draws a revolver, know that
few men, if any, have odds against him with
fire-arms. Still—not one man in a thousand
would have walked up to this renowned des-

perado, waiting with a cocked rifle [held, now, in his left hand]."

"Get off your mule, John," said Howie. Wagner started to whip up the rifle, but Howie dropped a hand to his revolver-butt. Not much more was needed. Wagner instantly lowered the rifle and "looked stricken."

"Now give me your gun, and I'd like to see that hand."

For the first time in his career, Wagner meekly obeyed. He had defied Plummer, his defiance of a Higher Power had been widely admired—rhetorically rich and expressed in every good sentence. And yet, as he stared into Howie's "stern face and unflinching gray eyes," he quailed at last. No doubt he rued the loss of his Indian, who was believed to be across the mountain, shooting squirrels, no doubt shaking his head over the crazy pale-face.

Examining the injured hand, Howie said, "Yes, so the wound was described. You're wanted in Virginia City."

"I slept too near the fire and throwed one hand in," explained Wagner.

"John, we have many other charges, and wtinesses and confessions from your own rogues. The time's come to square accounts."

Here the historian feels a certain embarrassment. Howie's hastily gathered "Vigilantes" backed off in the crisis. They were not, properly speaking, authentic Vigilantes; they were, rather, a scattering of merchants and clerks not hardened to violence, and they'd heard, from a rider, that sixty of Plummer's men waited just down the trail. "Dutch John," they were told, "is up to be freed." Now this amateur posse suggested to Howie that John Featherston, a rancher of proved courage, was camped nearby with a train. Featherston readily enlisted and, with Howie—and Wagner riding ahead—passed on toward Virginia. They ignored Plummer's men, who stood aside, uneasy about Howie's and Featherston's revolvers.

The weather was deadly-cold, with frozen streams and a sprinkling of snow, and the three stopped often to thaw at a makeshift fire. Wagner made one break at freedom, and never tried again. He dove for three rifles stacked against a tree and heard two simultaneous "clicks." His normal sardonic mien having revived, he grinned and said, "Boys, you're quicker than storm lightning. I reckon I'd better throw in my hand. To be candid, I never seen two more cussed varmints, and if you don't mind we'll have a drink on it."

"John," said Howie, "try it again, and we'll kill you." Then, no one minding, they drank from the same bottle and pushed on through the snow.

Without further trouble they delivered the prisoner to Vigilantes at nearer-by Bannack, the feat having the effect of uniting Howie and Featherston in a professional-lawman friendship that endured through Montana's growth into territorial status and statehood. It was one of those friendships perhaps not fully comprehended apart from the frontier. Each man, in a crisis, would probably have given his life for the other—"the two forever joined in a community of sentiment, hardship, danger and mutual devotion," as someone wrote.

Wagner awaited trial while the Vigilantes—real Vigilantes now—decided suddenly to strike at Plummer himself, with his two chief deputies, Buck Stinson and Ned Ray. The move was prompted by news that those leading scoundrels were planning to vacate the area. Plummer was not, of course, fully sane, but with devlish cunning he sensed that it was time to call a good thing finished.

By coincidence—in this January of '64—the Sheriff and his deputies had business in Bannack, where Dutch John now languished in a locked empty cabin. Evidence appeared, by the way, that he tried to gnaw his way out. He was immensely powerful, as suggested, and his teeth being especially sound, he patiently set to work on a weak lower log; he had, in fact, made real progress when he was finally interrupted. He complained, with some excuse, that "a hell of a lot of work's gone for nothing here. You boys ought to be ashamed. I could a been snoozing."

Plummer's "business" could be said to sum up his whole deranged career. As a red herring (seeing how things were going) he'd arrested a confused fellow on a trumped-up charge. After chaining him, he promised to hang him next day (Sunday); then he had several deputies start building a scaffold. In his twisted way, Plummer doubtless saw this lynching to be as a sop and comfort to the community. He was wrong. In Bannack, as in Virginia, the grapes of wrath had lain too long.

Early Sunday morning the programs for capture proceeded without fanfare. First it was learned where Plummer and the two aides stayed. Then their horses were silently removed from sheds and led away. The weather had continued severe, still with snow and cold, and a man, even a wily schemer like Plummer, was helpless without transport.

Plummer, Stinson, and Ray were regarded as "corraled," and the Committee called at the Sheriff's house first. His door was kicked open, to reveal the tidy official, wearing his concealing plug hat and shaving. He remarked with unconcern, "Good morning, gentlemen. Please make yourselves comfortable." ("Gentleman," with its plural form, was a pet word of Plummer's. One of his highest satisfactions, as he strolled Bannack's and Virginia's streets, was that all women to whom he almost lifted his hat thought him "a perfect gentleman.") Informed that he was wanted, he proceeded to wipe his face and hands, saying, "I'll be with you in a minute."

Most men at the scene saw him as chastened and resigned, but they might have known better. A veteran of unexpected crises—many having to do with a husband, Plummer, *sans* trousers, and a squalling nude wife on a bed—he tossed down his towel and advanced toward his coat. Then he made a dive for a revolver barely visible in a pocket. When a Vigilante stepped up fast to stop him, Plummer turned pale but maintained enough poise to converse in his usual measured tones. "With his expertness in the use of that weapon," observed Langford, "he would doubtless have slain some or all of his captors."

Ned Ray was taken from his familiar place of rest in Bannack—asleep on a gambling table in Goodrich's. Stinson was found drinking at the home of an innocent friend named Toland. The deputies were cut of a piece, "ordinary cutthroats and villains," as an historian wrote. If Stinson had an identifying mark, it was his habit, in drink, of going from saloon to saloon, modestly announcing in each: "Whoop! I'm from Pike County, Missouri; I'm ten feet high; my abode is where lewd women and licentious men mingle; my Parlor is the Rocky Mountains; I smell like a wolf, and I drain a creek dry like a horse. Look out, you bastards! I'm fixing to turn loose!"

Both men, seized, resented it in suitable language. Ray struck a Vigilante in the face for emphasis. Even so, they were marched off, with Plummer, a short distance out of town where the gallows had been arranged. A row of Vigilantes held back a fast-forming crowd.

Here Stinson and Ray stepped up their vilification, as the charges were read, while Plummer took a different line altogether. This man, whose record was crowded with slaughters, who'd never shown a sign of remorse, in California or Montana—the master planner in murder now presented arguments why he should be spared. Several were puzzling in the extreme.

First he begged his captors to "cut off my ears, and cut out my tongue, strip me naked and let me go!" The response being negative, he screamed that, at the least, they could let him see his "sister-in-law," who was believed to be in England. The visit was denied. Then Plummer pleaded for time "to settle my business affairs," but someone remarked that these were being resolved at the moment. "That is exactly your sort of business" a Vigilante told him.

"Now," said the *Post*," "the deranged and unfortunate creature fell to his knees, tears streaming from his eyes. But not a man of those who knew him was touched. A more desperate and bloodthirsty life was never seen in the Rocky Mountains!"

Plummer's last appeal defies reason by any standards, Arising, his composure restored, he announced, as if his verdict were final, "I'm too wicked to die. I cannot go bloodstained and unforgiven into the Eternal presence," and he prepared to leave, feeling that the issue was settled. But he was forcibly restrained to watch the disposition of Stinson and Ray, who blasphemed and struggled to the end.

In Ray's case, "he merely doubled, or tripled, or increased by some multiple known to the Almighty, his suffering from the rope." When the noose was adjusted, and his box kicked aside, he somehow slipped the fingers of one hand between the strand and his neck, and so, swinging, thrashing, kicking, he choked to death over a period of minutes. Two or three Vigilantes, having meant to snap his neck, with no pain, were upset to the point of nausea.

But the person most noisily moved was a 'Madam Hall,' a noted courtesan of the town and mistress of Ned Ray—that is, of Ray and any other Bannack male with five dollars. This creature, her dyed red hair streaming, broke free of restrainers and ran up to the gallows-scene.

"Where's Ned?" she shrieked. "Where at's my my Ned Ray?"

A Vigilante pointed to the object dangling from the rope, and then fell back, amazed. From the Madam issued a "volcanic" stream of abuse so foul and skilfully composed that several men confessed later that her technique surpassed

their own—a confession hard for a miner. Apart
from her other line, she was mistress of the
idiom, and there was talk of escorting her to her
cabin, or place of commerce, and leaving her a
purse, out of respect for her tongue.

"There goes poor Ned Ray," whined Stinson,
who a moment later dangled in death agony
beside him. When Stinson was being hoisted, he
exclaimed, "I'll confess!" and Plummer
promptly spoke up, "We've done enough already, twice over, to send us to hell."

His utterance was believed to be the first open
penitence of his life. Plummer's time had come,
an inevitable milestone in the evolution of Montana order. To me, there was something terrible
in hanging such a man. Though sunk in infamy,
he was a person of intellect, polished, genial,
affable. But now he awaited the end.

Last to the scaffold, Plummer removed his
usual necktie and tossed it to a young boarder at
his house, saying, "Keep that to remember me
by," and then, turning to the Vigilantes, "Boys,
as a last favor, give me a good drop!"

To oblige, insofar as possible, those nearby
lifted him high, and then let him fall. He died
quickly, without a struggle. The bodies, soon
stiffly frozen, were left to swing three days in the
winter winds.

After those rude Sunday devotions, the crowd
was released, and people singly, in pairs, and in
groups, walked out to the cluster of pines, solemnly gazing at what one of their number wrote
down as "the wages of sin." Another man, a
typically offhand miner who'd suffered from
Plummer's band, observed in a Diary note: "If

we'd had a church in Bannack, I doubt if anybody would of turned up that day. There was
better entertainment down toward the Gulch."

It would be worthwhile to be able to say that
Plummer died with his celebrated hat on, or off,
but no one I talked to remembered.

Against this disappointment may be set a
more important footnote. Some days before, the
Sheriff had written his brother and sister in New
York City, saying he feared for his life because of
"my allegiance to the Union." This was about as
thin a ruse as possible; his politics, if any, had
never been discussed.

But the brother and sister, on hearing of
Plummer's death, swore vengeance; and in 1869
wrote that they were soon headed, by rail and
stage coach, for Virginia City. It happened that
Mr. Langford was in New York on business and,
with a former Bannack resident named Purple,
called on the kinfolk, finding them "well-
educated, civilized people." Nevertheless they
meant soon to board a train for Ogden, Utah, as
being the first leg of their ill-advised trip to Montana.

Langford's and Purple's first diplomatic pleas
not availing, Langford, "with great reluctance,"
gave them Professor Dimsdale's *The Vigilantes
of Montana*, published in 1866 from his notes
and articles in the *Post*. Besides a chronology of
Plummer the Road Agent, it contained a police
sketch of the Sheriff's swath through California.
Convinced at last, the brother and sister burst
into tears and "begged everybody's pardon concerned," which Purple later wrote "would include half the population of Montana, and a
heavy bloc further West."

On the morning after that January Sabbath of '64, the Committee met to weigh evidence against both Dutch John and another favorite of Plummer's—a Bannack nuisance called, affectionately, "The Greaser," a nickname that seemed to please him. This was Greaser Joe Pizanthia, a Mexican who looked hurt, always, if someone omitted the prefix. He was, in fact, a crude specimen of the pleasant land dozing south of the border, and had long ravaged Emigrant trails, killing and robbing under Plummer's captaincy.

It's unwieldy to include all details of the Vigilante cleanup, though it extended for a period of only five weeks. The disposition of Wagner and Pizanthia, however, had points of singularity. A miner told me about it later. The "Greaser" was approached first, crouching in his cabin, which he'd heavily fortified. When a cry to come out was ignored, Vigilantes named Smith Ball and George Copley tried to break in but received a thundering fire. The two staggered out, Copley shot through the chest with a buffalo gun and Ball struck in the hip. (To avoid gangrene, the leg was later removed by a surgeon.) Copley, with his terrible chest wound, died while being led off by friends. A crowd had gathered, "and the excitement rose up to near about madness," said the miner, looking pleased. From here on, Vigilante command went to a Civil War officer whose campaigns had dried up back home. This forthright fellow took over briskly. First he ordered a mountain howitzer jettisoned by an Emigrant train; then he aimed it at the cabin, calling out, "Fire!"

A ball did actually emerge from the elderly

piece, which sat on a box, its carriage cast aside. But spectators waited in vain for that tell-tale second concussion so dear to the artilleryman's heart. In short, during the emotional fever, the shell's explosive fuse had not been cut, and it pulled free.

The ball passed through the wall, sending up a geyser of chips. The officer, only slightly daunted, slammed in another shell, and this time improved the occasion, though not very much. He'd ordered the range shortened, and the projectile traversed the house and exploded outside, not far from a group of spectator whores. These squealed and "stepped daintily back."

Now what Greaser Joe, in his eyrie, thought of this hullabaloo of bombardment was never stated. However, being a Mexican, he must have considered that a revolution, ever popular at home, had broken out. The third shell cleared things up a trifle, for the officer militarily surmised that the Greaser might be standing in his chimney, and it was there that the last shell found him. No sound issuing, the cabin was stormed by a detachment under Smith Ball, who dragged his doomed leg, vowing to "get the Greaser or die." His somewhat crippled spirits brightened a moment later when Pizanthia was seen lying injured on the floor. Into the prostrate body Ball promptly emptied his revolver.

Here somebody yanked down a clothes line and fastened it around the prisoner's neck. Greaser Joe was pulled to the top of a planted timber with what was described to me as a "jamb hitch." While he swung thus, secured but not properly hanged, the crowd burst out of hand and began to even old scores. Nearly all persons with guns fired dozens of rounds at the unhappy Agent.*

The action certainly accents a weakness of Vigilante justice, but Bannack had long been hazed, and "An account of Greaser Joe's offenses would have filled a set of ledgers," wrote a Bannack citizen, partly, no doubt, to extenuate the undisciplined frenzy. (Among Pizanthia's many other distinctions, he raped then choked to death two Coeur d'Alène girls of eight and nine.)

Whatever else might be said of Pizanthia, he was tough as the average *vaquero* who, on the Mexican range, spends twelve to fifteen hours in the saddle, often without food or water. Midway through the wild melee of shooting, he called down from aloft—and witnesses agreed on his verbatim remark: "Say, boys, stop shooting a minute, will you?" Seconds later he was lowered to the ground, dead, after absorbing enough punishment to wipe out a platoon. His corpse was hurled into a bonfire, and in the morning some brothel novitiates panned the ashes, hoping to find gold in his purse.

The Southern officer was congratulated on his inspiration about the howitzer; he modestly accepted the homage, and the crowd dispersed.

* * *

Dutch John was escorted from the makeshift jail where John Featherston now acted as guard. In the meanwhile, the Committee had met again and could find no cause for reprieve. Wagner's crimes were known to all and had been witnessed by many. Oddly, after Plummer's pleas,

---

*This marked the only occasion during the campaign when the crowd boiled into active participation.

Dutch John suggested a hanging substitute that centered around amputations.

"Why don't you cut off my arms and legs and let me go?" he suggested. "You know I could do no harm then."

Finding death inevitable, Wagner showed no more signs of weakness. He wished to send some last messages and called for "a Dutchman who can write in my native language." A strong impediment to creation was, of course, that all fingers of his right hand were wrapped in bandages, from Lank Forbes' rifle shot.

Obligingly, the Vigilantes found an "amanuensis" who, at Wagner's dictation, set down what must be regarded as among the most imaginative lies ever dispatched by a doomed man. In a letter to his mother, he admitted to borrowing a few "knicknacks" from a wagon train, to give a sick Indian, and had suffered a "knuckle-dusting" for his pains. He was pretty much dedicated to good works in general, with a compassionate eye to the poor, and, in short, had probably been one of the finest men in the Rockies. Curiously mixed in with this rubbish were contradictory (and vague) admissions of guilt.

Wagner was marched to an unfinished building, a rope thrown over a cross-beam, and the prisoner allowed to pray. While the noose was adjusted, he inquired with casual interest how long it usually took a man to die; he'd never seen a hanging. He was assured that the time would be brief. Then he ascended to a barrel, the words "All ready!" rang out, and the barrel was pulled away.

Dutch John had been misinformed. In his

case—a powerful, iron-willed giant—all agreed that the great sinewy neck snapped. But his life-thrust was too fierce to be stopped by such an injury. For whatever reason, he kicked and struggled for an astonishing time, "the cold blue eyes gazing at us in reproach." Professor Dimsdale, while sorrowfully but firmly in accord with the execution, observed, almost as an epitaph, "It was a matter of general regret that Wagner could not be saved for his courage."

CHAPTER XXIII

DURING THIS RIOTOUS time, I stuck to the forge. Most Virginia City miners left their claims and collected in saloons, or stood in the cold streets, talking and awaiting news from Bannack. The invitation to Madison lay fresh in my mind, but, Bostonlike, I appraised it cautiously. As things turned out, I'd only wasted time.

Early on that day, an Indian boy rode in with a carelessly scrawled note that might have attracted students of psychology. Its composition had been wrought, I concluded, with an artist's charcoal pencil: "Not today. Sleeping. Saturday—unless strain too great!" This last was puzzling until I recalled her possibly humorous reversal of my age. The implication, now, was that my advanced years made such a trip unlikely.

It was a remarkable note; her first inertia overcome, she'd gone ahead and decorated the paper with surprisingly astute pictures from the blacksmith's art: horseshoes in the top corners; and down the sides an anvil, tongs, a swage, a hoof-parer, and a "ball-pein" hammer (as Mr. Smithers spelled it).

At the bottom of this rich, creamy paper was a depiction that I failed to grasp, until I showed it to my boss, who (for inspection) wiped his hands

on his apron, which was harmlessly afire in two
or three spots.

"Why, son," he said, "that there's a lamed
blacksmith a-shoeing a horse. Very prettily
drawed, too. But being as I'm the only such creature present, I wonder how she knowed? Still
and all, she's sprightly to recall these decora-
tional tools, particular with her not active in the
trade. Unless"—eyeing me keenly—"I've been
misinformed. But whereabouts, we'll inquire,
did she lay sight on Ewing T. Smithers?"

"She meant it as a joke, aimed at me. It's her
way of sporting over my 'baby-face,' turning it
all around, you see. She doesn't know about your
leg."

"Well, now, son, you musn't judge her harsh. I
did gain this twister droll, if you reflect. A man
grown, rolling down a tent aisle! I see it differently now. I ain't—and hope the Lord don't
pluck my tongue out—quite so hipped as I was.
There's a happy medium," he advised me severely. "Think on it!"

I promised to do so, though he'd missed the
point. There was no use trying to explain it; I
hadn't the energy right now. I begged Saturday
off and, when it came, saddled up early and
headed toward Slade's, fearful but curious.

The weather had abruptly warmed, as it often
did in this region of streams and springs,
Chinooks and soft low valleys. Winter could be
fitful here. I enjoyed the scene, taking an Indian
trail improved when the Stampede began, so
that travelers could avoid dust on the main road.
No dust now, but deer after a mile or two, a small
black bear absently pawing at a stream, not con-

vinced of the fishing, and, in the open places, high dark circles of vultures. "In this place and period," Grantly once wrote, "the odds are about even whether soaring scavengers mean an animal dead or a miner slain, with a slight lean toward the miner."

Anyhow, I didn't investigate, but loped easily on, happy again to be out of town. I crossed and re-crossed slippery rivulets, the water gurgling beneath skin-ice that formed on these gradients.

I'd made inquiries, of course, and provoked suspicious stares that I was too innocent to notice. Perhaps Mrs. Slade had been right. Chronology aside, I *was* too immature to remember my present status very long at a time. Like some Agents (I found later), I was allowed to ride free until the Committee had decided whether or not I belonged in the area, or would be more useful banished.

I'd proceeded between eight and ten miles when I saw the Madison River, some distance off to the right. And not long after, a low stone house rose before a graceful stand of pines, the river behind, the valley stretched in a wavy white carpet to a series of white-streaked hills. It was a rare choice, this ranch staked out by Slade. From the outskirts of Virginia to here, I'd seen not so much as a wickiup, nor a house, nor cattle, nor even wagons holed up to wait out the snows.

Blue pine smoke curled out of his chimney, friendly and cheerful, and no sound disturbed the retreat. I trotted down a path, where snow had melted leaving hoof marks, then dismounted before reaching the house. I tied my horse to a hitching rail, rubbed him down, and pinned a blanket from ears to tail. The weather had eased, but an over-warm horse ridden this far could quickly take lung-sickness, despite the shaggy winter coat.

I approached the door, heart thumping. But my hand never touched the thick-hewn slabs. The door was suddenly snatched wide, and Slade stood in the entrance, pointing a cocked revolver. His thick yellow hair brushed his shoulders and the blue eyes looked clear—he was sober.

Frightened as I was, I stared back calmly, since I figured I was dead already. The truth is that his wife's careless note had aroused whatever it was that sent people from England, bound for risky shores, and who, in our case, built and sailed the ships that my father now ran with a hand resembling Mr. Smithers'. I looked down at the gun, smiling, and again at Slade's face, which seemed confused.

Not moving fast, I handed him my note. But before he could read it (if he meant to at all), the familiar laugh rang out, and my client of last week made herself known.

She came out of a back room, not adjusting her hair or clothes like other women; coolly regardless and wearing the same scant costume of the Forge, except that she had no shoes on. The omission gave her a curiously wanton air.

She took the gun from her husband, uncocked it, and tossed it across the room, where it fell to the floor with a clatter.

"I paid fifty dollars for that revolver," observed Slade. He appeared ill at ease, and added, addressing himself to me, "It has pearl handles."

I nodded understandingly, as if it were a secret between us two.

"So you came," she said, with the mocking look. "I warned you not to expect much. Do you feel like asking him in, Jack, or do you intend to stand there like a great gawking ape?"

I thought this speech dangerously casual, considering Slade's reputation for rages. But he seemed to shake himself out of a trance-like state. Certainly there was something wrong beyond my comprehension.

He said, "You'll have to excuse me. I—I've been unwell." What struck me as a normal enough reason provoked more laughter, this time light and lilting and with, I thought, a catch in it midway.

"Help him in, and put him near the fire. No, the leather chair. How's your lumbago?" she inquired with concern, her face close to mine.

I wondered how long the frail joke could survive, but I said, "Better, Ma'am, here by your fireplace."

"You see, Alison, he likes you," said Slade in a detached, even a pleased way.

"Older men often like young girls."

He said, "I suppose there's some private joke, one that I've missed? You talk in riddles as usual."

"She thought I was ridiculously young, shoeing her horse, and when I proved it by looking annoyed, she decided I was ridiculously old."

"I see."

"You're very well preserved," she told me seriously, seated on the hearth. And in an inspiration, "Would you like some sassafras tea?"

"You've run through that," said Slade without conviction, his mind obviously elsewhere. To my astonishment, he was deathly pale. And though she continued to try, offering me first a shawl, then a heated stone at my feet, and then, at last, an Indian cure for rheumatism—she finally burst into tears, putting her hands to her face.

I got up—sprang up. "I came on the wrong day. I'm sorry and hope I haven't—"

The master of this unhappy house fixed his full attention on me for the first time. "It's rude to have you embarrassed," he said in a low voice. "Now I wonder, I can't help but wonder . . . You see, we have no real friends. None but the riffraff I pick up in saloons, and the best of those would shoot me for a sackful of dust. And my wife won't have them, or—for a long time—anybody in the house—"

I disliked watching him go through such a struggle, for the West had never seen a more imposing, and attractive, and proud figure; historians would agree on that point. He was the handsomest man I'd met in my life, with his bearing and manners, and a kind of magnetism that even males felt.

"I'll come back another day."

He asked an odd question. "Do you like my wife, young man?"

I'd begun to wonder how people got buried in this climate, with the ground rock-hard, and thought it best to tell the truth, this close to the end.

I said, "Yes, sir"—without embroidery.

"You find her beautiful?"

"Very beautiful."

"Exciting?"

I turned pink and kept silent.

"But difficult?"

I mustered the courage to look at the subject of this catechism, and was surprised to see her awaiting a reply, lips slightly parted. Bracing myself, I said, "I think so. But I don't mind."

"You came to see her today?"

I said, "No, sir, I didn't. Only partly."

"What then?"

"From curiosity, and the stories I've heard. And because your wife makes me feel like a schoolboy. And now, Mr. Slade, if you're planning to shoot me, I wish you'd get it over."

His laugh was the first relaxed moment I'd had since entering the door. "You'll stay," he said with decision, getting up, "and we'll have a drink, as a welcome guest must—"

"No!"

"I said a drink. One only," he told her. "Now I'm going to take a liberty. It's bad taste to burden a stranger with confidences, but the truth is I'm to be put away—hanged—soon. We had an earlier visitor today. Perhaps you saw his tracks. I was advised to improve my ways. And they won't improve, of course."

"I'll be glad when it's over," she said with passion.

"No," he replied thoughtfully, returning with a bottle and three glasses. "No, you won't. You'll be lost completely, for a while, and that's my chief worry. For four years you've been dependent on me entirely, and you'll need somebody afterward."

I felt an angry flush rising.

"See here, Mr. Slade—" but he waved it away.

"Yes, yes; you're quite right. I should." He poured an ordinary amount of whiskey—

Scottish whiskey, such as my father drank—into my glass, very little into his wife's, and filled his own to the top. She walked over quickly, picked it up, and threw it into the fire.

When he seized her, his hands on her hips, I scrambled to my feet, glancing about for a poker or something with which to save her life. But he swung her high, holding her without effort. Then let her down and slapped her right buttock.

"There, Alison—or is it Maria or Virginia Dale today?—you have a knight to defend you. I really do believe," he told me, looking earnest, "that you were sent by Heaven."

It occured to me that, if this were true, I'd come perilously close to being sent back, with a little luck about routing, and the like.

"Tell him he can drink what he pleases. It makes no difference at all."

"You see? She talks to me through you." He refilled his glass, much as before.

I set to work on my courage again. "In that case, I'm bound to say that you may have treated her—"

He tossed off half the drink and said, "Shabbily. Of course. I've hurt her for years, and while she doesn't understand it, she's hurt me. But here"—he walked over and drew her to her feet—"I was joking. Playing a game, one of your kind, Alison." (The color had returned to his face, and I hoped he felt better.)

"Now, do you see this whiskey?"—the glass was nearly empty. "It's the last strong drink I'll take in my lifetime left. I won't be hanged, or shot, or harmed in any way. Only a weakling would bow to bad habits. So—listen," he told her. "Ugliness all gone, vanished, vamoosed. From this moment forward, I'm the man you thought you married. Believe it!"

When he drew back, after brushing her cheek, she stood regarding him in the same derisive light she'd shown at the Forge. But there was a glint of terror in it, too.

"Now, let's entertain our guest, and have some fun for a change. Come along," taking my arm firmly. "I'll show you the ranch."

One crisis presumably past, I glanced at the room, surprised by costly-looking furniture, silver carelessly strewn over a dark gleaming sideboard with burn spots and scratches, finely-woven Navajo rugs, and walls covered with rare skins and heads.

"We run down to the river," said Slade outside. "I bought the valley, or most of it, from Bannocks, but the title's probably worthless. Your horse is still at the rail?"

He made a tut-tutting sound, then led the animal to a series of closeable stalls behind the house, this area neat and clean. There was a corral, of stake-and-rider fence, and even a barn, the lower part stone, like the house. And beyond, in a wide fenced circle past the corral, a variety of jumps.

"My wife's a horsewoman." He thought this over and said, "She's more horsewoman than wife, in some ways."

We leaned against the fence, and I noticed that now, toward noon, the air felt colder and the sun had retreated into an overcast that blurred the tops of the hills.

"It might help you understand to know that her mother died in childbirth and that she was

reared—a good word—by a father of self-
indulgence, well, remarkably like my own. No
doubt that's why we married." I found myself
reflecting on the difference in his speech when
sober, and he reflected, in turn, "I don't believe
either of us quite managed to mature, and we
ceased helping each other years ago."

I wanted to ask a few questions, and sensed
that he might welcome them. But I shrank into
Eastern reticence, disliking myself for it.

Back inside, she was busy distributing plates,
of fine china though badly chipped, in a manner
that suggested a professional dealer at cards. She
was also humming, her spirits restored.

"Well," she said, looking me in the face at
close hand—a disconcerting habit—"did you
learn things? Did you hear about my father?"

"I think he was mentioned, Ma'am."

"And our romance begun in storied St.
Louis—paddle-wheeler, river darkies softly
singing, banjos, ugly old Frenchmen with flat-
boats? Why St. Louis?" she suddenly demanded.

"You've forgotten, Alison," said Slade mildly.
(He was at the sideboard, strengthening his last
drink on earth.) "Your father decided to go West
for his health."

"I hope the trip was successful," I said, trying
to contribute something after my silence outdoors.

"Entirely," said Slade with satisfaction. "He
died."

I remember Grantly saying that Slade was
known, when relaxed, as something of a wit; I
wondered if it all was as sharp-edged as this.

The girl had made several attempts with a
plate that refused to stop in place (she'd broken

one already), and I expected her to throw it at her husband's head. But she shrugged. "You've always been wrong about Father. He wasn't, and didn't."

"You're careless at delicate times, Alison. Especially when you've had more than one drink."

"I've decided to be Virginia. This isn't the sort of day for Alison."

"Virginia," said Slade. "Inappropriate, but Virginia it is. I must explain that Mrs. Slade"— he emphasized the words for obscure reasons— "uses three names, none of which, I believe, she can lay proper claim to. They are, in order of descent, Alison, Maria, and Virginia."

She'd placed the plate, now, and looked up to say, "I get tired of being me. Why should you have to be one person all your life?"

"I wonder," said Slade, with genuine interest, "what name the papers will give you after I'm hanged."

"All three, I hope. I'll be the mystery woman. The mysterious and elusive Mrs. Slade. Beauty and the beast. I know," she said brightly, spots of color in her cheeks, "I'll write one of those what-do-you-call-it pieces—"

"Obituaries?"

"I'll write a beautiful obituary to that what's-its-name paper—"

"*Montana Post.* My dear, you seem to have neither civic pride nor knowledge. You should get out more."

"—about Slade the curse of the Rockies, and a soft ode to his lovely, brutalized bride. Yes,"— she snapped her fingers, and now I noticed her own refilled glass. "That's *it!* I'll pitch the whole thing into verse, appeal to that wilting lily, what's-his-name, the editor."

"Professor Dimsdale is scarcely a wilting lily, Alison."

"Virginia!"

"On the contrary, he's an excellent young man of erudition and courage considering—"

"He has consumption, Ma'am," I explained. "Nobody thinks he can live much longer than a year."

But she was absorbed in the dazzling new venture, and I watched her empty her glass with a kind of practiced flourish.

"Tell him to wait. He can die later. Tell him I'll put that paper on the map. Anyway," she said, "I took a freighting notice in there once, and to me, Virginia, he wilted."

Out of nervousness I'd helped myself at the sideboard, and I murmured something to the effect that she'd caused me, blacksmith though I was, to wilt, too.

"You see, Virginia," said Slade again, in a tone he tried to make fatherly; "all men wilt when they see you. That should help, when you take up your new life in town, seeing people, bandaging miners, helping at the new Singing School. But tell me, do you plan to give us dinner?"

"I?"

"Or me, if you prefer."

She'd gone to a door and called, and I was agreeably surprised, on this jangling day, to see an Indian woman come in carrying a platter, followed by a shy, smiling, handsome Indian boy of seven or eight.

"I want you to meet our son," said Slade, drawing a chair around. "Jemmy, come here.

Yes, that's a good boy. Sit on my knee a minute."

Responding fondly, the boy leaned his head against Slade's chest, and his shiny black hair was gently smoothed.

"I killed his father. I don't remember the details. I was drunk. Two years ago."

"Yes, you might tell us why. Can you, Jack? As a matter of passing interest to the child." She beckoned to the boy, who glanced up and, seeing the nod, slipped out to run around and fling his arms around her neck.

"You can go back now," she said, and kissed him.

Slade turned to me. "Is there anything, Mr. Nickerson, more—"

"Ross!" I exclaimed, emboldened under the whiskey.

"*Can* there by anything—Ross—more soul-soothing than a scene of domestic bliss? The doting mother, the patter of little feet—"

"You know, Jack," she said briskly, addressing him directly now, "I was wondering, I really was wondering how many, if you'd adopted the progeny of everyone you've killed in rages, we'd have here on the old plantation." She waved toward a window. "Acres and acres of wickiups, wagons, nurseries going up. We'd have a town of our very own!"

From first to last, Slade never properly sat down, but she said suddenly, "I'm hungry," and after bringing the bottle to the table, began to eat what I took to be a stew of tender beef. Not the usual antelope, deer, bear, or other, lesser meat. I ate, in all, perhaps two or three forkfuls.

"I see this moment as ripe for divulgence." Slade perched himself on a chair pulled back from the table. "Our condition today is due to my misbehavior last week. You heard? No? I'm surprised. But perhaps you can help, for I assure you I would greatly dislike to be hanged.

"As nearly as I can piece it together, the trouble was started—"

"By you, of course."

"—in Skinner's saloon. I fell into argument with that noisy braggart, Jack Gallagher, and gave him, I'm afraid, a thrashing. Then came the Exchange, where, it appears, I turned round at the bar and knocked down my neighbor, a stranger, the act done without provocation."

He continued a recital of violence notoriously his own, leaving a trail of broken heads and property; and at last, he said, he assailed Mr. Langford about a purchase of lumber. He held nothing back; instead, I thought, making himself as guilty as possible. The voice was that of a penitent without hope of absolution.

"Langford!" he cried. "Of all men to abuse at this time in Virginia!"

The account (which I later checked) was remarkably accurate, though he left out whiskey-inspired boasts such as "You think you withhold lumber from me, you blue-nosed old bastard?" and "Stand apart—we'll swap lumber for lead!" and "You're talking to Slade of the Overland; maybe you didn't know it, you *look* ignorant enough!"—and worse.

Thinking it over, I said, "I'll speak to Mr. Langford, and tell other friends what I believe to be true. That you aren't responsible after drinking. That you have no idea what you do, or ever have done."

His wife sat studying him, but her eyes shone

and I felt, somehow, that she'd become excited.

There was no sign that he heard me. He'd opened a second bottle, and drank off nearly a full glass of whiskey. And his next words were changed—bitter and sarcastic, then gritted out. The imposing figure had begun to spark and crackle. I could think of no better description. A thicker blood ran through those veins.

"Yes, now, the brothers Lott! They've plagued me, shamed me, made me back down and look like a cur. Well,"—rising and taking a deep breath—"First things first. Who really minds Langford? Doddering old maid. [Mr. Langford, I believe, was then in his early thirties.] But those damned, infernal, swinish, crouching, black-guarding, bushwacking, counter-jumping Lotts! They—have—to—be—dealt—with! Nothing can happen until they're dosed with lead—my lead—and what better time than the present? Good! I needed that support, and thank you for it."

(I failed to remember giving support, and I didn't see how the Lotts could be called "counter-jumpers." They contentedly ran their store, happy with the side they were on.)

He looked exactly as he'd looked long ago, when he fell afoul of James in Bannack. Larger than life, eyes blazing, face flushed a dark, angry red—a man poisoned, and bent on murder. The descent from gentleman was complete, and had happened with shocking abruptness. Dimly, I saw the Indian woman open the kitchen door, then hurriedly close it.

I, and my companion, sat immobile while Slade strapped on his guns, wrenched his hat from a peg, and flung himself out.

There was a sound of stumbling in one of the stalls, oaths, and then the rapid thud of hoof-beats, fading slowly away. He'd left the door open, and outside I could see light snow falling again. It had a strange look, wholesome and normal.

Meanwhile his wife had neither moved nor spoken. Now she said (sobered, I thought, but changed in some kind of union with Slade): "Good. I usually ride, here." Despising me, she said, "You jump horses, I suppose?"

"Of course," I replied, offended. "Why not? Bring out a horse; I'll jump him, with room to spare."

"I'll saddle the fool's best hunter. Wait five minutes. Then come outside."

"I have a perfectly fine horse," I said with dignity. "I paid forty—"

"You have a mule. A burro. You know nothing. Five minutes exactly."

"I might remind you," I said carefully, tapping the table for emphasis, not certain she knew, "it was a cow that jumped over the moon."

The point was well taken. I savored it as she got up and left.

The fire was nearly out, and I crossed the room to throw on two logs, annoyed that a chair deliberately moved into the way. At the same time, I became aware that my mind was affected—for the better—by the unnatural emotions of the house. Then I heard a sound of galloping, and closing the door behind me went out, disregarding the cold and sifting snow.

My hostess, nude, was racing her black stallion round and round the ring. She went at a

reckless pace, saddleless, her thighs drawing
warmth from the horse, sensual beyond the average man's dream. And yet, I vaguely understood, without a hint of eroticism. She was, it
struck me finally, free, soaring above the real,
her own person, released now and, oddly, married.

Seeing me, she whirled and took a high jump,
the seat hardly rising, only the erect breasts responding. I mounted the horse she'd saddled
and tied, failing twice to find the stirrup; then
the chase was out of my hands. At some point—a
few seconds, an hour later—I saw the easy obsta-
cle, felt a strong lift, and fell into a painless void.

I awoke in the dark and lay confused, trying
to unscramble a nightmare. I remembered the
ring, with its pale ghost, and felt over my body,
discovering that I'd somehow been undressed.
But with no worse reward than bruises and
aches, and a certain damage to the spirit. I started
to sit up and stopped at the quick surge, shameful in these conditions. Then hearing a rustle at
the door, I saw delirium come in as a fixture.

A sweetish fragrance of ring and horse remained, but like a child she'd added scent, and
with this mingling an improbable future became
briefly distinct. But at a frenzied wild pace,
sensing my first chance at command, she
reached higher and higher, her head above the
pillow, then sank back and sobbed like a knife
thrust, "Jack!" She spoke the name three or four
times again before I moved aside at dawn, leaving her asleep, winner over nothing.

On the trail, halfway to town, a party of men
approached, and I stopped and waited. Four

horsemen led a buckboard on which Slade lay unconscious. I knew two of these—men of the Vigilantes—but no one spoke, and I continued toward town, worse off, I supposed, than before.

Slade had risen to new peaks of mayhem and destruction and had finally been paid for his trouble. Three miners, ridden down, had beaten him almost beyond recognition. A doctor had pieced him together, but his face would not heal for weeks. Probably, as the Duncans observed, it was as well he was beaten, for the Lotts had been alerted and stood ready. I thought he might better have reached them, in view of the inevitable reckoning.

"His friends warned him of the consequences," said a Journal. "But he spurned their advice, and, if possible, behaved the worse for it."

CHAPTER XXIV

FOR TWO DAYS I toiled away, finding little to say. Mr. Smithers watched me from the corner of his eye but asked no questions. I was aware that he had some notion of my ride, and recognized that I'd been hurt. Despite his often garbled speech, he was far from stupid, and he had instinct and intuition, with tact in equal degree. So—he bided his time.

Time, even a short time, is the only real healer, as many have noticed. By the third day, I'd only suffered a bad dream; none of it, in the late stages, had happened at all. Except for an irksome pain in the chest, I happily embraced this version and blamed everything on more whiskey than I'd drunk before in my life.

"Well, now, son," said Mr. Smithers, having worked himself up to it, "you apprehend the scrapes we nudge into. Your father being absent, unless he's staked out some ways up the Gulch, I'll step in as I know he'd prefer. Call to mind David—last name never divulged—Uriah the Hittite, and his thieved Bathsheba. The aforesaid killed off Uriah, as plain as a crowbar, and the Lord stepped in with fetters, destructive of the first son." Mr. Smithers thought this over, trying to piece it together, and added: "Disregard Solomon, the second son. In my view—and spoke in

342

confidence—he crept out accidental, while Providence was showing another horse, so to say."

"I'm sorry, Mr. Smithers. Try it again, please. My mind wandered."

"I recognized that it had, for I see you've taken and hammered out a heart, small but tidy, with an arrer pointed through it. We'll store it up for the Christmas trade, and come out on the long end, since requests for same are infrequent by the miners. But what I said was, reduced, look not on the wine when it's red, and uncovet your neighbor's wife. Both Biblical, true, and while I've loosed my grasp, they'd stand up in Court."

"All I meant was a friendly visit after being invited, you know."

"There are visits and visits. And when interested parties see a young friend, much as one of the family, drooping home from same caved in and shook, why, that's a visit in quarters dark and stormy—speaking poetic (as were often my weakness)."

The poetry escaped me, but I apologized for the heart, and dug in to make the hinge I'd been assigned. The pain was wearing off, and I had the helpful thought that I was too young to be so easily injured.

Other considerations fled when suddenly, once again, I noticed miners collecting in groups, with the familiar hum of low-pitched speculation.

"There's fret and holler in the wind, son," called Mr. Smithers in his cheery style. "Yes, sir, she's re-started over, and from what I hearn on Saturday, standing in this spot, it's no more than

expected. We'll close down for the day and stand
ready, if lawful citizens be required."

The Vigilantes had met in Executive Committee and voted for conclusive action. The members, said Grantly and James, had spent the previous night studying the files on the five leading
members left of Plummer's Agents. Much of this
material came from police in Oregon and
California—the territories fled by one or two
culprits before coming to Montana. Each man in
turn, and more often together, had terrorized
every settlement of the Virginia-Bannack area.
And one Boone Helm, in particular, had been
described as "an inhuman monster with no
single redeeming trait from birth."

Afterward I was allowed to make notes on
Helm's career. It made Henry Plummer, at his
worst, seem like a choirboy. I thought, and still
think, it important to offer these for persons
forming fair judgment of Montana's Vigilantes.
Helm was in truth a rare exhibit in the annals of
depravity. "Some men are villainous by nature,
others become so by circumstance," wrote
Langford. "Hogarth's series of pictures repre-
senting the careers . . . of two apprentices illus-
trates this truth better than words. Both commenced life under the same influences [but] the
one became Lord Mayor of London, and in the
discharge of his official duties at last passed
sentence of death upon the other."

Helm jumped off to a sound start in Missouri
(where the family had moved from Kentucky) by
knifing to death his best friend and neighbor, a
man with the euphonic name of Littlebury
Shoot. This latter's crime, or error, had been to
change his mind about accompanying Helm on a

rampage through Texas. Shoot's brothers, seeing the act as forward, tracked the promising youngster to an Indian Reservation, seized him, and brought him home for trial. Helm was found guilty, but he managed such an artistic simulation of lunacy that, on advice of physicians, he was confined in an asylum. So docile, yet strange, was his conduct that he was shortly allowed walks over the grounds, with a keeper of childlike faith. Midway through the third or fourth week, Helm had been hopping on one leg and quacking like a duck when he abruptly "dove into a willow copse." A search was quickly made, "but the bird had flown," as authorities aptly put it, no doubt relieved.

Most outlaws of the day saw California as sanctuary, and it was in that far-West land that Helm's tastes matured. Police reports showed that "he killed several men in personal rencontre"; that is, in duels at digs or shootouts in mining-town saloons. Then he absently shot a man in the back and moved north to Oregon, comfortably ahead of a posse. Soon after this, Helm concluded that Oregon lay too close to California. News and even drawings of outlaws had a way of drifting into the organized Territory. Perhaps a decisive factor was Helm's knowledge that California had recently issued a fugitive warrant for him.

So—he joined a group of honest men preparing a trip to Salt Lake, and during its course, seemed to delight in refreshing them with tales of his exploits.

He said, "Many's the poor devil I've killed at one time or another, and the truth is that I've been obliged to feed on some of them."

The group, exchanging looks, pressed him for details, and one of the number later made notes, as did others who met Helm in that period. So it was that a letter from John W. Powell, traveler and trader, formed part of the Vigilantes' dossier; in it Powell described an encounter with Helm on the trail during the following severe winter. Asleep in a lodge, Powell heard a "harsh, carrying voice" demand from outside, "Who owns this shebang?" On opening the flap, he saw a "tall, cadaverous, sunken-eyed man standing over me, dressed in a dirty, dilapidated coat and shirt and drawers, with moccasins tied to his feet."

This bleak intruder "described himself as one Boone Helm" and gave a disconnected story of traveling in Oregon, being caught in snows, half-starving, and, now, requiring assistance. He said a group he joined had eaten its horses, including an expensive and celebrated race-horse, and had made snow-shoes of their hides. Helm and a man named Burton alone survived the ordeal, said the visitor "with a wolfish grin." At the moment, Burton waited outside.

Helm and his companion were steered to an empty removed house and supplied with articles of travel. However, before Powell left, Helm rushed into camp to report that Burton had committed suicide. Powell expressed restrained grief, then made a quiet investigation. Through a window, Helm was observed sitting at a table and dining on Burton's left leg, much as a family might sit down to a ham.

In the interest of balance, Helm had also removed the right leg, which was strapped to his saddle—rolled up in a red flannel shirt.

As grisly as his file reads, Helm deserves mention in some detail, since he stands among the few natural cannibals in American criminal history. One can surmise that he saw his fellow men as a butcher surveys a steer—in choice cuts and condition. Human flesh was not then Government-graded U.S. Prime, Choice, and the like, but Helm himself chose succulence over sinew. (Grantly has attempted to strike that sentence; let it stand. I contend that the narrator deserves some release when considering a vulture like Helm.)

Incapable of quick decision, Helm wandered lonely as Wordsworth's cloud, though twice as black, here and there among the Rockies. In Idaho he forced combat with one "Dutch Fred" (it's remarkable how many persons bore the "Dutch" prefix in the early West), a decent fellow but a committed gambler, and who when roused "was a perfect Hercules in a fight," people said.

Threatened by Helm during a game, Dutch arose and whipped out a bowie, hoping to offset Helm's revolver. Both men were disarmed, the bartender consenting to keep their weapons during a cooling-off period. Helm left and returned in an hour, "contrite," drawing on his histrionic gifts of Missouri. But the instant he recovered his gun, he shot and killed Dutch Fred as he stood calmly, arms folded across his chest. The file does not imply that Helm enjoyed Dutch beyond the murder.

In 1862, a British Columbia paper said that "The man Boone Helm is at last in custody. He was brought to this city [Vancouver] last night strongly ironed." Helm, once again, had taken a companion, and reports of the two "trudging up the Frazier River on foot" reached the Canadian police, who knew Helm's tastes. Captured alone, Helm was closely questioned about his comrade of the road.

"Where is he?" cried the prisoner, vain of his palate, in the known style of gourmets. "Do you take me for a damned fool? I ate him." Helm was jailed (alone) but escaped, despite extraordinary measures by Vancouver.

So, by turns starving, killing, dining, Helm slowly made his way to Alder Gulch and Plummer. Upon this last he fell as being the man, the fellow-fiend with an organized brain, who at last could tell him what to do. It was, as someone said, "a wedding made in Hell."

That weary, way-worn wanderer had chosen the worst possible time for his promotion to Road Agent. But he quickly made his mark, bullying the region with Plummer's men, riding the wagon routes, robbing stages, cruelly beating both men and women, happy at admission to an exclusive club, after the years of loneliness.

Now, as Mr. Smithers had noted, something was in the wind. A kind of subdued excitement was once again swelling in the streets. But it was evening before the Vigilantes made their most dramatic move to date.

The remaining Plummer Agents considered most dangerous were Helm the cannibal; Jack Gallagher, murderer and highway robber; Frank Parish, accomplished horse-thief and accessory to murders; Hayes Lyons, who'd assisted Gallagher in murdering an informer named Dillingham, then completed other Plummer chores;

and Clubfoot George Lane, a committed villain with, apparently, no feeling at all.

At dark, on that January day, five hundred armed Vigilantes quietly surrounded the city, allowing no one to enter or leave. All five Agents were known to be in Virginia, hence the quick strike. During the howling winter night, I walked with Mr. Smithers, watching a cordon of men forming along the overlooking heights, having been alerted by Grantly about several decisions taken. Aside from the massive cordon, the Executive Committee sat in council, slowly examining evidence.

The reports I heard later conflicted on the order of capture, but I think Helm was taken first, in front of the Virginia Hotel. It was believed he was preparing to dine conventionally, there being nothing better at hand. Arrested, he seemed far from upset. He said, "If I'd only had a show, if I'd knowed the drift, you'd a had a gay old time taking me!" "His interest," said a young, perhaps plump and tender, desk clerk whom he chatted with, or appraised, "seemed aimed at the fight he could have made." His right hand was bandaged over a wound, and he slumped down on a bench in the building where the Agents were being taken.

Mr. Smithers and I approached the building and stood looking on. Helm was in a conversational mood and when told about his offenses said in a deliberate tone, "I'm as innocent as any babe unborn. I never killed no one, nor robbed nor defrauded him neither. I'll swear it on a Bible." A nearby Vigilante sprang into another room and came back with a volume of Holy Writ. Grabbing it, Helm repeated his oath, "invoking the most terrible penalties on his soul in attesting its truthfulness." Then, as a clincher, he gave the Book a resounding smack. "The Committee," wrote one of its members, "regarded this sacrilegious act of the crime-hardened reprobate with mingled feelings of horror and disgust."

Noting which direction the gage of battle pointed—that is, away from him and toward the scaffold—he confessed to several murders and stated, with pride, that he'd once dug himself free of "several stout jails out West." Thereafter, he passed the time before the execution in joking and cursing, frequently bawling for whiskey.

Jack Gallagher was found in a closed gambling hall, rolled up in bedding on the floor. His shotgun and revolver lay beside him, but he reached for these a little late.

Montanta historians have wondered why Plummer's tattered and remnant band, after his hanging with two Agents, stayed in the area at all. In the main they weren't stupid, and they must have known that the net was tightening. Indeed the Vigilantes prayed that Gallagher, Helm, and the rest would leave, preventing further action. The only possible answer lies in the outlook of Montana desperadoes then. By their reckless, debonair, even jocular attitude, they showed every disregard for human lives, including their own. It was the code they lived by, and most carried it over the final threshold of death.

After an interval of tears, Gallagher reverted to his old, breezy manner. He bounced into the Committee room, said Grantly, swearing and laughing as if the meeting was a game. He said,

"This is a pretty break, ain't it, boys?" But he would crack before the finish.

Lyons was approached in a miner's cabin while eating pancakes. Though the intruders offered to wait, he stated in candor that the visit had ruined his meal. (From first to last, prisoners were treated with courtesy, even with consideration.) Outside, he expressed resentment about his dinner: "You disturbed me in the first good meal I've sat down to in weeks. Pancakes, by God!" he said severely. Together with Helms, Lyons' attention seemed often fixed on his stomach, though Lyons leaned more toward the farinaceous.

Clubfoot George Lane was arrested at Dance and Stuart's Store, where as a red-herring he'd taken a part-time job. Informed of his plight, he fell penitent and asked for a clergyman. There were several (but no formal church) then in Virginia, one or two believed authentic, and a Reverend Straight was found in the Arbor Restaurant, next door to the "Shades," a popular whorehouse to which he'd devoted missionary zeal. Reversing his collar as he ran, he proceeded to Lane's side.

Frank Parish was taken in Meninghall's Store. He was examining guns, knives, and various solvents, such as lime. He showed very little fear, and inquired, "What am I arrested for?"

"For being a Road Agent, thief, and accessory to numerous murders and highway robberies."

"I'm as innocent—as innocent as you are!" he exclaimed with some heat.

But when the Committee read him its charges, he made a turn-about and confessed to even worse offenses.

All evidence weighed, the time had come for
the miserable finale. The dead-march led toward
an unfinished building, with an exposed ridge-
beam, that would soon be Clayton and Hale's
Drug Store, at the corner of Van Buren. By now
the streets were choked with people, and the
prisoners, two Vigilantes flanking each, were
halted briefly before the Virginia Hotel. Then
five dry-goods boxes were arranged inside the
empty structure. We stood outside, shivering in
the cold, me relieved that my case had not been
mentioned.

During the halt, Clubfoot George called to a
spectator friend, "Won't you give me a character?" The man refused. Here Lane, Gallagher,
and Lyons dropped to their knees, and Lyons,
asking that his hat be removed, offered up a
prayer, while Helm continued to crack jokes.
The prayer finished, Lyons begged to see his
mistress; this was the sole request denied; it was
thought unseemly to have women present.

Boone Helm, in high spirits, called to Gallagher after the prayer, saying, "Jack, hand me
that coat; you never give me anything yet." (It
was a handsome cavalry coat, trimmed with
beaver.)

"Damned sight of use you'll have for it!" Gallagher replied.

The two continued their short and pithy re-
marks to friends roundabout, crying such as
"Hello, Jake, they've got me this time!" and
"Skeeter, old cayuse, they've nabbed me sure."

As the wretched men climbed up on their
boxes, ranks of Vigilantes faced the crowd,
alerted for trouble. Gallagher began to rip and
rant, using the foulest oaths and obscenities.

Then, somehow freeing one hand, he found a knife in his clothes and yelled, "I'll not be hung in public! I'll cut my throat first!"

Two Vigilantes leaped forward to disarm him, and Helm said in reproach, "Don't make a fool of yourself, Jack. There's no sense being afeared to die."

The Committee chief now solemnly intoned, "You are about to be executed. If you have any dying requests, this is your last opportunity. You may be assured they shall be carefully heeded."

Gallagher, run out of oaths, which included an advice to the Vigilantes: "God blast you all, and I hope to meet you in the blackest pit of Hell!" heard the chairman's statement with relief.

"I want one more drink of whiskey before I die," he shouted, and a filled tumbler was brought him. His offhandedness returned, he said, "Boys, slacken that damned rope, and let a man take a last snort!"

Then the terrible words "Men, do your duty!" rang through the skeletal structure, and Gallagher's box was yanked aside. Helm, looking coolly at his quivering form, said to his dying friend and fellow cutthroat, "Kick away, old fellow. I'll be in Hell alongside in a minute." After this, the inexplicable creature jumped into space without assistance, before his box was touched. His last words were: "Every man for his principles! Hurrah for Jeff Davis. Let her go!"

After the hangings, a newcomer asked "X" Beidler, who acted as hangman, "Did you not feel for the man [Helm] as you put the rope around his neck?"

Beidler, worn out from his far-ranging search for evidence, replied, "Yes, I felt for his left ear."

Notwithstanding his part in bringing these criminals to justice, they'd appointed him, to a man, custodians of their property, executor of all last wishes. He was trusted by the lawful and lawless alike, and his response to the bystander was a reflection of the prisoners' own code.

Except for some undramatic tidying, the Vigilantes' work was finished—until the tragic, pathetic, divisive, and near-riotous valedictory of March 10.

With several of the victims—left swinging till friends came to claim them—law and order had failed in other Western lands where law theoretically existed, and numberless inhuman outrages resulted. Organized practical measures now succeeded in protecting the innocent. Even so, conversation, for the rest of that day, even in the noisiest saloons, never rose above the subdued. These crises had to be faced, but Alder Gulch deplored them.

CHAPTER XXV

Professor Dimsdale's new singing school was held at nine o'clock two nights a week at the Virginia Hotel. The hotel's dining room was the only spot in town sufficiently large to accommodate the students, who ranged in age from about three to ninety. A child of three, of course, can be chronologically placed without serious error; in the case of leathery old mountain-men, the span between seventy and ninety was a limbo of conjecture. After weathering five hundred storms, Indian fights, saloon brawls, panning in icy streams, and accidents of interesting kinds, their appearance crystallized into something indefinable. One old blister claimed to be 110, and another not only said he was 153 but had documents to prove it, though he never produced them.

To tell the truth, this second nuisance was not taken very seriously. He rarely uttered a sensible statement. He told all around town that his children were coming to visit him; he'd sent expense money back East—because he "liked to hear the patter of little feet around the house." His son, the "nipper," was 130, and the daughter, his "sprite," was 128. There was more, but it was so far-fetched and tiresome it's slipped my mind.

The Singing School had caught on swiftly. A

chief reason, of course, was the Professor himself. This tall, frail, myopic Englishman was as
tough in his way as the meanest roustabout. His
toughness sprang from determination, plus, no
doubt, inherited fiber. Of the many types at the
Gulch, Dimsdale was unique in brashness. He
held three jobs: schoolmaster, Singing School
master, and editor of the *Montana Post*. In this
last he ran pieces of spiky candor that would
have seen a less favored figure shot. But miners
and ruffians alike held him in a kind of reverence, no matter how he described them. His
"strangulation jig" remained highly prized, a
classic, by the ones for whom it was coined.

I myself saw Whiskey Bill Graves, in the only
urban haunt with which he was familiar—a
saloon—showing the clipping around with the
repeated observation, "Now, by God, that's *writing*! And you needn't proffer argyments about
writing, neither. I've knowed good from bad
since infancyhood; it's run through the family."
The fact that "jig" might apply to him made no
difference; he was proud of Dimsdale.

The Professor was known to have a fatal sickness of the lungs. As often stated in town, he
proceeded with no more physical store than
"grit," and a desperado laying a hand on him
would have been buried later that day. Like
most people of courage, he quietly went his way,
self-effacing, never presuming on his status as
Virginia City pet. "To study him," in Grantly's
words, "you tended to forget his condition and,
eventually, to place him among the toughest
miners; and while no gentler fellow ever lived,
he had all the easy bend of a black-oar spar."

On the other hand, Professor Dimsdale had a

few traits common to his title. He was slightly
absent-minded, gullible, sometimes confused,
in the immemorial style of the guild. The confusion was briefly signalized by a wrinkling of his
forehead; after this he took a deep breath from
lungs not quite able to deliver one, and carried
on without apology. He became confused on this
Thursday evening at the hotel. The Post had
announced, "The Singing School offers an out-
standing attraction for this week's second assembly. Maestro Guilio Borgia, fresh from
triumphs at the Zanzibar Municipal Opera, has
consented, through a friend at whose wakiup
[sic] he graces our city, to render a program of
popular favorites . . ." etc., etc.

Typically, the Professor hadn't bothered to
check the artists but took a miner's handed-in
note on faith, of which he, Dimsdale, had a painful amount. (I should say that the sessions were
held on Tuesdays and Thursdays; the miners
were drunk on weekends, and some on Fridays
when they knocked off; and on Mondays they
were not regarded as being in prime melodic
shape, either.)

Well, a big crowd showed up, including several Hurdies who found business dull where
they practised. The Smithers were there, with
the daughter Daisy, as well as the yellow-haired
girl I'd taken from the Indians. She'd been provided the name "Faire," which was Mrs.
Smithers' mother's name, and she was learning
to talk English. Or maybe English was returning
from some childhood elsewhere. She was a
grave, beautiful girl with wide gray eyes that
seemed anxious to absorb and remember everything.

The dining room had a round black stove, and what with foot-thick walls, the place was comfortably warm. A Mrs. Biggs, wife of a clerk at Meninghall's, worked a harmonium, and did it very well. And Professor Dimsdale, at the classes, generally stood beside her, holding a stick, with a dozen or so hymnals on a stand. Other hymnals were scattered here and there, the lot ordered from St. Louis by Dimsdale himself, out of his own pocket (which Grantly once guessed "had no bottom." He'd come out here for health, not riches; and Grantly added that families which took degrees at Oxford seldom found it necessary to dig for gold while standing in frozen streambeds).

The tables were stacked on one side, and benches were added to the dining room's thirty or so chairs. The Singing School was popular. Anyhow we were packed full by nine, with an uncommon number of miners, many seated on the floor against one wall. I noticed that Professor Dimsdale's hair was standing on end—a sign of mild bewilderment, as if he wondered whether he'd put on his trousers, or was in the wrong building. The place was bulging. But he took a look at those squinty, sober-faced mountain-men, sighed, straightened up with decision, and rapped on his stand for attention. He repeated his promise for the "special treat" printed in the *Post*, then said we would lead off with No. 63 in the *Everyman* nondenominational hymn book, "Just as I Am, Without One Plea," and he hoped the far row of miners would see fit to remove their wolfskin caps, to avoid frightening the children, since a cap of that kind, added to a "thicket of uncombed whiskers," ruled out positive identification.

Well, his jokes loosened up the crowd, making everybody laugh and slap their knees, and the miners rolled over on the floor. I heard one say it was "the primest bolt placed betwixt this chile's ribs since I broke my leg last spring." But when the caps were off, another had been scalped, somewhere along the way, and his red peeled head might better have stayed covered, in my view. Especially because he'd had a tattooer in Salt Lake stitch a wobbly blue arrow down the middle, so people would understand what had happened. Drunk at the time, naturally.

But he, like the rest, boomed out on the hymn, after Mrs. Biggs hit the opening chords, and people felt grateful to hear voices lifted eager and joyous after all the troubles. Professor Dimsdale, waving away, shook his head a time or two, because the words "without one flea" did seem to rise from those pests along the wall; however, they were drowned out, mostly, so he was pretty soon easy again.

As a rule, Mr. Dimsdale provided musical tutelage between numbers, for this *was* a school, and now (with an apprehensive but firm glance at the wall) he told about the octave being divided into eight notes, with both sharps and flats, and after a miner remarked that this seemed only fair, he went on to describe music sung in "rounds." He said it was "contrapuntal and, in fact, close in structure to the fugue." Another of the incorrigibles stated that he "knowed *that*"—counterpointed was the only kind of music he cared to sing, generally. Then he subsided after some muttering, though the group wasn't corked up entirely, of course.

Professor Dimsdale gave as a sample the old English folk tune, or nursery rhyme, "Three Blind Mice"; and he split the class into men, women, and children, to show how the exercise was done. This went off remarkably well, considering that the miners insisted on singing through all three parts, imitating in hideous falsetto both women and children. At the conclusion, to vigorous applause, a miner stood up and suggested—looking meek and apologetic— that he'd conferred with his group and they'd never seen any blind mice, "neither here or anyplace else," and wondered if Professor Dimsdale wasn't referring to moles.

Mr. Dimsdale said, "Thank you, Mr. Hendricks. We're most grateful that you caught this regrettable error," and he promised to write back to England so they could alter the original text.

This over, the Professor (sardonically relieved) announced the "pièce de résistance" of the evening, "the very gracious expenditure of time and talent offered by"—he consulted a card—"the well-known, the greatly sought-after, and, we're sure, the highly paid virtuoso, Maestro Giulio Borgia, of the Zanzibar Municipal Opera"—and it was here that I saw him frown, as if he'd given his first solid thought to the Maestro's origins. However, as was his way, he braced his shoulders and said briefly, "Thad, or Thaddeus, Foss, of the Lively Lady claim, has volunteered to introduce our distinguished guest."

There was a bustle in the rear and a miner that all of us knew walked to the front and cleared his

throat. He was, barring none, the worst gasbag in
Virginia City, perhaps because he'd acquired a
scattering of education in the far-distant past.
Though normally as ratty as his kin, he now
wore a frock coat without a tie and held beside
him a shiny tall hat—both plucked from a wagon
road.

But he started off in an untroublesome key,
addressing the group as "Ladies, gents, and
papooses"—waiting for restrained titters that
died early. Then he apologized for his lack of
necktie, saying he "reckoned it was stole" during the previous week, when he was up the
Gulch visiting his wife's relations. "Both my tie
and dress shirt, which was imported and will be
missed." With unnecessary candor, I thought, he
said his wife's connections, an offshoot of
Crows, were not much worse than their tribe,
"but you take the most of them and they'd steal a
stove and come back later for the smoke."

He particularly regretted the deficiency because of Maestro Borgia, who moved "in circles
where formal dress was expected and followed,
even at breakfast in his castle at Zanzibar,"
where he, the speaker, had once visited and was
introduced to the Rajah. From what little I knew
about Zanzibar, it hadn't any Rajah, or any cas-
tles to speak of, and not much else but a gang of
thieving Arabs that rounded up Negroes and
sold them off as slaves. And pretty soon I wished
they'd sold Mr. Foss, too, because he fell into a
vein he was proud of, and practised (and had
taught some to me) in which the remarks waxed
and waned, you might say, sounding sensible
one minute while losing their meaning the next.

Shaking his head slightly, he grasped one

lapel and acknowledged that he'd strayed off the
subject, which was "aimed to describe the Maestro's foreground and musical development,"
and said that Signor Borgia (he pronounced it
"Sig-nor" in the way of aggravation) was, at the
start, and farther, a member of the accomplished
Borgia family of Genoa, where his grandfather
was a friend of Christopher Columbus and
helped discover America, apologizing for it later
"when the two was throwed in jail. Does that
demean and downgrade Virginia City?" he
asked. "Not while it stands as the Garden Spot of
nowhere, since we ain't been declared a Territory or anything else but a hunk of land roosting
on mountings without names to the eternal
shame of men like Nathaniel Langford and Sam
Hauser.

"But what, you inqure, has that got to do with
the early Signor Borgia? Everything, because he,
too, hadn't got a name for six or seven years. Yes,
it's true. The Maestro was born out of wedlock,
which lies south of Naples, and it was only after
Queen Isabella herself heard him sing that his
career officially begun."

Here the old fool stopped and asked for a glass
of water, but there wasn't any and by now nobody would have budged if there had been. So he
produced a pint bottle and refreshed himself.

"But to proceed with our guest. It was now a
matter of studying under one European teacher
after another, to wit: [and he had the impudence
to consult a card] Peter the Hermit, a Mr. Smith,
or Smythe, third violinst to the late King Cole;
Jo-Anne Sebastian Brahms"—at this point
Professor Dimsdale rose and started to call a halt,
his face badly flushed, but the reprobate boomed

on over him—"Sir Harold Harefoot, and others equally endowed. As to the Sig-nor's later triumphs—carried on shoulders away from La Scaler, the Pope kissing his toe, crowned heads reeling, women propelled beneath the carriage—well, you've likely read it all, and so, in person, and sorry the introduction never come up to snuff, the speaker has the honor, the very high honor, to give you, at 135 pounds—Maestro Giulio Borgia!"

We now had a second convulsion at the rear, and there was hoisted to his feet and pushed forward a skinny little rooster, and I'm a giraffe if it wasn't a Chinaman! I'd seen him working in the Gulch toward Bannack, and it was true; he sang all the time he panned, and was known for it.

Professor Dimsdale sat studying the miner and the Chinaman, who wore his native costume, except that those mischief-makers had added a flowing black Ascot—a ridiculous sight—and hung a lorgnette around his neck. With a re-signed but sarcastic expression that I'd often seen on his face, the Professor let the oddity take the reins, seeming curious about what he might do. And the rest of the class, by now, had over-come their peeve and begun to enjoy the outrage.

Well, sir, that Chinaman hadn't the least no-tion of anything wrong, and laying back his head commenced a kind of sing-song wail that sounded to me and others like the noise you hear in a sawmill. Where the saw strikes hard and then soft spots, and complains about it, the rack-et rising and falling. At first, Mrs. Biggs made an attempt to accompany, but she quit soon; the harmonium wasn't up to it. Professor Dimsdale let him saw for three or four minutes; then he sprang up and thanked him, shaking his hand and steering him firmly toward the rear. And after that, he seized the opportunity to explain that the Oriental scale first had sixty-four and then eighty keys, the scale set in "fifths," and the whole laid down by pitch-pipes, clearing this up with further remarks. So, he made educational material out of it, just the same.

And concluding the Doxology, with everyone filing out, he stood at the door as usual, bidding people goodbye, and listened patient but weary when the miners offered admiring statements, saying things like, "Well, I've never heard a more harmonious evening, Professor; we ain't apt to forget it!" and "When it comes to music, give me opry every time, and this specimen here couldn't be beat."

Mr. Dimsdale replied on the order of "I'm so very touched and grateful that you enjoyed yourself, Mr. Mullins. You must come again soon, possibly in the late spring, or next year. Yes, to be sure, good night to you too." Following such exchanges the evening ended, and it occurred to me, walking home with the Smithers, that everybody had genuinely been refreshed. Their minds were taken off the depressing events of the last few weeks. All, that is, except the Chinaman; he would have gone on happily singing until dawn, and probably expected to.

CHAPTER XXVI

IN THIS PERIOD, I was told that the Vigilantes were considering my case—my connection with Plummer and friendship with Slade—and I became daily more apprehensive. The other authenticated Agents had quietly been rounded up and hanged: Steve Marshland, William Bunton, Cyrus Skinner, Alexander Carter, John Cooper, George Shears, Bob Zachary, and Bill Hunter. This completed Plummer's gang. None of the above were executed in Virginia City; they'd been caught in remoter places like Hell Gate, Frenchtown, Deer Lodge, Fort Owens, and Gallatin.

As for me, banishment hung over my head like a rain-cloud. I kept trying to make plans, should the blow fall. But to return to Boston, virtually an outcast, was too much to bear. It was Mr. Smithers, of course, who kept me going, relentlessly cheerful, always optimistic, making observations like, "Son Ross, that Committee's merely aiming to spruce up your attentions, in the way of reckless," or (happily clinking away at iron), "Worry never soothed a treed cat, as the saying goes, and you've got friends with voices loud and clear. Rest easy, else we'll have *two* blacksmiths plagued and ailing."

Well, my visits to his house, the frequent

meals there, the family chatter did rest my mind;
it was, after all, the only close family I'd known,
and the warmth of those friends and fireside kept
me hopeful and sane.

* * *

Meanwhile, Virginia City was growing, adding amenities to the crude hotels, saloons,
stores, and houses with which it started. Perhaps
Professor Dimsdale's regular school (tuition two
dollars a week) fanned the first faint winds of
civilization. A certified conveyor of the gospel,
"with unforged papers to prove it"—a Reverend
A. M. Torbett—set up shop in a cabin and then
commenced building a church in Idaho Street,
with the help of three Indians who turned up
drunk every two or three days—this despite the
fact that Torbett pelted them with some pretty
threatening prayers. He was the first real Protes-
tant minister in Montana.

Inevitably a Catholic priest showed up soon
after, "not wishing to see old Torbett hog all the
business," a miner wrote. But the Catholic was a
good fellow, and popular—Father Giorda, who
claimed he'd previously been a missionary. Still,
those miners weren't civilizable, not yet, anyway, and they noted out loud that Giordia never
said where he'd been a missionary. So they
speculated on this awhile, and decided it was
either New York, or, more likely, Washington,
"where it was needed worst." They were down
on both places, having contempt for any region
outside Montana. They'd buttonhole Father
Giorda, trying to make him feel at home, and ask
him questions like, "Pretty fur cry from New
York, ain't it, Reverend?" and "I'll bet the Presi-

dent couldn't haul up a nugget in thirty year—
what do you say to that?"

Giordia, amused, took it in stride and was apt
to buy a drink when they ran down, joining for a
modest sip of beer. I noticed that this had the
effect of deflating them briefly.

And then, with Plummer's rowdies gone,
never to return, the town began holding "socials" and even dances here and there, the children usually brought to be bedded down in back,
with the people taking turns to watch. The dancers were happy to pay five dollars a couple, for
which they received supper at midnight and the
opportunity to dance until dawn. "It was pleasant to participate in these frolics," said a Journal,
"and walk home with some chance of not being
robbed or hit over the head."

A Mr. J. B. Craven and his wife came along—
from St. Louis—and gave "theatricals" in whatever big room might be idle for an evening. They
were both skilled and had several trunks full of
properties like wigs, and costumes, and lath
swords, and putty noses; and people enjoyed
their offerings, mostly. But Mr. Craven was
hipped on Shakespeare, and for a production of
that kind, he enrolled amateurs, which occasionally meant miners, and sometimes the results were indifferent. *Macbeth* was his favorite,
and in the first try he ran into a sort of trouble
that became familiar later. Since the play was too
ambitious to be done entirely, it was Craven's
practice to lift out scenes that he thought dramatic, and these were generally soliloquies by
himself.

The citizens paid three dollars each to attend,
and the hall was always jammed. Not only for the

performance but to see what the accursed miners would think up next. In a sense, Mr. Craven, and his wife, too, were as gullible as Dimsdale, and both finally took on similar expressions—suspicious and sarcastic but still determined to win. Mr. Craven gave *Macbeth*'s best soliloquy, standing on a platform they'd rigged. He had a wig, of course, and black pantaloons, with a sword that unfortunately dragged the ground, since they'd temporarily misplaced three other swords, and a short velveteen jacket, and if Macbeth ever looked like that, it came as news to me.

Anyway, he stepped out, hollow and gloomy, holding a borrowed bowie knife and cried in his rich, stagey voice: "Is this a dagger which I see before me, the handle toward my hand?"—and set off speculation in the front row. Some miners thought it was, some thought no. They finally decided it was a butcher's knife, and said it wasn't "appropriate on the boards." A second clique claimed it was a letter-opener, and if he, Macbeth, had received bad news, it was best to use the opener and get it over. Thus he could "know how to deal with it, before his pesky wife came sneaking and slithering back in, confound her hide!"

"Tomorrow and tomorrow and tomorrow" went off very well, I thought, because these miners were decent men, basically, and interested in Lady Macbeth's funeral. And if a few asked him to nail down the actual day without further dilly-dallying, so they could arrange their schedules, it seemed only fair.

But Craven had hired six miners, the poor, misguided man, for the last big scene in which Birnam Wood came to Dunsinane. I heard he'd

encountered obstacles in rehearsal, for the new
players (at five dollars a head) agreed right off
that the action was absurd, pointing out that the
woods east of town had remained stuck since the
Stampede, and probably before—"not a tree
shifted around, nor likely to." They recom-
mended that both Shakespeare and Macbeth be
confined, until doctors could take up their case.
Mr. Craven finally drilled the trick into their
heads, and they went off straightaway, satisfied
and eager, to chop down some runt pines and
attack the castle.

When the moment arrived, they crept in a back
door, hiding behind their trees, and things
looked smooth and silky, except for one man that
had a tree about twenty feet high, so that he had
to take a hatchet and trim it to stand upright.
Everybody waited, laughing, except maybe Mr.
and Mrs. Craven. But directly on Malcolm's cue
of "Now near enough, your leavy screens throw
down," they moved forward, though declining
to cast aside the trees, and commenced to run
into each other, with complaints of "Now, you
watch out, Tom, and I ain't apt to tell you again!"
and "Stick a branch in my eye, will you Dub
Boomer?—Well, two can play at that game!"

And then they seemed to forget about Mac-
duff's situation and fell to twirling around back
and forth, to rake each other with limbs, one or
two men falling down; until Mr. Craven stepped
in at last, ignoring the heaving undergrowth,
and made a graceful, good-sporting little speech,
in which he told the audience that he'd heretofore considered Macbeth to be one of the sub-
limest tragedies on record, the noblest creation
of the Bard, but now he'd been made to see it was

a comedy, and he would henceforth play it that way in Virginia City.

He'd even call in *all* the miners, so they could get their chance; that is, until the hills were skimmed off bare, when they could switch to an offering slightly lower down, or to the miners' taste.

Meanwhile Lady Macbeth had somehow become involved in the forest, causing her skirt to be ripped and her hair bedraggled, with pine needles showing through, and she stamped out in a huff. But she got over it next day.

As to the miners, they felt guilty for a change, and had Mr. Smithers strike off a beautiful dagger at the Forge, and even talked him into welding (which he disliked) so that the finished product had a hammered brass handle and scabbard. And at the next play they presented this to Mr. Craven, and gave Lady Macbeth an expensive new costume bought in Ft. Benton. Mr. Craven tried to make a speech of thanks but was overcome, blinking, and sat down, to a perfect storm of applause.

Other favorites acted out by Mr. and Mrs. Craven, with various supports, were "The Courtship of Miles Standish," "Ten Nights in a Barroom," "The Deacon's Masterpiece," "Evangeline," and, to be sure, "Uncle Tom's Cabin," which caused another ruckus. The majority of miners being Southerners, they laid back their ears and balked. They discussed it at a meeting, then told Mr. Craven he could produce it but only after they, the miners, did some "editing." So they took the manuscript and studied it, those that could read, and changed things con-

siderably. The overseer turned out to be one of
the saintliest persons around, while Uncle Tom
emerged as mean as a snake. For this last part,
the miners went up to the Gulch to fetch Black
Sam, a strapping big fellow from Alabama, heavily muscled, yet easy-going and gentle as a deer.

I have no notes covering his response to being
drafted. I did hear he'd stressed the self-evident
point that he was a miner, not an actor. But they
talked him into it, being good friends, and on
opening night they had him topped with a
snow-white wig, which looked odd on a young
man of twenty-five. Mr. Craven had planned to
play the part himself, but he wearily took a back
seat and contented himself as Simon Legree.

Mrs. Craven had a double role. She was that
sanctified bore, Little Eva; then she blacked herself up for Eliza. And now *she* demurred, for the
miners had written a whole new part, practically, which had Eliza trying to slide across the ice
toward the South, where she felt comfortable,
and safe. In other words, *away* from the North,
where she'd been "abused"—the script didn't
say how. Mrs. Craven's objection was chiefly to
the lines, which emerged as pretty ignorant
miner slang. And at the rehearsal Black Sam
threw down the whip he'd been given to hold,
during the chats with Little Eva, and said he'd be
"dad-dratted," or something like, if he'd spill
out any such mixed-up garbagy trash. But the
performance went ahead, and Sam was right—
the thing *was* confusing; the miners had garbled
the message to a degree where nothing made
sense. Curious, I read the book for the first time,
and was so embarrassed I wondered why Mrs.

Stowe wasn't run out of town. It was indeed garbage trash, no matter what her purpose in writing it.

Nobody really won, unless you counted continuous audience convulsions as an asset. Mr. Craven had failed to get his way, all right, but the miners also ran into difficulty trying to "strengthen" the plot—"where the writer fell down on the job." They'd offered to saw a hole in the dining room floor and have Eliza disappear through it, while crossing Mr. Craven's silvery cloth, but the hotel owner sailed in and stopped them. And Mrs. Craven wouldn't do it anyway; said she'd break her back. The play only ran one night.

A photographer named A. M. Smith came along and set up in a room above Con Orem's Saloon. "He took tintypes," a Journal peevishly said, "then put them in black cases lined with velvet and called them 'daguerreotypes.'" I, myself, was never able to see any difference between the styles, and was puzzled by the writer's imputation of fraud. Smith's venture, at first, caused a second Stampede. People flocked in to have their pictures taken—very clear likenesses—and send them back home, for a price of five dollars. While the shop was much frequented, Smith never became over-popular personally. He had the common fault of photographers of confusing himself with Leonardo da Vinci, and flaunted airs unsuited to Virginia in that period. He wore a flowing cape, and a skull-fitting French cap called a "beret," and affected a clipped spade beard, which stood out amongst the tangled wildwood that passed for whiskers here.

These quirks were forgivable, but he was touchy, and his professional directions (and tantrums) were what caused the trouble finally. The trouble was mild, but it whipped him into Virginia City shape, and once again it was the miners. Smith had a plush armchair with a strong back-clamp for the victim's head, and a tripod with a black tent under which he focused. For children's trade, he placed a home-made over-sized monkey suit on his left hand, and wiggled it to catch their attention. Then he cut loose, raising whitish smoke with a powder rack.

Well, the miners, uncomfortably fixed in the vise, put up with Smith's screams and foot-stamping and other Old-Master genius for a while, as meek as could be. And then, when they spotted the monkey, they paid him double to photograph it, head in the clamp, and after "treating" the photographer in a saloon (which he surveyed with distaste, holding his nose), they eased out his home address, together with his mother's name. This done, they sent her the monkey's picture, with a note (from Smith) that he'd been sick but was now believed "gaining in strength and weight and should be up to my former health soon. Love—Arvin." He got back a pretty testy letter, in which she demanded his return. This only stepped up his irritations.

"No, no! Mr. Alworth—I believe you go by the nickname of 'Hogwaller'?—sit *still* in the clamp and, yes, by Jehosophat, you've done it again! Another plate ruined! What is it you *see* on the ceiling? The Second Coming of Jesus? Do you itch somewhere?"

I was on hand, and Alworth said mildy, "Why,

no, sir, they's a hole up there, and a rat was working hisself through—"

"A rat!" and Smith bolted downstairs to Orem's. When he came back, Mr. Alworth sat patiently waiting, and now he said, apologetic, "Mr. Smith, I dislike to upset your shebang, but I don't believe I could make her go without you trotted forth the monkey. It soothers me down."

Under this constant hazing, the artist worsened, of course, until he really *was* intolerable. The miners talked it out among themselves, saying they hated to see a young man get off to a bad start in the community. What he needed, likely, being "a city feller," was diversion. So they substituted blasting powder for the sort of powder used in the rack, and singed his eyebrows and part of his hair, and peeled a trifle of skin off his nose and forehead. And when he peered into a mirror, that spade beard might have had a tornado rip through it. Weeks passed before it resumed its old shape, and some claimed that, as a showpiece, it was finished.

"The explosion appeared to have probed down into the roots," a miner said. "It disrelocated the streambed." But sporting as always, as he stood weeping, they dosed him at Orem's again, until he could barely support himself at the bar; then they finished off the evening at Moll Featherlegs' popular new whorehouse. One of the miners told him, at last, clapping him on the back, "Son, you're shaping up neat as a nugget. You take your average municipal Emigrant and he undergoes worse adjustments. No, you've sunk down to Virginia level in record time; all the boys say so."

Then a Thomas White, point of origin unknown, opened a hair-dressing parlor on Jefferson Street. He ran some fancy ads in the *Post*, along the lines of "White's Beauty and Restorative Salon; Hair-trimming; Shaping and Dyeing—Black and Brown a Specialty. Ladies—Look twenty years younger! Miners, come out from behind your tattered pennons! (Price adjustments for Children and Servants!) Appointment preferred."

Curiosity ran high, with women venturing in at first, expecting "to get skinned," as a husband put it. But White was a skilled workman, and a Journal notes that "[he] soon resurfaced Virginia and Nevada as neat as a group of artisans might have done. The place took on a new and tidy appearance, and we were better for it." Then the miners, noting these improvements, decided to submerge their notions about "sissiness," and spruce up a little. What interested them was not hairclipping or whisker-trimming, but dyeing. The idea hadn't previously struck them.

So a third Stampede took place. One week a group would pound in to be dyed brown; next week they'd return to be changed black. Since a good proportion were middle-aged, they had gray-streaked hair and beards, and this gave Mr. White considerable leeway, as they told him, provoking no enthusiasm. Like the photographer, almost in tears, he tried to explain that while brown could be transformed to black, the opposite wasn't possible, according to his standards. After this, following custom, things got slightly out of hand. A miner would have his graying hair dyed brown and his beard blue, half killing the hairdresser with the esthetics of it. And other combinations were swapped around.

Then they brought in Beaver Charlie Baggott, who hadn't any hair at all; bald as an onion, even on the sides. His hair appeared to have gone to his chin and chest.

"Now here's old Beaver Charlie," the men told Mr. White. "You've got to rig up something— look him over. Ain't that a sight?"

"I can scarcely be expected to correct the whims of Nature," replied White a little coldly. "What do you suggest?" (I should explain, in his defense, that he was on the brink of prostration, what with the recent demands.)

"Well, ain't you got a wig, or whatever they call them hairpieces like old Louie the Twelfth wore? Now one without fleas, mind! Old Charlie's sensitive; you can tell by looking."

"My nose had arrived at the same conclusion," replied Mr. White.

The speaker snapped his fingers. "That's it! By God, you've prospected the first step. Give him a bath! And then take up the question of the knob. How long since you had a bath, Charlie?"

Scratching his bald head, Mr. Baggott tried to think back, and decided it was in the summer of either '61 or '59.

"We have no facilities for bathing here," said Mr. White stiffly, "and the Salon's supply of wigs ran out last week. It might be months before I get a new shipment."

The miners drew off for consultation.

"Then paint him. It's the only solution. You're a human and observing young man, Mr. White. Everybody says so. Old Charlie's cold, lacking a carpet. You wouldn't want him to freeze on your hands, would you?"

"On my hands! I fail to see—"

"What colors have you got in store, at the moment, I mean?"

Mr. White said, "I'm extremely dubious about the physical result of painting one's head, though it be of solid rock, as I suspect in this case—"

"Now you've gone and hurt old Charlie's feelings! I tole you he was sensitive; he's like a new bride along them lines."

(This was certainly untrue, since Baggott was more drunk than sober.)

In the end, over Mr. White's anguished representations (and after implied threats), they gilded Beaver Charlie's head out of a pot the hairdresser commonly employed for fingernails, among the Hurdies. Again, he was near tears when he finished. But they filled him up with Tanglefoot, and after that had no trouble dyeing Charlie's beard and chest red.

Mr. White showed unexpected spirit when he sobered up the next day. He marched into the Sheriff's office and reported a case of "intimidation, kidnapping, forced feeding of poisonous spirits, and theft of irreplaceable Salon materials."

In the face of this, the miners saw no course except to send in Billy Wallers, who hadn't any hair either but wore, in cold weather, under his cap, a Blackfoot scalp he'd taken some years before. He appeared for "a mild hair-trim, without removing too much off the top." Right away the scalp lifted in Mr. White's hands, not being glued or nailed but fixed with a paste of flour-and-water. Uttering a shriek heard at Mulvany's Claim, he ran—this time without persuasion—down to Orem's unaccompanied.

As in the case of Smith, he settled down by and by, and became a favorite of the Gulch, though he categorically declined to ride out to claims for "house calls," after a downpour or an accident of tripping up in the streams. It made no difference; the miners admired him for it.

A pawn-shop came along, too, with three burnished balls hanging out in front. It did a pretty brisk business, and was in the right place for it. The balls were much admired. I wondered how many citizens realized that they traced back to the first, forceful Medici, who was equipped with same. I have no evidence to prove that his were burnished.

CHAPTER XXVII

SLADE WAS IN TOWN, drunk and "cutting up." Everybody knew, and wondered what might happen. He and several companions were turning the place upside down. The noisy row went on all night, and I stayed out of his path but kept close enough to watch developments. In the morning, J. M. Fox, the new Sheriff (popularly appointed) met him, arrested him, took him into Court, and began reading a warrant. Midway through the reading Slade blew up, seized the writ, shredded it, threw it on the ground, and stamped on it. Here a number of revolver locks audibly clicked—these from his friends—and Fox backed off from a capture.

"Being at least as prudent as he was valiant," wrote an historian, "The Sheriff succumbed, leaving Slade the master of the situation, conqueror and ruler of the courts, law, and lawmakers."

Slade's act was a declaration of war, and was so accepted. The Vigilance Committee now felt that the question of order and safety for lawful citizens had to be decided once and for all.

Thus approached Montana's most dramatic and tragic episode. Slade had finally gone too far, and his rages, with their wake of destruction, had increased rather than diminished during the month following that January 14, when Plummer's power was broken at the scaffold. Adding to Slade's mania was the fact that he'd been driven into debt, where once he was considered canny in business. Hardly a week passed without riotous scenes he'd stirred up. Salde's suicidal conduct troubled us all, but he was unapproachable in drink. Many tried reasoning with him. Even I considered trying, knowing what might happen. It was no use. We could only stand by, looking on, while he destroyed himself. The Committee, I heard, shied off at extremes in the case. All duties they'd performed seemed pale compared to the task now at hand.

"But we [the Committee] had to decide and that quickly," a member told me afterward. The Vigilantes had lately set up a "People's Court," with Judge Alexander Davis presiding, a jury, and both defense and prosecuting attorneys. All lawful citizens had been content, eager to abide by its decisions. This was the nearest approach to social order that conditions allowed, and though the Court lacked strict legal sway, the people were dead-set on enforcing its decrees, But the present case, all agreed, called for a popular canvass, with special reference to the miners, who had suffered most grievously at Slade's hands.

Well, this crisis caused all stores to close, miners to leave their claims, and the largest crowds yet to collect. First off, there was little more than rumor and report. Slade was mentioned, in whispers, but it was thought that a wider action—involving his cronies—had helped swell the uproar.

Of all the paradoxical figures produced in the Rockies, Slade was unique. He had a great many friends who remained loyal to the end; he knocked down and beat one of these—for no reason at all—but when the verdict came, the man wept bitterly and begged for his life. The point could be made that Slade now kept Virginia City and Nevada in continuous terror. It had become common, when he was engaged in a one-man riot, for shopkeepers and citizens to draw shutters and extinguish all lights, fearful of some senseless attack. For his wholesale destruction he was willing to pay when sober, if he had the money, but more and more people considered payment not enough.

There's no way for a lame pen to describe Slade's furies. The terrible things he did seemed to whet his lust for worse. Some are described here, but the record was limitless, damning for a man who "among gentlemen was a gentleman always . . . generous, warmly attached to his friends (when sober) and happy in his family."

On one occasion while bargaining for some hay, he found it filled with bushes. Enraged, he chained the ranchman, threw him into the hay and prepared to burn both. He was dissuaded when several persons pleaded for the man's wife and children. Slade reluctantly freed him, on his promise to vacate the West, as he did without delay.

Slade himself had fled his native Illinois—to begin his nightmare trail—after a murder of ingenuity. Losing a fist-fight with a brawler of similar outlook, he humbly acknowledged defeat, then picked up a stone and brained the winner, who was occupied in what proved to be premature boasting.

In one breath, years later in Virginia, Slade would describe that incident, and in the next, correctly describe himself as a "Vigilanter." Never did a man have two more separate identities at war with each other.

On the night before this final arrest, Slade and a retinue of thugs had rampaged through Virginia and Nevada, leaving a scene of desolation. No single saloon escaped their drunken mischief; even the unafraid Orem found himself out-numbered. And now the citizenry were fed up with Slade's next-day reparations and apologies.

His ultimate blunder, during this last spree, was to lead his rowdies into that new, ornately appointed brothel of the woman implausibly named Moll Featherlegs. At a time when Virginia, or a segment of it, was turning to churches and socials, the miners still required bawds. And they were proud of "Mrs." Featherlegs' gleaming establishment. Many persons had asked her about the unusual name. This evoked only laughter, or, if she'd been drinking, an offended dignity with the assertion that the name was not only real but distinguished.

"Where at, Moll?" I heard a miner say, having dropped in from curiosity.

"Philadelphia, that's where!" and she flounced from one part of the parlor to another, producing rustling noises from her costume, which reached the floor but left anatomy peeking through at key points. Mrs. Featherlegs was

believed backed by "eastern money"—a curse
then in Montana—but she cast out hints of inheritance. "The Featherlegs are Philadelphia,"
she once said, smarting under the questions.
"My old grandfather, Amos Featherlegs —rest
him—was one of the city's first mayors. He'd
make you look like dirt!"

"I reckon he musta run a right-down cham-
pionship whorehouse, Ma'am, to leave you fixed
like this."

"My grandfather," she said with contempt,
"wouldn't have spat on a 'whorehouse,' as you
call it. He was—an—importer! Yes, that's
exactly what he was!"

"Brought in Irish and German girls for the
trade, did he? Well, they's the best, Ma'am, and
he certainly to Jesus handed his talents on down,
if you don't mind, we'll have a drink on it."

I heard, and recorded, the above conversation,
and it was here that Mrs. Featherlegs gave up
and ordered champagne to be served those ras-
cals, to shut them up. There was no way to
squelch them; besides they spent lots of money,
much gold dust, at her place of business.

Normally—and she seldom drank past control—she was a good-natured creature, with
hair dyed red, a bulging but not displeasing figure, expensive gowns altered to suit her impressive bosoms and thighs. These costly dresses
ran chiefly to silks and satins, with assorted
maribou boas. Her girls, twelve to fifteen in
number, were young, lovely, prim, and lady-
like—"coached in manners" by Mrs. Featherlegs
herself. Furnishings of the "recreational
lounge" were elegant and rich, the emphasis on
tasseled crimson plush with strings hanging

down, tall Italian mirrors, and, of course, solid
brass spittoons kept at high polish.

It was these last fixtures that, at some point in
their drunkenness, attracted Slade and his aides
in demolition—Naylor Thompson and Bill Hardin, a pair of misbegotten rounders. Slade (I
clearly heard, on that wintry night, standing
among onlookers) snapped his fingers after
wrecking the last open saloon (Coleman and
Loeb's) and said, thickly, "Boys, that strumpet
Moll Featherlegs is up there, showing her parts,
with a museum full of things we may need. Let's
go visit—pick and choose. And not feel sorry
about it. She's sitting on her best asset, and can
gather more."

But once he forced his way in, with sidekicks,
Slade fell into a rollicking vein and, literally,
took the place apart. I watched, depressed, while
they stole what they wanted and destroyed the
rest. It made a fine, moonlit sight, those wild
men packing erotically decorated chamber pots,
gobboons, paintings, beaded lamps, chalk dogs,
and other treasures back and forth to the snow.

After the first thefts we heard sounds of splintering furniture, to shrill female protest; then
Slade, Thompson, and Hardin brushed past the
pile outside, their interest waned, and headed
downhill toward town. Mrs. Featherlegs kept on
hand a huge, swarthy, unobtrusive bouncer
(popularly considered her lover), but he took one
look at these intruders and dove out of a back
window; then he lit out toward the woods.

When morning greeted Virginia's ruin, all decent residents, including the miners at Moll's,

were overblown with outrage. None, however,
for fear of reprisals, appeared at the People's
Court—excepting, that is, Mrs. Featherlegs herself. Despite her professional stance, she was not
the breed to take this sort of thing lying down.
She filed any number of claims, writs were issued, and the Vigilance Committee, meeting in
"regretful" session, made the decision to place
the issue before the people. Plummer with his
organized and cold-blooded murderes was one
matter; Slade—well-liked and admired when
sober—was quite another.

I saw crowds jamming up further in the
streets, as reports reached outlying claims and
miners headed in. Many of these, to be sure, were
friends and even advocates of Slade. Tough
themselves, they admired anyone that suicidal.
"In their brief history, the sister-towns had never
seen anything remotely like this," wrote a
freighter named Daugherty. "It had its fascina-
tion, but it was sobering as well. These passions
ran deep."

All merchants, saloon-and hotel-keepers, and
other victims in commerce voted for the extreme
penalty. Then several hundred miners, themselves often filled with mischief, unanimously
agreed on execution. A quotation shows how the
sentiment lay: "If a chile cain't stand at a saloon
without fear of having his head crunched or his
dog shot, then it's time to haul in."

Judge Davis, once a lawyer in Ohio, now presiding at the People's Court, was a friend of
Slade's, but when he presented the writs (advising Slade to go home, recover, and make all
possible apologies), Slade shredded the papers,

as he'd done with Sheriff Fox. Then he aimed a derringer at Davis' head. "I'm holding you as a hostage!" he cried.

In recent weeks Slade had appeared at the Court to pay small fines, without resentments, and with expressions of remorse. Now he'd descended below that rational level. Standing far back, I witnessed the incredible scene. Davis made no resistance, and while it seemed that everyone held his breath, Slade, with (to me) the familiar look of confusion, lowered his gunhand. Unknown to him, his execution had already been set by popular vote of both towns. The final deliberations took place behind a wagon, where the Ohlinghouse stone building now stands.

Slade sobered the instant news was conveyed him by a friend. He quickly walked into P. S. Pfout's store, where the Judge had gone, and apologized, crying, "I take it all back!" But the reformation had come too late. A column of men filed into Wallace Street, and the Executive Officer—Beidler—stepped forward and arrested Slade.

He was informed of his doom and the question asked whether he had any business to settle. The pathetic figure—a friend of mine, too—appeared stunned. He refused to consider business and began begging for his life and to see his "dear wife." Then he called to a friend in the crowd, "Bill, for God's sake, ride after my wife; maybe she can save me!" The messenger, whoever it was, sprang on his horse and clattered at a wild gallop down the street toward Slade's ranch.

I stood behind the main mass of people,

watching the rider. His hat blew off, and his hair
flew wildly in the wind.

But Slade's exhortations had now reached the
point of tears. He promised never to drink again,
abjectly pleading for mercy, and I turned away,
with Mr. Smithers, whose face had gone
chalky-white. He liked Slade who, curiously,
had never made a threatening gesture near the
Forge and addressed him always with courtesy.
Mr. Smithers, looking suddenly older, walked
slowly off up the street, but I stayed on a few
minutes longer. Among the last sounds I heard,
trying to leave the scene, were Slade's "My God!
My God! Must I die? Oh, my dear wife!"

Here another, smaller, column—Slade's
friends to the end—advanced on Pfout's, and a
comrade who had dropped to his knees in
prayer, which failed to take hold, leaped up,
tossed away his coat, and, doubling his fists,
shouted that Slade should be hanged only over
his dead body! The raising of a hundred rifles
brought him to his senses; he seemed glad to
escape after an assurance of future saintly be-
havior. The man staggered away, "pulling out a
handkerchief and weeping like a child."

Near Pfout's was a stone building that had a
corral with high, strong gate-posts. Across these
a beam was laid and a rope fastened, and a dry-
goods box pushed underneath for a platform.
Here I fought free of the crowd and stumbled
away; I'd seen all I could stand, and must let
others tell the rest.

"To this place," said the *Post*, "Slade was
marched, surrounded by a guard composing the
best-armed and most numerous force that ever

had appeared in Montana . . . Judge Davis now addressed the crowd in almost unaudible tones, suggesting banishment instead of death, but his words fell like water upon adamant."

It had been concluded, "with bitter reluctance," that Slade, elsewhere, would provoke the same kind of trouble and that banishment would work unfairness on innocent communities. His life pattern, never stable, often murderous, "had sunk beyond hopes of correction. All lamented the stern necessity which dictated the execution," added the *Post*, and others, too, turned aside before the last act.

Everything being ready, the command was given, "Men, do your duty!" and the box was jerked from beneath his feet. Slade died almost instantly.

But the high drama of that day was not yet finished. As the body was being cut down, for removal to the Virginia Hotel, Slade's wife galloped, "flew up the crowded street like an avenging angel. She was thinly clad and her hair blown, and her grief and heart-piercing cries were terrible . . ." Hearing the extraordinary sound, I turned back. She was riding at breakneck speed, knowing, as the *Post* said, "how to use the rifle and revolver, and [able] to perform as many dexterous feats in the saddle as the boldest hunter that roamed the plains."

"Why, in the name of God," she cried to the people around her, "why didn't some of you, his friends, shoot him down, rather than let him suffer on the scaffold? I would have done it for him. No dog's death should have come to such a man!" Many expressed angry agreement, as she slowly, painfully regained control. Her anguish was too hurtful; I left—this time for good.

Later she had the body placed in a tin coffin filled with alcohol, after which a wagon was hired to convey it to the ranch. In his vest pockets were two dried and curled ears, posthumously removed from an Indian who once offended him, somewhere along that dim, bloody trail when Slade worked for, and maintained order at, Overland. Ironically, he'd kept these as good-luck pieces.

Mrs. Slade rode alongside the wagon, "head up and eyes flashing fire, as a heavy pall settled over Alder Gulch."

CHAPTER XXVIII

NOW THE VIGILANTES considered their work done, and they disbanded with relief. No action was taken against Slade's fellow-rowdies. These either drifted off to Hell Gate, or Gallatin, or north to the new Prickly Pear mines, later the site of a great quartz discovery—the Last Chance Gulch. The ones who stayed in Virginia underwent a miraculous change of manners. They turned courteous, meek, chastened. And then of course they spilled over, two or three joining Reverend Torbett's church, where they sat in the back row and concentrated on singing. The Reverend looked more and more suspicious, until they turned up drunk one night and howled like hyenas, holding the hymnals upside down, and the congregation got up and pranced them out of there.

But in the saloons—restored, now—their deportment was adjusted to the usual run; that is to say, fair. One, oddly enough, was Bill Fairweather, who made the find at Alder Gulch, during James' long-ago trip to the Yellowstone. Fairweather had enjoyed raising hell with Slade and had attempted to prevent arrest; it was he, I learned, who rode to fetch the wife (being outpaced coming back by a better horseman, or horsewoman).

My thoughts turned to a girl riding nude in a snowstorm, dissecting each detail, remembering her words at the Hotel—and fell at last silent at the Forge.

Once again, Mr. Smithers noticed my mood, and at length laid down his pincers, since nobody was present.

"Son Ross," he said, "I'd like to thrust in un-invited and made a seggestion. Based on observations by family, brace of daughters included." (He'd taken steps to adopt the little Indian captive legally, going through the People's Court and Judge Davis, who signed the papers. Only trouble was that neither the Smithers nor Judge Davis could decide on a permanent name. Faire had given way to Alice, and then to Mary, which they said was Biblical, and back to Faire, and on to Ann, so that Ann it was at the moment.)

"We mislike to see you unhappy, son, and wonder why you don't take and call on your friends the Duncans. Opposite this old Pounder, without eddication, or wisdom to match, those stand-up [he meant "upstanding"] citizens are, well, they're"—he groped for a word—"yessir, they're Oraculous!" Liking the sound, he repeated it two or three times. "Oraculous as ever was, and Oraculous in a pinch, unlike Uriah, who wasn't Oraculous and come out on the bottom. They might have ideas meritorious."

Having unloaded all this, he beamed, to show how friendly he felt.

"James is off on another Yellowstone expedition," I said wearily. "And Grantly's at their place in Deer Lodge. Besides, as you know, my status with the Committee has never been cleared. I dislike to embarrass friends and Council members."

"That's what I was coming at!" he cried with satisfaction. "I couldn't a said it better myself!" (Since this made no sense whatever, I remained silent.) "Mr. Grantly Duncan was right here this morning—a-honoring this old Forge—and requested your presence, *at subject's convenience!* Only at convenience—he stressed it."

"Is it convenient now, Mr. Smithers?"

He consulted a gold watch on a heavy chain. "Right smack on!" (He failed to say what; the hour was 10:15 A.M.) "Now if *that* ain't a coincidence! Go ahead, son, and feel free to dawdle. These miners," he said, himself seeming subdued, "they ain't to say bounced back. *I* ain't, if it comes to that!"

We stared at each other, then I removed my apron and headed off toward Grantly's, uneasy.

I found him at home, since many places kept desultory hours at the moment. He was deep in conversation with Mr. Meninghall, whose principal store was in Bannack, though he'd lately opened a branch in Virginia. The new store was holding a sale, with red-and-white signs that said things like "Closing Out!", "Everything must go!", etc.

Grantly motioned me to a chair, and said, "Now, Meninghall, you really must confess that a 'Going out of Business' sale is, in fact, a little bizarre for a brand-new business."

"A technique, a device. A means of catching the eye. Is it dishonest? Is it unethical? No! In the long run, I die, and we *do* go out of business. So, where's the deceit?"

"Well, dammit," replied Grantly, leaning forward, for they were forever debating merchandising tactics, "you'll admit this—and I think you're aware I intend no offense: a continuous close-out sale over, say, a period of thirty years is a, well, tribal rite."

"Tribal, shmibal! Now I mean no offense, but the establishment, I should say establishments, of J. E. Meninghall are prospering, thriving, and I'd like to see the store of an old friend prosper equal. Hold a sale, Grantly! And if you forget to take the signs down, well, is it commerce? Is it successful? It is, and that's the long and short of it."

Grantly sighed. "It would be idle to try and fool you, Jacob. Our store *has* been laggard of late. A little tribal enterprise might be the answer. I'll confer with Brother James."

Mr. Meninghall, rising, slapped him on the knee. "When it comes to the signs, call at the Emporium of J. E. Meninghall. The lettering's important, and so is the angle pasted on. People enjoy craning their necks. Exercise stimulates the appetite to buy—remember that." To me, on his way out, he said, "There's good news for you today, Ross. Right here in this room. No, no, my friend"—to Grantly. "The boy's long enough dangled in suspenders, to refer to a garment presently pushed at Meninghall's Now tell him the rest."

Mr. Meninghall was popular. People poked fun at his "sales," as everything was made sport of here. But during the dreadful winter of '65, when food and supplies were nearly nonexistent, he gave his stock to half-starved miners, until he was broke and could give no longer. Was he daunted? Hardly. By some means he

arranged credit at Salt Lake, and when the tide
turned, residents flocked in to buy, putting him
back on his feet, even if they had to borrow.

As to new signs he'd made, with ridiculously
low prices, the miners crossed those out and
chalked reasonable tags on everything.

"I suppose you know what Jacob meant," said
Grantly. "From the start, the Committee regarded you as guilty mainly of inexpereince.
Gullible youth, we might call it." (There it was
again; I figured I'd be unable to outgrow it if I
lived to be 110.) "They saw you caught, en-
tranced by two of the most engaging men in the
West. One happened to be a villain, the other a
blend of good and evil. It's too bad, but Slade's
death may stand as a deplorable act performed
by bloodthirsty irresponsibles—a 'lynch mob,'
extremist rogues who 'took the law into their
own hands.'

"Well, what law? Territorial status is coming,
and constituted law, we hope, will follow
shortly after. Vigilante justice is not the answer,
if you have alternate means. But I needn't remind you that these 'low rogues' were, are, the
best men in Montana; let's hope history treats
them kindly. However, there will always be a
group of mule-headed fools, ignorant of our
problems, by whom 'Vigilantes' will be hissed
out like a curse. And yet, as Dimsdale wrote in
the Post, they'd be the first to cry 'Protection!
Help at any cost!' if their own lives, families,
property were threatened.

"So be it—fanatics committed to a single
wrong idea will sap progress like a cancer. It's

regrettable," he added, musing, "that they usually thrust themselves into posts where their ignorance is transmitted to the coming, still childish generation. I forsee a day when this mindless bias may bring the nation to its knees. Long-range vision is not an attribute of these people, nor can they learn any lessons of history. And in the end, they themselves usually fare worst from lax laws and morals.

"On the other hand," he said, hopefully smiling, "I could be mistaken. The Committee thought best, in your case, to let you worry awhile. We grieved for you, Brother James and I, but there was nothing we could do. Meninghall, among the stoutest of Vigilanters, begged to ease your mind, but he was overruled.

"And now," he said briskly, "it's come to my notice—oh, never mind how; ours is a small community, and like other small communities it's cemented together by gossip—that you have a different concern."

"What would you do?" I asked.

"You ask me? Among those conspicuously unqualified for the role of conjugal sage, I stand alone. During my adventures in wedlock, I have suffered [he produced a list from his pocket] the loss (by runaway) of seven squaws, ranging in age from eleven to nineteen, forty-three horses, cattle in numbers undetermined, several bags of dust, the largest moose-rack in Montana, a beautifully-tanned grizzly-hide, two pairs of snow-shoes, one truss, with straps, cigars, a ladder, assorted kitchen-ware, a breech-gapped rifle that I hope blew up soon, a leatherbound volume of Homer, twenty-four pounds of seed and several patches of skin, with an indented forehead. I believe I failed to mention gray hair—"

"But now you've married Aubony."

"Yes, Aubony makes up for them all. I consider my finally legal wife," he said, "to be the best, the most intelligent person I've met in a lifetime spent among questionable types. They tell me the Indian falls short in capacity to the white. I assure you that this is false. It is dramatically so in the case of Aubony. At the least, she disproves the rule. Frankly," he said, sounding like his old self, "I consider myself the luckiest fellow alive."

"And I the unluckiest!"

"Not necessarily. Perhaps a period of time should elapse. I'll say this in confidence, my boy: A Committee member who recently rode to that ranch, hoping to offer counsel, help, was greeted by what he considered to be—returning with one boot—rifle fire of accuracy unsurpassed in the region.

"He regarded the fact of his getting home at all as a miracle, and he's not a religious man. Now there are many kinds of courtships, the majority, I feel (though I have no data) not involving gunfire. I see this as a wooing that requires delicacy. A suit of plate armor might help, and as a blacksmith you're well placed to turn one out. In all decency, you might consider a metallic cover for your horse as well, at least in front.

"No, the usual flowers, bonbons, gifts of silk kerchiefs would be peculiarly, perhaps suicidally, weak. A side of venison, a Blackfoot scalp, a stuffed and mounted big-horned sheep—these could serve to draw off fire until verbal passage could be managed—"

He was wound up now, and I was curious about the limits of his invention. Sitting in what the books call a "brown study," the firelight flickering across his face, he looked much older than when we'd met five or six decades ago in California. He still looked, I thought, like a man who would never quite get what he wanted from life, pan the wrong stream, plánt the wrong crops, buy cattle in the worst and unexpected season.

Aubony had come in, on soft cat's feet, and after a gentle smile for me, placed both tea and a bottle of Spanish sherry before us, the tray resting on the hob. Unlike Grantly, she knew precisely how I felt, and it struck me she had more sensitivity than all of us together. Leaving, she touched my shoulder lightly, to show that she understood and that everything would find a happy ending.

Grantly glanced up fondly before she closed the door. Then—it was almost possible to see behind the furrowed forehead and watch the wheels at work—he resumed in the vein not completely stripped.

"You'll have some tea, my boy? No?"— startled. "Sherry, then, As you know, neither James nor I have bowed to the need for liquor. We thought it best, in these settings, never to start, and so, in short, we haven't. But your case. We were discussing ways and means, and enjoying it, I recall. Ah, yes—I was about to suggest that, for your first call, you might cross the Madison at Hobson's Ford, six miles out, and ride *cautiously up the other side!* Tether your horse in willows, well hidden, and swim—wade—across. Then—carrying your rifle—inch toward the house on your stomach, silently, silently, wary for twigs and other breakables. The element of surprise, Ross; it's important here! I shouldn't go so far, speaking of a lady, as to use the vulgarism, 'getting the drop on her,' but—"

"Tell me, Grantly," I broke in. "Do you see this as comic?"

He looked even more startled; then he eyed me keenly.

"Blast my loose mouth! I believe I've offended our young friend! Now, Ross, you'll have to forgive an aging man's—"

"How long ago was it that you and James took me from the Indians and nursed me back to health? In California, I mean," for his expression was bewildered.

"Why"—he frowned deeply—"that must have been, yes, I'm sure I'm right—sometime in '57?—'59? Over six years?"

"How old was I then?"

"Your age? I don't believe—"

"Seventeen. I'll be twenty-four next month. You'd be the last man on earth I'd deliberately hurt, but Grantly, I'm not a 'boy' now. I'm grown—six feet two inches tall, weight 185 pounds, and the arms are blacksmith's arms. The soft innocent's gone, and he has an unfunny problem—a man's problem."

He sprang up and embraced me, the picture of chagrin. "Confound me for a fool! My b—, my very dear young—yes, by God, I'll stick to that from my height of years.

"My esteemed young friend, I have a habit of

letting my tongue waggle in advance of my
sense, granting that any exists. But Ross, we
can't, we simply can't start thinking of you—
closer than a son—as middle-aged. You'll have
to concede us parental privilege. As for 'my
boy'—"

"I was upset," I said. "I've been upset of late.
Not only the problem but distrustful looks on
people's faces. Frankly "—I looked up and
smiled—"if I may borrow from a selfless man I
know, I'd *miss* being called 'my boy,' at least in
this home. And just for the record, I *do* look
uncommonly young, twenty-four or not. I've
noticed it in the mirror."

Grantly rattled his teacup to show his composure; then he fell into thought. "There was something more; I know I'm treading on fragile
ground. But I feel it my duty to speak, and I
represent James as well. I've never been convinced," he said slowly, carefully choosing his
words, "that the young lady in question—she's
little more than a child; younger by fifteen years
than Slade—that, in effect, she hasn't some of the
traits of her husband. That is—wild, fierce in
passion, possibly ungovernable. Unhappiness
may lie there, my boy, or, rather, son—"

"My boy will do."

"—a lifetime of agony and grief, of ups and
downs, instead of the peace-filled home that I've
found at last. Brother James and I would dislike
to see this happen. (I offer these remarks as coming from a man with an indented skull.) But you
must understand—she has beauty, grace, flair,
and abandon, and I imagine, excitement for a
young fellow your age. These are suppositions
only. She never mixed with the town; no one

knows her. She could almost be," he said, "a creature of the imagination. Slade's good or bad angel.

"Are you certain," he asked at last, "that you can't turn your mind to something else? Someone else?"

"I don't know," I told him truthfully.

CHAPTER XXIX

I LET ANOTHER week pass, and then started—early as before— toward the Madison. April had come now, and the long thaw had started, though the run-off was still distant. I proceeded at an easy canter and covered the twelve miles in something over an hour, slowing to cross rivulets and climb shaly banks. And my heart thumped away as before. Blue smoke curled normally from the chimney, and, at a few hundred yards, I reined my horse to a walk, determined as flint (if flint is determined).

And then, sure enough, I heard the crack of a rifle, and saw stones bounce up, not twenty feet from my side. Sweating, I rode on forward, and a second shot fell closer. But she was within view, now, dressed in the same clothes—jeans skintight at the thighs, blouse careless, black hair pulled sleekly back and tied. I cried out: "Fire away! I've come to see how you're getting on. Send me back in a wagon if you choose."

She leaned her rifle against the corral and stood waiting, neither grieved nor unhappy. She looked merely—interested. And bearing out Grantly's appraisal, much like a child.

"Well?"

"It's a tradition to ask visitors in, if they've come to pay respects."

"What respects?"

"Respect for your trouble, Ma'am. I'm sorry. Everybody is."

"That's why they hung him from a rope. Because they were sorry. You might have shot him, but I never saw you around. I would have shot him," she said, reflecting.

"I apprehend you said so at the time. Or so I was told."

" 'Apprehend!' You're beginning to talk like a miner."

Nothing—nothing at all—could surprise me further here, and I said: "Yes, Ma'am; that's true. When in Rome. Besides, I'm a blacksmith, practically the same thing."

"Rot. You look as much like a blacksmith as *he* does."

"Who? Where?"

"In there," waving toward the house.

At this point I had some notion of turning back. But curiosity, and something else, drove me on. I took a deep breath and said, "You look chilly, without moccasins, no coat, and the rest."

"What rest?"

"Well"—expecting to be shot—"you might wear something under that blouse. Or anyway button it up."

For a second she looked angry; then she laughed. "Do you think I *care?*"

"No, Ma'am," I said promptly. "I wonder if you care about anything."

This time I got a different look, one of speculation.

"You know," she said at last, "you're pretty special, in the way of impertinence. Come in," she added, "or stay out—just as you please."

Closing the heavy door behind me, I glanced round and froze. Lying on the table was Slade's tin coffin, with its lid removed, so that the occupant floated in his alcohol, horribly, the face still congested, the neck grotesquely angled, and the yellow hair streaming out like the tendrils of some ugly sea creature.

I sank into the nearest chair, one of several fashioned of sinew, that Slade had bought or wrested from northern tribes during his mad, lonely travels. The girl seated herself on the hearth and studied me, amused.

"Why?"

"When I come down in the mornings, I greet my former spouse and remember to hate a lot of people."

"What happened to Jemmy, and the woman?"

"She took him back to her people. She thought this"—inclining her head toward the coffin—"unusual. Too unusual for children."

I got up, found the lid and the screws, and, trying not to look inside, fastened it down with a screwdriver lying on the sideboard. I made it too firm, I hoped, for her to remove it again. Throughout, she sat and watched, showing no emotion.

"Insane? . . . 'his lovely and devoted wife remained loyal to the end—wild ride to town—tearful supplications—bitter recriminations . . . oh, why didn't you shoot such a man? . . . during his maniacal career, Slade's love for his wife never wavered . . .' et cetera, et cetera, et cetera—*Montana Post*. I could write the books about 'this tragic figure of the West.' "

"I don't know about 'insane,' " I said slowly,

my back to the table. "But why do you care what's written about *him*, if it's true?"

"I like the part about love never wavering. It came out strong in Mrs. Featherlegs whore-house." She moved to a chair, laughing.

"He was drunk."

"He was drunk all the time. Mainly a matter of degree."

I spoke up, half-angry. "Haven't you the de-cency to cry?"

"Cry! I caught up with that years ago."

"How can a woman love a man as deeply as you did Slade, or 'Jack,' as I remember you called him, and show complete indifference, flippan-cy, even? Your mind must be deranged, as peo-ple feared in town. I hope the books make that clear. Fact is, I'll see to it."

This was a pretty reckless speech—the place bristled with guns—but I was angry now and meant to have my say.

"Young man, you've placed yourself in a posi-tion to hear a sad, sad story. Do you wish to take it standing up? Or would you prefer it over here?" She patted a chair beside her.

"I'll sit there when you've buttoned up."

"It bothers you? Why?"

"There's too much of you. And I'm normal, fully grown—"

"I see. Then we'll get rid of it," and she took the blouse off.

I sat watching and waiting.

"Oh, I'll put it back on—buttoned. Under-stand, first, that I *like* to torture you. Jack taught me torture. How would you enjoy," she went on, colding sane, "seeing your husband cut the ears from an Indian still living? Would it enliven your day to watch him scalp an employee for a trivial act of carelessness? How about burning a man alive in a haystack? That's right, it was lighted and flaming before I stamped it out. Shall I go on?"

"I've heard the stories," I said with a touch of sullenness.

"Then how could you, and hundreds of other fools, surmise what went on this house?"

"I don't know," I said, sitting down beside her, finally alerted. "Maybe you'd better not tell me."

"By what lunacy did people conclude that the bold, swaggering Slade could be a devil in town and a saint at home? In the nest with his loving and loyal wife? I never knew the meaning of hatred," she said thoughtfully, "until I realized, after a few months, what kind of sadist I'd married. In some ways he was, and continued to be, a man—hence the devoted wife's ride and piteous accusations. In most ways he was Satan come up from Hell.

"Magnetism! Hypnotic influence over friends and enemies! Magnetism died for me in the dozens of large and small tortures he found in this and other homes. 'Homes!' They were battlefields, though they never saw open, honest war. It was more subtly horrible than that"—pointing. "It was slow acid, perversions of a sick child poking out the eyes of rabbits.

"The first time he struck me, I found a way to strike back. I was a better shot than the Swaggering, and I promised to kill him if his hands touched my throat again. I meant it, convinced him. That was the end of violence for me. In or out of liquor, rages notwithstanding.

"I struck back in other ways, too. He tried to

make me a drunkard, but I'd pour the whiskey in the pickle jar and laugh as he changed from human to demon. Why didn't I 'mix' with people in town? Easy. I couldn't suffer the mewling about our 'devotion,' and ever-so-touching 'love'—the pride of Virginia City! Now what did *they* know?—I believe I asked you that. In God's name, what did they think I was doing while my husband spent his time in brothels? Knitting? Making samplers? 'God Bless Our Home' would have been perfect. Did they think that, after the brothels, after the dashing nights at Moll Featherlegs'—is that a made-up name?"

"It'll be in the books."

"*After* Featherlegs, what? (Maybe a good title for a novel?) Did they see the patient little wife, rocking away as age crept on? Well, yes. Home, in a day or two, to throw his drunken self on a bed and sleep. Attend the devoted wife? Hardly. Then, finally, even at his remorseful best, I responded not at all. And I craved more release than the usual healthy wife, in this house of strain and tension.

"It took the form, among other forms, of riding my horse nude. Abnormal or not, I felt free, and sometimes I felt a fine physical release, too. He knew it and hated it, but he didn't dare touch that horse, or me. And then, when he infrequently needed me, I'd laugh in his face, often as not. The blouse—for which I'm sorry—was calculated cruelty. When my *spouse* fell into need, I had ways to delay and tease. The blouse was only one. If he had a grain of devotion—a word I've heard till I'm sickened—it was to that toy garment. It drove him wild, and I enjoyed every look.

" 'Jack?'—I remember crying it out. That was something he taught me early. Why?—vanity pure and simple. 'Jack' was not the world's supreme lover, you'd be surprised to know. Too much whiskey had gone down that throat, too many demands on a mediocre body. But 'Jack!' became a habit, I suppose, when I was young in marriage and obeyed.

"And he had a streak of cowardice, had the Swaggering. He killed Jemmy's dog, in a typical fit of temper, and hadn't the courage to admit it next day. He blamed it on me; said I'd had an accident. People were proud—all of them—of the smashing, injuring, even killing. So—the 'host of admiring friends.' And they were too stupid to consider that these things always took place in drink, or in mania. What he minded most, I'm convinced, was that I knew it!

"How he must have cursed himself about the brothers Lott! They were not afraid, but Mr. Slade was afraid of them, at his drunkest. He knew they'd kill him, and he was afraid! I used to sit here and taunt him—now you'll see the demon he turned me into—about why not ride the much-sung horse in their store? 'Why don't you call on the Lotts today, Jack?' I'd ask him. 'It's not fair to smash every other place and ignore them completely. They'll feel left out, as if blackballed from a club.'

"Probably, at times like these, he'd have murdered me if he could. I'm surprised he didn't do it in my sleep. But we slept apart, and I kept a revolver under my pillow. And the door, of course, locked. So—you can see what I've become. A nightmare for any decent man. Why keep the coffin here with the lid off? I enjoyed

seeing that blotched face and crooked neck! And
that, I'm afraid, is what Mr. Joseph A. (called
'Jack') Slade has created. There's more, worse,
but that's all you'll hear today. Or ever. And
having heard so much, would you like to ride
back? It's all right—I've spent a lifetime
alone—waiting. Waiting and hoping. I'm used to
it."

I made the decision, turning my back on caution. I got up and said, "It's time for a drink. And
then food. And after that *I'll* talk."

"No! You've heard about two sides to every
story? Right now I feel virtuous, self-righteous,
while probably I could have helped. With a
drink I might lose it. Slade failed to make me a
drunkard; sometimes I wonder how close he
came."

"Yes, Ma'am. Then I'll have a tumbler for myself. I need it, and I need it very seldom."

"The sideboard, unless the beauty in the box
whisked it down before his arrest. Not widely
known among his admirers, but his saddlebag
carried two bottles. To polish the swagger."

From a half-empty bottle, I splashed whiskey
into two glasses, placing one beside her without
comment. When I felt the fire work its way
down, I said, "I've considered your case,
Ma'am—"

"You can stop calling me Ma'am. It doesn't go
with your face."

"—and you can start over, as I see it. How old
are you?"

"Exactly the same as yourself—twenty-three.
But you'll be twenty-four this month."

I must have looked thunderstruck.

"Oh, from Slade. He had ways of finding

things out. He was jealous of what happened to you here. Jealous of everybody, jealous of my horse."

I was about to speak but didn't, and drank down the drink instead. I was relieved to see her sip at hers. Something had to free the emotion, and I hoped Slade's whiskey might make a start.

"It was the only relaxed night I'd known in years," she said, thinking. "But don't worry,"—looking away—"it won't happen again."

"You need to make plans, Ma'am. You can't go on here alone. Crows, Sioux, Blackfeet are moving in, and they aren't friendly. I'll help you decide what to do. That's why I rode out."

"Liar! Besides," she said, "I've got plans. I figured them out in my own little head, with support from the coffin."

"What plans?"

"I'm leaving. Anyone can have this ranch that wants it. Nothing!" she cried with passion, finishing the drink, "nothing could make me stay here any longer." She glanced up and said, as if inspired, "Do you want it?"

"Of course," I replied in good humor. "That was the real reason I came. To cheat the grieving widow out of her ranch."

"I mean it. You can buy this place, legally, or I'll leave it to the porcupines and squirrels. Or anybody that rides along."

"Then, later, you'll change your mind and—no ranch, no roof, nothing. By the simple act of burying that"—pointing—"and maybe cleaning up a bit, this can become, overnight, home. Not a nightmare home. And it is beautiful, the best valley up and down the river."

"I don't want to come back, ever. Don't want it possible. I believe a dollar's the legal token of sale—"

"How about ninety cents? Think it over."

"You may be joking; I'm serious. All right— I've handled such things when Slade was in business, and if he had anything at all, he was shrewd about money. Until lately."

She strode to a desk and took up a pen. "Let's see—'For the consideration of one dollar,' etc., etc.,—'to Ross Nickerson,' and the description, with the deed or claim—"

"The joke's worn out. What's more—"

"Sign here and put the papers in your pocket. Details later." She tapped a foot with impatience.

Crossing the room, willing to indulge a whim, I signed my name in a great looping flourish and said, "There you are, Ma'am, all legal and—"

"The dollar! It's my pound of flesh. I'd like him—you!—" addressing herself to the table— "to understand what value the devoted wife placed on her tranquil and solitary nest."

"I'll tear this up on the way home."

"Suit yourself. And now," she said, the color back in her face, "maybe I can drink a bottle of wine and enjoy it at last. A whole bottle, without holding back and feeling my stomach in knots because of some dirty little game." Forgetting the wine, she re-filled her glass with whiskey; then she got more from the shed.

"There's champagne here," she called. "Don't you think, could anyone deny, that this is a God-given chance to launch that tin pumpkin for the long warm trip ahead?"

"I deny it. That fact is, I won't permit it."

She came out, eyes blazing. Then she sat down and laughed. "You probably think I'm drunk. Not that I owe you, or any living person, an explanation, but I haven't touched alcohol since the hanging. I've been afraid to. But I've earned the right to get a little drunk now."

I leaned forward. "Before you do, promise me something. I signed your document, now you sign mine. This is Tuesday. I owe Mr. Smithers help in clearing things up. I'll be back Friday evening—to stay. It makes no difference what people say, or think. Besides, it's the custom here—"

"Like a squaw?"

"Not like a squaw. You know the reasons. You've understood them, and me, since you rode into the Forge."

"Tell me the reasons."

"I'm no good at that; I lack practise."

She said, "You might get down on one knee," but her face was troubled, and the tears came when I picked her up and, sure of myself with the buttons, released what Slade had unsuccessfully sought in his wildness.

When I left, near sundown, she was riding her horse, clothed, the stallion with a saddle, a soft look of things remembered on her face. She blew me a kiss as I closed the front gate, and I rode toward town on a trail paved in gold, aglow with a new kind of peace.

I told Mrs. Smithers, and Grantly, and both said something like, "I'm glad for you, son," and during my three days at the Forge, I'd never done work half so well. Everything I touched (for a change) turned out perfect, or nearly so. The tools seemed to leap forward toward my hand, without Mr. Smithers having to say, "That's a flatter you've lifted, son, not tongs. Your mind appears to be off frolicking again."

And the people in town, who'd nodded curtly for weeks, while my case was under scrutiny, went out of their way to stop me on the street, conversing in friendly effusion. The invited me to 1) dinner, 2) Singing School, 3) Mr. and Mrs. Craven's Theatricals, 4) the Social-Dances, and 5) everywhere else. And if the invitations came largely from parents with unmarried daughters, why, I decided, that was normal, to be expected.

I was so buoyed up that I might likely have burst before Friday, except for the miners. They'd heard the news, of course, and did it change their humbug? Not at all. As I look back, it was the miners who kept me on my feet, so to speak. Before, when I was suspect, they'd spoken civilly, not one saying an ugly or accusing word—in short, being, I believe, the fairest minded men I knew. Not once, I repeat, had they made me feel like a kind of criminal on trial.

Now that was changed. Since I was cleared they took the line that I'd been guilty all along, and commonly ate miners for breakfast. I'm convinced the buzzards could have thrown a monkey wrench into the Last Supper. I knew these men and liked them. But if I went into a saloon, now, a dead hush fell on the place, and the ones playing cards were apt to stop and place their hands above the table, slowly, looking apprehensive.

In Orem's at noon, to drink a glass of beer, as to calm down a little, I stood at the bar beside Jake Silvie, and I'm a Chinaman if he didn't draw his

gun and hand it across the Con Orem, saying,
"Now, I'd be obleeged if you'd just grapple that
hogleg, if it wouldn't distress you. You take and
a ruckus starts, I don't want no trouble with
him!" And when I tried the Exchange, worn
down with nonsense, Pee Wee Slater (six foot
five) turned, almost crying, and told me, "I never
said it! You got to believe that! No matter what
people reported, I ain't opened my mouth. Now
don't back me into a fight; I ain't got the stomach
for it!"

I sighed. "Pee Wee," I said, "you've run out of
jokes. You ought to ride down to Salt Lake and
get a new batch."

Well, this broke them all apart, some throwing
their cards on the floor; and as many as a dozen
crowded up to "treat" me, and said they
wouldn't take no for an answer, but meaning no
offense by it.

When I finally wobbled out, glassy-eyed, they
were still telling how Pee Wee had got his "de-
serts," and that jackass was in agreement, nodding and saying, "Oh, I figured it'd come from
him. He's unpeeled dynamite, and it ain't Pee
Wee Slater that's apt to light the fuse!"

After that I stayed out of saloons. There might
have been some way to reform that bunch, but
nobody had found it out yet.

Mid-afternoon on Friday, Mr. Smithers urging
me to take off early, since "we've cinched the
main bulk" (by no means true), I went to my
cabin and hitched up the wagon I'd bought and
loaded. Then I locked the door, for I intended us
to keep this place in town, too, while doubtless
building a better one by and by. In my father's

last letter (which I'll get around to soon) had
been a draft for a thousand dollars; and I'd saved
considerable from the Forge as well. Any
number of people—friends—waved as I drove at
a medium clip out of town, my horse tied to the
back, this time following the easier but longer
wagon road toward Madison.

It was one of those early spring days when, in
my humor, you heard each individual bird sing
and chirp, and the streams made a new kind of
music. I thought: This is a high point of my life;
we'll discuss it in the years to come. They had
the prospect of being good years, after her alone-
ness and—I'll say it once—mine for a long time.
Truth is, the vision was such that I had trouble
holding the draft horses, not to hurt them with
their heavy load.

It was two hours or so, and seemed like a week,
before I rounded the last curve, climbed the last
knoll, and came within sight of Slade's valley. I
frowned—I'd remembered wrong. Unhappy
wanderer, it was his valley no longer and in a
way never had been. The thought was briefly
sobering, so that I missed seeing that no blue
smoke now curled out of that chimney. No
blooded horses stood in the corral, no sign of life
came from Slade's stone house.

For it was his after all; I began to grasp the
truth. During an almost hopeful moment, I
thought of Indians, but I knew it wasn't so, and I
drove slowly on to the gate. A leaden weight
filled my chest, and climbing down from the
seat, I stumbled and fell.

The door hung ajar. Inside, the memorable
table was bare, and nothing—no clothing, silver,
household belongings—remained, upstairs or

down. After their manner, two porcupines had
taken up lodging in the shed. These I shot—the
noise startling loud—and carried to the stream
in a broken snow-shoe. Then, expecting nothing, I searched for a note, something scribbled
on a wall, anything to give life to this ghost-
haunted castle. But I'd been wrong to expect
nothing at all. Lying on the hearth was a small,
gay sprig of wild flowers woven into the shape of
heart.

After a while, I sank down in a sinew chair
and, in half an hour or so, dozed off. But I shortly
awoke and knew what I needed—badly needed
for the first time in my life.

In a dark corner of Slade's sideboard remained
an opened bottle of whiskey, and I drank this
deliberately while the jumbled pictures ran
through my mind, less rapidly soon, the procession slowing to a walk, changing at last to a
solemn cortege. It was confusing but familiar
. . . on either side the river lie, long fields of
barley and of rye . . . but in her web she still
delights, to weave the magic sights . . . she
loosed the chain, and down she lay . . . and as
the boat-head wound along . . . they heard her
singing her last song. La Belle Dame? No. I
struggled, but it was hard to remember.

I felt better before the deep sleep came, con-
gratulating myself on solving a simple mystery;
near enough to touch yet millions of light years
away.

CHAPTER XXX

"—AND SINCE LAST Christmas we've had the extraordinary fortune to hear from you twice—three times at the most—and I've concluded that your 'news,' if I may call it so, might fit neatly into a thimble, leaving room for one's thumb.

"You report that your present domicile in one 'Virginia City' (not included on my maps), is in the throes of 'religion almost orgiastic' and that a 'professor from Oxford' is teaching the young 'at a minimal charge.' Well, I feel it my duty to tell you that, in my lifetime, I've avoided 'orgiastic religion' like the plague (from which it differs only in outline) and that the marvel of having an Oxford scholar in southern Montana greatly relieves my mind. 'Oxford' where?—Colorado? Utah? Or do you refer, perhaps, to a federal prison in California? I must add that I consider this utterance to be a lie, substantially like your other statements, and I remain determined to visit your dubious retreat.

"I have heard, to be sure, of the gold strikes in Montana, but my best information is that all significant fortunes will be made in something called 'quartz-mining,' an operation which calls, of course, for Eastern capital. I believe that our Gianini family of bankers, friends in this city, have interests in one or more ventures, each

bearing, in part, the unlovely name of 'Gulch.'
What, precisely, is a Gulch, and in how many of
these cornucopias have you and your Duncans
invested? Do your Gulches prosper? Or do they,
like your other ventures, represent success of
Tomorrow? And if you retain, after this time, a
trace of family feeling (which I doubt, while your
sister ascends in hierarchic importance), you
will send me a full profit-and-loss statement,
together with a capital accounting—the two
done by a reputable firm of accountants (possibly Indians in your area).

"Now I must touch on a disturbing story that
came to my ears from a nephew of Eliah Gould,
first mate of the *Southern Cross*. He claims, in
sum, that a friend (people here make friends in
boyhood, and keep them!)—a friend of the
nephew, I say, descried you, he afterward decided, at work as a common blacksmith! His
recognition came after he'd departed your town
(no doubt in a hurry), his first vision failing to
penetrate what he described as 'the rough and
villainous garments' of your trade. He further
represents you, or whoever, as wearing a 'hideous wolfskin cap' and said, in conclusion, that
you appeared to have 'an elderly, one-legged
partner of distinctly piratical mien!' What he
said of the region in general I'll spare you, for I
am, after all, still your father.

"Since the nephew is presently at Harvard
College—and *doing well*—I'm inclined to
believe him implicitly. (You won't, I'm sure, be
offended when I remind you that I, in my time,
graduated third from the top in my class.) The
nephew convinces me more than ever that the

time is ripe for a visit, and if you require release
from jail, I shall, with reluctance, arrange it.
Blood is regrettably thicker than water, and cold
blood is thicker than both, and I, at least have a
sense of obligation—shrunk now, in your case,
to the size of a pea. Meanwhile, again, if it requires a month of your valuable time, prepare a
list of all gambling debts. Toward these I
enclose—in my folly—a third draft for a
thousand dollars—" etc., etc., etc.

It was easy to tell that my father was annoyed,
and after he'd continued (in this longest letter
he'd written) about the blockade hurting business; the line's reluctance to convey goods to
England, because of "the usual contrary spirit
there"; and the fact that my Uncle Abner had
suffered a wound "in his left buttock" during
some battle or other, he closed with a testy quotation from King Lear.

Well, as unhappy as I was, I couldn't avoid
feeling my outlook brighten at one item. My
Uncle Abner was a persimmony old deacon, and
mighty critical of me, forever tapping me on the
head with his long-handled collection plate—
when I appeared to doze (thinking). A wound in
the buttock shouldn't faze him, for he had bulk
there, and I recalled , further, that he must have
been running *away* from the field, which was
typical. I wondered why they signed a man of
that age in the first place—he was nearly forty.

I was interested in my father's reminder of his
college record, for it was stressed in each of his
letters, though the number had crept up from
twelfth.

Then I fell to worrying about the chance of his making a visit and decided that it might be time to go home. I'd failed in Montana, and, for another thing, my father was so eruptuous and hasty that he might look Virginia over, dislike it, buy the whole works, and burn it. After that, of course, people would blame it all on me.

But people, right now, were being unusually kind, in their diplomatic way. Neither Mr. Smithers, nor his family, when I took a meal there, acted out of the ordinary. They were as cheerful, and warm, and kinsmanlike as always, but not overly so. They had tact, and no mistake, and that included, now, the previously addled Daisy, who'd been attending Professor Dimsdale's school, with her "sister," re-named, permanently, Faire, and was practically normal. (About the name: they had to settle on something, and do it quick, because when Mr. Dimsdale called on somebody, she generally stood up—Mrs. Smithers' fire had been just scattered.) The Professor, hearing Mr. and Mrs. Smithers' explanations and deciphering them, had worked hard, giving the girls special attention, and they attracted notice from various swains in town. This included the yellow-haired child, who I was shocked to learn would soon be fourteen.

And Grantly behaved almost the same, never referring to Slade, or his wife, or the ranch on the Madison. James was back from Yellowstone, now, and said, in his laconic style, responding to questions, that "the trip cost two thousand dollars, and we lost a number of men." Grantly was unhappy about it, but he never pressed him for

more, and neither, of course, did I. Occasionally
I caught both eyeing me, as if they'd like to have
a long, helpful talk, but I avoided giving them
the chance.

One weekend I rode out to the ranch. Sitting
my horse atop the knoll, I saw it as it was when I
left—empty, removed silent. On impulse, taking
a deep breath, I walked down and spent the day
cleaning, straightening, boarding up windows,
and nailing shut the door. She would be
back one day, and I wanted the claim intact.
Moreover, I was leaving Virginia City, probably
not to return. So I tacked up a notice, putting
forth all information from the documents and
adding, as an afterthought, a guide for her alone,
in pretty dismal French, about the key to Slade's
heavy brass padlock.

And when I reached town I thought about that
deed, and asked Grantly and James to write
themselves down as witnesses. They did so
without comment, and I tried to pay Judge Davis
to re-record the claim, or deed. He waved away
the money but did what I asked, and I placed
both papers and key in a vault at Mr. Hauser's
bank. And so, I felt she was protected.

The episode changed me, as the Duncans said
years later. And of course, for a long time, my
chest seemed wrapped around with chain, and
while I never got drunk, I drank more than beer,
now.

As for those miners, they'd changed even
worse, or better, than I had. To a man, down to
the most impious nuisance, they gave me exactly
the respect they gave each other, to use the word
loosely. Not one ever bought me a drink for no
reason, or in any way referred to my setback. If,

on the contrary, when playing cards, I found one of my boots afire, it was no more than Grimy Joe Bates had found a minute before.

I began slowly putting my affairs in order, arranging my goods, ready to rent my cabin. But then talk of Territory filled the air, the feeling, even in the papers, being that it was a matter of weeks. So—I decided to wait for the celebration. After all, I'd been a pioneer here—and of Bannack and Deer Lodge before that—and I was curious to see what might happen. Montana was my home, whether I left it or not, and down inside I knew it always would be, in some way. For one thing, I'd left a part of me on the bank of the Madison River.

CHAPTER XXXI

TERRITORIAL DAY! THE government in its conde-
scension had seen fit to wrench us out of that
expanse of mountain and plain called Idaho, and
give us separate entity. The three men mainly
responsible were Colonel Sanders, our lawyer
and now-acknowledged head of the Vigilance
Committee; Mr. Sanders' uncle, Sidney Edgerton, of Bannack, who'd been named our first
Governor; and an Ohio Congressman friend of
Mr. Edgerton, James Ashley. Grantly peevishly
thought the act pretty tardy, or late, and expressed us as "ripped untimely out of Mother
Idaho's womb," referring to some poet or other.

The vote had passed Congress, or the decision
made by President Lincoln—I've forgotten
which—on May 26 ('64), but news traveled slow,
without telegraph or train, and the town settled
on July Fourth to be Celebration Day, thus "killing two federal hogs," said a Southern ig-
noramus, confused about national holidays. He
told me, "confidential," that "When the Guvi-
mint freed the [Negroes] on July Fourth, they
done a underhand disservice that ain't apt to be
forgot for four hundred year."

I refrained from asking why he wasn't back
fighting tooth and nail to help un-free the Negroes. That kind of question was never asked in

these parts; besides, he was a decent fellow
when sober. Each man here had his reason, aside
from lost battles that saw men drift off without
leadership or orders, and nobody's reason was
cowardice, as people well knew. This applied to
both South and North.

Well, the Celebration was going to be "monstrous," and plans got under way in a hurry. And
then, when additional news arrived that a Chief
Justice—a man named Hexekiah Lord Hosmer—would show up soon after, so that
Montana would have constitutional law, a kind
of lunacy seized the town. A collection was tak-
en, and the sponsors were appalled to find
within a week that their kitty totalled $43,247,
plus 12½ cents. (I should explain that the old
English "bit," or half a quarter, was still in use,
so that half-cents were not uncommon.)

When the brass farthings, counterfeit Lincolnskins, wooden nickels, and further annoyances were raked from the pile, there was
still $35,000 left, and a meeting was called to
dispose it.

The miners, being in the majority, ran all this.
The leading merchants threw in their hands
early, concluding to let the miners have their
heads. Considering all they'd suffered, it seemed
only fair. But their ideas of celebration took some
pretty wild turns at first, and then eased off, as
people usually do. First off, they sent five wagons to Salt Lake and bought 450 cases of champagne. Then, the drivers having money left
after those cheats gobbled up what they could,
they invested in eight barrels of Valley Tan, the
regular Mormon brew. While several men were

put to knocking off barrel-heads and fishing out things like spiders, beetles, and old wheel-iron, Dink Smothers stole one of Brigham Young's wives—a girl he'd lately taken on, scarcely knowing he owned—so that the wagons rolled out at fast clip.

Red, white, and blue bunting festooned the fronts of all stores, saloons, and public buildings, with rubber-balloon "effigies" of Uncle Sam floating here and there (filled with gas, "which seems appropriate"—Grantly). Then a pretty seedy band was recruited from up and down the Gulch. Some of these men hadn't touched their instruments in years, and the racket of practising—from as far off as Bannack— would have deafened a bison. Things like tubas, and flutes, and bass fiddles, and trombones, and French horns, and, of course, any number of harmonicas—some two feet long—emerged from hiding and began to take punishment, you can believe me. One man found mice in his trombone, and another removed a dead squirrel from a dented tubalike horn that lay at the bottom of a busted old trunk. Even his squaw had complained about the stench, and most Indians, commonly, ignore smells that don't boil water.

They almost came a cropper when Paddlefoot Gates discovered that his kettle-drum's head had rotten into shreds. Professor Dimsdale's suggestion that the traditional "Spirit of '76" be enacted, including a boy beating a drum, a fifer with his head bandaged, and an old man with a flag, met unbridled applause, the miners clapping each other on the back and saying, "And him an Englishman, which we whipped to make it possible!"

A moist resolution was promptly drawn to cast Professor Dimsdale in full-sized bronze for the "Public Square" (there was none). But when a group insisted on placing it before Moll Featherlegs' brothel, "so it would look down and over the town, like a Angel," the plan frittered away. It was ridiculous; he'd never been near the place in his life.

That kettle-drum was a stumper, and the miners solved it in their way. Wong Chee Chee (correct name unknown, or ignored) was a fat, roly-poly, popular free-Chinaman in the Gulch, and a crafty and master card-player to boot, the target of limitless practical jokes. But he'd died two days before, when a boulder fell on his head. After a sober and lengthy council, late at night, the miners broke up satisfied, feeling they'd done the right thing. I heard one say, "Old Wong would a wished it thataway; there wasn't no finer specimen ever come to this Gulch, and I'll fight the man to deny it!" And another said, "Me, I'm glad he'll participate, him that's done so much for the town—it ain't fair he didn't live to see the Celebration." (I wasn't quite clear what he'd done for the town, aside from winning money playing fan-tan and making odd noises singing in Reverend Torbett's church, to which he'd been the most generous contributor of other people's cash.) But he was a sunny-natured fellow, fiercely patriotic of his chosen new land—a favorite of everybody—and I supposed that was enough.

So they stripped a sizable piece of skin off his stomach, then got Mr. Smithers—jawed him into it—to patch up Paddlefoot's drum, and she came up with an interesting boom, except in the center. It was almost as good as new; Gates said so himself. Moreover, they said, it was "the right color, where an elk or a antelope would have appeared sickly, if large enough to start with."

Professor Dimsdale's Singing School was scheduled to march in the Procession, and Mr. and Mrs. Craven would present a condensation of "Our American Cousin," which was as near as they had in their files. And not a soul, North or South, complained about it; spirits were just that high.

A jolt occurred when notice arrived that Bannack was named the Territory's first capital. But after Colonel Sanders assured everyone that this would be changed soon to Virginia, and was a "token tribute" to Bannack's Governor Edgerton, who lived there, the citizens calmed down. (It was a scarce few months before he was proved right, by the way; comparatively, Bannack was played out.) And in any case, all Bannack planned to come down for the Celebration.

I wrote my father, explaining that, due to events unforseen, I had to postpone coming home for a while to help organize Territorial Day. I admitted past errors and said I realized that my place was in the family business. "I've sowed my wild oats, Father," I said, "and they seem to have grown up weeds. I'm not over-happy these days, but I'll discuss that later. Meanwhile I hope you'll try to understand." And I expressed concern—perfectly bogus— about Uncle Abner's left buttock, and inquired about everybody else. To wind up, I urged my father not to attempt a trip to Montana at this moment, for we were in the midst of an Indian war—between the Choctaws and Utes (Eskimos and Aztecs would have served equally well)— and there was no chance to get through. After writing this last, which I couldn't help, I reflected that a good deal of Montana miner must have rubbed off on me.

There was more, none of it very bright. To tell the truth, I couldn't concentrate on writing letters just now.

Several Journals contain criticism of Territorial Day at Virginia, but these were mild on the whole, and others saw the Celebration as amusing, and even healthful, after the awfulness of Plummer and Slade. It had been a dreadful winter, and its memory was by no means faded. Grantly and James contended that the miners did their best, and if things went awry here and there, it was nobody's fault, really. At the very least, the residents were given something to talk about, other than murders, holdups, and hangings.

July Fourth dawned blue and sunny, and the colorful bunting cheered people long before the regular events started. There were to be speeches, on a platform near Pfout's, by Mr. Edgerton, Colonel Sanders, Congressman Ashley, and one or two others with "oratorical gifts," but only after the Procession reached there. "The Honorable" Thadeus Foss (self-proclaimed), the wiseacre that introduced "Maestro Giulio Borgia," wanted to be a speaker and was backed by several miners; others thought it a poor idea, so they rigged up a fake telegram which had been carried pell-mell from Salt Lake by a former Pony Express rider. It said, "YOUR

UNCLE JUST DIED HERE, LEAVING FORTUNE IN GOLD AND PART OWNERSHIP OF BREWERY AND TEMPLE. CAN YOU RUSH TO SUPPORT CLAIM?—RUFUS T. APPLEGATE, ATTORNEY-AT-LAW."

The Honorable remembered no such uncle, but he couldn't "afford to take chances like that," as he said, so he saddled up and lit out. Another pest disposed of.

I think the overall confusion was caused by a shipment of whistles that arrived at Pfout's the previous week. A good many children bought them, but Mr. Pfout had forgotten, and now he distributed whistles to the Procession's Marshals. These included Professor Dimsdale. I suppose you'd call him the Grand Marshal, for he organized the placement of units and his whistle, from about 9:30 on, worked overtime.

They had no rule about units joining—there were three from Bannack—and I'm dead-beat if those Sons of Temperance didn't show up wearing white sashes, as pious and saintly as priests—twenty or more. Mr. Dimsdale put them at the end, but they edged up, somehow, and in all the uproar, with instructions shouted and whistles blowing, the Hurdies (in long dresses, also white) wound up next to the Singing School children.

By this time, Professor Dimsdale's hair was standing erect, and his whistle sounded hoarse. But it was all right; the Hurdies behaved motherly and concerned, helping the children with their costumes, where underwear had hit the street, and along that line. The band, of thirty-two pieces, was in the middle, and when the Bannack Volunteer Police and Firemen, and the Nevada Upward League, and the "former

Claim-jumpers Association" (an outfit that told competitive lies), and the Hurdies, and the Singing School, and the Sons of Temperance, and so on, eventually became arranged at the foot of Wallace Street, it made a noble sight. Nearly everybody, including the Chinese Association, waved small American flags, and, naturally, a number of Southerners had got some Confederate flags, and many persons were provided with both.

Whistles were going all the time, by children on the sidelines mostly. But when Professor Dimsdale—a reddish-looking color in the face—was heard over all, Paddlefoot Gates thumped Wong's stomach, there was a respectable fanfare (these miners had been practising), and the Procession stepped off. The first melodic offering was the Upward League's "Abide with Me, Lord," and it rang out to warm your heart. This was followed by a rain-dance, in full regalia, by combined Snakes and medium-friendly Crows (very rare, at least nobody got hurt), and a thunder of applause burst from under the store awnings.

The day had warmed up by then, and a freak frost had given way to mud, which discolored the Singing School's white shoes. It made an odd sight, all the gumbo against the dazzling dresses above. But Virginia people were used to mud, ice, slush, and water in the streets, and blood pretty often, so nobody minded.

And then Professor Dimsdale, waving his arms, tried to divert sections to the board walk and around a big hole (a person could disappear in it—a left-over from when the Stampede had hit town-center) and the marchers mixed things up. It was too bad, because the plan had gone splendidly that far, with onlookers practically clapping their hands off.

A whistle from somewhere forward swung the band into a fighting rendition of "Yankee Doodle," and directly in the middle, Wong's stomach broke. It turned out unimportant because half the band had changed to "Dixie," anyway, in good humor but preferring their regional song. Wong failed to hold the unit together, but it wasn't his fault, and nobody blamed him.

Forseeing trouble, Professor Dimsdale ran up and stopped those tunes, substituting "Mine Eyes Have Seen the Glory of the Coming of the Lord." Then the musicians, commenting over their shoulders, decided that "Lord," of course, meant Hezekiah Lord Hosmer, the new Chief Justice, and they reminded each other that "Lord" also appeared in "Abide with Me," and they took it as a sign. They agreed, one and all, that such a blessing, possibly Divine, had to be toasted. What's more (being in front of the place) they said there was no doubt about it; the hymn made it plain—the "grapes of wrath" were stored in Orem's, so they wheeled and marched inside, followed by the Sons of Temperance.

Out in ten minutes, to find the Procession pretty far ahead but scrambled a little, now. Some brat, near the detour, had imitated Mr. Dimsdale's whistle and, with a stick, pointed the Singing School up toward Moll Featherlegs'. The scandalized Hurdies were close behind, trying to point them back. And you can say this for Mrs. Featherlegs—she and her girls rushed out and helped steer the children right, and gave them all cookies.

After this, with people holding their sides, the Procession reached the speaker's platform, and I'm confounded if a grizzly bear didn't amble out of Van Buren Street, looking curious, and maybe annoyed at the disturbance. Much of the crowd dove for shelter, but more, I believe, stayed to watch. And I'll pay tribute here to Mr. Edgerton. After being introduced by Colonel Sanders (who cared no more for grizzlies than he did for Plummer), he took up some papers and told us how glorious a day this was for Montana, and what it might mean for the future, and he was glad that a Congressman from his own state had persuaded Mr. Lincoln.

Then he made further gracious remarks, but the speech seemed to have an underlying Northern tone. The grizzly apparently thought so, too, or didn't care for politicians, for after listening closely, sitting back on its haunches, it wheeled with a snort and left. It was the first adult grizzly bear ever seen in the shopping district of Virginia City.

Well, other speeches proceeded without incident, and all were happily received, especially by the Sons of Temperance. They interrupted with "A-a-men!" and "Let her rip, Governor!" and further impudence.

"The festivities of Territorial Day," said the *Montana Post*, as written by a new young reporter, "were a brilliant success, though they might have seemed unusual when weighed by New York standards. Great credit should be given to the *Post's* own Professor Thomas A. Dimsdale,

Oxon., new Superintendent of Public Instruction," etc.

At the Post Office, Bannack's Volunteer Police and Fire Department raised a new flag, sewed by ladies of Father Giorda's Catholic Church, and everyone shifted to tables set up on a lawn, or stubbly grass-patch. There we enjoyed a barbecued steer, donated by Coleman and Loeb's saloon. Nothing was served except beer, with lemonade for children and temperance folk, but some private bottles were going, as peaceful as a christening. Then, toward evening, with the champagne, dancing commenced at the Virginia Hotel and continued till dawn, with a minimum of rowdyism. The Sheriff's office reported only twenty-two arrests for the whole day and night.

A footnote was the fact that several Church people, around sundown, took Paddlefoot Gates' kettle-drum and quietly buried it on the Hill beside the rest of Wong Chee Chee. (The popular Chinaman's name, incidentally, was later inscribed on a tablet with others of that landmark day.)

CHAPTER XXXII

IN THREE WEEKS the great news arrived, Chief Justice Hosmer, bringing law to Montana, was expected in Virginia any day. True to Colonel Sanders' prediction, the capital was being moved to Virginia (where it would remain for twelve years), and "incorporations" were under way. The appointed new Governor brought a legislature, or "assembly," into existence, the People's Court was made official, as others were, and all was ready for the descent upon Virginia, and Bannack, of the now legendary Mr. Hosmer.

If anything else was discussed in town during this phase, I never heard it. Speculation ran most nearly wild in the saloons. I'd estimate that 90 percent of the miners—converted mountainmen—had never laid eyes on a Chief Justice, and there were those to whom the title itself was unknown. The majority were convinced that he could not be ordinary, in even a physical way, and a small group clung to the Divine theory as expressed during the Procession.

Wandering from place to place after hours, I gathered information denied to the general public. Certainly the newspapers collected by Grantly failed to mention these scraps, perhaps from lax reporting. I'd been unaware, for instance, that Judge Hosmer was eight feet tall, a fact let slip and then insisted on (with a promise of fisticuffs) by Smiley Klein.

"I'd heard it was well over seven," a drinking friend said, "but eight foot tops anything in *these* parts. You don't catch *me* tangling with him!"

It was newsworthy, I thought—this from a professional Georgian—that Mr. Hosmer was a mulatto and had served two terms in a federal penitentiary. "I don't mean it to disqualify him," said the Georgian, "for I ain't small, but you'd think, by Jesus, they'd trot out a specimen with a medium clean slate."

"And so it went. In the Exchange, I learned that Justice Hosmer, altogether, had killed thirteen men and was considered to be the "fastest draw east of the Mississippi," but this was absurd that the man who uttered it fell apart, convulsed, and later, after more Tanglefoot, reduced the number to nine. A miner who'd made a trip back East, the year before, said that he, personally, had seen Mr. Hosmer lift an anvil weighing 385 pounds and hold it at arm's length for five minutes.

"Where at, Jake?" asked one of the few skeptics.

"Where at? Why, in Washington, where he works!"

"Speaking specific—where *at* in Washington?"

"In his office. You didn't think he'd keep it in the parlor, did you? With the President likely lolling around there and all?"

"All right, now you anser me this: What's a Chief Justice doing with a anvil in his office?

Surely he ain't operating as a blacksmith on the *side!*"

"Oh, shucks, Curley Knowles, you wouldn't believe it if he come walking down Idaho Street 'with the anvil a-top his head!"

Things were getting pretty thick, so I left. Half this material was the poorest kind of jokes, of course, but the rest—including the estimate of Mr. Hosmer's height—was taken as approximately correct. They preferred him that way.

Well, all residents agreed that some sort of welcome must be arranged, though not on the same scale as Territorial Day. So they sent one man riding to Fort Benton, to check on steamers (sometimes we had news of passengers or cargo from part-way down river, when the boat slammed into a bar, or sunk, and a person or two got off with horses), and another rider went to Salt Lake to ask about Stages. But he found the Prophet in such a peeve—having found that he'd lost a plump young wife worth a hundred dollars—that the man didn't stay long. He had to make tracks to get out in time.

Anyway, it was learned which Stage Mr. Hosmer was coming on, from Fort Benton, and a delegation went to meet him. An election was in progress, having to do with Congress, but they persuaded "Judge" Filbert, an impressive but not wholly authenticated lawyer, and some members of the Upward League, and others that knew protocol to ride out and escort Judge Hosmer into town.

The miners had located a one-pounder brass cannon, and when the Stage rolled in, the cannon was fired, fully loaded, and the ball went ricocheting off through the trees, barely missing the wickiup of Filo Skeggs, down with a sprained ankle. He hobbled out and shook his fist and uttered some interesting combinations. But the Judge never batted an eye, and a miner surmised that he owned such a cannon back home, and was accustomed to the noise.

To people's amazement, when he climbed down and pointed to his bags, he seemed perfectly normal-looking. His hair was graying beneath a fedora, he wore golden prince-nez, and everything else was average: height, weight, feet no larger than common, none of the things ascribed him of late. So—seeing he hadn't flinched at the cannon (while many did, for it was supplied twice the usual dose of powder), the miners took an opposite tack entirely.

Judge Hosmer was the personal embodiment of courage, and had been picked for it. "That feller's all grit; you can see it from his face" was the consensus, and it stayed that way through his tenure. Certainly Judge Hosmer's face was unfrightened, though there was enough in southern Montana to scare off a Zulu. The bare sight of a miner, in from his claim without washing up, would have floored most men, Chief Justices or not, and sent them hiking back to Benton.

Some leading citizens stood in front of the People's Court to greet him, and these, followed by others, headed toward the Virginia Hotel, where "light refreshments" were consumed. Grantly then tapped on his glass, arose, and made a short, graceful welcoming speech, and Hauser, Langford, and Sanders added their bit.

Then Judge Hosmer got up and spoke in a dry,
polite way that I realized meant business from
first to last. What happened to him, finally, was
regrettable, but his purpose was to bring law,
and justice, to Montana, and nobody denied that
he tried hard.

His arrival was on a weekend, and the main
entertainment was a prize fight, for a purse of a
thousand dollars, between John Condel Orem,
who ran the saloon, and Hugh O'Neil, an especially tough young miner. This "Attraction" had
been set for Sunday, but Mr. Dimsdale persuaded the sponsors to delay it till Monday, and
not "desecrate the Sabbath with anything so
vulgar."

So—at noon Monday, the town (with a rather
bewildered Hosmer) repaired en masse to a ring
roped off in the new Leviathan Hall, on the north
side of Jackson Street. At 1:15 Hugh O'Neil arrived and threw his sombrero into the ring, followed by "one hundred ninety pounds of as
good bone and sinew as one could expect to look
upon." Then Orem appeared and "deposited his
castor*" over the ropes. He weighed 138
pounds, so he said, but he had an uncommon
history of professional fighting. His father (an
Eastern blacksmith) had taught him to wrestle,
in the teen-age stage, but the lessons were so
onerous that Orem left for the Rockies as soon as
possible. There, in Colorado, he switched to box-
ing and fought anybody willing to tackle the
small bundle of fury—for trifling purses. He

*"Castor" dervies from the Greek "Kastor," meaning
beaver.

worked as a blacksmith in Denver, when fighting was slow, and gained reputation as a buffalo hunter and expert rifle and pistol shot. He neither drank nor smoked (nor swore) and made a fetish of keeping in rock-hard condition. This gave him an advantage over miners whose off-hours were limited to drinking whiskey and reveling in brothels. He won most bouts in two or three rounds. A Denver account said that his training, in part, "consisted of fighting bears, using only a knife to even the odds." Now, in Montana, at thirty, he was, as reported in the *Post*, "A model of symmetry and form, wiry, healthy, with a boxer's eye." He gave out (modestly) that he'd moved to Montana because Colorado bears "were becoming scarcer and scarcer."

O'Neil took his training casually, continuing to pan, and if it suited him, to run once in a while. He was extraordinarily strong, and, prompted, performed lifting feats after a few drinks. Outside the ring both were mild and easy-going—close friends—and O'Neil spent much time chatting in Orem's saloon, the two on opposite sides of the bar. Orem's reputation as a fighter was well-known, newspaper accounts having followed him to Montana, but O'Neil was so obliging that, when asked to join the fiesta for Hosmer, said merely, while leaning on a pick, "Sure enough. Let me know when to turn up."

I had a seat down front and was as excited as the crowd packing the hall. Another, and better, band had been recruited, with an occidental drum-head, and the group produced some fairly creditable noises as the crowd bulged in. "The fair sex was not unrepresented," said the *Post* in

its delightful style of employing double nega-
tives, and the entire first page was given to the
fight that week. This included highlights of each
round, descriptions of the men, and a summation that set off a row, as I'll mention in a minute.

The fighters' costumes were of interest.
O'Neil, entering the ring, was wearing green
trunks—a testament to his Irish birth—and these
were adorned with a harp and several stars and
his name embroidered in full on a belly-band.
Orem had on black trunks with a single star and a
broader band around his waist that had both
stars and stripes and an eagle, besides the motto:
"May the best man win." They were a gaudy
sight, and the "seconds" of both were dressed in
whatever finery they could scrounge—Indian
feathers, bear teeth strings, and the like. Each set
of seconds had five or six sponges, and buckets
of vinegar to dip them in.

The crowd's humor was noisy but controlled,
for Virginia City, and a hush fell when the referee, a Mr. Wilson, stepped out in the middle,
introduced the fighters, who shuffled their feet
on gravely-sand strewn over the floor, and then
cried, "Ladies and Gentlemen, we're observing
the London Prize Ring Rules in this contest of
fisticuffs—"

There immediately rose a chorus of boos and
protests from miners, who yelled, "Let's keep
this ruckus home-grown; there ain't a particle of
use wandering over to London for their views on
the subject!" and a smelly old fellow sitting beside me said, "I've knowed old Wilson for years;
now ain't he the one to tell us?" and he started to
throw a bottle he'd been consulting, but I
grasped his arm. He stared at me, blinking, not

certain what he'd done wrong; then decided to drop the matter, since somebody had struck a bell and the fight was on.

Well, I can't tell it all, of course, but it continued for exactly three hours and five minutes, or for 185 rounds. Orem, fighting as gamely as anyone could against such a tough and conspicuously larger man, went down repeatedly and many times resorted to his wrestling tactics; but in O'Neil he was dealing with a miner of immense strength, and, more often than not, these failed.

Both men wore unlined buckskin gloves and a round, as I got it, was called when a man hit the floor or flew out through the ropes. (At least half the time the two went down together and had to be unscrambled.) Within twenty minutes the faces of both were macerated, and "ruby" (*Post* expression) was much in evidence.

I tried to keep track of the rounds, but gave up fitting the number to what happened, so I'll borrow scraps from the paper: "Round 7: Con laid his sinister mauler on Hugh's knowledge-box"; "Round 37: Hugh took a pull from the bottle with revivifying effect"; "Round 60: Orem returned to Mother Earth for the finish"; "Round 86: Many exchanged on the mug"; "Round 145: Con popped his right to O'Neil's olefactory department."

Such statements as the above led, later, to literary howls by the *Salt Lake Union Vedette*, and then to a more general fuss, an enduring curiosity of what may remain history's longest, and bloodiest, prize fight, despite conflicting statistics from other, better-known parts. The Salt Lake reporter claimed that the *Post* language

was "not that of the manly art of self defense."
Our local story was unsigned, but it was pre-
sumed, on examination, to have been written by
the ubiquitous Dimsdale, and the wording did
sound a trifle odd here and there.

After the 185th round, the backers of both men
agreed to call the fight a draw. Bets were declared off, and the purse equally divided. But it
was the *Post's* summation, mostly, that kicked
off the Salt Lake feud. "The referee was persuaded by all backers to stop the fight," said the
Post, among other syrupy phrases. "Both men
were still game and ready to go. This was accord-
ingly done to the satisfaction of most people
present."

"That account is inaccurate," claimed the Salt
Lake paper. "The decision was heavily weighted
in favor of Orem." Well, the *Union Vedette's*
man was right; I was near enough to see and hear
what happened. Orem being all but pulverized,
the time-keeper (Grantly) and other officials sent
a man to O'Neil's corner, asking whether he
wanted to "kill a friend for a thousand dollars."
O'Neil replied, "Of course not," and the fight
was stopped.

There were complaints about the bets, but they
died out soon. Even the bettors disliked to see
further punishment of an esteemed citizen like
Orem. That cocky but unfortunate battler was
(covertly) carried home in a blanket, while
O'Neil, not in the primest condition, had the
blood sponged off, an ear pumped out by a doctor, unguents applied, and plaster laid over both
eyes. Then he strolled with friends to Orem's
saloon, where he spent a couple of hours, in the
sunniest of humors, before retiring to his cabin.

Chief Justice Hosmer left for Bannack the next morning, escorted by several of Virginia's influential men. For some reason, I thought, he seemed glad to go. Or perhaps he merely enjoyed travel.

CHAPTER XXXIII

I WROTE HOME again, restating my reasons for delay, while urging my father not to budge—the Indian wars, now, "had spread out of hand"—so that I was present when Judge Hosmer moved to Virginia with his retinue and began operations in the Territory's new capital.

Meanwhile the Indians *had* got out of hand, to the point where Grantly and James signed 330 volunteers and raised $300 for an assault on the Pend d'Oreilles, who were mainly responsible for a "breakout" that saw repeated raids on outlying ranches and stock. And there were attacks on wagons that came through in unusually bland weather. At the last minute, however, the volunteers elected to stay home and prospect their claims. (This was a mistake when one considers the Indian troubles that developed soon.)

But life for Virginia brightened when Justice Hosmer took up his new place of business. Now here I'd like to pay tribute to a serious and dedicated man, a man of stature, politican notwithstanding. Mr. Hosmer's sole aim in leaving the comfortable East to buck the roughest region this country's ever known was a desire to serve his nation. His pay (I was told) was insulting, less than the take of a semi-successful panner, and he had no love of power. He meant, simply, to give Montana a start, at least, toward full legal justice; and if the barriers were insurmountable for one man alone, it was scarcely his fault. And in any event, he showed successors the way. The Justice empaneled a Grand Jury that was, as the *Montana Post* said with pride, "the first Grand Jury ever assembled in the new Territory." But Montana *still* had no law of its own, so the poor fellow relied on Common Law and Idaho's "Civil Practice Act," with occasional reference to California's precedents in water-rights cases. And the sole copy of Idaho's Act was, as he said, "so worn and dilapidated, dirty from constant use, and scribbled over with notes that its original color was hardly discernible."

Perhaps his principal headache was—lawyers. A single scene, which I witnessed, will give a notion of what Hosmer faced. Not everyone favored all of his actions, needless to say; and the worst critic was the visiting Pennsylvania writer (and lawyer) Alexander McClure.

The first courtroom was in a big loft over a half-finished hotel, and contained one long table, and one smaller table, with the Judge on a stool. "Prisoners, jurors and even dogs mingled together in incongruous confusion," as Mr. McClure gleefully stated. Prisoners, of course, were taken by volunteer police and were lodged in a cabin called "the County Jail." If a sentence was for under three years, the criminal remained in jail; if it exceeded that time, he was sent to the federal penitentiary at Detroit, an expensive and dubious trip. Also, it should be said that many merchants, and others, favored releasing County Jail prisoners, to save the cost of feeding them.

The new Chief Justice (in a larger hall, packed

to the rafters) delivered a first Charge to his Grand Jury; it was acclaimed as a gem of sensible oratory. The *Post* printed it in full. Among his remarks, Hosmer said: "Gentlemen of the Jury: It is no part of the business of this Court to find fault with what has been done, but to laud the transactions of an organization, which, in absence of Law, assumed the delicate and responsible office of purging society of all offenders against its peace, happiness and safety . . . [These] are the first measures reported to by well-intentioned men, to free themselves of that vile class of adventurers which infest all unorganized communities for purposes of fraud, robbery and murder. The sources of official power had been monopolized by the very class which preyed on Society! The greatest villain of them all—hands reeking with the blood of numerous victims was the principal ministerial officer of the Territory and had at his back a band of wretches who had become hardened in their blood trade, years before they came here to practice it. In this condition of affairs there could be but two courses to pursue—to hang these offenders or submit to their authority, and give the Territory over to misrule and murder. Happily, the former course prevailed, and the summary punishment, visited upon a few, frightened the survivors . . . and restored order and safety—"

Well, the Justice could hardly have stated the case better, and everyone said so. Even the miners failed to dredge up a single joke about it; they were impressed.

In the same speech, Judge Hosmer observed correctly, as people also agreed, that "Much as we may approve the means of self-protection thus employed, and the promptitude with which they were applied, our admiration ceases when they assert an authority defiant of *Law*, and usurp offices which belong to the Government itself. We give them all the credit they deserve, and praise them for what they have accomplished; but they have fulfilled their work."

The speech, or Charge, ran to three columns of fine type, and was intelligent, erudite, and far-seeing. It seems a pity that such a man had to find himself tangled hand and foot by lawyers so shady and troublesome. His work thus became badly crippled. "He started wrong at the outset," wrote the terrible-tempered McClure, "like a timid driver failing to wield the reins of a vicious team, and the team has measurably driven the driver ever since. Stern in his integrity, and well versed in the law, he does his part creditably in all things, save in exercising with firm purpose the high prerogative of a Court of Justice."

The courtroom scene I mentioned, and to which McClure naturally took exception, being there, was in its way comic but disgusting. In this case, Justice Hosmer had indeed let the lawyers get out of hand, and at the end of that day, he understood Vigilantes even better.

When I dropped in, the tableau was roughly this: The Chief Justice was stretched out prone on a green carpet-covered sofa, his expression exhausted, himself as near defeat as possible. Milling around the room, shouting, waving papers and books (with markers showing "precedents," perhaps from the Magna Carta), often shaking their fists in each other's faces, were upward of thirty "lawyers." Befitting his high post, Mr. Hosmer's sofa was elevated on four blocks from a nearby carpentry; occasionally he tried to rise from his horizontal sprawl. But it was done without success; his strength was depleted. Under the newly-organized rules, he had no power over the juries that formed (after the Grand Jury) to try specific cases. He insisted, only, after a classic row, that legal points be asked of him. (Mr. Hosmer, supporting at least some of Mr. McClure's peeve, had so far given in.)

The lawyers made long-winded speeches, and the cases more or less wobbled to the juries, where they were knocked about by shysters, as like as not. Half a dozen lawyers spoke at once, or shouted, and pummeled foolish technicalities. I grieve to say that Hosmer let the silly show go its own way.

A part of the loft was set aside for dances, sermons, itinerant shows, and the like, and a side door led to billiards, drinks, and "short" cards. Lawyers visited the bar with regularity, hoarse from argument (and ignorance), and returned wiping their chins with brocaded kerchiefs. At intervals, Chief Justice Hosmer dispatched a Negro boy to the bar where, after protest, he was supplied with lemonade, the Judge being "temperance." He often had trouble getting this down, out of pure exhaustion, for a portion of it spilled down his waistcoated front. Occasionally, at last, he made a real effort to restore order; but he sank down, as before, dazed.

The cases, if sent to jury by the Justice, could

go to higher courts, at some distance removed. But the choices caused ill feeling, as Mr. Hosmer decided appeal merits from his sofa. One example I saw aroused noisy anger, for reasons lost to me. It involved the replevin of a borrowed pickaxe and ended in "a free fight," as the miners used the term. The Chief Justice lay and fanned himself with a doily until it was finished, with the ugliest lawyer present, I thanked God, sporting a swelling black eye. Over this, the man instantly sued, of course, his opponent countersuing, thus adding stupidity to the docket.

Mr. Hosmer took it all in stride, if I may use the phrase for a man horizontal, but McClure appeared to be maddened. "If I'd been the judge, during my four days at court," he wrote, "I am sure that half the liars—or lawyers—would have been in jail the first day, and the residue stricken from the rolls before I was through!"

Certainly the writer, himself an attorney, had a valid point. On another day, when he was absent, I saw a litigant keep his rifle pointed at the Sheriff, pending disposition of a claim.

These ravenous pleaders also managed to sow discontent in the Legislature, whose first act had moved the capital from Bannack to Virginia. Well, the lawyers stirred the people so, causing them uncertainty how to vote, that the Legislature itself fell into a Stampede. In the matchless jawboning of the guild, the lawyers nit-picked, and objected, and pointed to previous cases having no bearing on Montana (one was in Havana, dealing with cigar-wrappers), and made speeches for and speeches against, and at last they objected to everything, whether they favored it or not. Or so it appeared. They hashed out Mr. Hosmer's local application of the Common Law, Idaho's Practice Act, and California's Bill of Water Rights, and as nearly as I could tell, expressed themselves as being on both sides of each. Finally the lawyers persuaded this befuddled Legislature that Justice Hosmer's "modes of thought" were "entirely beyond legal bounds," and prompted a Resolution asking him to resign!

But they'd badly misjudged their man. Worn out as he was, he coolly declined, tapped his gavel, and said, "we will pass on to the next business."

In a sense, this show of courage, and contempt of troublesome lawyers, turned the tide. He not only refused to step down but occupied the post for four more years. The action was so valiant that the miners got together and elected to "tote them lawyers up toward the mountains, where they ain't seen the view yet," and give them, to a man, a sound and corrective thrashing. Somebody—probably Chief Justice Hosmer himself—talked them out of it.

"But I have no doubt," Grantly told me later, "that he was mightily relieved when years later he threw aside his robes [these didn't exist, by the way] and settled down to relax as Virginia City's Postmaster."

CHAPTER XXXIV

GRANTLY AND JAMES, the Smithers, and others saw me off, by stage to Salt Lake City, the first leg of my journey home. It was winter, now, and we stood shivering. Mr. Smithers made me a gift of a beautifully-wrought iron plaque that he must have worked on for hours at night. It had an anvil at the top and (welded) the words, "Ross, Son as Ever Was to the Family of Ewing T. Smithers"— this followed by all their names.

The Duncans gave me, beside a body-lift from James that put a shoulder out of joint, a wolverine hide tanned by Aubony—a rare skin, for you never saw those devils abroad in daylight. Professor Dimsdale was on hand, blinking and looking (as usual) slightly bewildered and unwell. And then Con Orem and Hugh O'Neil— who fought the prizefight—turned up to shake hands; and there were others, including a Chinaman I played draughts with. Then the Stage pulled out, with my stomach in knots and me miserable.

I won't go into my trip, which was dull except for routine breakdowns, and Indian scares that came to nothing, and a few hardships of winter travel by Stage in those days.

We had snow off and on—bad snow—and followed the custom of transferring often to lumber-sleds drawn by four or six horses, depending on the drifts. Where snow was deepest, the Line had caused stakes, in the form of pine boughs, to be set, marking the route. They looked odd—waving green sentinels stretching across the un-tracked white plains. They looked, in fact, more like palms, as if awaiting a eucharist or royal procession from ancient times. On previous occasions, though, people had wandered off, lost, then froze to death, if they started in winter before these wands were placed. Still, the passengers cursed and made threats when they had to pile out and help the driver transfer a ton of mail to the sledges.

Hostler stations were eight miles apart, and at these we dined, if such trash could be dignified so. For the sum of $1.50—gold—we were provided sow-belly, black "coffee," and baking-powder biscuits (which might have been useful in a rock fight). We endured this morning, noon, and night, the station-hostler doing the cooking, and absorbing—with a startled and aggrieved look—a range of sarcasm and invective to shrivel a mummy.

But the dietary scourge, we decided, was offset near Salt Lake at a "hotel" kept by a Mormon bishop's wife, of which he had a surplus and so could spare one to be innkeeper. This excellent lady gave us roast chicken, light rolls, fresh butter, pure cream, and excellent coffee, all for the modest sum of one dollar—in green-backs!

After a span of time that seemed pretty short, for my thoughts were behind me, I arrived at St. Louis, on a different Stage. Then it was a ride by trains sitting on seats that seemed too soft, now, to New England and home.

My mother having died when I was small, I remembered my father as fierce, but he was surprised, and cordial, and we shook hands and had dinner alone in our big old gloomy house on Beacon Hill. I'd thought about sending a telegram from St. Louis, but decided that, in the interval after he got it, he might work up a new set of resentments, and I wasn't in the mood.

He said, "Well, son, you've grown and you look—different."

He himself looked older, I thought, and felt guilty about not being around to help. In the next few days I greeted all the various uncles and aunts and cousins, and my sister, who'd been in New York on business, and I resolved to dig in and try. At first, this was in an office where I started at the bottom.

Then, by and by, I read in Mr. Bennett's New York paper (which my father took by mail, because it made him mad) a speech by "Montana's Chief Justice Hosmer," who was East on a trip.

It was a good speech, I thought, made before the Travelers' Club of New York, and described Montana and its people with accuracy and more detail than I thought one man might absorb in that short a time. He even explored the changeovers in mining, pointing out that it was "usual, now, for miners to prosecute their labors under some company's patronage. Many are often destitute of means to purchase a meal. They lead a life of constant exposure, sleeping alone on a mountain side, living upon the plainest food,

and many times working for months without
success."

I thought nostalgically back to the Stampede
when all prospectors, then, had money, and gold
grew on the trees left at Alder Gulch. Today
panning had given way to quartz lodes that
called for new processes, costly crushing
machines; and "a new class of people had
flocked into the Territory," among them "professors, assayers, and Eastern operators. Prospecting is now conducted on a large scale, and a
considerable quantity of quartz has passed into
the hands of men who can control it."

He was right. It was happening when I left,
and I hated to see it, for it represented the passing of a picturesque life we may never see again.
Even so, his description of the country and manifest love of Montana were phrased with such
skill that nostaglia rose almost to stifle me.

Justice Hosmer's speech also repeated his remarks about the early Vigilantes and praised
Virginia's leading citizens, who had "with sober
restraint" made the community fit to live in.

I worked hard, though my attention often
wandered, returning to old friends and sights
and even the profession I'd left behind. And my
father watched me, I knew, with speculation. At
length he sent me on a voyage of nearly two
years, around Cape Horn in a square-rigged ship
that carried supplies to California—dried cod
and other dried foods, seed, mining machines,
rum, iron, tools, sailcloth, and even lumber of
special hardwoods, sometimes hard to buy, and
always expensive, on the Pacific slope.

I remember standing at the rail with the purser—little more than a child as I saw him now—studying the California shore while dockhands unloaded. He said, "I wonder what it's like in there—wild, I'll bet!" and I replied, "It's probably worse than you think."

On this ship—the *Melissa B.*—was the same Uncle Abner who suffered the rearward wound in battle. He was First Officer, while I'd been named, by my father, "Special Super-cargo," under orders of a round-shouldered bully, bald, hairy at the chest and back, pocked with small facial scars, and resentful of upstarts like me. This was the boatswain, or "bosun," named Lyman Bone, of ferocious reputation. Hardly a day passed without curses for my ignorance and slowness, and I began to be cuffed now and then.

In the words of an English writer now become popular, I didn't "vally bullying a marlinspike," as sailors called such discipline; and one day, absorbing a blow to the head, I said, "Don't strike me again, Mr. Bone. Ever. Do you understand?"

Not before in history, I suppose, had a bosun stepped back more surprised.

"What'd you say, Favorite?" he cried. (It was his way of addressing me, because of my position in the family.)

I repeated my low-voiced advice, but deckhands heard and dropped tasks assigned them, mouths open.

"You may rank special ashore," said Mr. Bone, "but I happen to know sea-rules, little Mr. Lickspittle, and *here* you take orders my way, without no complaint. You better learn it fast, hear?"

I was no longer "little," weighing 195 pounds and standing six foot two and a half now in my socks. And there were additional factors. Once, in a summer before I entred college, my father had engaged a "professor" to teach me fisticuffs, and then, of course, finding himself interested, he'd gone on to teach my sister, too, though what she was supposed to do I had no idea. But there was more. For nearly seven years I'd lived in the Rockies, enduring most hardships of the miners, and I'd been, beyond that, a blacksmith.

"For your impidence, you can take that to warm up on, as refresher for future!"

The blow never landed. Altogether, as the ship watched, I knocked him down fourteen times, or until he gasped out, sprawled against an anchor-coil, "Enough!"

There was no pleasure in the ruckus, but my tensions had been building up. And this particular bully never struck another hand.

As for Uncle Abner (not actually an uncle, but a middle-aged cousin), he'd detested me from childhood, and I couldn't stand him. Now he came forward—rare, for he feared seamen—and said, "I've a mind to place you in chains. It's within my province, and you've got it coming. Yes, I think so."

But my blood was up, and I said (to my shame), "Ab, I'll own this ship some day, and you'll be the first to go. And you'll get no further berth, not anywhere. Now hump yourself back where you belong!"

Nothing came of the incident, probably because the Captain had a bellyful of that bosun too; and a move to punish me, beyond that, might have made men restless. They enjoyed it, and one asked me to do it again; they'd collected up a pot.

Once home, and squared away, I was summoned to my father's inviolable study before dinner. It was the first time I'd properly seen the room—gleaming with reddish furniture and wall panels, rows of leather-bound books filling shelves, two or three deep leather chairs, a globe, and a desk the size of a wagon.

He was seated behind this, smoking a cigar; he said, "Sit down, son," and I braced myself for a sermon.

"Have a cigar"—holding out a humidor embossed with his initials.

Startled, I said, "Well, yes, thanks," and, noting that they were *puros*, from Havana (superior to kinnikinick), I took two.

"Son, I've kept an eye on you, since you returned, and God knows I've made every allowance to which"—he coughed—"a somewhat hasty nature can aspire. Your sister says she's been watching, too, hoping you'd settle down and be happy. But you don't belong here. To put things clearly, this isn't your home—"

Booted again, I thought, not surprised, and made no response.

He leaned back in his swiveled chair and said, the expression a little sad, "No. Everything about you, your apathy ashore, the things you don't say, your determined look to succeed, tells us you belong in Montana. I'd hoped and prayed," he continued, "for a son to take over what I've built since your mother's death. However, it doesn't pay to cross Nature, and I trust

I'm not so bad a father that I'd arrange a young man's life to make him miserable. Have another cigar."

I hadn't finished the one I'd started, but we saw no cigars like these in Virginia, so I took three more.

"Go on back, Ross. Go home. We'll miss you, of course, as little as we see you now. Life can be lonely," he said slowly, "when one's work is done and age creeps stealthily up—"

Here I argued that I *would* stay on, and do my job, and probably come to love it, but he waved the protest away.

"Oh, you can cheer up. I'm not trying to arouse sympathy. Or your sense of duty, either. And you might as well get apprehensive again. I *will* make the trip out, exactly as announced. Assemble your gear, and go back where you belong. I'll grubstake you—right word?—until you can get properly started. You might have another cigar—"

I took five this time, but I wasn't joyous, and said, "I'm sorry. I wish I'd done better."

"Nonsense. You've done well, considering. You musn't forget that. Now, a couple of points: first off, your Aunt Rachel forgave you for stealing her bracelet—before she died. She would have given it to you anyhow."

Then: "How many times did you knock old Bones down? Was it fourteen?" he asked with satisfaction. "Did you injure—that is, was he damaged?"

"Well, I—"

"Could he have required the use of a dentist, let us say?"

"A dentist might have been handy."

"Were there, ah, other cuts, abrasions, lacerations? Much blood?"

"I really don't remember, Father. I was busy—"

"To be sure, to be sure. Now you'll be surprised to know that I myself thrashed that hound, years ago in a waterfront tavern. Why do we keep him? Well, he's one of the ablest sailors alive, and good A.B. seamen aren't tossed up on beaches. Oh, don't look shocked. I haven't spent *all* my time in church, despite your mother."

We exchanged a few other remarks, and an embrace; and I had a long talk with my sister, and said goodbye to various cousins I liked. And after that I had a tearful farewell from old Hawes, the butler, who now was so near-sighted he had trouble finding the present of pipe tobacco (and pouch) he'd bought me. I wondered, again, about the quaint English custom—handed on down—of not allowing a butler to wear either spectacles or a moustache. No one in history had seen such adornments on a butler, either in England or here, as my father once stressed, describing these lacks as "traditional." And likely they never would in the future.

Then—I was aboard the cars again.

Three years had passed. It was early summer, with the Missouri at high flood, and I recall to this day the names of towns, or "landings," en route to Fort Benton: "Sawyer's Bend," "Gasconade," "Saline River," "Bluff Port," "Maxwell's Landing," "Little Platte," "Leavenworth," "Kickapoo," "Hole in the Wall," and maybe a hundred and fifty other stops; then, finally "Maria's River" and "Fort Benton."

Of paddle-wheelers, I had my choice of the *Benton, Yellowstone, Effie Dean, Cutter,* and *Mackinaw No. 5.* I chose *Mackinaw* because an elderly St. Louisan, at the foot of Market Street, said it was "less apt to blow up" than the others. After this remarkable news, he took a Bible from his pocket and swore to it, saying that most boats hadn't much chance to get above Little Sioux before exploding.

When we pushed off, however, I noticed him busy with our lines, so he had a stake in the matter after all. And I wasn't entirely at ease about *No. 5;* what happened to the first four?

CHAPTER XXXV

THE BOAT-RIDE properly ended not far from Helena, which was built at the quartz-find known as Last Chance Gulch. The place bulged with people—too many people. It was new and raw and I badly wanted to leave for Virginia. But I had a commission from my father. He'd given me a draft for ten thousand dollars and told me to "buy in to one of the Quartz companies. Let's assay your business head." And then— surprising as usual, he scribbled down the name of a man in a Helena bank. You never could tell about him; he always knew more than you thought.

I won't bother with details, but I finally invested the money in Grizzly Gulch, and eventually it made my father (and me) about ten times the sum. Meanwhile, fretting, I stayed on to see lawyers, sign papers, and go through other such rubbish.

But my mind was on Virginia, and I worked up a little peeve at my father. No matter where you were, he always seemed to wind up boss.

My letters from Grantly had been infrequent, for his immersion in "new projects" had been "entirely absorbing from sunrise to sundown." He'd given me news of the Smithers, of course, and of other persons I knew, and had perhaps omitted Professor Dimsdale by oversight.

Pretty well exhausted at last, I slept nearly two days in my room at a Mrs. McGinnis's, who ran a boarding house. I had worked hard for my father, hoping to erase delinquencies, and the trip from St. Louis had failed to help.

The fact is, despite the "non-blowing-up" qualities of *Machinaw No. 5* it seemed to me that I—and other passengers—spent a lot of time prying ourselves off sandbars, log-piles, wrong channels, and the like. The Missouri had been high when we started, but water petered out when we neared the Platte, thrashing into the hot, dry prairie. And the Captain and crew were mighty careful not to buck rapids and crossings over-steamed; people recalled the *Chippewa* blowing sky-high, not much farther up-river.

Helena was Montana's future capital, but it had defects at this stage. The town was encircled by "Gulches," that is, big quartz lodes run by the Syndicates—"Belmont," "Whippoorwill," "Penobscot," "Blue Bird," "Black Alder," "Lexington," "Grizzly," to name a few. And Syndicates owned the quartz lodes farther south, too. One day I saw some miners from "down under" bring in a wagon loaded with a million and a half dollars in dust. The new machines could crush unbelievable amounts in a day's time. And they had additional gear for extracting *all* the gold. It was here, during this last step, that lone miners lacking capital failed. What machinery they acquired loosely separated the metal, but the average miner's zeal for this was never very high. And when prospecting, panning, gave way to the drill of quartz mines, mountain-men miners fell careless and apathetic. It became equally so in Virginia. But the Syndicates made things up in a money way.

The traveling Alexander McClure arrived before my business was complete and resumed his newspaper squalls.* He wrote that "half the cabins are groggeries, many others are gambling saloons, and a good percentage are occupied by 'those fair but frail ones' who ever follow mining camps. The people are of all classes, from the 'fast boys' to the gentle sex even faster, but all appear to have the vim, restlessness, extravagance and jollity of a new camp. I see here more substance and pretense, more virtue and vice, more preachers in groggeries than at any place visited before."

Since Mr. McClure had seen (and abhorred) Virginia, I wondered why he bore down so heavy on familiar sights, rackets, and contrasts. But when I met him in Schwab and Zimmerman's Bar—a pompous, white-haired foghorn idiotically garbed in a frock coat, striped trousers, and silk hat—I found that his peeve (always near the surface) had been caused by bedbugs.

He was, he told me, bitten "from scalp to toenails, sir—bites that have risen and festered—" and his recovery seemed "dubious." He spoke in a flowery, grandiloquent style, and I learned that he'd acquired political ambitions in Montana.

The bedbugs were blamed on his landlady, whose place was at the outskirts of town. "The

---

*These were sent down to Virginia's *Montana Post*; Helena's new *Herald* refused to print them.

unlovely slattern admitted to me, sir, came out
and confessed it, that she 'hadn't washed her feet
since spring.' Then she proceeded, and I'll
mimic her frightful speech—a gift I own," he
confided with swollen aplomb, "in well-
developed degree. 'Bedbugs are aw-ful critters!'
quoth this stirrer of cauldrons. 'They do beat me,
whichever I muster to roust them. You'll likely
puke when I say there hain't a spring in this
house free of swarms, and if they don't tote the
beds off for auction, I'm busted!'

"Now what do you think of that, sir, for an
address to a probable future governor of this
Territorial endeavor?"

I was about to reply that I thought it very
appropriate when a skulking sort of cadaver ("in
charge of my campaign, sir") caught his arm,
and I left.

The bartender told me a local election impended, and "if that braying donkey McClure
garners ten votes, I'll enter Dee-troit prison,
both gratis and voluntary."

This struck me strong, but sure enough, on
that same evening I strolled down Main Street
and saw an unearthly glow before the Last
Chance Hotel; there was Mr. McClure, perched
on a box, attempting to make a political speech.
The cadaver, with aides, had lighted two woolly
balls soaked in coal oil and hung them atop a
pole. They cast a sickly glare over the candidate,
who, hatless, his cottony hair disheveled, strove
red-faced against odds.

For one thing, he'd placed his elocution stump
next door to a dance-brothel, so that the cries of
"Single turn, gents! Who'll call the step?" and
"What girlie catches your fancy?" all but

drowned out his remarks. During one lull, a miner thrust his head out of the brothel and shouted, "Why don't you dry up, old Blossom Top?"

Mr. McClure (he lost the election, handsomely) left Helena three days later, his immediate reason being that the citizens refused to let him bray on Sunday. I, too, thought the decision odd, since other activities proceeded as usual. He raised a howling fuss and wanted to know if Helena considered political oratory "the social inferior of whorehouses and saloons?" Several responsible persons eased his mind on the point; they said yes.

CHAPTER XXXVI

THE PRINCIPAL "STREET" then in town went directly by, or around, the Last Chance mine. Later, with the Golconda spent, leaving stores, hotels, and saloons clustered all about, it seemed only natural to name the thoroughfare "Last Chance Gulch," and thus it remains to this day.

"Helena's people are sojourners—there's frolic to everything they do," reads a Journal, and that brings me to a surprising encounter, early in my stay. When the Journal, in its curious way, speaks of "sojourning," the writer undoubtedly meant the main recreational boon—the warm, hot, and cold baths that lay four miles south.

Such streaming and bountiful pools graced the valley that some enterprising gentry had added the grace notes of a European spa. On Sundays especially, people of all classes took picnics and went to the Springs "for bathing, dancing, drinking and flirting." In the largest hall, besides the long shiny bar, there was a dance floor, a veranda with tables for picnickers, an inside door leading to a gaming room where monte, faro, and other card games proceeded beneath clouds of tobacco smoke—and, upstairs, rooms in files up and down the halls. An attempt was made to keep order for family visits. A free lunch, costing $2.75, was served across from the bar, and a single over-sized plateful was adequate to any family: venison; beef; vegetables staged in from Salt Lake; double bread loaves baked of coarse, inferior flour that yet had good flavor; occasionally bear meat and moose-noses; and desserts of pies and cakes bought at a new town bakery. Tables stood helterskelter at two walls, and the attendants at these were female—"waitresses"—rather than male.

I put the word in quotation marks, for I never quite determined the niche occupied by these scantily-clad girls. All wore thigh-length black silk stockings and provocative blouses, but over their brief skirts had demure and spanking-clean aprons. Walking toward you, a girl aroused no special interest, unless she bent over. Going away, apronless behind, she left little to be imagined.

Each waited on tables and was, besides, available for dancing, at a fee. As to their further functions, I have no fixed idea. Doubtless they sported upstairs; if true, it was adroitly managed, and families with children were not offended.

On Sundays the road to the Hot Springs from Helena was lined for outings, with people of every degree, many of these families that chose a spring, "frolicked," and picnicked after the week's work. Oddly enough, while the halls were rowdy, within limits, the bathing was troublefree. It cost nothing to change one's costume behind willows, step into a pool, and feel the exhilaration—especially in brisk weather—

of swimming in some tepid but strangely bracing bath.

All pools gurgled toward the Missouri, or a
tributary, and they gave off a feeling of freshness
always. It was just as well. Miners came down to
scrub up after (in many cases) long periods of
wallowing in ravines. One old fellow—of the
breed that enlivened Alder Gulch—told me he'd
lately come from "Californy," and had not, to his
best recollection, bathed in two years. It all
began sounding familiar. When I saw his singlet
and drawers (which were sewed and required to
be cut free), I believed him. His reason, he said,
was "paregoric"—meaning therapeutic, I suppose—though he had reservations.

"I don't hold with water on the hide, never
did," he said, grimacing as he dipped a toe in
(here) sulphur water of about eighty degrees
Fahrenheit. "Some folk appear to favor it, without deeleterious effect, and I'd be the last to
stand in their way. But me, it brings on an
epizootic."

I said, "Surely not in this bland weather, Mr.
Parks"—that was his name, or so he claimed.

"Weather ain't a factor," he advised me severely. "Else I'd a removed the top-soil previous.
It's agin natur to prospect the pelt with a
flume-nozzle. Now you answer me this: you ever
see a owl a-washing his face? Or a antelope
scraping lye-soap twixt its legs?"

I was about to comment on the raccoon's
habits, and those of birds that splashed down to
bathe, but decided against it. You can't teach a
mountain-man to argue; Montana hadn't devised a way yet.

He fought free of his under-garments (which he buried); then he waded in waist-deep, protesting his discomfort. While his stringy chest had wispy gray hair, his stomach was ornate with a tattoo of what appeared to be a compass-rose, and, above it, the initials "E.S.," with a blue anchor-and-line. It seemed reasonable that, at some point, he'd been to sea. But when I complimented him, he stated that he'd "acquired it in San Francisker, whilst in town on a spree." And he said, further, typically warming up, that he wouldn't take any money for it, that three museums had "come down handsome," with offers "to choke a buffler." Thinking this over, while dabbling at the water with distaste, he said he'd concluded to leave the masterwork to his "daughter back in Loosianer." She'd be rich, and could buy a plantation. I left, nostalgically feeling that an eternity had passed since I'd heard such warming piffle.

This old fellow was not the symbolic local miner; Helena's population were mostly Johnny-come-latelies to Montana's mining scene. There was a swashbuckling air that contrasted strangely with the reckless tomfoolery of our prospectors down below. The men were "cavaliers"; they wore rowel Spanish spurs, with bells, and considered themselves very gay blades.

On this Sunday at the Springs, I sat feeling strangely un-well at a table of the Hall, drinking raw, heady beer from St. Louis, absently watching the dancers. The day was fine, and the belled "cavaliers" were making the hall ring. Even the musicians—two fiddlers, jew's harp, drummer, piper and piano—seemed in good fettle.

It was an enjoyable place to be, if I hadn't been so anxious to leave. I'd never realized how much time was required to invest ten thousand dollars. Each day, it seemed, brought new red-tape to delay me further.

Without glancing up, I motioned the waitress who'd served me, pointing to an empty beer-glass, unmoved by the figure she presented from the rear. But when she returned, I lifted my eyes, for no reason, and my insides congealed.

"I wondered if you'd say hello."

Staring, I finally managed to speak. "Now what are you doing here?"

She said, "I can sit, if you pay for my time."

"Do your mother and father know about this?"

"Not entirely. It's a mixed-up story."

When she sat down, bending slightly forward, I thought that Daisy had grown up at last, perhaps mentally but certainly physically.

"Oh, it's not what you think. I serve drinks and dance—downstairs."

I said, "You'll be promoted in time—they all are."

The girl blushed, to her half-covered bosom, and said, "Probably I should slap you for that. But you have a right to think so."

"Start at the beginning," I said—when one of Helena's swashbucklers approached our table.

"Dance, little lady?" He was swaying back and forth to the rhythm, dressed in full regalia and wearing, besides, a look that suggested he was fatal to women.

I waited, watching her face.

"No. That is, thanks. I've met an old friend."

"Well, we won't mind that, will we?"—he started pulling her up. "Your job's dancing with the customers, or maybe better"—with the leer of the self-confessed lady-killer. "And dancing with Jack McGivern's regarded as a treat!"

"The little lady said no," I told him politely, or as politely as I could.

"So-ho! We have an old friend here in dude cut-and-cloth, and he's raring up like a regular he-man grizzly."

It was true that I lacked the cavalier costume, my clothes still suggesting the city man not long off the boat. But I'd added the usual revolver-and-belt, after taking a room with Mrs. McGinnis, and was happy to feel my dude coat tight across my—or Mr. Smithers'—shoulders.

Mr. McGivern himself now leaned across the table, his rakish hat touching my nose. "Now, 'old friend,' we don't want a spanking here—right here in public—do we? Not before all these nice people. I asked the young lady to dance and"—giving a tug at her arm—"dance she's a-going to do. You stick to your ledgers, or peddle your turnips and beans, and keep free of the boys with the spurs. Likely you don't know our ways here, Sonny, and that's why you ain't chawed up a-ready."

As I studied him, beneath the brim of my hat, he seemed almost prissy, when I thought back to Virginia's wild days; and I guessed that he, too, hadn't been long off the boat. I noticed that the music had stopped and most people were looking on; these included the bartenders, who stood frowning.

Carefully, as if I valued it highly, I laid aside my hat—imported from Locks' and bought in Boston—and stood up to face him. He was perhaps five foot eleven, in his boots, and

feminine-slender, and I towered over
him. Another time I might have let such a girl
handle her own problem, but I was angry, from
the fact of this girl being here at all. I said, in
tones that I meant to be heard: "Outside—heel
and toe? Or do you prefer a handy ravine, with
guns?"

The cavalier stepped back, his color drained
away, the silly bells and garnishments jingling.
My action smacked of the bully, for the odds
were plainly against him; I sensed, too, that
without the hat I no longer looked like a dude.

He stared, and what this poor, posturing,
dangerous new accretion to the West saw
was—Montana. I'd been here too many years; it
must have shown. Backing still farther, he said,
managing a grin, "Old friends is old friends. I'm
afraid I didn't catch your drift, partner. No hard
feelings."

I glanced around the room, as if to inquire,
"Anybody else?" (which might have turned out
badly), and, as nobody moved, and the bartenders' frowns only deepened, I resumed my seat
and picked up my dude hat. To tell the truth, I
felt ashamed of it, in this setting, and resolved to
leave it behind when convenient.

She leaned far back, to appraise me coolly.

"It seems I'm not the only one grown. You
have changed!"

I said, "I'm not very proud of that scene; I lost
my temper. I've lived pretty hard of late, and that
dandified fop scraped my nerves."

"He's the great lover here—from *Indiana!*
Most of these men are rough, and pleasant. *That*
one's a pest to every girl in the Hall."

I took a deep breath, calming down; then I

said, "Now try it once more—from the start. Not religion, I hope?"

"Maybe the tailings of religion, as a miner might say. Let's see—Ross?—how long?"

"I've been gone three years; and it's time you were unconfused; it went on too long. But this!"

"When you noticed (and it took a while), you probably did expect the half-addled infant you saw at Daddy's. But after Professor Dimsdale took my sister and me into the school, he worked long and hard. In my case especially. He 'vowed,' I believe he said, that he'd make a student of me if it killed us both. Poor sick man! He finally realized that the effort was wasted. What people wrote in books never stuck in my head; it isn't apt to. Something happened when the tent-shouters seized this religion one day, and another the next, and the threats and mentions of brimstone—what's brimstone, by the way?— and my own parents screaming and wrenching themselves about, calling on the Lord—"

She stopped and said, "You know, I don't believe any such creature exists. If there is one, why so much misery and trouble?"

I replied carefully, "I believe the popular view claims we're repaid after death for the suffering here below."

"Then why not skip 'here below' and start off 'above'?"

"Well, even primitive peoples all have gods, and worship them, or something. The Aztecs cut people open alive and pulled out their hearts. That was worship for them. Maybe best to believe. It may turn out safer. After all, it's harmless."

"Not harmless!" she cried. "I spent my childhood crouching in the dark, afraid of that son of a bitch's wrath. I heard about the wrath, nine or ten times a day, while being told that we, here, should control our wrath. Well, why? Mother and Daddy and their 'evangelists' always said we were made in God's image. Why not be wrathy in the image? The whole nightmare left me twisted for years. I take back 'son of a bitch,' " she said, thinking. "I'm not *that* untwisted."

The word had shocked me, but I said, "You might consider that your mother and father have done some growing up, too. They see their backwoods religion better, and when I left, at least, they were trying to make it up."

She looked off into space. "They're the very best people ever. I see that now. Can you imagine what it took to step up and toss out a lifetime of nonsense? Not one in a million could do it—and mean it.

"Religion lies back there," she said, waving at the gambling room, with its cries that rose over the music and the dancing. "It's people trying to copper bets—about having to die, in religion's case. Mostly it's 'the leavings of superstition.' I read that in a book," she added, with a smile, a sweetness of expression I hadn't noticed. "Here, not in Virginia."

"Are you *sure* Professor Dimsdale failed on the books? Did you try?"

"Oh, a day came—glands—I've seen it in others—when I grew out of 'girl.' My mind, or something, wandered off the books, and classes, and even Mr Dimsdale. I was thinking about other things. Mama, at least, understood.

"Virginia started its family dances, and after the years before, it was real life. Excitement,

music, the looks on men's faces. I suppose it
sounds like a tart."

"Not yet. You may be brighter than you think,
or anyway bright enough for me. Then what
happened?"

"I was finally allowed to go 'walking out'—in
the safest possible way—and then I met Con
Orem—"

"The saloon-keeper and prize-fighter!"

"Not the saloon-keeper and prize-figher! A
good man, temperance man, no-tobacco man,
who doesn't gamble, who never even swears like
Daddy. He does what he can for the town."

"You met him. Where?"

She laughed. "I met him in Reverend Torbett's
church. Religion again."

"And saw him afterward."

"Several times. I lied to my parents. He—I
mean Mr. Orem—wanted to call at our house and
explain, but I was afraid.

"Then they found out. And, suddenly, after
all, he was a saloon-keeper and prize-fighter.
Religion has snobberies; ours lacks Christianity—your friend Mr. Duncan said that."

"And then?"

"Professor Dimsdale had a young lady assistant who decided to start a school of her own,
here in Helena. Mr. Dimsdale helped her. She's
not attractive to men; afraid of men. But she's a
good teacher, and a teacher for life, they all said.
Then they agreed that I should come along with
her. Where others had failed, she might get my
mind off dancing, men, clothes. So—off we rode
on the Stage."

"Well, where is she, dammit? Surely her classes aren't held here! Which one is she?" I said, peering around. "Over there with the red garter?"

But she'd gone too far to be offended, and she laughed again.

"*She got married,* if you please! Once removed from the Church, she married the first miner that asked her. And he had a squaw already, and two children. That was four months ago. For a while I worked for a Syndicate, trying to keep books, afraid to go home—"

"Pretty silly."

"Yes. Well, the Syndicate—my head wasn't turned to figures—not their kind. They let me go, after several proposals about another kind of figure."

"I see what they meant," I said, appraising. "I can feel a certain sympathy. But how long here, at this job?"

"A week only. I hoped Mr. Orem would come get me, but—"

"You like it here?" I looked upstairs and she blushed.

Her reply was defensive, uncertain, despite the new girl. "Yes. I like to dance—it's more than than x plus y equals boredom. But I'd like to go back, and I haven't been upstairs. Not because I haven't been asked," she said, arranging her costume and glancing around.

"All right. Listen carefully: it's important not to lie. Do you understand?—don't lie! You're beautiful, what they call nubile, now, and—"

"What does it mean? The last."

"It means staying a long time in bathrooms. Now, are you *sure* you want to go back?"

"Lend me Stage fare! Then you'll see!" She leaned forward, waking feelings that I'd forgotten. "I'll pay it back."

"For what day?"

"Tomorrow!"

"You don't feel like giving notice here? It's the custom, usually.

"None of the girls do. They—float off."

"Well, then. Be at the Stage office tomorrow, an hour early. I'll arrange it all. If you don't show up, frankly I'm not sure—"

She arose, kissed my cheek, and I crossed the room to address the head bartender. "I've taken up your waitress's time and spent very little. How much do I owe?"

"Not a farthing, Mr. Nickerson," he cried, polishing a glass. "All on the house, and it's a service you've rendered the girls this day!"

"You're sure?"

"Have a drink, sir, before you leave, and come back often." He reached over to shake hands. "I'm Irish, sir, but not brag-Irish. would that be clear?"

"Perfectly," I said, "and I've been brag-English today. But that needn't stand between us."

"Not so long as Bill Muldoon has a spark in his fist or a penny in his pocket!"

(I ascribed this speech, in part, to a popular now meaningless slur picked up by mountainmen: "No Irish need apply!" They'd eyed with routine suspicion a whole new wave of Emigrants. The King of Prussia, with his court, would have been treated precisely the same.)

I walked away, wondering why bartenders, as

a breed, were the kindliest and most patient of men.

Before I could get through the door, the shapeliest possible girl, dressed differently from her sisters, though not overdressed either, bounced up to hand me a small jar filled with minted gold coins. "Our appreciation, sir, for stopping the Plague of Helena. I don't think he'll be brash again soon!"

"You'd like me to have this?"

"With our thanks."

"But you work hard," I said, trying not to look aloft, "and I don't need all this money."

"You may value it later," she told me, and she was right. The jar stands in my study as I write these notes.

And to this day, I have no idea how the bartender knew my name. But nothing about bartenders could surprise me, ever.

CHAPTER XXXVII

AFTER DAISY HAD gone (somewhat to my surprise), I wandered around town, cursing bankers, lawyers, and Syndicates. For some reason I felt more alone than I'd felt in my life. And then, my mind awhirl, I fell sick, critically sick, for the first time since the fever in California.

I'd been strolling near Murphy and Neel's, hatless, on a blazing day, when I looked up to notice that the sun was not properly a sun any longer but an enormous angry whirl of red and white gasses. The sensation was odd, remindful (in my state) of De Quincy and his ability to narrow perceptions. I observed without hurry each component, which ceased whirling if I stared directly. I reflected that Galileo, when the Catholics talked of putting out his eyes, had probably seen the sun like this, as he did research that rivaled the Church.

Excited, I dissected the drifting orange wisps; then, suddenly, I could see nothing clearly, and I heard—off in the distance—a voice that said, "Are you all right, sir?"

I said, "I'm not certain. Something's happened to my vision. But I've seen a fine thing, all the same."

Apparently I fainted here, for I awoke at Mrs. McGinnis's, staring at her unscientific ceiling.

My landlady stood by my bed, looking worried and piteous. Near her was an impressive man in frock coat and pearly-gray trousers, a man with a thrustful medical beard, curled hair, and golden pince-nez, a man whose opinions one might shrink from opposing.

On a contrived bed-stand sat a black homeopathic kit, as well as two or three glasses of fluid and opened boxes of capsules.

"Now, Mr. Nickerson," said Mrs. McGinnis, wiping her hands on her apron—a habit she had—"you musn't fash yourself. Lie as quiet as a lamb, there, and let the doctor ask questions. Dr. McPheeters it is, not long in this town, and him with certificates to stagger a king."

"How long have I lain here, Mrs. McGinnis?"

"How long is it? Near on to a week, the poor lad, and never a move or a sound."

"But someone had to nurse me—was it you? With all you've got to do? Maybe you'd better say what happened."

"Some gentlemen—and bartenders amongst them; I'll not deny it—carried you home from where you collapsed in the town. They tried to pour whiskey down you, meaning nought sacrilegious, but the liquid came back up, a-gurgling from the sides of your mouth—choking you were."

"Thank you, Mrs. McGinnis. I've been a trouble to you. I feel very warm," I added. And indeed I felt distinctly un-well.

"To be expected—*expected at this stage!*" assured the doctor, producing a fever-gauge. "If my diagnosis is correct, we must take steps, and take them quickly. Ah-*ha!* You'll note your

temperature, sir"—showing me the reading of
104 degrees. "For one of your age, that touches
danger-line. A fever, sir, with complications that
I withhold *at this point*. We must have ice, and
that without delay!"

"The Kruger boys' ice-house, blocks sawed in
the winter, for supply to the saloons," quavered
Mrs. McGinnis, wringing her red, cracked
hands. "It's as near as you could wish, and the
Lord's work, as plain as—as—daylight is!"

"No doubt, Madam, no doubt, but we'll give
this same Lord a hand. You must consider," he
told her severely, "how many cases for simultaneous treatment Providence has in—well, let
us call it His Clinic. Some on crutches, others
with a foot dangling, sprains and fractures,
tumors, Ma'am, and boils, and dessications, and
affections from far heathen places. He requires
help, Ma'am, and it's here that Dr. Filbert T.
McPheeters steps in."

(The name fell uneasily on my ears, but I made
no comment.)

When Mrs. McGinnis fluttered out, to find her
Indian boy (likely asleep) and hand him a bucket, with instructions, Dr. McPheeters said, professionally clearing his throat, "First we must
throw up a protective shield, sir—the enemy,
we've found, tend to work and wriggle their way
into the skin, or epidermis, as we of the Hippo-
cratic faith know," and, my ear alerted again, I
watched him remove from his bag a common
nostrum known as "Merchant's Gargling Oil,
Good for Man or Beast" and containing, among
other unmentionables, oil of cloves, castor
beans, arsenic, and a weak solution of acid, with

a substantial base of alcohol, as all remedies were based then.

"But doctor," I protested feebly, trying to rise, "I have a fever, and don't think I need Merchant's Oil—without meaning offense."

"We use Merchant's Oil before advancing an inch! I wouldn't give so much for your chances"—snapping his fingers—"without it!"

Docilely, I swallowed a tablespoonful of the hideous mixture, and promptly felt worse. Before, my head had swum, and my body was afire; now my stomach burned and I was nauseated besides. Even so, Dr. McPheeters commenced a head-to-toe examination, clucking and talking aloud and seeming to include himself in my dilemma, as doctors generally do when they have little notion of the problem.

Producing a heart-cone, he listened with care; then he remarked (cheering me up) that, "Heart trouble—that is, over-thin ventricles with enlarged aorta—is, I think, hereditary in your lineage. At what age, sir, did your maternal grandfather die?"

"Ninety-six," I told him truthfully. The old gentleman, who'd seen his first child born when he was fifty, fell off the stern of a Nova Scotia boat while scalloping.

"That bears me out. Now, sir, a poor toiler in the vineyard of Aesculapius asks—what are these?"—rubbing a finger along my left hip.

"Arrow wounds, acquired in California."

"I don't wish to alarm you, but I see significance here, and danger. How long ago acquired, you said?"

I hadn't said, but I told him approximately seven or eight years.

"Indeed! the precise span after which such wounds become toxic! Can we conjecture what noxious extract of the woods might have poisoned those primitive barbs? Negative. As Dr. Filbert T. McPheeters views this aspect, the punctures were aimed to mature, or explode, later. On the order of a long-fused bomb. The scars look ugly, sir, I won't deceive you. They must be treated apart." He fell to humming, entirely self-satisfied, while I had a few doubts by now (ablaze, it seemed, with fever).

"You perhaps recall, sir, Dr. Abercrombie Sneed's ground-breaking monograph on subcutaneous injuries by Indians? No? He was the forerunner; others trailed behind. But we of progressive views took pains to equip our kits with Dr. Sneed's anodynes. Now, sir, if you'll re-open your mouth for several hard-hitting capsules. Excellent! Pink-and-Senna. Oil of Wormwood. Vermifuge. Quinine and Strychnine. Pulverized Os. And a final capper of Jalap-with-Turpentine. If they fail to fetch us, I suggest that you summon your attorney. A proper Will—"

To my relief (though I rejoiced at the mention of Quinine) Mrs. McGinnis arrived with ice, and the Indian boy, himself looking concerned, had a second bucket. Never did an application strike a suffering body more gratefully. I felt the coldness fight its way into my bones, which I figured were melted by now, but no sooner did my temperature plunge than I grew violently hot again, soaked through, so that the near-tearful

Mrs. McGinnis had to change the sheets (probably for the ninth or tenth time).

"Normal and expected," said Dr. McPheeters, snapping shut his kit. "My boy, from here it's a matter of time, one way or another. Not meaning to frighten, if I were a betting man, I'd take the nether view. But we all have to go. Good day to you, sir, and happy to be of service."

He collected ten dollars and left, in something of a hurry. I concluded that he preferred to be absent for the finish.

"Mrs. McGinnis," I said when he shut the door, "I believe that man to be an imposter and humbug. Merchant's Oil!" Then I leaped out of bed and dove for the outhouse, anxious about mortuaries in a town so new.

On my return, Mrs. McGinnis said, "I sensed it myself, sir. As soon as he opened his poke. And his manner! He was that oily, was he not?"

"Merchant's Oily, which has now, if you'll excuse it, been disposed of."

"I've a mind to hound him down, sir. A twister!—He'd steal the charley from under the Pope's bed!"

She looked sheepish, color deepening her reddened skin. "From a saloon, sir, the Lord forgive me. But he had a wagon out front, handsome it was, with the lettering and all—"

"Is there a regular doctor in town, Mrs. McGinnis? A man of reputation?"

"Well, sir, whilst you lay unconscious I got in Dr. Fleesum—drunk from morning to night—and all he said was 'Imagination! Pure imagination—a classic sample of hypochondria.' Them were his very words, strike me dead.

"And there was another, sir, a partner of Dr. Fleesum, and he could scarcely get himself up the stairs—"

"And *his* view?"

" 'Hopeless!'—the single word: 'Hopeless!' and him scarcely looking in your direction. Then he fell down the stairs on his way out. And there were two before that, sir. I looked high and low, that I did, if you'll believe it. One man could only say 'Hmmmm'—not another sound out of him—wobbly in the head; that's my belief, sir, not able to talk at all. He wandered to the window and seemed taken with me dried butterflies. And the other man—rolled up in a carriage and pair—said he'd need fifty dollars before he'd open his kit! I showed him the door, tempted to give him the rough of me tongue!"

Toward nightfall there arrived a man dressed differently from most doctors I knew. By now, I was pretty well out of my head, not fully conscious. But this fellow was wearing a long white coat—of a kind we call a "duster"—and he never removed his hat, which I recall thinking needed repairs worse than I did. His kit, too, was above the common, being upward of two feet long, with several odd tools showing at both ends.

"Evening, Ma'am," he said to Mrs. McGinnis, who looked deeply suspicious. "Dr. McPheeters wanted a second opinion, as stated; we discussed the case in Schwab's. He was shook, Ma'am, badly shook."

For some reason, I had the impression that Mrs. McGinnis held a broom, and the Indian boy stood behind her with a bow-and-arrow.

"Hmmmmmm!"—exactly as before, I supposed—then he produced a themometer the size of a walking-stick, started to roll me over, changed his mind as my landlady lifted her broom, and thrust it under my arm. I remember smelling his atrocious breath, and wondered how long he'd been in the saloon.

"Fever, serious fever—distemper would be an apt guess. However, we've had three epizootics here and must be sure. First, Ma'am, is to get him on his feet—"

"Why, whatever for?"

"Routine in such cases. There, good, and we'll just walk him around. So—so. Now tell me, have you run him any distance without placing on a blanket? After lathering, that is."

"See here, sir"—but he seemed not to hear. "Stay on the feet, by all means—Whoa, boy! Easy there, steady! I'd stand from behind, if I were you Ma'am. He's weak but he's skittish; we can't take chances here. He hasn't been a-gorging on apples, would you say?"

"Apples!"

"I've seen them swell up and bust, you'd scarcely credit it. We'll need a good worming; that goes without saying, and isolation, of course. If it's a plague, I don't want no gun-toting ranchers down on my neck. Would you have a good stout key for that door?"

"Well! I must say—"

During the walk, he'd felt me over, for "distended stomach," as he said, and searching for "fistula" (likely joking); and then he asked Mrs. McGinnis: "Ma'am, while not aiming to discomfit, have you noted symptoms of scouring? Or a drying of the nostrils?—'Scouring?' It means a loosening of the bowel—common knowledge, Ma'am"—and he gave her a reproachful look.

"Now?" asked the Indian boy, raising his bow, but she held him back.

"Very well—return to the straw for the moment."

I sank onto the bed, half dead from exertion. Meanwhile, the doctor had taken out a pad and pencil "It's best, Ma'am, if possible, to get the patient's full history—difficult if rounded up on the range. But I think we have a thoroughbred here. Would you know the name of Dam? Or even Sire?"

"Now, sir, I've heard about enough—"

"Hereditary pips are not unusual here—weak lungs, strangles, rump-sprung, sway-back. Oh, they're handed down; you'd be surprised. Well, then," producing two bottles, one containing "summer linament"—which had the worst stench I'd encountered since the wickiups—and the second filled with white pills the size of walnuts.

"Let's see where we're at. Rub every three hours with linament, head to foot and covering"—he glanced up—"*all* ground—then apply pellets till he pukes. Finally"—even more reproachful—"whatever you've been feeding, *switch to oats!*"

It was here, I sensed dimly, that Mrs. McGinnis raised her broom, causing the mischeivous horse-crook to leap up, grab his bag, and dart down the stairs. I heard him shouting, over his shoulder, "Frankly, I came a-hoping not to shoot him, but—" His voice rose to a comforting shriek as the Indian got in a good, solid *thwack*, and I figured he'd be having troubles soon along the line of Uncle Abner's.

"Now, sir, I think you know I never fetched that filthy limb of Satan. He appeared on the scene unbeknownst and—" She choked up, wringing her hands.

"It wasn't your fault, Mrs. McGinnis," I said weakly. "Don't worry about it. What we had, you might say, was the welcome voice of Montana—" I mean to to say more but drifted off to sleep, done in for a while.

Next day, as I lay freezing and sweating, while my landlady and the boy worked like slaves, a pale, concerned young man, a recent arrival in Helena, quietly came in, pulled up a chair, tested my temperature and pulse in silence, and, sitting back, said, "Tell me, Mr. Nickerson, have you had emotional upsets of late? Excitements? Have you, well, been living under strain?"

I thought this over, wet to the skin, and said at last, "Yes, I believe I have. Possibly for three years or more. Dr.—"

(I liked both his looks and manner.)

"Stern. I thought it possible. Now list for me, if you will, the various—ah—remedies you've lately been given."

"By other doctors?"

"Exactly."

I told him what I could remember, and his high fragile forehead flushed a dark red, almost purple.

"Criminal!" he gritted between his teeth. "I'm afraid we'll have to purge those from your stomach. You see," he went on, "My opinion is this: you've taxed your mind beyond its power to hold fast. Oh, no—I don't mean you're mentally 'disturbed.' We call it, now, 'brain fever,' and it deserves a better name some day. The sun brought it all to a head, if I may state it so; then residues of old malarias—you've had them? Mildly, you say? I thought so. These were dredged up to cause a climax. They'll probably do so, at intervals, the rest of your life.

"But we'll have you right in a few days. We'll lean on the quinine, adding calomel as a mercurial. And, of course, ice for fever. You're fortunate in your landlady," he said, smiling, and Mrs. McGinnis writhed with pleasure.

I said, "Doctor, this is the first sensible talk I've heard up to now. I'll follow your instructions to the letter; Mrs. McGinnis is a noble woman, and what's the charge for your visit?"

He waved it aside. "Oh, I'll be back. Let's get you up and around."

Of the first string of doctors, I'll explain that many such sifted through the Rockies in those days, often with a posse close behind. There was no real way to check their credentials, or even their intelligence. For a man with an infusion of liquor can seem brighter than he is. But the majority, I'd venture, had only the background of wagon-borne medicine man; these, with the incompetents, and, worse, the ones ravening for riches, doubtless left a well-marked trail of crosses.

CHAPTER XXXVIII

RECOVERED, I COMPLETED my father's business; then I bought three horses, and after giving Mrs. McGinnis a present that made her cry, and not neglecting the young Indian, I left for Alder Gulch by way of Bannack. I still felt weak, and wanted to regain my strength before Virginia.

But Bannack was a mistake. What I found was a ghost town. Le Grau's Bakery was boarded up, and Skinner's Saloon, of course, was closed, fallen in, and the late proprietor, I judged, was having no trouble these days with cold weather. Goodrich's appeared to exist, but it had an air of desolation, and I passed it by, though I wanted a glass of beer. Hank Crawford's butcher shop, empty, stared me in the face, and Davenport's Boarding House was turned into a dingy Chinese restaurant. I peered through a window; two gloomy Chinamen (much different from our rollicking Chinese of the Gulch) sat at one of the three or four tables.

I searched out the cabin-store that James and Grantly and I once shared and found the roof caved in, blocking the entrance. Pushing past two fallen logs, I looked in and saw nothing but five or six porcupines in a corner. The sole object intact was the "meat" pole outside, to the top of which James had started to pull the 300 trout, in that starvation winter of several decades ago.

From first to last I never saw a faimiliar face among the few persons wandering along Main Street, and I left, sobered by memory.

Along Alder Gulch an unaccustomed silence lay beneath the tall and now broody pines. The great days of panning were over; all had surrendered to the new search for other slopes, other ravines, the quartz lodes where machines removed the fun with the gold.

In Virginia City a different bustle, one of commerce and politics, had replaced the joyous racket of furniture smashed, windows knocked out, and blows exchanged. Or so it seemed to me. Grantly, briefly a "cattle-baron"—prosperous at last—was absent in Deer Lodge, I heard, and some heavy news awaited.

Professor Dimsdale, the good and strong-hearted man, had died not long before, giving in to those frail lungs that saw him farther than the stoutest miner might have survived. Everyone able to walk had come to the funeral, and the miners cried like babies. The Reverent Torbett had recently been replaced by a new minister who'd seemed confused at this emotion from such sinewy, ill-clad roughnecks.

But worse was yet to come. Heavy-hearted, I rode up Idaho Street toward the Smithers'. Passing the Forge, I felt something turn over in my chest. The fire-bed was cold, its warming glow gone, and no one was around. A sign had been posted, but spurring my horse, I passed it by without looking. A black wreath hung on Mr. Smithers' door, and I knocked, hardly able to summon the force.

Mrs. Smithers fell into my arms, clinging with her always astonishing strength, and then, breaking free, put her apron to her face. Mr. Smithers had apparently given up that last, muscular breath, cheerful (I was told) to the end. If I'd bypassed Bannack and come direct to Virginia instead!

At the moment of her divulgence, the bedroom door opened, and a doctor came out, carrying his kit in one hand and a hat in the other. He was dressed with a good deal of care, in a frock coat and what once had been spruce striped trousers, now badly faded, the stripes all but vanished.

Mrs. Smithers looked up, miserable.

"He should pass within the hour, Ma'am," said this new adornment to Virginia's medical clique. "The rattle's started, and we generally figure on forty to forty-five minutes. Barring obstructions."

"You mean Mr. Smithers isn't dead yet?" I asked, aghast. I could have said it with more finesse, but my recent bout with doctors had left me intolerant of the breed.

"Dying, sir, dying. In extremis. I could not, to answer your question, certify him dead as of this moment."

"Then what in the name of decency is that black wreath doing on the door?"

Mrs. Smithers now looked stricken. "The girls tacked it up, son Ross. I know I shouldn't have let them, but they thought Ewing might like it displayed as soon as convenient. You see, he picked it out himself and said to get as much wear as possible. He grumbled—I'll make no bones about it—he grumbled about the price."

"I'll be back before the end, Ma'am," said

the doctor, consulting a hunter watch that I figured he'd rescued from a patient in approximately Mr. Smithers' present condition.

"I promised to look in on a Cedar-head
Knowles, just across the street. He broke two
bones in his foot while kicking a mule. And he
won't—he will not, despite advice—leave off
scratching under the splints with a wire."

I glanced up sharply, flushed, for his com-
ments had a familiar ring, but his face was grave,
even sad, as if he were a genuine sharer in grief.
When he left, I spoke to the girls, who were
seated, in tears, on a bench beside one wall.

I might never have recognized the girl Faire,
who was a woman now, lovely and slender, and I
gave a small nod of reassurance to Daisy, whose
eyes, I thought, held a faint, mute appeal She
was engaged, said Mrs. Smithers, to her temperance Con Orem, and by a stunning coincidence,
the sister was "walking out" with none other
than that second wildcat of the celebrated scrap
in Mr. Hosmer's behalf—a greatly subdued
Hugh, or Hughie, O'Neil.

"Someone should be with him," said Mrs.
Smithers, drying her eyes on the aprin again. "It
would be wicked and ungodly to let a man like
that go out alone, but I can't bear—" when there
came a knock at the door and the two swains,
their faces slightly, or picturesquely, marked
here and there, in tribute to Montana's first Chief
Justice, stood awkwardly in the doorway.

Being apprised of conditions, and shaking
hands with me, they—that is (I believe)
O'Neil—said, "We'll go set with him, Ma'am."

Orem began, "A finer man never—" and came
to a stop; resuming, he added, "We'll call if

there's any change; don't fret more than need-ful."

We sat waiting, having little to say except, now and then, speaking in brief undertones about some feat or other of the dying blacksmith, trying at once not to hear the hoarse rasps as he fought for his final breath. And then, quite suddenly, the sound stopped, and Mrs. Smithers cried, "Oh, merciful Lord, he's gone! Gone, and I should have been at his side!"

We stood up as Mrs. Smithers, deathly pale, started toward the door, but her progress was impeded by that of her husband emerging. He was gaunt and the face blanched, but his expression was determined and cheerful, and it seemed to me, the color was returning by the moment.

"I couldn't do it, Harriet. I know it's expected, with cash down, but I laid there thinking about them ox-shoes half finished for Jeeter McQueen, and there ain't a ox alive can track on a half shoe, them being clove—so stated Biblical; and bless my soul if it ain't Ross son!"—here he collapsed onto a stool, making gestures toward a niche in the sod that, remembering Plummer's long-ago extraction, I finally realized was known to no outsider except myself. I fetched the bottle, to a shocked gasp by Mrs. Smithers, and he gurgled down about half a pint.

"We tried to pin him, Ma'am," said O'Neil, "but he was too strong for the pair of us. He's bent on getting well, and I'll fight Satan—without purse—to back that statement up!"

"Ewing Smithers, you mean you've been a drinking man all these years and I not knowing? For shame!"

"I acknowledge it looks bad, Harriet, but it was

for the tooth abstractions, mainly, with an infrequent gollop to cut phlegm—but only lately."

She nestled his head against her bosom and said, "Well, it don't matter. I'm glad to have you, you can drink a hogshead a day—"

"Well, now, I don't believe I could drink a hogshead, not in five year, less I give up the Forge and made it a all-out career—"

"Oh, piffle! You tangle and mix up everything's said, and besides," she said, looking at Orem, "we're not entirely temperance, here, no matter who spurns drink. What's more," she added blushing, "it's a good saloon, and to tell you the truth, I like a little beer myself."

Mr. Smithers, thoughtful, took advantage of this unexpected notice to bite off another leg of the hogshead, looking better every minute, when the doctor came back. He directed a keen look at his patient, then took his pulse, tapping him here and there. Mr. Smithers apparently thought he was trying to take his bottle, which he shoved in a quick lurch beneath his chair.

"I'm not surprised, Ma'am," said the doctor in a professional tone, the unctuous bereavement gone. "It often happens this way. We see it over and over in our practice. You may recall that I predicted—"

"You did no such thing," said Mrs. Smithers, bridling. "To hear you tell it, he was dead day before yesterday. Of all the unmitigated humbugs!"

The man seemed unruffled, and said, "Let us thank the blessed Lord for stepping in at the threshold, so to speak. This, Ma'am, was one of those cases that passed to the Higher Realm—it went to the Supreme Court, you might say. And now I'll just take my leave. I've got a bullet to extract—Duke Ogilvey, result of a disputatious inside straight."

"Harriet," spoke up the blacksmith, "wasn't there money paid to the new undertaker and preacher? I believe they're partners of yours, sir," he said to the doctor, "and a finer combination I can't hardly perceive—usher a man out, head him right whilst doing so, then plant him. But according to this old noggin, we've got a altered situation—"

"A hundred and twenty-five dollars," said Mrs. Smithers. "Funeral with Church sermon and trimmings, embalming, hardwood box, guaranteed 'worm-proof,' and service at the grave. And yet, it included the doctor's visits as well. As if they was worth a sprig of bunch grass," she added, beginning to look more indignant.

"I know nothing of business!" cried the doctor quickly. "To be candid, I have no interest in money, Ma'am. None of we physicians do. The only thing that counts is the helping hand to bleeding mankind. How my part—associates—view such cases is—"

"Fiddlesticks. Partners was the right word, or maybe fellow-thieves is better."

"Harriet, you know me for a generous man, and son Ross, you'll back that up—openhanded, even reckless with legal tender. [This was not strictly ture; Mr. Smithers was regarded as honest but, perhaps, a trifle "close."] But it don't appear fair to squander gold on a cancellation funeral and interring. Now I've never drawed off from a indicated bill in my life—pay up, cash on the spot's been my motto, no matter if my father was disposed to malinger—but this! Well, I'm corralled if it ain't a mite too much. To boil down, I've a mind to balk."

O'Neil rose here, and Orem got up a second later. "We'll just step down and recover the sum, sir, said O'Neil. "Don't stir yourself. To buy a cancelled-out funeral stretched anything I've heard of, and we'll set it straight in a jiffy. Keep calm and quiet; put it out of your mind. And you, sir"—to the doctor—"take a seat near the chimney. I'd like a word when we return. No, never mind the bullet. Duke Ogilvey's full of bullets; has been since he was fifteen. One additional won't matter, not for an hour or so."

"Lodged, sir, near the fifth upper vertebra, as near as I can make out. There's danger there—one heave of the shoulders—"

"Sit down and shut up!"

Within five minutes after they'd left, Grantly appeared at the door, having heard the news. He was on business from Deer Lodge, and come to pay respects; James was off on another expedition. Grantly's face was beet-red—a sign of anger—but he greeted me warmly, shook hands with Mr. and Mrs. Smithers, spoke to the daughters, and addressed the doctor, who, huddled in the corner, had lost his professional pomp.

"Of all the cruel and rascally pieces of incompetence in my experience, this certainly heads the list. I think," said Grantly to my surprise, for he was normally quiet under pressure, "I'll just ask to see your credentials. Produce something, a card, a fob, a prescription pad, anything that might set you apart from a plumber," and he started in the trapped man's direction.

"I'd do it, sir, in a minute, but alas, the entire lot, including my diploma, which I normally carry on my person, was soaked and destroyed only last week in a cloudburst."

While reading books at college, and thereafter, I'd often encountered a character who said "Humph!" and in fact, discounted the comment as an actuality of life, but Grantly, pausing, distinctly said "Humph" at this moment, adding, "Very likely. Very likely indeed." And then, seating himself beside the blacksmith (who, slightly awed, tried to arise, only to be pushed gently down), said, "Mr. Smithers, I, too, am not a drinking man, but I'll join you in a pull from the bottle I see beneath your chair. If it wouldn't inconvenience you."

"Glasses!" cried Mr. Smithers, who now had a very good color. "Three of your sainted father's best glasses, Harriet; and Harriet—wouldn't you, and yes, the girls, cover the bottoms of additional, mixed with sugar, of course, in the way of—I lack your oratoricals, sir [to Grantly], but what I mean is, well, it's in the way of Jubilee."

"What the girls drink is their own business, up to a point," said Mrs. Smithers, not at all awed, "but I'll have a cup running over, as the man says in the Book. He failed to say running over with *what*, I'll remind you!" She was still seething.

Mr. Smithers only sighed.

O'Neil and Orem returned in half an hour. Both looked sheepish.

"Just place the dust on the table, boys, and take the thanks of this blacksmith today. Now, mind, it ain't the tender that plagues me; it's the principle. If there was one thing my daddy taught me, it was, cling to your principles." He frowned. "I'll add that he hisself hadn't no more principle than a tomcat, on occasion, that is."

"We failed to get it, sir," said Orem. "When we busted into that coyote's den, he crouched behind an iron stove with a double-barreled shotgun. And since his place lacks any see-through windows, we were naked to barrage. I'll catch him out after dark; bank on it."

O'Neil said, "On retreat, we considered burning the parlor, him in it, but it wouldn't scarcely serve." He looked more crestfallen than I thought possible to those 195 pounds of bone and muscle. "What's more, you take with a sod top, and weeds growing, it wouldn't burn down too handy."

Mr. Smithers had lost a faint trace of new color, but after thinking a minute, he straightened up and said, clapping his knee, "Boys, I don't want you to grieve and fidget. I've hit on the only rightful solvent, and I think Mr. Duncan, here, and Ross, son, will toe-up and agree. A funeral paid for points to a funeral held, and we'll go right through as arranged—"

"Ewing Smithers!"

"No, you needn't stand astride, Harriet. For once I've made my mind up. We'll have that money's-worth Departure, corpse or no corpse. I'll show him, with his shotgun; him and the new preacher both."

"Well, I never heard of such a thing in my life! We'll be the laughing stock of Virginia City," but both girls giggled, and even Grantly tried to hold himself in. So it was plain to see she was outvoted.

"Doctor," said O'Neil in an almost cooing voice, "I wonder if I might consult you professional, behind those cottonwoods along the Gulch."

"Now just a minute," said Orem, stretching up to his full five nine. "If you think—"

"The notion crossed me first: Not to say," said O'Neil, "that you can't make an appointment for later. They tell me he's got a Blackfoot nurse, if you can call her that—begging your pardon, Ma'am and ladies. Get her to consult her book; if there's anything left to make an appointment *with*, I mean."

Here Grantly stood up and took over. "Let him go, boys. He's not much worse, or better, than the rest. I don't see Mr. Smithers as a violent or vengeful man; the fact is, he's a man of God, I hear, and God's supposed to be forgiving. Though I confess," he said, in the old musing study, "that a close reading of the Old Testament fails, in my view, to turn up convincing samples. Offhand, I recall just the opposite—"

I could see that, as usual, he was about to wander off on a tangent, and as Daisy had half risen to express *her* ideas, I got up and said briskly, "It's an inspired idea, Mr. Smithers, a sublime and groundbreaking idea, if you'll excuse the phrase. Leave it to us—we'll work out all details."

And to his wife (red-faced again): "It would be an act of kindness, Ma'am, a boon to the town. As I understand matters, entertainment's been lacking here of late, an explosive situation—I *know*!"

"Now Ross son's hit it right on the nail-head! We don't hold dress-up parties, Harriet, nor announce oyster spreads at the hotel. This is our chance to pay off debts. Don't you line up likewise, sir?"—this to Grantly.

"I'm fully in accord," said Grantly, his expression determined, though reminiscent of reproductions I'd seen of the Mona Lisa, a painting in Paris—serene but laughing inside. "A large funeral without, ah, the central figure, is precisely what Virginia City requires at this moment."

The girl Faire spoke up for the first time. "Daddy, don't you think we might at least take down the wreath on the door?"

"Now, Faire child, I wouldn't be too hasty about retiring that adornment. It's a pretty thing, and hardly wore at all. No, I was counting on leaving that displayed till Christmas, to fall in with the holly and all."

"Ewing T. Smithers, I do believe what little senses you had have skittered up the chimbly. The minute this poppycock's finished, that ugly thing's coming *down*! It's my door, too, and I'll have my way on *that*, or there ain't a further meal to be cooked in this house!"

O'Neil and Orem offered one ray of sunshine; the undertaker said he'd knock $32.50 off the overall bill, since Duke Ogilvey had just expired and was the right size for the box; and he promised a bang-up eulogy from his associate, the cleric, together with a suitable service at the grave. So we let it go at that.

CHAPTER XXXIX

WELL, THE NEWS got around pretty fast, and no-body appeared to think it odd. So many unusual things had taken place in this gulch that Mr. Smithers' ante-humous funeral struck every-body as only sensible in the circumstances. From first to last, I never heard a soul laugh, and the miners, naturally, assumed that look of pesky solemnity that they used for occasions. The fact is, those last took a special fancy to the program and admired "the resurrected" for sticking to his rights, and they said that if this new preacher "didn't trot out a rouser of a memorial," they'd "take and hop-scotch him out of town, along with and in particular that skunk of an undertaker."

The church service was held at a new place of worship built by the usual groups that had splin-tered off the other churches formed in the past few years. It was the most commodious one-story structure in town, and the *Post* mentioned with admiration, plus its customary sarcasm, that "the benches even have hard backs, thus putting the votaries in a more heavenly frame of mind." It also pointed out that "the ritual of kneeling is not included in the new All Souls Reformed Church's theologic schedule, the omission causing some complaints among merchants."

Well, it's true that over-kneeling can wear out trouser-knees, but I never heard any merchants complaining, and I think the editor threw the last part in simply because the idea occurred to him. The Post was a marvelously relaxed publication, there being no such thing as reprisal by suit, and when one of the congregation called at the office with a dog-whip, the editor sent up word that he was re-adjusting some pied type. This seemed to appease honor all around. "Well, now, I ain't apt to be the one to withhold news from the town," said the dog-whip man. "There's such a thing as freedom of the press, and I'll stand out for it, personal grievance aside."

The editor had a creaky old flat-bed press in a half-basement, with some overworked type, and it was touch-and-go every week whether an edition would make it or collapse on the floor.

A crisis developed in the Smithers home when the near-deceased announced that the family would attend the funeral en bloc. I was on hand for dinner, and Mrs. Smithers kicked up a first-class fuss. She really laid her ears back.

"Right there you've gone a step too far, Ewing Smithers," she said. "We're mortified bad enough already, I and the girls, without trooping down that aisle like a ghost with hand-maids. Not to mention an ugly black wreath drooping from my door at this minute."

"Why, Harriet," said Mr. Smithers mildly. "I'd hope you proud to appear there triumphant,

your wedded spouse back from the grave and all.
Why"—he grew a little excited—"it comes
thundering close to the case of Lazarus and his
four-poster. There ain't a particle of difference,
barring Jesus at the scene."

"Lazarus, my granny! Like as not, he slept on a
pallet and wasn't dead at all"—but Mr. Smithers
failed to hear, being in what's known as a brown
study. "No," he said at length, "it ain't in the
realm of possibles. Our bed's nailed to the wall,
and if you count in the springs and slats it
couldn't be done, not without help, in my
plight—"

Mrs. Smithers arose from the table and flung
down her napkin. "That was the furthest you
needed to say. Yes, by all means, walk down
dragging a bed. Lay a hand on one slat, just one,
and I'll shop for separate quarters—"

"Why, Harriet," said her husband again, "I've
already sidetracked the notion, and stated so out
loud. As to the funeral, the family's *expected*;
people would look on peculiar, what with
money down."

She stood a moment, doubtful. "I'll budge this
far," she said at last. "If Ross will step into town
and ask one or two, picking those with brains in
their heads—I'll think it over. After dinner, I
mean, and a sorry dinner it's been, thanks to the
numbskull I married."

I walked along Wallace Street, wondering
how to tackle the problem, when it finally occurred to me that a miner carrying a few drinks
might be the easiest solution. But when I stepped
into the Bale of Hay and approached Dick Worthington, I recognized that I'd braced the wrong

man. This was a miner who'd been responsible for about half the mischief in town, in former times, and he hadn't changed any.

"Present?" he said, in a voice so loud I winced. "There wasn't no question of it, not in the minds of them I've heard. Now lookee here—Newton Smithers was a man, and a man ain't going to pull leather on his friends. But what's more important and vital"—he took me by a lapel, becoming confidential, almost pleading—"a funeral without a corpse won't *draw*! I misdoubt a dozen mourners would arrive. You don't expect a preacher could work hisself up to empty air, do you? And I'll just sum up, speaking individual: if the family ain't on hand, you needn't look for Dick Worthington. Think it over!"

Well, I went back and reported to the Smithers, maybe wishing to see the fun myself, after going so long without any, and the funeral was set for next day.

The church was packed when Grantly and I arrived, with townsfolk looking slightly uncomfortable and miners wearing long faces and their usual squinty expression. Some wore black arm-bands, and many brushed away a tear or a fake tear, now and then. The congregation had imported a real organ, hand-pumped from a back room, to lord it over the Baptists (which had a harmonium), and this was going very low, worked by a Mrs. Appleton, when we sat down in a back row. She was playing "Nearer, My God, to Thee," and it did have a soothing effect, unless you examined the circumstances, which were absurd. There was no excuse for the miners, of course, except that they seldom behaved any other way.

Among other nonsense, they'd littered the place with flowers. The whole dais was practically buried in bouquets of wild flowers and roses they'd lifted from women's gardens, I reckoned, and there were several potted plants—also stolen—and leaning against the altar was a giant horseshoe fashioned out of wire and wrapped in things like daisies and buttercups and clover, with a ribbon across that said, "Good Bye, Old Pard."

Here and there, mostly along the walls, were clumps of grass, with some tumble-weed, and blue-green sage-brush, nicely tied with ribbons and bearing cards with three or four signatures, like the other bouquets. Times had lately been dull in Virginia, a man told me, and people were ready for this sort of thing. It brought back memories of the old days of the Cravens' theatricals, and Professor Dimsdale's Singing School sessions.

Well, it was all comfortable and happy, despite the crocodile tears, but I noticed that Grantly, inspecting a card on some sage-brush, flushed a soft pink and remained thus through the service. The card had several characters like "夕亍兒癸" and was signed, "The Honorable Chinese Association"—prompted by people like Worthington, I supposed.

But there *were* some Chinese there, probably not knowing why, and they mostly sat in a group, and so did the Chileans and Mexicans and others. I tried to find out who devised the arrangements but never managed to pin it down.

The left front pew was held vacant, by one of the undertaker's men, armed, and this was draped in black crepe—the only really offensive exhibit on view.

The place was jammed before the Smithers came, and when the undertaker saw them he went softly, whispering, leaning over, unctuous and polite, yet fully in charge—distributing some hideous black plumes. Several persons refused them, I noticed, and Grantly tossed his on the floor with a snort of disgust.

The Smithers' entrance caused a stir, naturally, with Mr. Smithers walking in front and the others bright with embarrassment, dressed in black; and the organist switched to music even more doleful, while the miners burst into a freshet of grief. At the same time, several arose to shake Mr. Smithers' hand. It was about as outrageous a sight as ever I saw. As for Mr. Smithers, he appeared to be having the time of his life. No such notice as this had ever been paid him, and he made the most of it. Moreover, because of his sickness, he hadn't seen many of these people for weeks, and what with exchanging pleasantries along the way, and stopping to promise a farmer the ox-shoes previously mentioned, the procession went pretty slow.

When they were finally seated, there was the usual bustle and coughing and sneezing and rearranging that you hear in church; then the undertaker held a finger to his lips, hissing out "Sh-h-h-h-h!" but smiling, too, and a Reverend McAfee slipped to the altar from the back room and gazed around, sorrowful but trying to bear up. He was a handsome-appearing man, tall and

broad-shouldered and wearing a tail coat with a
black silk tie.

He began by reminding the family of the great
loss they'd suffered [here Mr. Smithers turned,
beaming, to agree with the crowd]; that we'd all
suffered here in Virginia, and then he seemed to
think a small but tasteful joke was called for,
saying it was hard enough to *ride* a horse here,
let alone *shoe* one. After Mrs. Smithers had restrained her husband from rising, to explain
about ravines, Reverend McAfee acknowledged
that he'd known the departed only a short time,
more was the pity, but that many, many people
had come forward with facts about his life and
character, and these persons, of course, included
the family. Mrs. Smithers, like Grantly, turned
pink here herself, but it got worse by and by.

Mr. Smithers, he said, had sprung from poor
but reasonably honest parents back East, and
even as a lad had been noted for his support of
somewhere between nine and fifteen different
churches—"scattering his fire, which may be the
best system, only the Almighty knows." This
held a grain of truth—the blacksmith *had* been
religiously mobile for several years—but it was a
trifle impudent, too, and so was that "reasonably
honest." But the "churches" made a hit with the
miners, who turned to each other and said things
like, "Didn't I tell you? He couldn't a done
different—it came natural," and "If Ewing T.
Smithers had a fault, it was flinging money right
and left—Jesus or no Jesus," and one old fellow,
middling drunk, rose to refresh Mr. McAfee on
"what you may not have knowed," that the
blacksmith, once in Salt Lake, had tried to "or-

ganize a church for horses, but Indians sneaked in at night and stole the entire congregation." This last appeared too much even for the miners, and several hauled him down with mutters and a threat or two.

" 'Man that is born of woman hath but a short time, as the sparks fly upward,' in the Good Book's word, and when I add ashes to ashes, it might strike even the knot-headedest among you [looking at the squelched miner] as peculiarly appropriate. The passage might have been *wrote* for him."

Now an interruption came when the undertaker was caught trying to pass the plate, but O'Neil tripped him up, sending him sprawling, and order was restored.

During the next few remarks, I realized that the Reverend McAfee didn't know any more about the Bible than a goat did. Either that or he strove on purpose, for his statements came out scrambled, and not necessarily Biblical. After mentioning an orphans' home Mr. Smithers founded, near Pittsburgh, he consulted his Book and cried, "Wherefore art thou, Ewing T. Smithers?" but a miner took exception and said, "In Virginia City, Montaner, and another slip like that might provoke trouble. Watch it!"

Reverend McAfee ignored him, mooning on, flipping the pages at random, it seemed to me, though he had inserts here and there. " 'Yea, though I walk through the valley of death, I shall fear no evil, for without are dogs and murderers. Is not the gleaning of the grapes of Ephraim better than the vintage of Abezier?—' "

Some of the miners thought yes, and others no, and one said he'd have to try both crops on *the same day*, otherwise the test wouldn't mean anything.

"—the Lord opened the mouth of the ass and she said unto Balaam, 'What have I done unto thee?' "—but *all* the miners bridled at this, and one, standing up, said, "Now, you take one more swipe like that at a corpse, in no ways situated to defend itself, and we'll convert them swaller tails to laundry. He ain't no more an ass than you are—less, likely."

"—whatsoever parteth the hoof and is cloven-footed and cheweth the cud among the beasts, that shall ye eat—but not the hare, because he divideth not the hoof—"

"Well, you've come a cropper now for sure. There ain't a soul in this settlement don't eat jack-ass rabbit stew, and I've saw your Reverence do it yourself, at the Virginia Hotel."

It was pleasant to hear the tommyrot; I'd missed it more than I realized. Half the congregation was bent double by now, and the other half—miners—had worked up a full head of peeve. An outsider might have considered them dangerous.

For the first time, Reverend McAfee responded directly. "The Scripture is, as you suggest, a trifle obscure in the passage, Mr. Slater. We do eat hare; I acknowledge it. But if you check Leviticus 11:13, you'll find the same proscription applying to the camel—"

"I've never et a camel."

"Perhaps you haven't checked today's menu at the hotel," replied the minister with his first trace of bitterness. But this was uphill going, as many another before him had learned. He took a deep breath and bulled on with "I am the rose of

Sharon and the lily of the valleys," arousing the single comment that he didn't look it, when a blast came from the back room that almost shook down the building; bits of plaster fell from the ceiling.

"Got him, by God!" came a cry from the region. "One shot with a hand-gun .45 Colt. Now *that* ain't *bad!*"

A number of men leaped forward to inquire. That organ pumper, spotting a fat deer through a clear glass window, had opened fire, as a matter of course. The season had been scarce of wild game, the river was too low now for boats, and Brigham Young had cut down supplies, so the man was congratulated, and shaken hands with, and asked whether he would sell some meat, and then, eventually, the undertaker got everybody to their seats. Nobody mentioned the wrecked window.

Anyhow, this charade was about finished. Reverend McAfee said we could join him in prayer, and dropping to one knee (no doubt relieved), he offered up a surprisingly eloquent and touching memorial to Mr. Smithers, who broke down before it was over, and at the end, Mrs. Appleton played a soft, mortuary tune while the family filed out first, escorted by the undertaker, and Mr. Smithers, recovered, greeted people at the door. Then the undertaker cried, "Hold on, all! Up the hill and show plumes!"

Well, they could hardly bury Mr. Smithers, so the group strolled up out of curiosity. And, once there, they had the surprise of their lives. Several men were barbecuing half a steer on a spit, and others were opening a keg of beer, and, yes, Mr. Smithers had helped organize the whole entertainment. He'd bought the steer out of his own pocket and provided the beer as well. (Privately, I thought it probably strained him slightly.)

I heard people say, "Well, if that isn't the handsomest gesture I ever run across!" and "The dear, good man, to take the trouble, in his shape," and, "This beats anything in Virginia since I arrived! Thoughtful?—Well, I guess so!"

For my part, I felt a surge of relief. Mr. Smithers was eccentric, but I'd never considered him a lunatic, to hold his own funeral while still alive. And when I shook his hand, as he stood beaming, he said, "Fooled you, didn't I, Ross son? My thinking run approximately so: If the Lord in His bounty seen fit to spare me, I might acknowledge it public, to speak in figures. Step in line for some meat, son; it didn't come cheap."

Well, everybody had a good time. The Hurdies were there, embarrassing Mrs. Smithers briefly, or until she got some beer down, and the group sang the old tunes, happy to be out in the open again, even in a graveyard. I noticed that most temperance people had a sip of beer, too. Nobody got drunk, there was no rowdyism, only a general, heartwarming get-togetherness, with Mr. Smithers the hero of the day.

From start to finish, Grantly, while enjoying himself at last, eyed it all as if he meant to write it up some day, and he finally did, the article appearing first in Mr. Greeley's paper and then in *Harper's* magazine. As for the *Montana Post*, it gave the funeral a column of type on page one, under the headline: MOURNFUL OCCASION TURNS INTO FIESTA.

In the late afternoon, with people drifting away, I felt an odd sense of bereavement. I wondered whether anything so enjoyable and crazy might happen in Virginia again. I'd been diverted for a while, but nothing, really, had changed for me.

To shorten things, for I've gone on long enough, I rode back to Deer Lodge with Grantly; we had several fine talks, he and I, with Aubony in the background, lending some sort of primitive and subtle help; and, for the while ("until you can find yourself again") I joined the "saddle tramps" that rode herd on Grantly's stock. I learned to sing the low, mournful songs, at night; the ones cowboys sing—to lull the stock. People tend to ascribe these dirges to some deep loneliness in the cowboy himself, as he follows his solitary way. But it's been found over the years that only this soft song, or lament, will keep cattle from growing restless and straying.

In a few weeks I undertook a mission to Virginia City for the ranch, and while there, on the sort of impulse that injured me always, I rode out toward the Madison. Watching the trail, with several new houses now, I realized that every rivulet, each stone and tree, was still familiar. More than three years had passed, as I said, and I expected to see Slade's sad failure of a house in ruins.

Breasting the last knoll, the pounding heart no less familiar, though I knew the uselessness of punishing myself further, I sat looking at blue smoke curling from that stone chimney. In the corral stood a pale horse, of a kind nobody else here would own. The season was early autumn, and the leaves had just begun to turn. Gazing round at this broad green valley, that had long awaited devoted and purposeful hands, I walked on toward what I saw as an end to loneliness of my own.

Afterword

A Roaring in the Wind follows the journals and adventures of James and Granville Stuart, who prospected for gold in California and Montana, ran a Montana store, went into the cattle business, and tried other pursuits. They made their principal home in Montana's Virginia City—perhaps the roughest boom town in American frontier history. Living, on occasion, in nearby places—Bannack, Deer Lodge, etc.—they recorded the tumultuous gold Stampede at Alder Gulch and were present at the Popular Tribunals conceived by a Vigilance Committee in an area then without official law, and when all Montana mining camps were at the mercy of outlaws, notably the bloodthirsty Henry J. Plummer and his organized Road Agents.

Here the fictional brothers Duncan are meant to resemble the Stuarts only in very broad outline. Many other journals, diaries (day-notes), letters, newspapers, and contemporary volumes help detail the unfolding events in Montana of the 1860s, before the region won Territorial status. (The author being devoted to lists, a number of these sources are herewith appended.)

All journals agree on southern Montana's early acute need for Vigilance, and the first

Territorial Chief Justice—Hezekiah Lord Hosmer—paid high tribute to those pioneer strivers for decency (who quickly became Montana's elected leaders) in his Charge to the Territory's first Grand Jury, December 5, 1864, and in his speeches made later in New York and elsewhere.

Justice Hosmer also stressed the danger of Vigilantes when acting simultaneously with an existing system of laws, which he theoretically brought to Montana. However, for some years, Mr. Hosmer was without police to back his valiant efforts, with the result that other, irresponsible Vigilance groups later formed—all turning sour, as most such bands are bound to do at last. Colonel Wilbur Fiske Sanders, head of the Vigilance group in that early wild time, became a United States Senator when Montana achieved statehood (1889) and remains the state's most revered historical figure, as a bronze statue in Helena's capital building suggests.

He deplored and detested his brief role as Vigilante leader (hence the near-duel), continually strove for moderation during those few terrible weeks, and, at their end, when official law impended, warned against resumption of a system "inherently immoral and evil." Nevertheless, he did what he saw as his duty at the time and disbanded the group as promptly as possible. Throughout his life, Sanders was a man of stern integrity and common sense, and his service as senator was of a kind not always seen in these days.

In a few instances, a journal entry has been rearranged by a word or two, in the interest of clarity. In no case has the sense of any quotation been altered even slightly. For narrative purposes, one or two trivial liberties have also been taken with chronology.

The author is greatly indebted to Yale University; to Dr. Archibald Hanna, curator of Western Americana collections at Yale's Beinecke Library; and to Dr. Hanna's excellent assistant, Joan Hofman. Mrs. Harriet Melroy, librarian of the Montana State Historical Society in Helena, generously made available the intact files of Virginia City's *Montana Post* and the *Helena Herald* and helped with many valuable manuscripts and volumes. The author's wife, Judith Martin Taylor, again functioned as helper-in-research, editor, copyreader, and target of much complaint from a worker perhaps uniquely peevish.

BIBLIOGRAPHY

Abbott, E. C. (Teddy Blue) and Smith, Helena Huntington. *We Pointed Them North; Recollections of a Cowpuncher.* New York, 1939.

Adams, Ramon F. *Six-Guns and Saddle Leather.* (Bibliography of Books and Pamphlets on Western Outlaws and Gunmen) University of Oklahoma Press, 1954.

Bancroft, Hubert Howe. *History of Washington, Idaho and Montana.* San Francisco, 1890.

Bancroft, Hubert Howe. *Popular Tribunals.* San Francisco, 1887. "The Banditti of the Rocky Mountains and Vigilante Committee in Idaho." Chicago, 1865.

Bealer, Alex W. *The Art of Blacksmithing.* New York.

Beaverhead County, Montana Recorder's office Document of Recorded Claim (no. 7) Kearsage Lode, by Sidney Edgerton. Bannack, Montana, 1864.

Beita, Lester V. *Treasury of Frontier Relics.* New York, 1966.

Bierce, Ambrose. Route Maps of a Journey from Ft. Laramie and Dakota Territory to Fort Benton, Montana Territory. 1866.

Black Hills Placer Mining Co., Rockerville, So. Dakota Transit Book.

Boller, Henry A. *Among the Indians: Eight Years*

in the *Far West. (1858-1866)*. Philadelphia, 1868.

Boyce, James Richard. "Facts about Montana Territory and the Way to Get There." *Rocky Mountain Gazette*, Helena. 1872.

Broadside, Bannack Theatre. "A Grand Bill Tonight. On Saturday, October 16, 1864 'The Tragedy in 5 Acts of *King Edward IV*.'" Other Broadsides, 1864–1867.

Bullion Mining Company of Montana. Prospectus. (Organized under laws of the State of New York.) New York, 1865.

Burlingame, Merrill G. *The Montana Frontier*. Helena, Montana. 1942.

Camp, C. L. "Chronicles of George C. Yount." *California Historical Quarterly*, April, 1923. "The Song of Hugh Glass" 1915.

Campbell, John L. *Idaho: Six Months in the New Gold Diggings*. (The Emigrant's Guide Overland.) New York, 1864.

Campbell, John L. "Montana. The People of Eastern Idaho as affected by House Bill No. 15." Washington, 1864.

Cooke, Lt. Col. *Adventures in the Army, or Romance of Military Life*. Philadelphia, 1857.

Daugherty, Captain J. F. Description of Route from Ft. Benton to St. Louis.

Daugherty, Captain J. F. Across the Plains to Virginia City.

Deer Lodge County Recorder's Office. Record of South East Claim, Lomax Lode, Deer Lodge County, Virginia City, 186—

Delano, Alonzo, *Life on the Plains and Among the Diggings*. Ann Arbor, 1966.

Dickson, Albert Jerome. *Covered Wagon Days*. Cleveland, 1929.

Dimsdale, Professor Thomas J. *The Vigilantes of Montana, or Popular Justice in the Rocky Mountains.* Virginia City, Montana, 1866.

Edwards, Horace. Letters.

Edwards, John E. Papers as a Crow Indian Agent. (Montana, 1883-1902.)

Fisk, James Liberty. Circular. "Northwest Expedition being Organized." Written for Yellowstone Town and Mining Co. Washington, 1865.

Granville, Stuart. *Forty Years on the Frontier.* Cleveland, 1925.

Hardy, William. Scrapbook of clippings from newspapers about Montana mines 1863-1868.

Hauser, Samuel T. Papers, Montana 1862-1890.

"Historical Sketch and Essay on the Resources of Montana." Helena, 1868.

Hosmer, Chief Justice Hezekiah Lord. "Montana," an address before the Travelers' Club, New York City, Jan., 1866.

Charge to the Grand Jury of the First Judicial District, Montana Territory, December 5, 1864, *Montana Post,* 1864.

Hosmer, J. B. *Genealogy of the Hosmer Family,* 1861.

Hunt, Thomas B. Letters 1861-1871. Helena.

Irving, T. (Broadside.) Grant of Power of Attorney to Sam T. Hauser, Wm. Wyke, T. C. Everts, and H. S. Hosmer for the purpose of selling certain mining districts. Virginia City, 1865.

Isaacs, James P. (Complainant) Copy of Judgement Roll, Territory of Montana, County of Madison. James P. Isaacs vs. Alexander McAndrew and M. J. Isaacs for recovery of unpaid wages. Virginia City, 1869.

Jenkins, J. Geraint. *Traditional County Craftsmen*. New York.

Johnson, Virginia Wesel. *The Long, Long Trail*. New York, 1966.

Kent, Ruth. *Great Day in the West*. Oklahoma University Press, 1963.

Langford, Nathaniel Pitt. *Vigilante Days and Ways*. Boston, 1890.

Langford, Nathaniel Pitt. *The Wonders of the Yellowstone*. New York, 1871.

Lavender, David. *Land of Giants*. New York, 1958.

Lavender, David Sievert. *Westward Vision*. New York, 1963.

Laws of Fairweather Mining District, Enacted September 16, 1864. Virginia City, 1864.

McClure, Alexander Kelly. *3,000 Miles Through the Rocky Mountains*. Philadelphia, 1869.

McKey, Francis S. Journal 1863–1866. Detailing his Journey by the Overland Route to the Montana Gold Fields and Return Trip by Flatboat down the Missouri in 1866.

McTucker, James. Montana Journal. 1866

Mathews, Alfred E. *Gems of Rocky Mountain Scenery*. New York, 1869.

Mathews, Alfred E. Interesting Narrative: The Journal of the flight of Alfred E. Mathews from the state of Texas . . . on foot and alone over 800 miles . . . to Chicago. 1861.

Mathews, Alfred E. *Pencil Sketches of Montana*. New York, 1868.

Meagher, Thomas Francis. *Lectures and Speeches of Governor T. F. Meagher in Montana*. Virginia City, 1867.

Mining Bureau of Montana. Prospectus; by-laws, officers and members. Virginia City, 1866.

Mining Deeds of Madison and Jefferson Counties. Virginia City, 1865.

Montana Post, Virginia City, Montana.

Montana Territorial Government. Message of Governor Thomas Francis Meagher to the Legislative Assembly. Virginia City, March 6, 1866.

Montana Territory Auditor's Office. Report of the Auditor and Treasurer of the Territory of Montana, 1865–1866.

Montana Territory Laws, Statutes, Resolutions and Memorials of the Territory of Montana. Passed at regular sessions of the First Legislative Assembly, 1864–1865. Helena, 1865.

Mumey, Nolie. *Alfred Edward Mathews: author, traveler, map-maker.* Boulder, Colorado, 1961.

Neally, Edward Bowdoin. "A Year in Montana." *Atlantic Monthly*, August, 1866.

The New York *Herald*. New York, New York.

Potts, Benjamin Franklin. *Climate and Resources of Montana.* Deer Lodge, Montana. 1876.

Raymer. Montana, *The Land and the People.* 1930.

Root, Frank A. and Connelley, Wm. E. *The Overland Stage to California.* Topeka, 1904.

Russell, Charles Marion. *Studies of Western Life.* New York, 1890.

The Sacramento *Union*. Sacramento, California.

Sloane, Eric. *A Museum of Early American Tools.*

Strachan, John. "Blazing the Mullan Trail." The

Rockford (Ill.) Register. 1852.

Strahorn, Robert E. The Resources of Montana Territory, Helena, 1879.

Stuart, Granville. Diary and sketchbook of a journey to "America" in 1866 and return trip up the Missouri River to Ft. Benton, Montana. Los Angeles, 1963.

Stuart, Granville. Montana As It Is. New York, 1865.

Stuart, Granville and James. Letters and Papers.

Stuart, Granville and James. Uncatalogued Field Diaries.

This Fabulous Century. Time-Life Publications. New York, 1972.

Thompson, Judge Francis McGee. "Reminiscences of Four-Score Years." The Massachusetts Magazine. Salem, Mass. 1912.

Tunis, Edwin. Colonial Crafts. New York, 1961.

Tunis, Edwin. Frontier Living. New York, 1961.

U.S. Army. Report on Construction of a Military Road from Ft. Walla Walla to Ft. Benton. Washington, 1863.

U.S. War Department. 1862 Expedition from Ft. Abercrombie to Ft. Benton. Report of Captain J. L. Fisk. Washington, 1863.

Vaughn, Robert. Then and Now; or Thirty-six Years in the Rockies. Minneapolis, 1900.

Voorhees, Abram. Journal (undated) A trip to Idaho from Menden, Michigan.

Wilkinson, E. Letters from Virginia City. 1867.

Wolle, Muriel Sibell. The Bonanza Trail. New York, 1963.

The Yreka Union. Yreka, California.

Winners of the SPUR and WESTERN HERITAGE AWARD

08383	**The Buffalo Runners** Fred Grove	$1.75
13905	**The Day The Cowboys Quit** Elmer Kelton	$1.25
29741	**Gold In California** Todhunter Ballard	$1.25
34270	**The Honyocker** Giles Lutz	$1.50
47082	**The Last Days of Wolf Garnett** Clifton Adams $1.75	
47491	**Law Man** Lee Leighton	$1.50
55123	**My Brother John** Herbert Purdum	$1.75
56025	**The Nameless Breed** Will C. Brown	$1.50
71153	**The Red Sabbath** Lewis B. Patten	$1.75
10230	**Sam Chance** Benjamin Capps	$1.25
82091	**Tragg's Choice** Clifton Adams	$1.75
82135	**The Trail To Ogallala** Benjamin Capps	$1.25
85903	**The Valdez Horses** Lee Hoffman	$1.75

Available wherever paperbacks are sold or use this coupon.

ace books, Book Mailing Service,
P.O. Box 690, Rockville Centre, N.Y. 11570

Please send me titles checked above.

I enclose $. . . . . Add 50¢ handling fee per copy.

Name . . . .

Address . . . .

City. . . . . State. . . . . Zip. . . . .